Caroline Anderson is a [...] gardener, unofficial tearo[...] of lovely cakes. Not nec[...] Caroline loves: her fami[...] Writing contemporary love stories. Hearing from readers. Walks by the sea with coffee/ice cream/cake thrown in! Torrential rain. Sunshine in spring/autumn. What Caroline hates: losing her pets. Fighting with her family. Cold weather. Hot weather. Computers. Clothes shopping. Caroline's plans: keep smiling and writing!

Emily Forbes is an award-winning author of Medical Romance for Mills & Boon. She has written over twenty-five books and has twice been a finalist in the Australian Romantic Book of the Year Award, which she won in 2013 for her novel *Sydney Harbour Hospital: Bella's Wishlist*. You can get in touch with Emily at emilyforbes@internode.on.net, or visit her website at emily-forbesauthor.com.

THE MIDWIFE'S MIRACLE TWINS

CAROLINE ANDERSON

THE PERFECT MOTHER FOR HIS SON

EMILY FORBES

MILLS & BOON

First Published in Great Britain 2022
by Mills & Boon, an imprint of HarperCollins*Publishers* Ltd,
1 London Bridge Street, London, SE1 9GF

www.harpercollins.co.uk

HarperCollins*Publishers*
1st Floor, Watermarque Building,
Ringsend Road, Dublin 4, Ireland

The Midwife's Miracle Twins © 2022 by Caroline Anderson

The Perfect Mother for His Son © 2022 by Emily Forbes

ISBN: 978-0-263-30113-7

01/22

MIX
Paper from
responsible sources
FSC™ C007454

This book is produced from independently certified FSC™ paper
to ensure responsible forest management.
For more information visit www.harpercollins.co.uk/green.

Printed and Bound in Spain using 100% Renewable Electricity
at CPI Black Print, Barcelona

THE MIDWIFE'S MIRACLE TWINS

CAROLINE ANDERSON

MILLS & BOON

Huge thanks to Carol, who fed me cake and
helped keep my midwife on the straight and narrow,
and to John, as ever, for his endless patience.
Love you.

CHAPTER ONE

'DO YOU NEED a man?'

Absolutely not, and particularly not the owner of the low, soft voice with a hint of laughter that came from behind her, but she'd exhausted all other options, so she stopped wrestling with the lid of the peanut butter and turned to face him.

He was propping up the door frame of the ward kitchen, arms folded and looking sexier than a man had any right to look in scrubs, and as she met his eyes a lazy smile tipped his mouth and tilted her heart sideways.

He had heartbreaker written all over him and under any other circumstances she would have run a mile, but right now she was too tired and hungry to refuse. She thrust the jar towards him.

'Do you know what? I've tried everything else. Knock yourself out.'

The smile tilted a little more, and he shrugged away from the door frame and twisted the lid off with ridiculous ease.

'It's all in the wrist action,' he said, that sexy mouth

twitching, and she rolled her eyes and relieved him of the jar, stifling her smile.

'I think you'll find it's brute force, but thank you anyway.'

His lips twitched again. 'You're welcome. My brute force was happy to oblige,' he said, and she stuck a spoon in the jar and put it in her mouth before she could make another smart retort.

He gave a startled laugh and pulled a face. 'Good grief, you must be desperate,' he said, but she was past caring.

'Hungry,' she mumbled, her mouth all stuck up with the peanut butter, and he laughed again, this time with a hollow ring.

'You're not alone. If I didn't loathe it, I'd grab a spoon and join you. Someone nicked my lunch out of the fridge. I'm Dan, by the way. Dan Blake.'

As in Daniel Blake, their new consultant? She nearly choked.

'Georgia Seton, aka Georgie,' she said, throwing the spoon into the washing up bowl and sticking out her hand. 'I'm a midwife.'

'I'll look forward to working with you, then, Georgia Seton,' he murmured as his hand grasped hers in a firm yet gentle grip that sent interesting tingles up her arm.

Well, that was one way of describing them. Dangerous was another. Their eyes met and locked, his a cool grey framed by dark lashes and the crinkle of laughter, and her heart hitched in her chest. She ignored it. She wasn't ready for that kind of interesting. Not now, not ever.

He dropped her hand and she turned away from

those mesmerising eyes, plunged herself wrist-deep into the washing up bowl in the sink and washed the spoon—and her hands, to get rid of the feel of his warm, firm grip as much as anything.

'Back into the fray?'

His voice, like dark, melted chocolate, teased her nerve endings again. 'Hopefully not,' she said lightly. 'Paperwork on my last delivery, then home for something proper to eat before I keel over. And with any luck I won't be three hours late again today.'

He snorted. 'Good luck with that. They broke me in gently with a nice simple elective list today, then chucked in a couple of emergencies just to mix it up, so I'm only running an hour late so far. I thought I'd come and introduce myself to whoever's here on the labour ward on my way home, see if there's anything useful I can do before I leave. Apart from opening jars.'

That made her smile. 'Good idea. They'll appreciate it. And thank you again for rescuing me.'

'You're welcome. Just don't dream up a crisis before I get out of here.'

She gave a hollow laugh at that. A crisis was the last thing she needed tonight. She'd been running on empty for hours. 'I'll do my best.'

She flashed him a smile, squeezed past him in the narrow kitchen and caught the scent of his skin as her nose skimmed by his chest. No way. She was not interested.

Absolutely not...

'Ah, Georgie, there you are. Can you do me a favour? Kat's had to go home, she's got a migraine, and we've got a primip who's walked in with a slight bleed and everyone else is tied up. She's just moved here, so we don't have a hospital number for her yet but she'll have her handheld notes with her. Room four. Her name's Susie.'

Her heart sank at her team manager's words. She'd only just finished writing up her last delivery, and she was about to go home. Or not, by the sound of it…

'Is there really nobody else, Jan?'

'No. I'm really sorry, but the night shift'll be on soon and it's probably nothing to worry about.'

Don't say that!

She sighed and closed her eyes. 'OK. I'll go and see her.' She shut the file and headed for what Jan seemed to think might be nothing to worry about. Which had probably jinxed it utterly.

She went into the room and found a young woman sitting cross-legged at the top of the bed with her eyes closed, a man, presumably her partner, sitting beside her stroking her hair back off her face.

They looked up as she closed the door, and she smiled at them. 'Hi, my name's Georgie, I'm a midwife and I'm going to be looking after you. You must be Susie?'

'Yes, and this is Rob. He's my partner.'

'Hi, Rob. Good to meet you. Susie, I understand you've had a bit of bleeding. Is that right?'

She nodded, her hands stroking her abdomen in a gentle rhythm, her eyes a little worried. 'Yes. I think I've just been overdoing it with the move, but I thought I should get it checked out. It was just a few spots, but my placenta's low so I thought it was best.'

The shrill scream of alarm bells rang in her head. A low placenta. Fabulous. Jan had definitely jinxed it.

'OK, well, let's have a look at your handheld notes and see what they've got to offer.'

Susie shook her head, her eyes welling with tears. 'I don't know where they are. I put them down somewhere and I can't find them because the house is in chaos—we've only just moved. My section was due next Friday and I was going to come in tomorrow to see someone but we didn't know we were going to be moving so soon and it was such a rush and now I'm bleeding...'

Great. It just got even better.

'Don't worry, we'll sort it out,' she said calmly, handing Susie a tissue to blot up her tears. 'We'll need your name, date of birth, hospital number and so on so we can contact your old hospital and get the notes sent over. Rob, I wonder if you could go to the desk out on the ward and give all that information to the ward clerk while I look at Susie? And tell her I said it's urgent. Is that OK with you both?'

'Yeah, sure,' he said, and dropped a kiss on Susie's forehead. 'I won't be long.'

She smiled at him, and Georgie picked up her pen. 'Right, Susie, as we don't have any notes for you I need to take some details and then do a quick scan to see what's going on. Did they give you a grade for your placenta previa?'

She gave a little shrug. 'I don't know. They never said.'

'Has this happened before? Any spotting, pink discharge, anything like that?'

She shook her head. 'No, nothing. I've been fine and I've felt OK till now, but...'

'Do you know your due date?'

'Yes. The twenty-fifth of August. I'm thirty-seven weeks and five days. I don't know if it's significant but I've been having a few—not contractions, really, I don't think, but sort of tightenings?'

The alarm bells got louder. 'Braxton Hicks contractions, probably. That's quite normal. It's your uterus toning up ready for the main event, but tell me if they get worse. Right, I need to do a scan so we can see what's going on, but before I do that I just want to put this clip on your finger. It monitors your heart rate and your oxygen saturation, so it'll give me an idea of how you're doing. Have you had any blood pressure problems?' she asked, strapping on the cuff.

'Not as far as I know.'

Well within the normal range, and her sats were ninety-eight per cent. All good so far.

'Right, let's have a look at this baby. Have you felt it moving today?'

'Oh, yeah. It wriggles all the time, and sometimes it jerks.'

'That's probably hiccups, it's quite common. Could you pull your top up, please?'

Susie hitched up her top and wriggled her jeans down, and Georgie could see at a glance that the baby was sitting very high. She laid her hands on the taut swell of her pregnant belly, feeling the smooth curve of the baby's back, the hard jut of its little bottom up under Susie's ribs, the sharp point of a tiny heel on the other side as it stretched, but the baby's head wasn't engaged in her pelvis, even though it was head down. She pressed gently on the baby's bottom, trying to coax it down, but it didn't move at all.

Not good news. Her placenta must be very low.

'OK, let's have a listen to baby's heart, shall we?' she said, and moments later the steady swooshing sound filled the room.

One hundred and fifty-two beats a minute, which was spot on. Small mercies. 'Well, that's all good. Right, let's do an ultrasound scan now, so we can find out a little bit more about what's going on in there and get a look at this placenta.'

'Do you think that's caused it?'

She smiled reassuringly, trying not to stress her. 'It might be, but you're both doing well at the moment so I'm not worried for now.'

'Oh, I'm having one of those things again. The Branston Whatevers.'

Georgie paused the scan. She could see the tightening of her uterus under the skin, the changing shape of Susie's bump, and judging by the look on Susie's face it wasn't a Braxton Hicks.

'Breathe, Susie. Nice and light, quick little pants and an outbreath, again and again until it eases. That's lovely. Well done.'

By the time it had worn off Rob was back in the room, and he settled himself back beside Susie, holding her hand and looking worriedly at the screen as Georgie ran the transducer over her lower abdomen.

She felt her heart kick up a notch as the image appeared on her screen. The placenta was very low, spanning the area of the uterus that was starting to thin and stretch. Grade Three, and she was in the very early stages of labour, but the baby's heartbeat was strong and steady, and so was Susie's. For now.

She took a photo of the image on her phone, wiped away the gel and smiled at them both. 'OK, Susie, your uterus is starting to pull up at the bottom where your placenta is, so we're going to have to deliver the baby now. The first thing I'm going to do is take some blood and get that off to the lab, then book Theatre for you, OK?'

Her eyes widened and she reached for Rob's hand. 'Is my baby all right?'

'Yes, it's fine at the moment. Nice strong heartbeat, which is what we want to see, and you're OK for now, but your placenta is very low, which is why you've had that bleed, so I'll get a surgeon to have a look at it and get the ball rolling, OK?'

They nodded blankly, and she put a cannula in her hand, took all the necessary bloods and handed Susie a gown.

'I won't be long. Could you undress and put this on while I'm gone? I'll only be a minute.'

She slipped out of the door and hurried to the work station. 'Can you get these off to the lab now for urgent cross-match and group and save, and page the on-call registrar for me, Sally? I've got a mum with a placenta previa who needs an emergency section.'

'She's helping Samira with a breech—she's only just gone in. Patrick's here somewhere?'

The F2 who'd been with them a week. 'Damn. No. I need someone more senior. She's contracting. Is Mr Blake still around?'

'I thought I told you not to dream up a crisis?'

She turned, and he took one look at her face and the smile faded from his eyes. 'OK, what is it?'

'Grade Three placenta previa, twenty-five-year-old primip. Thirty-seven plus five weeks. They've just moved and she's lost her notes, so we have no records for her, but she's had a slight bleed and she's starting contractions. The move was a bit rushed, I gather. Here, I took a photo of the scan.'

He glanced at it, and his mouth tightened a fraction.

'OK. She needs an emergency section. Have you told her?'

'Yes, and she's stable at the moment, but it won't last. Do you want to check her now?'

'No, I trust you and I've seen enough. Go and prep her for surgery and get her consented, I'll kickstart this and come and join you.'

'OK. I've done bloods for cross-match and group and save.'

'Good. Thanks.'

She left them to it, his voice following her.

'Can we get a crash section team on standby, please, and a Theatre ready asap? Theatre One should be free. They were cleaning it when I left. And activate major haemorrhage protocol.'

The door closed softly behind her, cutting out their voices, but she was relieved to hear him sound so controlled and in command. And he trusted her judgment.

Letting out a quiet sigh of relief, she went over to them and perched her hip on the bed and took Susie's hand. 'Right, I've had a chat to Mr Blake, one of our consultants, and he wants to do your Caesarean section now. He's going to pop in and talk to you in a minute, but in the meantime I need to fill in the consent form and I'd like to put you and the baby on a monitor, just so we can keep an eye on things until Theatre's ready.'

She shook her head. 'I'm so sorry. This is my fault. The move was so difficult, it went on too long and I knew I should have contacted you but I didn't have time, and now I've done too much and I can't believe this is happening—'

Georgie squeezed her hand. 'Susie, stop. This is not your fault, and you're here now, you're safe, and we'll look after you. Don't worry. It'll soon be over, and you'll make a quick recovery and your baby will be OK and you can all settle down in your new home.'

She put her on the monitor and everything looked fine. So far, so good. She rapidly filled in the notes, assembled all the things that would be needed, drew up the consent form, talked Susie through all the possible things that could go wrong, gave her a pen to sign the form and then handed her a tissue when she started to cry.

'I really can't believe this is happening. I thought I'd be OK.'

'You are OK,' Georgie said firmly. 'We just want to make sure you and your baby stay that way.'

She printed off a host of labels for all the things that would need them, and then glanced up to scan the monitors for the hundredth time. Nothing drastic in the way of change for either mother or baby, but they were both subtly different, and she felt a flicker of unease.

'How are you feeling, Susie?'

'Not great. I'm having one of those Branston things again and I feel a bit woozy,' she moaned, her face wincing, and Georgie checked the monitors again and felt the flicker of unease ramp up a notch. There'd been nothing to worry about a moment ago, but now the baby's heart rate had dropped a little, and Susie's blood pressure was down slightly while her heart rate was rising. Not much, but enough, and Georgie was reaching for the alarm button when she heard the door open behind her.

'Hi. How are you doing?'

Dan Blake's steady, reassuring voice came from behind her, and she turned and met his expressionless eyes.

'Minor decels,' she said quietly, knowing Susie wouldn't understand that she was talking about the baby's falling heart rate, and his eyes flicked to the monitors, an unreadable expression in them as he took in the non-reassuring trace.

'Are we good to go?' he asked.

'Yes, all done, she's consented. She's ready.'

'Good. Thanks.' He looked beyond her and smiled, his face all calm reassurance now.

'Hi, Susie. I'm Daniel Blake. I'm one of the consultants here, and I'm going to be looking after you.' He stood at the foot of the bed, keeping the monitors in view as he spoke to them. 'I understand Georgie's told you that we need to deliver your baby now by Caesarean section?'

'Yes. Please get it out safely.'

'That's what I'm here for,' Dan said, and it sounded oddly like a vow.

Georgie took her hand and gave it a gentle squeeze.

'It's OK, Susie. You don't need to be scared. We're looking after you. I just need to get another line in, and we'll take you straight up to Theatre as soon as they're ready for you.'

'I want my mum. Can we wait for her? She's on her way.'

Dan shook his head, his voice gentle but implacable. 'No. I'm sorry. We need to move fast, and I know it will all seem like a bit of a rush, but it isn't, it's all under control, we do this all the time. Trust us, Susie. You're in the best place.'

Georgie saw Susie's shoulders droop in resignation. Thank goodness.

'OK, sharp scratch coming,' she said, and as she finished inserting the port, Susie's eyes widened.

'Oh. I think I've wet myself,' she said weakly, just as the alarms on the monitors started to beep. There was a dark, spreading stain on her gown, her blood pressure fell off a cliff, and the baby's heart was racing.

'Right, let's go,' Dan said crisply, and knocked the brakes off the bed as Georgie hit the alarm button again and it all kicked off.

Rob leapt to his feet, his eyes wide with fear, and Georgie unhooked all the leads and tried to reassure her terrified patient and her equally terrified partner as the team leapt into action and they ran for the lift.

Someone was holding the lift doors open, and when they opened again seconds later she was whisked into the waiting Theatre, Rob running with them to the doors, his hands knotted together in fear.

'Don't let her die. Please don't let her die.'

'It's OK, Rob, we've got this, it's what we do,' Dan said quietly, giving his shoulder a quick squeeze, and they wheeled Susie through into the theatre suite and handed her over to the anaesthetist, the doors swinging shut behind them.

There was no time to scrub, just a massive dollop of hand sanitiser up to the elbows, then gowns and gloves and they were in there with the hastily assembled team, Susie already anaesthetised and draped, a nurse on each side of her squeezing in O negative blood, a TXA infusion going into another vein to stop the bleeding, oxytocin to contract her uterus, the neonatal team hurrying in around them as Dan picked up the scalpel and glanced at the anaesthetist.

'Are we good to go?'

'Yes, but don't hang about.'

'I won't. Right, let's get this baby out.'

It was the fastest section she'd ever witnessed, and it wasn't subtle, but in moments he'd pulled out the floppy, grey baby boy and handed him to Georgie. She cut the cord and handed him straight to the waiting neonatal team and turned her eyes back to Dan's hands.

He'd removed the placenta, but it wasn't intact, and he was searching for the missing fragment while the inexperienced F2, Patrick, was trying his best with the suction.

'BP's falling. Fifty over thirty-five,' the anaesthetist said.

Dan swore, clamped both hands around her uterus and held it firmly while they squeezed more blood into her.

'OK. It's picking up. Seventy-five over fifty.'

'Right, I'm going to have one more go, and if I can't find this bleed in the next few seconds she'll lose her uterus,' he said grimly. 'Suction, please.'

He let go, but the suction failed to keep up and she could feel the tension in the room.

Jo, the registrar joined them, hurrying in to take the suction off Patrick, who was clearly panicking. Jo tried to clear the field for Dan to see.

'Don't you dare die on me,' he said under his breath as he struggled to find and stem the bleed, but for a few seconds Georgie really thought she would. Either that, or lose her uterus and with it the chance of any further children. And there was still no sound from the direction of the neonatal team.

'How's the baby?' Dan asked, as if he could read her mind.

'Alive but unresponsive.' The terse reply came from the other side of Theatre, and he swore again.

Then a tiny cough, so small they nearly missed it, and then the merest hint of a wail, and she saw the tension pour out of his shoulders.

He closed his eyes for a moment, sucked in a deep breath then started again, finding the last scrap of placenta and removing it, giving the oxytocin a chance to do its job. The flow stopped, her blood pressure picked up and once he was satisfied it was all right he nodded and started to close.

Georgie felt the tension drain out of her, and her eyes prickled with tears.

'I thought we were going to lose them both,' she said softly, her voice shaking.

'So did I and we could have done. You should have called me sooner.'

He was blaming her? 'This is not my fault, Mr Blake,' she said quietly but firmly. 'I'd only been in there a very few minutes, and as soon as I'd scanned her I came straight out to alert Theatre. It's not my fault.'

'No, of course it isn't. Sorry. Bit of a sore point. I apologise.' He met her eyes, his filled with an expression she didn't really understand. Something to do with that sore point? She gave a tiny nod of acknowledgement.

'Good. Accepted—but for the record, I don't over-
look things.'

'I'm glad to hear it,' he murmured, and carried on
suturing, layer by layer, the concentration pouring off
him in waves.

'Right, that's her uterus and muscle layers done. Jo,
can I leave you to finish off, please? I want to go and
talk to her partner.'

The registrar nodded, and they left her closing the
skin and went out to give Rob the good news.

He wept with relief when he was told they'd both
made it so far. Georgie could empathise with that, she
was pretty close to it herself, and she didn't think Dan
looked too great, either.

'Right, I need a shower and then I'm going home,
and I think you ought to do the same,' she told him after
they'd checked on Susie in Recovery, and he nodded.

'Good idea. Thank you for your help.'

'You're welcome.'

She spotted him in the ward kitchen ten minutes later,
and she was shocked. His hands, rock steady while
he'd been operating, were trembling so hard he could
barely hold the glass of water in his hand, and his face
was as white as his shirt.

'Are you OK? You're shaking.'

'I'm fine. Just low blood sugar. I'll be OK once
I've eaten.'

'Are you diabetic?'

'No, I just haven't eaten since breakfast, but I'll be
fine. I'm sorry I bit your head off,' he added, and she
decided to cut him some slack.

'I'll let you off this time. Want some peanut butter or will it choke you?'

He gave a short grunt of what might have been laughter. 'I think I'll pass. I'm going home. It's only a twenty-minute walk and I've got food in the fridge. I'll be fine.'

He didn't look fine, far from it, and it didn't sound as if he had anyone at home to feed him, either.

'I've got a better idea,' she said. 'I've got a massive chilli in the slow cooker, a fresh loaf of tiger bread, and I live just round the corner. Literally five minutes and you can be eating it. What do you say?'

He hesitated, long enough that she knew just how bad he must be feeling, so she pushed harder.

'I've got a sticky toffee pudding in the freezer. We could crack that out, too. Look on it as a welcome to your new job.'

She saw him buckle, and heaved a silent sigh of relief.

'Sold,' he said crisply. 'Now let's get out of here before anything else happens.'

He wouldn't have made it home.

His whole body was shaking, he felt sick and light-headed from low blood sugar and a massive adrenaline surge, and underlying it all was a tidal wave of emotion that was threatening to swamp him at any moment.

Of all the things to happen on his first day...

'Right, we're here. Come on in.'

As she opened the door, his nose was filled with the delicious smell of chilli, and he followed her through the hall into the little kitchen.

It was clean, tidy, unassuming—a bit like her, he

thought. She'd been calm and unflappable throughout, but with a hint of iron. Like when he'd accused her of not calling him soon enough. She'd put him firmly in his place. He liked that. Less keen on the fact that he'd been so quick to accuse her of incompetence...

She handed him a knife, a board and the loaf of tiger bread. 'Right, you slice the bread while I dish up. And don't be coy with it, I'm ravenous.'

She opened the slow cooker—not massive, but certainly more than big enough for two—and spooned out two huge dollops into bowls while he sliced the bread into big fat chunks.

'Cheese, yogurt?'

'Anything. It smells amazing.'

His stomach growled audibly, and she laughed. 'Here you go. Grab the bread and come on through.'

She led him into the living room at the back of the house and he followed her, his legs like wet spaghetti, and dropped into a chair at her dining table. The chilli was hot and fragrant, and he forked it down as if his life depended on it, mopping it up with chunks of soft, buttery bread until the bowl was wiped clean and the bread was all gone. Then he sat back and offered her a rueful smile.

'That was delicious. Thank you.'

'You're welcome. Feeling better now?'

'I'm getting there. I can't believe someone nicked my sandwich.'

She laughed and got to her feet. 'I can. Sticky toffee pudding?'

'Absolutely. If you can spare it,' he added as an afterthought, but she'd already walked out with their plates, so he stayed where he was and looked around him, taking in his surroundings for the first time.

It was a typical little modern town house, with the kitchen at the front and the living room behind it running the full width of the house, with French doors that led into the little garden. It was tiny, hardly more than a courtyard, and fully paved, but she'd made the best of it. It was stacked with pots overflowing with colour, and it looked fresh and inviting. His eyes tracked inside again, scanning the artwork on the walls, the choice of furniture, the soothing colour palette with little pops of vibrant colour that echoed the planting outside.

There was a crumpled throw over the back of a sofa, and a magazine lying open on the coffee table, as if she'd just got up and walked away. It was homely, welcoming, the house of someone who cared where they lived.

Unlike him. He didn't really care about anything, not any more. So long as he had a bed to sleep in and a sofa and TV and a kitchen to hold body and soul together, he was OK. It was the garden he cared about, the only thing that mattered to him, because being outside surrounded by nature brought him a glimmer of the peace he yearned.

That and work, only not today. Today was the worst kind of day, the kind that pushed all his hot buttons.

He shut off that line of thought as she came back in with two steaming bowls of sticky toffee pudding topped with a scoop of vanilla ice cream.

'That looks amazing.'

'Don't get too excited, it's not home-made. I tried making it once and it was hopeless, so I buy it now. Comfort food, for the days when it all goes haywire.'

He grunted at that. Haywire was putting it politely.

'I owe you dinner,' he said, changing the subject, and she met his eyes.

'I'll hold you to that. Eat up,' she said, and threw him a mischievous grin that stirred something deep inside him. Something vibrant and sweet and carefree that he'd lost long ago.

He picked up the spoon and turned his attention to something safer.

CHAPTER TWO

THEY ENDED THEIR meal on the sofa, her curled up in her usual corner, him slumped at the far end, the remains of a box of chocolates between them and giant mugs of coffee cradled in their hands. Decaf, although she wasn't sure all the caffeine in the world would keep her awake after the week she'd had.

'So what brought you to Yoxburgh?' she asked him round a dark chocolate truffle, and he picked up a hazelnut caramel and shrugged.

'Luck, really. I was looking for a change, they were looking for another consultant and Yoxburgh has a great reputation, so I just applied. It was a bit of a wild punt, but it paid off.'

'It's quite quiet here.'

'It's fine. I like that.'

I, not we, or he wouldn't be here, not if there'd been anyone with a meal waiting for him. Not that she was about to ask, but he volunteered it anyway in the next breath.

'I don't have anyone else to consider, my parents live near my sister and her family in Scotland, north of Inverness, so it's a long drive or a flight to visit them wherever I live. And I was ready for a consultancy. Why not?'

That surprised her. 'So is this your first?'

He gave a soft laugh. 'Doesn't it show?'

'No. I wouldn't have guessed. That was pretty dramatic with Susie, but you didn't hesitate.'

'There wasn't time to hesitate. It helped that I'd been in the same theatre all day with some of the same people, but it's not the first time I've done a crash section by any means.' His eyes met hers, then flicked away again, their expression unreadable. 'Sadly it doesn't always go so well.'

'No. I was so glad you were there, though, with Jo busy, because there wouldn't have been time to get anyone else.'

'No, there wouldn't. It was too close for comfort as it was.'

'But you saved her. Her and the baby.' She smiled to lighten the mood. 'I'd congratulate you on that again, but it might well swell your head.'

'What, because I did what I've spent years training for?' He shook his head and gave an odd little laugh. 'Unlikely. And *we* saved her. If you hadn't moved so fast it could still have been very different. And I'm really sorry I called you on that. You did well.'

She smiled at him. 'Thank you—and it's OK, you can stop apologising now, you're forgiven.'

'Thank you.' He was silent for a moment, looking lost in thought, then he sucked in a breath, put his mug down with a little clunk and got to his feet. 'It's time I went home,' he said. 'It's getting late and I've taken enough of your time and your hospitality.'

She followed him down the hall, pausing by the door as he turned towards her with a rueful smile that didn't really reach his eyes.

'Thank you for feeding me. You're a lifesaver, I wouldn't have got home without keeling over.'

'You're welcome. And I'll get my own back. You owe me dinner, don't forget.' She smiled up at him, studying his face at close range, seeing the light change in his eyes.

'I won't forget,' he said softly, and with a tender, slightly wry smile he bent his head and feathered the lightest of kisses over her lips, like the touch of a butterfly's wing.

And then they froze.

She had no idea how long they stood there, eyes locked, neither of them breathing, but then slowly, inch by inch, he lowered his head again and touched his mouth to hers, sipping, stroking, while her breath was trapped in her chest and her heart was beating a wild tattoo against her ribs.

Wow, he knows how to kiss, she thought, and then she stopped trying to think and gave herself up to the moment.

It really was only a moment, and then he lifted his head, his breathing fast, his eyes on fire as they burned down into hers. He dropped his arms abruptly and took a step back.

'I need to go.' His voice was taut with tension, his eyes a little wild, and for a second neither of them spoke. And then…

'You don't have to.'

Was that her? Must have been, there was nobody else there, and for what seemed like an age he said nothing.

Then he let out his breath in a gust and met her eyes again.

'Are you sure?'

His voice was gruff, laden with emotion, and she nodded, suddenly more sure than she'd been of anything for years. And why not? He was alone, she was alone... Why not?

She held out her hand, and for the longest moment he stared at her, then he took her hand in his and let her lead him up the stairs.

She turned on the bedside light, and the soft glow highlighted her tumbled bedding, just as she'd left it sixteen hours ago. It didn't matter. In a few moments it would be tumbled again, and anyway, right then being houseproud was way down her list of priorities.

She turned towards him, and he cradled her face in his hands. They were warm and firm, gentle, but with—not a tremor, exactly, more the hum of the tension zinging through his body and connecting to hers like a high voltage wire, every stroke of his thumb against her cheek sending shockwaves through her body.

And his eyes—they searched hers intently, looking for what? Hesitation? Regret? So she smiled, and laid her hand against his cheek, feeling the rough rasp of stubble against her palm, curiously intoxicating and reassuring at the same time.

'I want you,' she said softly, and she felt as much as heard his breath hiss out against her hand as he turned his face into her palm and pressed his lips against her skin.

'I want you, too.'

'That's always an advantage,' she said with a smile, and he gave a strangled laugh and she felt the tension go out of him.

He delved in his pockets, pulled out a wallet, rummaged in it for a moment then handed her a foil packet. 'Here. We'll need this.'

She put it down on the bedside table under the light, although there was a pain inside her at the needlessness of it. There was no way he was going to get her pregnant. No way he *could* get her pregnant.

She put the painful thought away, reminded herself that there were other reasons for using protection, and pulled her top off over her head and dropped it on the chair.

Something inside him seemed to snap at that, some last vestige of control finally giving way as he tore off his clothes and reached for her, drawing her up against his hot, naked and very willing body.

Hot. So hot. Hot and firm and taut with need, humming with that electric charge that seemed to fill them both. His hands ran over her back and stopped at her bra strap.

'You've got too much on,' he growled, and dealt with it, unclipping her bra, sliding down her jeans, hooking her underwear on the way so she ended up as naked as him, steadying herself with a hand on his head as he crouched down and peeled her jeans off one foot, then the other.

He worked his way slowly back up her body, scattering kisses all over the place, turning her knees to jelly as he paused here and there for a little extra attention until they buckled and she sat down abruptly on the edge of the bed.

He tipped her back, rolled her over into the middle of the bed and followed her down onto the rumpled bedclothes, pulling her into his arms so they lay together face to face, toe to toe, heart to heart.

She could feel the thud of his heart against her ribs, the jut of his erection against the bowl of her pelvis, the rasp of his hair against her legs. Eyes locked on hers, he ran his hands slowly down her back and eased her closer, threading a leg between hers, a hand following it with unerring accuracy.

Too much. Too intense, too...

She closed her eyes, focusing on his hand, his body, the nudge of his erection as she rocked against his touch.

Her hands were exploring him, too, tracing the taut lines of his muscles, the jut of his hipbone, the texture of his skin, coarse here with hair, then silky smooth there, burning hot and humming with tension.

He shifted, bringing a hand up to her breasts, rolling her nipple between thumb and forefinger as his mouth laid a line of hot, moist kisses across her collarbones, up her throat, behind her ear.

She ran a hand up his back to cradle his head, threading her fingers through soft tousled hair as his lips found hers in a kiss that spiralled instantly out of control.

He wrenched away, breath hot against her face.

'Two seconds,' he muttered, and rolled away, groping on the bedside chest for that elusive foil packet. She heard him swear softly, then the tiny sound of tearing foil, and he was back, nudging her legs apart for him.

She was ready—so ready, but as her body welcomed his it took her breath away. His too. She heard his breath hiss out, and she gasped and clung to him as his hand found her again, his touch sure and deft. She felt the tension building in him, then a rising tide inside her as he thrust deeper, deeper and took her over the edge.

She bit his shoulder to stifle the scream, felt him stiffen, heard the deep, guttural groan of his climax as he shuddered in her arms, and then he dropped his head against hers, his breathing ragged, his heart hammering against her ribs as they came slowly back down to earth.

In more ways than one.

As their hearts slowed and the passion cooled on their skin, common sense resurrected itself.

What had she done?

He was a consultant in her department, for heaven's sake! And it was his first day, she knew nothing about him, he knew nothing about her—she must have been mad! And work was going to be so, so awkward…

He'd rolled away, and he was sitting up now on the edge of the bed, looking at her over his shoulder. 'Hey. It's OK,' he murmured. He reached out a hand and touched her cheek lightly, and then stood up and walked into the bathroom, closing the door behind him and leaving her there sprawled naked and sated on the mess that was her bed.

What had she done?

He closed the bathroom door behind him and caught his reflection in the mirror over the basin. There were toothmarks in his shoulder, and he couldn't meet his own eyes.

What had he done?

She was a midwife, and he was going to have to work with her over and over again, and he'd slept—no, scratch that, he'd had hot, hot sex with her. On his first day, for heaven's sake! He knew nothing about her, she knew nothing about him—not that there was a lot to know, apart from the fact that he'd used her to blank out the memories...

Don't think about it.

He pulled himself together and dealt with the condom—and stopped, horror washing over him. It was torn. Only a slight tear, but enough to have consequences.

As if it weren't already bad enough...

He washed his hands and went back out into her bedroom. She'd straightened out the bed and she was sitting up against the pillows, messy hair tumbling over her shoulders, the duvet hauled up around her like a force field, eyes wary as she looked at him.

He reached for his shorts. 'We need to talk,' he said bluntly, starting to pull on his clothes.

'Do we?'

'Yes. You need emergency contraception. The condom tore.'

Her gaze was steady, but there was something odd about it, about the way she held his eyes. Almost defiant.

'It's all right. You can't get me pregnant, if that's what you're worried about.'

He'd heard that before, and he searched her eyes for more clues. 'Are you sure?'

'As sure as I can be, and I haven't got any STIs you need to worry about either. I had all the tests in the world four years ago after my ex confessed he was having an affair, just to be on the safe side, and I haven't done this since, so—yeah. You're safe. I can't get pregnant, and I can't give you anything nasty. Your turn.'

He felt the tension leak out of him like air out of a punctured balloon. Or a ripped condom...

He shook his head. 'You won't get anything from me. I'm fanatical about it.'

'No other ruptured condoms or intimate disasters in your history?'

He could have laughed, but it wasn't funny. 'No ruptured condoms.' Just a catalogue of failures leading to the ultimate disaster...

Her shoulders dropped a fraction. 'Well, that's all right then. We're both off the hook. You can relax.'

Hardly, not while she was sitting there warm and rumpled and sexy as hell, her hair a tumbling waterfall of gold that made his fingers itch to touch it. He held her eyes for a moment longer, then nodded. 'OK. I need to go,' he said, and she looked away.

'Yes, you probably do. I've got an early start and I don't...'

He had no idea what she didn't, but he needed to fill the void in this conversation, say the words that still remained unsaid.

'Georgia, it's OK. This doesn't need to make life difficult. We're both adults. We can deal with this, but not now. I need to get back to the hospital and check on Susie and the baby.'

'Really? You could ring.'

'I could, but I'd rather go in. The registrar's overstretched, the F2 doesn't know one end of a baby from the other yet and I'd rather trust my own judgement.'

He reached for his trousers and pulled them on, tucked his shirt in and looked back at her.

'Are you in tomorrow?'

She nodded. 'Yes. I'm on at seven.'

'OK. I'll see you there. Maybe we can catch a coffee if there's time.'

He heard a little huff of laughter.

'In your wildest dreams. But yes, that would be good.'

She looked up again, and in her eyes there was understanding and maybe a tinge of regret. In a moment of impulse he leant in and touched his lips to her, then straightened up.

'Thank you.'

She raised an eyebrow. 'What for? Specifically?'

He felt his smile. Was it as crooked as it felt? Probably. 'Everything. Acting quickly with Susie, being there in Theatre, feeding me before I fell over—and this...this, whatever it was.'

She smiled back as crookedly as him, and shook her head slowly. 'I'll see you tomorrow.'

He nodded, picked up his keys, phone and wallet from her bedside chest, ran downstairs and let himself out.

And then stood there, his brain a mess, utterly disorientated. He had no idea where he was, where the hospital was, and how to find his way back there. With a sharp sigh he pulled out his phone, clicked on the map and followed it.

She slept like a log, to her surprise.

She hadn't thought she would, not after what they'd done, but clearly she wasn't as troubled by it as she probably should have been. Either that or it was the flood of endorphins he'd released in her.

She rolled out of bed, stretched luxuriously and headed for the shower, and half an hour later she walked onto the ward to find him standing at the central desk talking to Ben Walker, of all people. Clinical lead, highly perceptive human and husband of one of her friends.

Great, she thought, and braced herself for the inevitable awkwardness.

'Morning, Georgie. Have you met Dan?' Ben greeted her with his usual wide smile, and Dan looked round and gave a tiny nod of recognition. He looked as awkward as she felt, and every bit as appealing as he had last night.

She plastered a smile on her face and tried to ignore the hitch in her pulse. 'Yes, I have. Morning. So how's today shaping up so far, Ben? Chaos already?'

'I don't know. Probably, but Jan was looking out for you,' he told her, so she went to find her, glad of an excuse to get away because it was even more awkward than she'd imagined it was going to be, and she had no idea what to say to Dan. Easier to ignore it—and him.

She spotted Jan halfway down the corridor, just as her phone started ringing in her pocket. Livvy. She'd call her in a minute. 'Hi, Jan. I gather you want me.'

'Yes, Livvy Hunter came in a few minutes ago in established labour. I think she'd like you to deliver her, if you're happy to do that.'

Which explained the call. She felt a little bubble of excitement and beamed at Jan. 'I'd absolutely love to. Has anyone started with her?'

'No, not yet. I've just got her notes up from the clinic. Her husband's with her. She's in Room Four, settling in.'

Susie's room. Hopefully it wouldn't be a bad omen. She popped her head round the door.

'Hi, Livvy, hi, Matt. How are you doing?'

Matt and Livvy both gave her a relieved smile.

'Oh, Georgie, I'm so glad you're here,' Livvy said. 'I just tried to ring you. It's happening so fast. Can you be with me?'

'Yes, I've already cleared it with Jan. Give me two seconds to change. I've literally just walked onto the ward.'

'Don't be long. I've got contractions every two minutes.'

'I won't be. Just keep breathing.'

She went into the locker room as Dan was leaving.

'Are we OK?' he asked, his voice low and all chocolatey again, and her heart did a silly backflip.

'Yes, of course,' she said, not at all sure and trying hard to ignore her heart and meet his eyes. 'Busy. One of our ED doctors is in labour, so that's my day taken care of.'

'You never know, it might be quick.'

She rolled her eyes. 'Now don't jinx it, you should know better. Jan did that to me with Susie. How is she, by the way? Did you see her last night?'

'Yes, and again this morning. She's doing OK, and the baby's fine, he's all good, feeding well, no apparent neurological deficit. She asked me to thank you. You should pop up and see them when you get a minute. And shout if you need me.'

'I will.'

She didn't need him.

Well, not for Livvy. For herself? That was a totally different question, and not one for now, when her friend was in labour and moving very fast, unless she was mistaken.

Livvy was lying on her side facing Matt and getting a bit stroppy with him by the time Georgie went back in. Matt was trying not to smile and doing his level best to be supportive, but Livvy wasn't having any of it.

'You're doing really well,' he murmured, and she glared at him.

'No thanks to you. It's entirely your fault I'm in this mess, and I don't want to do it any more. I'm going home. I'm too tired to do this now. I didn't sleep all night, and I just—aahh....'

Georgie went over to her and laid a hand on her side. 'It's OK, Livvy, breathe through it, nice gentle little pants—'

'I am breathing!' she snarled, and Georgie met Matt's eyes and smiled.

'Transition,' she mouthed, and he grinned.

'Looks like it.'

'Will you two stop whispering about me and shut up?' Livvy yelled, and Georgie reached over and pressed the call button to summon another midwife for the imminent delivery. A few seconds later she heard a soft knock and the click of the door opening.

She looked over her shoulder and found Dan there, one eyebrow slightly raised. 'Anything I can do?' he murmured.

'Not unless you're a midwife.'

He smiled slightly. 'Sorry, no, but they're all tied up according to Jan. Will I do instead?'

'I don't know. Looks like we'll find out,' she said with a wry smile. 'Livvy, Matt, this is Dan Blake, our new consultant. He obviously doesn't have enough to do today, so are you OK if he hangs out with us and plays midwife?'

'He can hang out wherever he likes so long as one of you useless people gets this baby out!' Livvy snapped over her shoulder, and then she reached out and grabbed Matt's hand and Georgie saw him wince.

She turned to Dan and threw him an apron. 'Here you go. You can see how it happens when you're not needed.'

He chuckled softly, snapped on a pair of gloves and did as he was told, which was more than Livvy did when she examined her.

'Stop doing that, I need to push!'

'Not yet, there's a tiny lip of cervix left, Livvy, just keep panting for a moment, it's nearly gone—'

'I don't want to pant, I want to push and it's my baby so I'm going to push!' she growled, and then she grabbed Matt and pulled herself up onto her knees and flung her arms around his neck.

'Ow-ow-ow, it hurts,' she wailed, and he rubbed her back and murmured soft encouraging words in her ear as Georgie crouched down and checked the baby's progress again.

'Steady, Livvy, you're nearly there, the baby's crowning now. Soft pants, no pushing—that's lovely, Livvy, that's brilliant, nice and gentle—and here we go,' she added, catching the baby and passing it through Livvy's legs as she sank down onto the bed.

'It's a girl. Time of birth: seven-thirty-eight a.m.,' she said to Dan, and he nodded and handed her a warmed towel to wrap the baby in as Matt lowered Livvy gently back against the pillows.

'Hello, my precious one,' Livvy crooned softly, and

Georgie lifted the baby and laid her on her waiting mother's bare skin, tucking the towel in round her. She let out a wail, then another one, her skin pinking up instantly, and Matt bent over and pressed his lips to Livvy's hair, his eyes squeezed tight shut.

'Well done, my love. You were amazing.'

She looked up at him, her eyes sparkling with tears, and smiled. 'I don't think I was. Was I horrible?'

'No, of course you weren't horrible, you were brilliant,' he murmured, and Georgie turned away, partly to give them both a moment and partly to hide her smile.

'Apgar ten at one minute,' she said, and Dan nodded again.

He'd already done it, she could see it on the screen as he filled in the notes by hand and onto the computer. He'd also drawn up the oxytocin.

'Thanks. You're actually quite useful to have around,' she said with a wry smile, and he raised an eyebrow and his eyes crinkled at the sides.

'Likewise. Nice delivery, by the way. You're good.'

'Just doing my job,' she said, but she turned back to Livvy and Matt with a warm glow inside, still smiling at his words.

'Oh, she's beautiful. Congratulations. Does she have a name?'

'Esme.' Livvy smiled and looked up at Matt. 'Esme Juliet.'

For Matt's first wife, Amber and Charlie's mother. 'Oh, that's lovely,' she said softly, swallowing a lump, and she wrote the baby's name on her label, slipped it into the tiny name band and clipped it around the baby's ankle.

'Well done, Livvy, I'm so happy for you both,' she murmured, and Livvy gave her a wobbly smile and reached out an arm and hugged her.

'Thank you so much. That was amazing. I can't believe we've actually got a baby...'

She started to cry, and Matt wrapped his arm around her and hugged her against his chest. They'd been through so much between them, both separately and together, and to reach this point was little short of a miracle, so it was small wonder they were both in tears.

She'd be in tears under the circumstances. Not that it was ever going to happen, not to her...

'You OK?'

Dan's voice was the merest murmur, and she blinked hard and nodded. 'Of course. Why wouldn't I be?' she murmured back, and busied herself with the notes, glad of something to do.

She heard Dan's phone buzz next to the computer, and he met her eyes.

'Are you OK if I go? Someone needs a ventouse by the sound of it. I shouldn't be long.'

'I should think so. You could bring us all back a cup of tea when you've done it. We'll be ready by then.'

His mouth quirked and he rolled his eyes, waved his fingers at Matt and Livvy and left, and Georgie turned her attention back to Livvy and the baby.

'OK, little Esme, let's have a look at you, shall we?'

She did a rapid check to make sure all was present and correct, clipped and cut the cord and put a nappy on the by then furious baby and handed her back to her mother. She instantly started rooting, her little rosebud mouth nuzzling at her mother, and Matt lifted a hand and stroked her tiny head.

'She's hungry,' he murmured, and Georgie nodded.

'She is. Livvy, have you had any more thoughts about breastfeeding?' she asked gently, deeply conscious of her breast cancer history and her concerns about whether she'd be able to manage it, and Livvy nodded.

'I want to try,' she said. 'This cancer's taken enough from me, but if I can't, I don't care because we've got our baby and that's all that really matters.'

'Well, let's see what we can do,' she said, and calmly and quietly positioned the baby and helped her latch on. It took two attempts, but then she was there, suckling hard, and Livvy's eyes filled with tears.

'Wow. Oh, clever baby!' she whispered, and she took the baby's tiny hand in hers and held it as she fed.

Her tiny rosebud lips went slack after a few moments, but Livvy held her there, staring down at her with such love that Georgie had to turn away.

She went back to the paperwork, leaving the three of them bonding, but she couldn't see. She blinked hard and tried to blot out her thoughts, but it was hard when all she could think about was the futility of that torn condom, and the babies she'd never have.

Maybe she needed a man like Matt, a man who already had children, but that would do nothing to quell the biological ache inside her every time a woman gave birth.

Maybe she didn't need a man at all. Maybe she needed a different job so she wasn't confronted by her own sorrow on a daily basis.

But for now she had this one, and she owed it to Livvy to do it properly. The baby was still suckling in between little moments of sleep, and judging by the look on Livvy's face everything was right in her world. Not so Matt's, she thought, catching a glimpse of another emotion on his face, and her heart ached for him.

'Are you OK if I go and grab a coffee, Olivia?' he murmured, and Livvy smiled up at him and stroked his cheek gently.

'Sure, darling. We're not going anywhere.'

'I won't be long.'

Georgie watched him go, then finished what she was doing and turned to Livvy.

'I just need to pop out for a minute. Press the call button if you need me, I won't be far away,' she said, and followed Matt out. She was almost sure he wasn't going for a coffee, so she headed off the ward and found him just outside, near the lifts.

He was standing by the window, staring out blindly across the car park, and she walked over to him and laid a hand on his arm.

'Are you OK?' she asked softly, and he swallowed hard and nodded.

'Yeah. Just—memories.'

Of the birth of his first two children, to the mother they'd lost far, far too young. 'Take your time,' she said gently. 'I'll be with her. She won't be alone.'

He nodded again, turning this time to hug her, his voice gruff. 'Thank you, Georgie. You've been a star.'

'Just doing my job, Matt.'

'Yeah, right,' he said, his grin a little crooked. 'I might go and grab that coffee now.'

'Good idea. You can always bring it back with you.'

'I might do that.'

She left him there with his thoughts, and headed back to Livvy. 'Everything OK?'

Livvy nodded. 'I've got the odd contraction, and I sort of feel I want to push?'

'That's good. Let's have a look. I expect your placenta's detached now.'

She'd just lifted it into a bowl and was tidying up when there was a tap on the door and Dan came back in.

'Are we ready for tea?'

She smiled at him. 'I was joking, but yes, that would be lovely. Dan's gone to get a coffee, but I'm always ready. Livvy?'

'Oh, yes, please. White, no sugar.'

'Ditto... Or I can make it and you can check the placenta?'

He grinned. 'You'd trust me?'

'With the placenta, yes. With the tea? Not so much.'

His lips twitched. 'D'you know what? You've got gloves on, I haven't. You do the placenta. I'll make the tea.'

The door clicked shut behind him, and Livvy gave her a curious look.

'You're getting on well. Do you know each other?'

Well, that was a loaded question, with a not so obvious answer. 'No, not at all, I only met him yesterday,' she said, trying to sound casual, 'but we worked together on a case. He seems OK. Good team player, very easy-going.'

'Hmm,' Livvy said, not sounding convinced, and Georgie ignored her and busied herself with the placenta.

'How are you feeling?' she asked, and Livvy gave a weary laugh.

'Happy? A bit sore? And very, very tired! I don't think I slept all night.'

'I'm sure. You've done really well. I'll take Esme off you in a minute so you can relax. I need to weigh and measure her, then clean her up a little and get her dressed, and Dan should be back soon with the tea.'

He was. She'd hardly said the words when he came back in, juggling three mugs and a plate of biscuits on a tray.

'Ooh, you found some biscuits.'

He looked a little guilty. 'Actually Jan found them.'

'So who made the tea? And don't give me the side eye, I'm only teasing.'

'You're rude. FYI, I made the tea.'

Livvy laughed and held her hand out for a mug, and he set the tray down, scooped up the baby with practised hands and passed her a mug, then peered at the placenta over Georgie's shoulder.

'Is it OK? As I have a vested interest, in that it'll be me dealing with the fallout.'

'No fallout,' she told him, and stripping off her gloves, she picked up a mug and peered at it. 'Well, there's a miracle. A decent cup of tea.'

'I am housetrained,' he said, sounding indignant, but she didn't bother to reply because Matt came back in then, with a coffee in one hand and a paper bag that looked suspiciously like a cake in the other.

'Here you go. A little present for the star of the day,' he said with a smile and handed it to Livvy, then took the baby from Dan, kissed her and tucked her into the crook of his arm like the seasoned father he was.

Dan picked up his tea and came and stood beside Georgie, so close she could feel the heat of his body, smell the soap on his skin, feel the drift of his breath against her cheek.

'Do you need me?'

Another loaded question.

'No, you're fine. I'm sure there are a million other things you should be doing, but thank you for your help with this.'

'It's what I'm here for, but you're right, there's a mountain of stuff I should be doing.'

He congratulated Matt and Livvy again and left, and she felt the tension drain out of her, but underneath she could still feel something unsettling, a seething, bubbling sensation of unfinished business between them.

Her own stupid fault. She should have let him go when he suggested it instead of dragging him upstairs and creating havoc between them. She finished her tea, put the mug down and got on with her job.

CHAPTER THREE

'JAN, I NEED a break. Can I grab half an hour? It's after one and I haven't stopped for a second yet.'

She hesitated, then gave a brisk nod. 'OK—but just half an hour, Georgie. I can't spare you any longer.'

'Thank you, you're a star.'

She headed off the ward, running downstairs before Jan had time to change her mind, and at the bottom of the stairs she bumped into Dan. Literally.

He caught her arms before she slammed into him, and grinned. 'Whoa! What are you running away from?'

She took a hasty step back, away from all that warm charisma. 'To, not from. I'm going for lunch.'

'Don't bother. The canteen's ramming.'

'Always is. I'm going to the Park Café. That's normally OK.'

'Really?' His eyes lit up. 'Mind if I join you?'

Did she mind? No. Was it a good idea? Big fat no this time, but she couldn't be that churlish.

'Sure,' she said, and let them out of the back doors into the beautiful park that surrounded the hospital, walking briskly over the grass to the Park Café near the back of the ED.

As she'd predicted it wasn't too busy, and she grabbed a banana and a muffin, ordered a cappuccino and plonked them on the tray next to his sandwich, black espresso and bottle of water.

'I'm getting this,' he said firmly as they reached the till, and she laughed.

'Go for it, but you still owe me dinner,' she joked, and then could have bitten her tongue off.

Why say that? Why poke the sleeping tiger?

But he just rolled his eyes, picked up the tray and raised a questioning eyebrow, and she led him outside.

'I need the shade, there's a bench over there,' she said, heading for a tree, and he followed her with the tray, swept a few crumbs off the seat and put the tray down between them.

'Good sandwich,' he mumbled round a mouthful, and she picked up her blueberry muffin and nodded.

'They are. I didn't want anything that healthy today, I just need quick calories. I haven't stopped since you left. Thanks again for your help with Livvy, by the way. You'll make a good midwife if you ever need a career change.'

He chuckled. 'You're welcome. It's nice to see it all happen as it should.' Then his smile faded and he tilted his head on one side and gave her a thoughtful look. 'So what's the story with those two? The atmosphere was loaded, and Matt looked—I don't know. A bit overwhelmed. Haunted, maybe, if that doesn't sound a bit far-fetched.'

She nodded. 'No, you're spot on, I think he was. He lost his first wife when his children were tiny, and Livvy's had breast cancer.'

His eyes widened and he went still. 'Whoa. Did he know that before they got married?'

'Yes. Oh, yes.'

He looked down, his face suddenly sombre. 'Wow. That must have taken some courage, marrying someone else who might die when you've already lost your wife.'

'But he loves her, and she'd had the all-clear, but one thing I know. Neither of them will ever take anything for granted.'

'No, I don't suppose they would.' He shook his head slowly. 'That's a heck of a journey to this point.'

'It is, but love can give you the strength to do all sorts of things. Anyway, this baby's really quite a big deal, and I'm so happy for them that they've been able to do it.'

He was studying her oddly. 'Are you?' he asked, and his words caught her by surprise.

'Well, of course I am. Why wouldn't I be?'

He shrugged. 'I don't know, you tell me. I mean, I'm sure you are, you're that sort of person, but for a second or two in there you didn't quite look it.'

She dragged her eyes away from his and drained her coffee. 'I don't know what you think you saw, but I'm fine.'

His voice was soft. 'Are you? Are you really?'

That again. She was opening her mouth to say something—she hadn't quite decided what—when he crumpled his cup and stood up.

'Look, I have to go, I've got an antenatal clinic in a minute, but I think we need to talk,' he said quietly.

'About?'

'Last night. It raised some—issues.'

'Issues?' she said, puzzled. She thought—

'Issues,' he said firmly. 'We need a conversation, but not here, we don't have time and it's too public for what I have to say, and anyway, as you quite rightly pointed out, I owe you dinner. Mine tonight, seven-thirty?'

'That was a joke.'

'Not to me. Please?'

She hesitated, not convinced it was in the slightest bit wise because last night was all she'd been able to think about ever since, and rehashing it seemed like the worst idea in the world. And anyway, she thought they'd already dealt with it.

'No strings, Georgia, I just want to talk to you,' he said, as if he could read her mind, and so she gave him her phone number so he could text her his address, threw her coffee cup in the bin and headed back to the ward, wondering what on earth she'd let herself in for.

Trouble, without a doubt, and she wasn't looking forward to it one little bit.

Livvy and her tiny daughter were discharged at three, and she escorted them to the door, watched as Matt clipped the baby seat with its precious cargo into the car, and kissed Livvy goodbye.

'I'll pop round and see you tomorrow,' she promised, and Livvy nodded.

'That'll be lovely. You can hold my hand and tell me it'll be OK.'

She laughed at that and hugged her. 'Of course it'll be OK. You're a natural. Go on, go home to Amber and Charlie and let them meet their baby sister.'

She waved them off and swallowed the lump in her throat. Was she the only person in the world who wasn't pregnant, smothered in tiny people or planning their wedding?

Laura and Tom were next in line of her friends, with a baby due in January. Another one she'd been asked to deliver, courtesy of their mutual friendship with Livvy Hunter. She didn't really know Laura, she'd only met her a few times, but like Livvy she seemed blissfully happy.

And Susie, too. She popped in briefly to see her on the way back to the ward, and found her sitting out in a chair with her little boy in her arms and her clearly besotted partner Rob at her side. They were the picture of happiness, and she was truly glad for them that it had turned out all right in the end, but still, under it all was that gnawing ache, the longing for what she'd lost when Mark had walked away. Although to be fair she'd never had it, but he'd just rubbed it in in the cruellest way.

You don't need a man in your life.

She didn't. She really didn't—especially not one like Mark, who hadn't even had the grace to tell her he wanted to move on until his girlfriend was pregnant. Or like Dan, come to that, considering she had to work with him, because the almost visceral tug between them was trashing her peace of mind.

Last night was *such* a bad idea. And now he wanted to talk about it?

She said goodbye and hurried back to the ward, for once in her life hoping it would be really busy, and she got her wish. Everyone in a fifty-mile radius seemed to be in labour, and she was straight back into the fray, which was just as well as it saved her from wallowing in self-pity.

Either that, or trying to work out what on earth Dan wanted to talk about, because she thought they'd dealt with the condom issue, and she couldn't think what else there was to talk about—apart from the fact that falling into bed with a colleague wasn't the smartest trick they could have pulled.

Still, four hours to go and she'd find out, and until then she was in charge of ensuring that other people got their miracle safe and sound. The miracle she'd never have.

She *really* needed a different job…

She was late leaving, of course. Only an hour, for a change, but she'd run home, had the quickest shower on record and pulled on the first thing she'd found that was cool enough, grabbed a jumper on the way out and left.

She turned into Brooke Avenue at seven-thirty-four and walked briskly along it, checking the numbers. Thirty-eight…forty—ah, here it was. Forty-two.

She stopped and stared at it curiously. It was Tom and Laura's house—or at least, Tom's old house. She'd only seen it once when she, Livvy and Laura had been out for a walk with Laura's dog, Millie, but she was sure it was the one.

It must have had a bit of a makeover in the last few weeks, though. The peeling woodwork had all been painted a soft grey-green, the rendered walls not quite white, and it was a charming, welcoming little cottage now instead of a slightly tired one.

She rang the bell, and after a second she heard footsteps running down the stairs and the door opened to reveal Dan barefoot, towel-dried hair on end, in the act of tugging on a T-shirt over his damp and really rather beautiful chest.

Don't bother on my account, she thought, and then spotted the bite mark on his shoulder before it disappeared under the T. Really? Had she done that to him last night? Heat washed through her at the thought, and she cut herself off before she lost the plot. She was there because he wanted to talk, not…

'Hi. Sorry, I got held up as I was leaving so I've only been home ten minutes. Come in.'

'I've only just finished, too,' she said, hoping her voice didn't sound as ridiculously breathless as she felt. 'It's been manic there today.'

'Tell me about it, but it doesn't matter, we're both here now and the food won't take long. Come on through, I'll get you a drink and you can talk to me while I cook.'

'What are we having?' she asked, to fill the void as much as anything. Not that she wasn't hungry—

'Mushroom stroganoff with wild rice, if that's OK, and I thought steamed veg. Green beans, tenderstem broccoli, sugar snap peas, julienne carrots—whatever you fancy, really. Is that all right?'

She gave a surprised laugh. 'Wow, that's a lot of options. Have you just been shopping or something?'

He chuckled at that and raked a hand through his hair. 'No. I had a delivery the day before yesterday, and I was going to cook last night except you got there first.'

And look how that went…

'It sounds delicious,' she said, cutting off her thoughts yet again before they strayed into dangerous territory, and followed him through to the kitchen.

'Make yourself at home,' he said, and delved into the fridge, so she settled herself in a chair and plucked a grape off the bunch in the fruit bowl to tide her over.

'So how come you're renting Tom Stryker's house?' she asked curiously.

'You know them?'

'Yes—well, I know Laura through Livvy, and I've seen Tom in the ED when I've been called down there. She's pregnant, too, due in January.'

'Another one?'

'Oh, it's rife.' Rife amongst her peer group, anyway. She couldn't get away from it, and every birth, although it brought her joy for her friends, just twisted the knife a little more. 'So how come you're here? I didn't know it was ready to rent, they've been working on it.'

He shut the door of the fridge and put a pile of things down on the worktop. 'Ben Walker told me about it. He asked if I had anything in mind when I was offered the job, and this came up a few weeks ago, and I love it. It's got a gorgeous garden, and it'll give me time to sell my house in Bristol and look for something more permanent. What would you like to drink? I've got wine, red or white, or pomegranate and elderflower cordial, beer with or without, tea, coffee?'

She debated the cordial for a second, then gave in and shrugged. 'D'you know what? I'm not working tomorrow, I have the miracle of a day off, so I might go for a white wine.'

Which was probably a mistake, because her guard had been well and truly down when she was stone cold sober...

Not an issue. For now at least he was busy chopping, slicing, frying, stirring, warming plates, so she stayed put and sipped her wine, raided the grapes and watched him, and within twenty minutes they were sitting down at a table in the garden with a steaming plate full of loveliness.

'Gosh, that smells good,' she said, and dived in. 'Mmm. Super-tasty,' she mumbled, and he gave a wry laugh.

'You really didn't think it would be, did you?'

She looked up and met his eyes, and they were oddly humourless despite the laugh. 'I didn't know what to expect,' she said, not only about the food but about him, what he wanted to talk about, what he wanted with her. If anything…

And then she couldn't wait any longer. 'You said you wanted to talk,' she said, and he put his fork down with exaggerated care.

'Yes. Yes, I did.' His eyes flicked up and locked on hers, oddly penetrating. 'You said last night I couldn't get you pregnant. You sounded very sure.'

She dropped her eyes back to her food, suddenly flavourless and unappealing. 'I am sure.'

'Why?'

'I just am.'

He gave a short sigh. 'Georgia, I need to know,' he said quietly, but with a thread of steel. 'If you get pregnant, it's on me, and I really don't want that to happen.'

'It can't happen,' she said, dropping her fork and meeting his eyes with difficulty. 'I can't get pregnant. My ex and I spent four years trying, and I mean *really* trying, and nothing happened, so I suggested having some investigations, and then he told me he was having an affair and his girlfriend was pregnant.'

His jaw dropped. 'While you were still trying?'

She nodded. 'Oh, yeah. Well, I was. He was just having his cake and eating it, only he preferred her cake. He said all we ever did was try and make a baby, but with her sex was fun, only apparently it came with a side order of an unplanned pregnancy.'

He frowned. 'It couldn't have been someone else's?'

'No. Oh, no, it was definitely his. She only lived round the corner, and he moved in with her after I kicked him out, and I bumped into them all the time. The child was the spitting image of him. That was when I moved here. I didn't need my nose rubbed in it every time I went out of my front door.'

'Hell, Georgie, that's...' He blew out his breath slowly, shaking his head. 'I'm sorry. Last night I thought you meant you were using some method of contraception, but after I saw you with Livvy Hunter...'

'Livvy?'

He shrugged. 'You had a look about you that I've seen before. A heartbreaking sort of "why not me?" look.'

She swallowed and looked down at her food. Was it really so obvious?

He reached out and laid his hand over hers. 'I'm sorry, I didn't mean to probe or upset you. I've got a few of my own hot buttons, but I sensed there was something about Livvy that touched one of yours, and it seems I wasn't wrong.'

No, he wasn't, of course, and every birth had an element of 'why not me', but it was an odd remark, something about the way he'd phrased it. Not the bit about her, but the bit about him and his hot buttons.

She studied his face, looking for a clue, and she found one there in the shadows, some hint of grief, perhaps, that she hadn't expected—and doing Susie's section he'd been weird, in a way, almost as if his emotions were shut down. And he'd talked about a sore point.

His hot button?

'What happened to you, Dan?' she asked gently, and he pushed his plate away and met her eyes.

'I can't eat this now. Let's go down the garden.'

He got to his feet, and she followed him past the late-blooming roses, the blaze of blue from the agapanthus, the brilliant white of the Japanese anemones mingling with them at the back of the border behind the delicate froth of baby's breath and the mounds of soft pink geraniums. There was a bench at the far end under a tree, surrounded by the sweet scent of nicotiana and night-scented stocks, and they sat down on it, tilted their faces to the evening sun and she waited.

And waited.

Then finally, when she was about to prompt him, he spoke, his voice soft and a little raw.

'I was with someone at uni. We'd been together for a few months, and we got careless. She was on the pill, but she'd had a bug, and we didn't even think about it, and she ended up pregnant. It couldn't have been at a worse time. We were about to start our first jobs, and although we were both in London we weren't in the same hospital, and living together would have meant a long commute. So I was in hospital accommodation on the other side of London, and we were hardly seeing each other and our relationship suffered. When she told me she was pregnant we even talked about getting married, but she didn't think it was a good enough reason and I agreed, really. I fully intended to have a relationship with my child, and I was there for all the scans and really looking forward to meeting the baby, and we were both OK with that, but not with us. We weren't really getting on by then and it wouldn't have lasted, but at least if we'd been together still I might have been there with her when it happened. I should have been there, and she should never have got pregnant, and that was my fault and I'll blame myself for ever.

'Anyway, it made no difference in the end. She was diagnosed with a placenta previa at her anomaly scan, which was pretty worrying, and she was booked for an elective section at thirty-eight weeks, with constant monitoring. And it was all going well, and then one day, when she was thirty-four weeks, I missed a call from her, and I didn't pick up her voicemail for half an hour. She'd started to bleed, and she'd called an ambulance. She sounded terrified, and I hadn't picked up because it was on silent and I'd missed her call.'

Georgie closed her eyes, not sure she wanted to hear what she knew was coming.

'I got there just as they were taking her to Theatre. She was still conscious, barely, and she made me promise I'd look after the baby if anything happened to her. I told her I would, and I told her she'd be fine, but she wasn't. I walked up and down outside Theatre, holding my breath for a little cry, but there was nothing, and then after an age the doors opened and the surgeon came out and told me she'd bled out. Her cervix had opened, and her placenta had pulled away and torn a major uterine vessel, and there was nothing they could do to save either of them.'

Horror washed over her at his quiet words, and her eyes welled. How on earth had he dealt with that?

'Oh, Dan, I'm so sorry. That's just heartbreaking.'

'It was. It tore me apart and it took a long time to put myself back together. And then Susie on my first day—that was just classic timing.'

'That must have been so hard for you.'

He gave her a sad, twisted little smile. 'It was, but it's why I went into obstetrics. I couldn't save them, but maybe I could save someone else. Someone like Susie, and her baby. That's why I was so determined to save both of them, because if I didn't I knew exactly what Rob would be going through. When that baby cried...'

'Yes. I think we all nearly cried with it.' She reached out and took his hand, folding it in hers. 'Did you see your baby?' she asked gently, and she felt his hand tighten.

He nodded. 'A midwife took me into a quiet room and gave her to me to hold. She was beautiful, Georgie, absolutely perfect, and there was no need for her to have died. If we'd been living together, if we'd got married, if I'd answered my phone that day, maybe I could have saved her. Saved both of them.'

'Could you? Could you honestly? It doesn't sound like it.'

'I don't know. They said not. It had been too quick, too catastrophic. The midwife was lovely to me, really kind, and I'll be forever grateful to her for that. She'd taken little footprints, and she'd washed and dressed her and wrapped her in a blanket, and she put her in my arms and sat with me, and then she held me when I cried. You know how it goes, I'm sure you've done it.'

Georgie felt her eyes fill with tears. 'Yes, I have.' She'd done the same thing for bereaved parents more times than she wanted to think about, and it never got easier. And he'd lost his partner as well, although they weren't together.

What an awful, dreadful tragedy for all of them.

'Holly's parents took charge after that,' he went on, 'and arranged the funeral at their home, and they shut me out. I think they blamed me for getting her pregnant, and to be fair I blamed myself, for that and for not being there for her when she needed me. I still do. I always will, even though she'd pushed me away. So I wouldn't have gone to the funeral anyway, but it hurt that I wasn't there to hold Holly's hand when it mattered most, and it really, really hurt that our baby died. I didn't know what love was until I held my daughter in my arms, Georgie, and I'll always be gutted that she'll never know how much I wanted her...'

'Oh, Dan, I'm so sorry.'

'Yeah.' His voice cracked, and he cleared his throat, paused for a moment, then went on, 'So, anyway, when I saw Susie, with no antenatal records on her and a bleeding placenta previa...'

'...it hit all your hot buttons.'

'Pretty much. Did it show?'

'A bit. You were very on it, and I thought, good, someone decisive, someone who knows what they're doing, but there was just something about you, an intensity, some undercurrent of something that I didn't quite understand.'

'Like you with Livvy.'

'Maybe. I understand a little of how they felt when they weren't sure if she'd be able to have a baby, so of course I'm pleased for them, but yes, I felt it. I always feel it, with every delivery. Don't get me wrong, I love my job, and I couldn't bear to give it up, but every baby

I deliver, a little bit more inside me dies. I didn't realise it showed, though.'

'Likewise.'

She laughed, but it was a sad little effort. 'We wouldn't be any good at poker, would we?'

He gave her a wry, sad little smile. 'Probably not. Anyway, I was a bit raw after all the drama with Susie, and you were there, and you were kind to me, and I didn't want to talk about it, but there was all that warmth and kindness in your eyes, and I just wanted to hold you and let it soak into me and blot out all the memories.'

He lifted her hand and pressed it to his lips, then laid it down and met her eyes. 'I used you, and I'm sorry. It won't happen again.'

She shook her head, lifted her hand and cradled his cheek against her palm. 'I can't let you take responsibility for that. I said you didn't have to go. You didn't use me. OK, you weren't up front about your personal history, but we'd barely met, and things like that— they make us vulnerable, and I think we have to hold onto them a little longer, until we feel safe enough to share them. Like I didn't tell you about my infertility.'

He nodded slowly, then searched her eyes. 'Does that mean you feel safe with me now?'

She smiled at him and dropped her hand. 'Yes. Yes, I do. Is it a good idea going there again? Probably not.'

'No. You're right, and I was coming to that. I—I really don't think we should go there again. I don't think it would be wise. I need to be able to concentrate on settling into my new job, and I'm not really in the market for a relationship, especially not one where we'll end up working together all the time. It's got too much potential to get really messy, but I can always use a friend.'

'Well, I'm here,' she said, and his mouth twisted into a sad little parody of a smile.

'Yes, I think you are. Thank you.' He gave a wry laugh. 'Given our histories, do you ever get the feeling we're in the wrong jobs?'

That made her laugh, too, because she'd had that very thought earlier, with Livvy. 'All the time, but what else would we do? We'd both miss it, you know that. At least this way we get to make a difference.' She tilted her head on one side and smiled at him. 'Do you know what? I'm hungry now. Shall we go and eat?'

His mouth tilted, this time into a proper smile. 'Good idea. I'll warm it up.'

He walked her home, but not until they'd talked more about their jobs, the people he'd be working with, the ethos of the department.

All nice and safe, one of them at each end of the sofa, sipping coffee and exchanging anecdotes.

Being friends.

Until they ran out of safe topics, and then all of a sudden the tension was back, that invisible tug that was so dangerous, so beguiling, so very much not a good idea. She got up to leave and he insisted on walking with her.

'I'll be fine,' she told him, but he shook his head.

'I've got enough on my conscience, I don't need you as well,' he said, and so she stopped arguing and let him do it.

Not that she could have stopped him. She might not

know him well, but she knew him that well already, and it was oddly reassuring.

They reached her door, and he stopped, just out of reach, while she slipped her key into the lock and turned it.

She left the door open and turned back to him with a smile, but something in his eyes stopped her smile in its tracks. A lingering trace of grief, of emptiness, of loneliness and longing that echoed her own.

For an age he held her eyes, then looked down, hands rammed in his pockets as if to stop them reaching out to her.

'I need to go,' he said gruffly, and she was so, so close to telling him to stay, because if a man ever needed someone to hold him Dan did then, but he took a step back as if he knew what she was thinking, and threw her a wry smile. 'Have a good day off.'

'I will. And thank you for supper. It was delicious.'

'You're welcome. Goodnight, Georgia.'

And without waiting for a reply he turned on his heel and walked away, striding off into the night with his back ramrod straight.

She could have followed him, called out, run after him—but she didn't. Her shoulders dropped, the tension of the moment leaving her, replaced in the nick of time by common sense.

He was right. It was too complicated, with them working together and him carrying the burden of his grief and guilt still, after ten years. He didn't need her, and especially not now while he was settling into a new role in a new hospital.

And when he did need someone there for him, it would be someone who could give him children. Someone who could give him the family he so deserved. That wasn't her, and never would be, but in the meantime she could be his friend.

Even if it killed her…

She went inside and shut the door.

Had it cleared the air?

He wasn't sure. He hoped so, but there was a niggle of regret that he hadn't taken her up on the invitation in her eyes.

Maybe he'd misread it, the light from her porch playing tricks with him. And even if he hadn't, it wasn't a good idea. Sleeping with a colleague that you had to work with all the time was never a good idea, and he really needed his mind clear to concentrate on settling into his new role.

Never mind the fact that once again he would have been using her to blot out the memories. Using her, after he'd promised it would never happen again.

He let himself in, closed the front door firmly behind him and set about eradicating all trace of her from the house. He loaded the dishwasher, tipped out the last dreg of wine from her glass, added it to the top rack and shut the door on it, then turned and spotted her jumper draped over the back of a dining chair.

She'd brought it in case it got chilly, but it hadn't, and she'd left it behind. He picked it up and buried his nose in it and breathed her in, then threw it down, cross with himself for giving in to the impulse.

It had only made it worse, brought back the memories of last night, the scent of her hair, the warmth of her body, the sound of her as she—

'Stop it! It's not appropriate, and anyway, you're broken, you're no use to her. Not going to happen.'

He turned on the cold tap, ran it for a moment, filled a glass with fresh water and took it up to bed. If all else failed, he could tip it over himself...

CHAPTER FOUR

SHE WENT TO see Livvy at eleven the next morning, armed with flowers, a present for the baby and a game for the older two, and found her resting in the shade on the swing seat at the end of the garden, her baby in her arms and a tender smile on her face.

'Olivia, look who's here,' Matt said, and she looked up and smiled.

'Georgie! Oh, they're beautiful. Thank you—and what are all these? You shouldn't have…'

'Rubbish.' She bent and kissed Livvy's cheek, and smiled down at the baby. 'Oh, she's so beautiful. Hello, little Esme.' She perched on the end of the bench and put all the presents down, and Matt rescued the flowers and took them inside, leaving them to talk. 'So, how's it going?' she asked. 'Are you managing to breastfeed her?'

Livvy nodded. 'Yes. I think it might be a bit more difficult when my milk comes in because of the tug on the scar tissue, but, d'you know what? I've had worse, and it's worth it, and I'm sure I'll soon adjust.'

'You can always talk to a breastfeeding counsellor.'

'I know. My midwife came this morning and we talked about it. I'm so glad it was you who delivered me, though. I mean, she's lovely, but I just felt you understood us and our situation and we didn't need to explain anything. Matt said you were really kind to him when he was having a moment.'

She shrugged. 'I just tried to put myself in his shoes. It must be very bittersweet.'

'Yes, it is. But he's so thrilled with her, he's utterly besotted, and Amber and Charlie are just over the moon. Especially Amber. I think she views her baby sister as a real live doll she can help to look after, and she's so gentle with her.'

'I'm sure they'll have great fun.'

'I hope so. It might take a bit of getting used to, though. So what's in here?' she added, putting one hand in the baby gift bag and pulling out the contents. 'Oh, Georgie! Oh, it's so soft and squishy! Thank you!'

She snuggled the little grey rabbit up against her face, and sighed. 'It's lovely. Thank you so much.'

'You're welcome. And that's just a little game for the other two to play when they get bored with Esme,' she said with a smile.

Matt reappeared with ice-cold glasses of elderflower cordial beaded with moisture and a plate of biscuits made by the children, taking the presents back inside with him and leaving them alone, and Livvy took a sip of her drink and leant back and eyed Georgie thoughtfully. Too thoughtfully.

'What?' she asked round a mouthful of choc chip cookie.

'This Dan guy. I know I was a bit distracted yesterday, not to mention a total diva, sorry about that, but—what is it with you two?'

'Nothing,' she said firmly, because it was nothing,

especially after their conversation last night, and Dan was the last person she wanted to talk about. 'Really, he's just a colleague—'

'Don't give me that. I don't believe it for a moment. You were both looking at each other, and the tension between you—well, I don't know, if you're not taking advantage of it you're wasting a golden opportunity, because he is seriously hot!'

She shook her head. 'It's not going to happen.'

'Why on earth not?'

'Because it's more complicated than that.' She had another bite of the biscuit, but Livvy wasn't going to let it drop.

'How complicated can it be? Crumbs, me and Matt are pretty complicated. It can't be worse than that.'

She wasn't sure, but she wasn't going to discuss it, even with Livvy. She swallowed, brushed the crumbs off her lap and took a drink. She hated lying, but...

'I'm not interested in a relationship, Livvy, and especially not with someone I have to work with. We're barely even friends.' And that was the way it was going to have to stay.

'If you say so.'

'I do. Mind if I have a cuddle with your little bundle of joy?' she said, changing the subject firmly, and Livvy smiled her understanding and handed the baby over. She settled her in the crook of her arm, and Esme immediately stirred and turned her head towards her, rosebud lips pursed, and she felt the familiar tug of yearning.

'Oh, dear, I think someone's hungry,' she murmured, and handed her back, leaving her arms empty.

Always empty, with an ache that nothing could fill.

She needed to get out of there, so she glanced at her phone. 'Oh, goodness, is that the time? I need to fly. I've got so much to do.' Which wasn't exactly a lie, more an exaggeration.

Livvy reached out a hand and squeezed her arm. 'Thank you so much, for everything. You were amazing yesterday. You made me feel so safe.'

'That's my job,' she said with a smile, and bent and kissed Livvy's cheek, laid her hand lightly on the baby's soft, downy head and left them to it before she started to cry.

Work seemed odd without Georgie there.

Odd, but no less stressful, because it was a crazy day with one intervention after another requiring his attention, on top of a gynae theatre list that had left him wrung out.

The list kicked off with removal of a cervical cancer in a thirty-two-year-old woman who had been trying to start a family without success. She'd missed the last two smear tests because she'd been on holiday, or too busy, and by the time she'd had one it had gone too far for a cone biopsy. He'd hoped to be able to save at least the top of her uterus in the long and complex operation, but when he opened her up it was worse than the scans had revealed.

Nevertheless, although she lost her uterus and a lot of associated structures and with them any hope of carrying a baby, it hadn't spread to her lymph nodes so at least she now stood a chance of making a full recovery. And he'd managed to salvage her ovaries by doing a transposition, re-siting them high up in her abdomen out of the field of any potential radiotherapy, so at least he'd not plunged her headlong into the menopause.

And there was always surrogacy. Small mercies...

She was followed in Theatre by a few routine ops, but his mind kept going back to her and he felt it acutely, and of course there was no one there to decompress with. Well, no one he knew, at least. Only Jo, his registrar, who'd assisted, and Patrick, who was observing and who'd also found it really hard to deal with, so he ended up counselling him instead.

Then he had to break the news to his cancer patient and her husband that she'd lost her uterus. It hadn't been unexpected, but she closed her eyes and tears slid down her cheeks, and he was gutted for her.

'Looking on the bright side, at least you haven't dumped me into the land of hot flushes, and there's always the possibility of harvesting my eggs, I guess,' she said with a brave attempt at a smile.

'There is,' he said gently. 'But give yourself time. I'll come and see you again tomorrow, and we'll talk about where we go from here, OK?'

She nodded, her smile wobbling, and as he walked away he heard a sob and the sound of her husband's voice trying to soothe her. Was that how Georgie felt? As if everything she'd looked forward to in life had been ripped away?

On the way out he dropped into the antenatal ward to check if he was needed, and was confronted by a frantic midwife who had an exhausted mother, a distressed baby, and Patrick on her hands.

'I was about to call you, Patrick's totally out of his depth and she needs intervention. I've done an episiotomy already, but I think she needs forceps, it's a bit high for the ventouse and he just can't do it and there's nobody else,' she said, and Dan gave an inward sigh.

'Let me have a go,' he said, and introduced himself to the exhausted woman, had a look at what was going on and within five minutes he'd lifted the baby out using forceps, and she had a healthy, squalling baby in her arms.

It was a lovely way to end the day, but by the time he left it was almost eight, and he walked home, opened the door and saw Georgie's jumper, waiting for him to return it.

He stood and stared at it. He could take it to work tomorrow. Or he could walk round to hers now, and drop it off. It was a beautiful evening, and frankly he needed something to do to chase away the shadows of the challenging day, so he ran upstairs, showered to wash away all traces of the hospital, pulled on jeans and a shirt and headed out, jumper in hand.

She answered the door in bare feet, a loose cotton shirt and cropped trousers with grubby knees. Her fair hair was scooped up in an untidy ponytail, gold tendrils escaping to frame her face, and he felt a rush of warmth, coupled with some good old-fashioned lust.

So much for friendship...

Typical. She was hot and sweaty, her clothes were dirty from gardening and she had no idea what her hair was doing, but Dan was standing there, her jumper in his hands, and he held it out to her with a wry smile.

'You left this behind yesterday,' he said without preamble, and she took it from him.

'I know, I realised this morning. You didn't need to bring it, tomorrow would have done.' She studied him for a moment, saw the shadows in his eyes and forgot about how she looked. 'Tough day?' she murmured.

He gave a short huff of what might possibly have been laughter, and nodded. 'Is it that obvious?'

'Absolutely. You look knackered. Want to come in?'

'No, you don't want me here. I'm not good company tonight.'

She tutted at him and stepped back. 'Don't be silly, I don't need entertaining. Come in and have a drink in the garden.'

He hesitated, then nodded. 'OK—but just one, and no alcohol.'

He stepped inside, shut the door and followed her into the kitchen, and she looked at him again. 'Have you eaten today?'

He laughed again, this time more recognisably, and gave her a wry smile. 'Not so you'd notice. I had a sandwich at some point this afternoon. Not sure when. But you don't need to feed me, a glass of something cold would be lovely. I can cook when I get home, I've got a fridge full of food.'

'Do you really want to be doing that? You're here now and I've got the last of the leftover chilli in the freezer, and some tortilla chips. Will that do?'

He held her eyes for a long moment, then gave a weary chuckle. 'That would be amazing. Thank you.'

She turned her back on him, digging out the chilli from the freezer, hugely conscious of his presence behind her in the small kitchen.

She could almost feel the warmth of his body drifting in the air, along with the scent of his shampoo or body wash. Subtle, masculine and doing nothing whatsoever for her peace of mind or their decision to be simple friends. Nothing simple about it.

At all. And as for her not wanting him there…

She put the chilli in the microwave, found the tortilla chips and the yogurt, grated some cheese and turned to find him propped against the wall, arms folded and staring into space with a sombre expression on his face.

She handed him a cold alcohol-free beer out of the fridge and met his eyes. 'Come on, let's take this outside,' she said, and piling everything onto a tray she led him through the living room and out into her tiny courtyard garden.

She had a little bistro set out there, and she plonked the tray on it, pushed it towards him and watched him eat mechanically. She waited until he'd finished and put his fork down, then she broke the silence.

'Want to talk about it?'

He met her eyes, smiled wearily and shook his head.

'Not really. I'm not sure I've got the energy.'

'Did you lose a patient?'

He shook his head again. 'No, and actually in some ways it was a good day. Bit of a curate's egg, really, but my gynae list kicked off with a young woman with cervical cancer that was diagnosed late. She's lost her uterus, but I did a transposition so I've managed to save her ovaries and there's a good chance she'll live, but it wasn't nice having to tell her that she'll never be able to carry a child. I think she pretty much knew it would happen, but there was a tiny shred of hope and I had to trash it. That was tough—but I don't have to tell you that.'

She felt her eyes prickle, and blinked. 'No. It's not something anybody wants to know, but I'm glad you've given her a chance of survival, and maybe a chance of a baby with a surrogate.'

'Yeah. Me, too. It was pretty major surgery and the prognosis is still guarded, but I've referred her to Oncology so it's all down to them now. She's only thirty-two, two years younger than me.'

And a year older than her. What a tragedy. 'You needed to talk to someone,' she said, and he laughed.

'I did. I ended up counselling Patrick after we finished in Theatre. He was observing the gynae ops, and it was a tough list with that young woman and it got to him a bit, but that's to be expected; he's only just started his obs and gynae rotation a week and a bit ago, and it's a steep learning curve. We've all been there. He just needs some experience under his belt. He'll be a good GP, I'm sure, and he's a great listener, but he's not a surgeon by any stretch of the imagination. And then when I was leaving I had to rescue him again.'

'Now what?'

He laughed, but it sounded weary and a bit jaded. 'A poor exhausted woman who just didn't have the reserves left to push the baby out. It was virtually there, Kat had done an episiotomy, but she still couldn't find the strength and she needed help, and Patrick was right out of his depth.'

'Oh, poor Kat. So what did you do? Use the ventouse?'

'No, it was too high, so I used forceps and it was all done and dusted in five minutes, but I could have done without it. Still, it was a training opportunity and it ended on a high, but it was a long day, one of those days that we all get from time to time.'

They did, and everyone felt the way he was obviously feeling. One of the drawbacks of being in a caring profession, and as for not getting involved, tell it to the fairies. They all did. Some just dealt with it better than others.

'I'm sorry I wasn't there for you.'

His eyes flicked back to hers and he gave a wry smile.

'Don't be. I'm a big boy now, I can cope. Anyway, enough of me. How was your day? Done anything interesting?'

She laughed at that. 'Oh, riveting. I stripped the bed, put the sheets in the washing machine, watered the plants, went and saw Livvy and took her some presents, came back via the shops to pick up some food and I've been out here mostly. I hung out the washing, did a bit of pot tweaking, deadheaded the rose, such as it is, and then I read a book.'

'That sounds lovely,' he said with a touch of envy in his voice. 'How's Livvy?'

'Doing well. Baby's gorgeous, breastfeeding's going well, so all good.'

'And you?'

She laughed again, a tiny huff, and gave him what had to be a twisted little smile. 'Dan, really, I'm fine. I deal with it every single day. It's what I do. I can handle it.'

His mouth was wry. 'Yeah, and I know how that goes.'

He looked away, glancing at her garden. 'It's lovely out here. I don't know what's in your pots, but they smell heavenly and they look gorgeous. It works really well.'

'Thank you. It does, but it gets really hot out here by the end of the day and I spend my life watering, so it's a lot of work. Your garden's so full and lush and pretty, and I'm really envious of your lawn and the bench in the shade under that tree, but this is fine for me, I'm happy with it. I couldn't cope with yours.'

He chuckled at that. 'It remains to be seen whether I can. I've only been there a week and Tom left it immaculate, but it's rapidly becoming my favourite room in the house—if you can call it a room.'

She could imagine that. Not that there was anything wrong with the house itself, from what little she'd seen of it, but it was simply furnished, white from end to end, and unlike the garden it was very much a blank canvas waiting for him to put his stamp on it.

If he did. She had the feeling he might not bother, not if he was planning on moving.

'So what kind of house do you want to buy when you sell your other one?' she asked, and he shrugged.

'I don't know. It depends. I haven't really looked, so I've got no idea what the local housing stock is like.'

'Pricey, mostly,' she said with a smile. 'This is very modest but it stretched me to the limit.'

'There's nothing wrong with it. It's a nice house.'

'I think so, and it suits me, but I don't think it would suit you, not with this tiny scrap of garden. Men always seem to want to cut grass.'

He laughed for the first time that day with a bit of genuine amusement. 'Bit of a sweeping generalisation,' he said, but he didn't argue, so she carried on.

'So where would you want to be? In town? In a village just outside, buried in the countryside up to your neck in nettles?'

'Probably not the nettles,' he said with a wry grin.

'OK, no nettles. How about overlooking the sea on the clifftop, or down by the yacht harbour near the river mouth? That's nice, and one of the ED consultants lives there. Livvy and Matt are on the clifftop in a gorgeous modernist house near Ed and Annie. You met Ed on your first day, he was looking after Susie's baby. That's the prime spot if you want a stunning sea view, but they're eye-wateringly expensive. If you like Victorian grandeur there's the old part of town. Ben and Daisy Walker have a massive house there stuffed with original features, so do Jake and Emily Stratton. You know them, they job-share in our department. And Nick and Liv Jarvis live not far from here but in a much more sensible house. You must have met them, too. He's an obstetrician and Liv's a midwife.'

'Yes, I've met most of them. So they're all pretty local, then?'

'They are. It makes being on call easier, and it's also a great community. Lots of social stuff. It's like one big family.'

He nodded slowly. 'I'm sure. It sounds like there's lots of variety to choose from when I get round to it, but I'm quite happy in the cottage for now. There's no hurry and it's not like I'm short of space.'

He glanced at his phone, drained the last dreg of his beer and put the can down. 'I need to go. It's getting late, and I've no doubt got another killer day tomorrow. I'm on take.'

'Oh, joy. I'm doing a double shift tomorrow. Seven till nine. I can hardly wait.'

He chuckled and tipped his head on one side. 'I'll be there if you need anything.'

Her heart gave a sudden thud and she ignored it. 'What, like my peanut butter opened?' she said lightly, and his mouth twitched.

'Something like that.'

He unravelled his legs and stood up, and she got to her feet and followed him to the front door.

And then they stalled, tension hanging in the air.

'I'm glad you came round,' she said, breaking the suddenly loaded silence.

'So am I. I'll try not to make it a habit.'

She laughed. 'Feel free. I'm never doing anything else.'

He hesitated a moment, then reeled her in against his chest for a gentle hug. 'Thank you,' he murmured into her hair. 'For feeding me again, giving me a shoulder to cry on—or whinge on, at least—you're a star.'

She wrapped her arms around him and hugged him back, her head resting briefly on his shoulder as she breathed in the scent of him, warm and clean and enticing. Too enticing. She let go and stepped away out of reach.

'You're welcome. You can return the favour when I need it.'

'It'll be my pleasure.' He smiled and opened the door. 'I'll see you in the morning. Sleep well.'

'And you.'

She closed the door behind him, rested against it for a moment and then shrugged herself away, gathered up all the things in the garden, loaded the dishwasher and went to bed.

It wasn't made, of course, because she'd washed the sheets that morning to get rid of the scent of his skin so she could stop fantasising about him all night...

She pulled fresh linen out of the airing cupboard, made the bed and crawled into it. Much better. Well, not better, but better for her peace of mind.

Except she went to sleep and dreamed about him anyway, which did nothing for her peace of mind at all.

He shouldn't have hugged her.

Stupid, stupid thing to do—but she'd been just there, right under his nose, with her messy hair and her gentle smile, and he hadn't been able to resist the urge.

He was glad he hadn't. It had been good to hold her. So good. And to talk to her. She was right, he'd needed to decompress, and she understood, knew what he was talking about, felt the same pressures and responsibilities. And one day no doubt he'd be able to return the favour.

He let himself into his cottage, walked straight through it and out into the garden, kicking off his shoes and grabbing a cold drink on the way. There was a white rose trained against the fence, the blooms almost luminous in the dark, and he headed past it to the bench under the tree, the grass cool and damp under his feet, and thought of her little paved courtyard garden filled with pots, and how she'd said she loved this garden. He loved it, too. It was a refuge from reality, a kind of sanctuary, and he'd be sorry to leave it when the time came.

It was dark now, with just the light of the moon to guide him, and the air was heavy with scent from the plants beside the bench. He didn't know what they were, but Georgie might know. He thought he recognised the scent from her garden. He'd have to ask her next time she was here.

He closed his eyes, letting the day fall away from him and the peace steal in to take its place, and all around him he could hear the rustling of tiny creatures. There was even an owl in the distance.

Bliss.

Maybe he needed to buy a hammock and sling it between the tree and the fence—except it might pull the fence over, but he could get one in a frame.

Or just go to bed.

He hoisted himself off the bench and headed inside.

She hardly saw him the next day.

He was rushed off his feet, she had two women in established labour that she was moving between and another being induced that she was monitoring for progress, and the day flew by.

Before she knew it her shift was over, and she walked home, let herself in, made some beans on toast and went out to the garden. It seemed empty without him, and it was oddly lonely.

That annoyed her. She'd never been lonely before, so why should she be lonely now? Ridiculous.

She ate her meal, watered the pots and went to bed, and again she could feel his presence. Or absence, more accurately.

She really needed to get a grip.

For the next two weeks they were like ships in the night.

He helped her with an awkward breech delivery, but apart from that she scarcely saw him because she had a week of nights in the middle of it, which was a killer. She even had to get Patrick to wrestle the top off her peanut butter jar, but at least he was capable of that. He told her that Dan had taken him under his wing and was mentoring him, so she had hopes for his progress. There was plenty of room for it.

But as for her and Dan—well, at least she was getting used to seeing him around, and with enough practice maybe her heart would stop doing stupid things every time she heard his voice. Not that he was unfriendly, far from it, he was just as busy as she was.

Then after her run of nights and her days off, she got sent down to his antenatal clinic because they were short of midwives and it was miraculously quiet on the labour ward, so she ended up working with him.

A new patient who was there for her twelve-week scan was worried sick because she'd had a little bleeding, so the first thing Georgie did was try and listen for the baby's heartbeat, but she couldn't find it.

'OK, I can't seem to locate it but that could just be the position it's in, so let's do a pregnancy test.'

She took a test strip out of her pocket where she'd put a few in case she needed them, stripped the wrapper off and dipped the strip into the urine sample the woman had brought with her, then waited until the first and then the second line appeared.

They didn't have to wait many seconds, and she smiled at her relieved patient.

'Well, it still says you're pregnant, so that's good news. I think our next move needs to be the scan. You're here for one anyway, so let me go and bump you up the queue and I'll come back to you in a moment. The consultant might want to have a look at you as well.'

She went out and tapped on Dan's door, and he opened it instantly, as if he'd been on the way out.

'Hello, stranger,' he said with a smile. 'Do you need me?'

That again...

'If you're not busy. I've got a worried first-time mum. She's twelve weeks, had a bit of bleeding, I can't hear a heartbeat but the pregnancy test says she's pregnant and I think her placenta is probably in the way. She's in for a scan. Do you want me to get that done first, or do you want to have a listen? There's a queue for the scan.'

'Let's do both,' he said, and followed her back in.

'Hi, my name's Daniel Blake, I'm the consultant in charge of your care. Do you mind if I have a listen to your baby?'

She shook her head, still looking worried, and he pulled his Doppler out of his pocket, wiggled it around for a minute, tried again in a different position and just when Georgie was giving up hope the room was filled with the wonderful whooshing sound of the baby's heart.

'There we go,' he said with a smile, and the woman burst into tears of relief. Dan slid the Doppler back into his pocket, handed her a tissue and winked at Georgie.

He opened his mouth to say something, and she gave him a look and he just grinned and walked out without a word, but she was too relieved to be cross that he'd found it and she hadn't.

That wasn't what mattered, and in the end the scan was fine, so the woman was sent off with her next appointment booked and a photo of her perfectly healthy baby. The rest of the clinic was busy but routine, with no dramas or crises, and she ended her shift only an hour late.

She went into the locker room to change, found the pregnancy tests strips still in her pocket and put them in her locker, then changed her clothes, dropping the scrubs into the laundry bin. Then she pulled out her bag and a tampon fell out. She bent down and picked it up, then stared at it thoughtfully.

Was her period overdue?

She wasn't sure. Her cycle wasn't an issue, so she never really bothered to make a note, but her periods usually started on a Tuesday, and it was Thursday.

Her heart gave a dull thud and she stared at it for another moment, then put it and the test strips in her bag and shut her locker.

There was no way she could be pregnant—was there? Surely not.

But all the way home her heart was racing, and the first thing she did once she'd closed the front door was run upstairs to the bathroom to do the test.

How could a minute be so long?

She perched on the edge of the bath, staring at the little strip and not quite sure what she wanted to see, one line or two.

One appeared instantly, to show the test was working. Not that anything else was going to happen—

Another line? Really? And a strong, dark line, too, not some vague little shadow.

She got up, her legs like jelly, and walked slowly out of the bathroom, sank down onto the bed and stared blankly at the test strip.

How could she possibly be pregnant? Dan had said it was a tiny tear, and she and Mark had tried for *years*. How could she be? Unless they'd just been incompatible, but even so…

She slid a hand down over her board-flat tummy. Was there really a baby in there? Dan's baby?

Please, no.

Please, yes!

But...

She'd have to tell him. Not yet, though. It might have been a fluke. She'd do another test in a while.

And then another one, until all the tests were used up.

Four of them *couldn't* be wrong.

She started to cry, great tearing sobs welling up from deep inside her where the pain she'd hidden for so long had festered like poison, and then the tears died away, leaving only joy.

She was having a baby, the thing she'd always dreamed of and had given up hoping for.

And Dan was going to be a father.

How on earth was she going to tell him?

CHAPTER FIVE

HE HADN'T SEEN her for ages.

Not really, not to speak to, apart from over that antenatal patient yesterday, because she'd been on nights. He told himself it was a good thing, they needed a little distance, but actually it didn't feel good, and in a strange way he missed her.

And he still owed her dinner, even if that had started as a joke. A real dinner, in a proper restaurant like Zacharelli's on the seafront, not whatever either of them could pull together.

No. Not Zacharelli's. It would feel altogether too much like a date, and that was dangerous.

A picnic, then, or supper in a pub. Nick Jarvis had talked about the pub on the other side of the river, overlooking the harbour and with great river views. Was that still too dateish? Because he didn't want it to be. No matter how much he wanted her, and he absolutely did, he didn't want a relationship.

Well, not that sort. Too messy, too much potential for hurt and disappointment, and altogether too complicated with them working together.

How would they both feel if it all went wrong?

Awkward. Hideously awkward. It just couldn't be

allowed to happen. But they could be friends, couldn't they? If they could make it work–

His phone pinged in his pocket, and he pulled it out and glanced at the screen. Georgia.

Can we grab a coffee?

He laughed. Coffee. That was it, perfect for a quick catchup. If there was ever a time when they were both free…

You read my mind. How about now? I'm miraculously free

It was a slight exaggeration, but her reply was instant.

Can you give me five minutes?

He checked the time. Just about, although it'd be a squeeze.

Sure. Park Café in ten?

Perfect!

He slid his phone back into his pocket, finished off what he was doing and sprinted through the park, catching up with her at the door.

'Well, hello, stranger,' he said, following her in, and she turned and smiled.

Or sort of smiled. There was something different about her that he couldn't quite work out. Something—

guarded? He cocked his head on one side and studied her.

'Are you all right?'

She smiled again, but it didn't quite reach her eyes. 'Yes, I'm fine. Why?'

'I don't know. I haven't seen you to speak to for ages. Are we OK?'

'Of course. Why wouldn't we be?'

'I don't know.' But he had a gut feeling something was wrong. 'Have I done something to upset you?'

'No, of course you haven't, but as you say it's been ages, so I thought you were avoiding *me* for some reason.'

So that was it. Relieved, he shook his head. 'No, of course I'm not. I'm just stupidly busy.' He hesitated, then confessed, 'I almost dropped in last night on my way home to say hi, but I didn't know what you were doing and I didn't want to presume.'

'Ah, no. I was busy last night,' she said, and turned to the person behind the counter. Skinny decaf cappuccino, please. Dan?'

'I'll have a double espresso, please. Since when did you drink decaf?' he added to her.

'I often have decaf,' she said, and turned and picked up a gooey pastry. 'Just in case I don't get a lunch break,' she said.

'Good plan,' he said, and reached past her into the grab-and-go chiller and picked up a coronation chicken wrap.

By the time he turned back she was at the till, card at the ready.

'My turn,' she said firmly, and paid, picked up the tray and headed out into the sunshine.

* * *

It was a glorious day again, and she went to the same bench that they'd sat on before, set the tray down in the middle and picked up her coffee, wondering where to start.

'So, how's it going? Settling in?' she asked, her voice sounding a tiny bit forced to her ears, and he nodded slowly.

'Yes, I think so. It's all good—well, so far. How are things with you?'

How could she answer that? *My world's just turned upside down, but apart from that it's fine?*

'OK. Stupidly busy, like you. How's the lawn mowing going?'

Oh, that's so inane...

'Good. Well, so far, but it hasn't rained a lot so it's not really growing. It'll be more of a challenge when it does.'

They fell silent, then—

'Dan, I—'

'How do you—'

They'd spoken together, and she laughed and waved for him to go ahead, glad of the reprieve.

'I was going to say, how do you fancy supper at mine one night? It's my turn and I was thinking—oh, now what?' he asked, pulling out his pager. He swore, got to his feet and shrugged helplessly. 'Sorry, I've got to go, I'm needed in the ED. I'll pop in tonight on my way home and we can sort something out. OK?'

'Sure.' She smiled, but it faded as she watched him go, heading towards the ED entrance, his coffee and wrap untouched. She'd take them up with her and put them in the ward kitchen, but for now she was going to drink her decaf coffee, eat her sticky, sugar-loaded pastry and regroup.

Just as well his pager had gone off when it had, because she'd been all ready to blurt it out, and if she'd just dumped that on him in a public place, it would have been really unfair.

Not as tricky as if he'd dropped in last night when she'd just found out, though. That was a narrow escape, because she'd needed time to come to terms with it herself before she dealt with his emotions. And goodness knows what they were going to be.

Better tonight.

And that would give her a little more time to work out what to say.

In the end it was easy.

He turned up at almost eight, apologised for the time, thanked her for putting his lunch in the fridge, and then he looked at her closely and asked if she was all right.

'You looked a bit strained this morning, and you weren't yourself. Is everything OK?'

She felt her shoulders slump, and gave up trying to word it any other way than the obvious.

'That depends what you call OK.' She took a deep breath, closed the front door and turned to face him. 'I'm pregnant,' she said quietly, and she watched the blood drain from his face.

He said nothing for an age, but his face said it all. Shock, disbelief, anger—with her, or himself, she wasn't sure—and then he shook his head.

'No. No, I can't do this again,' he said rawly, and turned without another word, yanked open the front door and walked out.

What? She'd spent the whole day trying to work out how to tell him, running through potential conversations in her head, dreading his reaction, but this was the last thing she'd expected, the absolute last thing.

She stood motionless, staring open-mouthed through the open door as he strode away out of sight, and then the dam burst.

She sank down onto the bottom step, great wrenching sobs tearing themselves out of her chest, and she clung to the banisters and sobbed her heart out. How could he do that to her? Walk away without even talking about it? It was his baby, too, his condom that had torn—and her denial that she needed emergency contraception. She'd been so adamant that it was unnecessary, and now...

'Oh, what have I done?' she whispered, and another wave of guilt and sorrow swept over her. She buried her face in her hands and wept again, the endless tears dribbling through her fingers and running down her wrists, and then she heard a car door slam and the front door close, felt gentle hands wrap around her shoulders and the nudge of a hip against hers, his arms easing her up against his chest.

'Georgia, don't cry,' he said, his voice rough and raw with emotion. 'I can't bear that I made you cry.'

'Why did you go like that? Why did you leave me?'

She felt the shaky breath of his sigh against her skin. 'I just needed some air, but I shouldn't have gone, I know that, and I'm sorry.'

'No, I'm sorry. This is all my fault,' she wept, but he hushed her and rocked her against his warm, solid body.

'No, it's not all your fault. If it's anyone's fault, it's mine. If I hadn't stayed…'

But he had, and that was her fault, and it set her off again.

She felt a gentle hand stroke her hair. 'Come on, Georgie, stop crying and let's talk about this calmly and rationally.'

She sniffed and scrubbed her face with her hands, easing away from him. 'What is there to talk about? I'm pregnant, it's your baby—what else is there to say? You said it all. You can't do it again. What more is there?'

'There's a lot more. Well, a lot I have to say, anyway, starting with a proper apology for running away just now. And I could make all sorts of excuses, but that wouldn't be fair. I still shouldn't have left you.'

'I thought you were angry with me.'

'I am a bit. I'm more angry with myself, but above all I'm worried about you, and about the baby. It's too late for recriminations. What's happened has happened, for whatever reason, and we need to move forward.'

'I didn't lie to you,' she said, finally lifting her head and meeting his eyes. 'I honestly believed this could never happen. We'd tried for years and nothing had happened and I knew it wasn't him, but maybe it was just incompatibility. If I'd had even the slightest doubt that I could get pregnant I would have done something about it immediately.'

'Would you? Even though you've always wanted a baby?'

She nodded.

'Yes, I would, because I knew you didn't. It was a one-off, we weren't in a relationship, and you told me the next day that you had issues, so I knew you wouldn't want a baby...

'No. I didn't want to get you pregnant. I never said I didn't want a baby.'

Hadn't he? Probably not, in so many words, but you couldn't have one without the other...

'Maybe not, but you certainly wouldn't want one with a random stranger, not after what you'd gone through—although I suppose that might be easier. If you didn't love someone it wouldn't hurt as much if it all went wrong.'

'That's not true. Being responsible for anyone's death or suffering is always going to hurt.'

He smiled, but it was a sad effort and it made her want to cry again.

He must have seen, because he gave her shoulder a little squeeze. 'Don't worry about me, I'm fine. You need to go and wash your face and dry your eyes, and we'll go to mine and have something to eat and talk about this, OK?'

She nodded, and he got to his feet, pulled her up and hugged her, and it felt so good she just wanted to stay there, but he dropped his arms and stepped back, and she went into the cloakroom, splashed her face, looked at herself in the mirror and could have cried again.

So many tears...

She patted her face dry, went out and found him standing in the living room, hands rammed in his pockets, staring out into the garden.

He'd said he was fine, but he didn't look it. He

looked as if he was staring into the abyss, and she felt another wash of guilt.

I can't do this again...

'I could feed us,' she suggested, but he shook his head.

'I've got stuff in the fridge that needs eating. If we go back to mine I can cook for you and we can eat it in the garden while we talk. It's more private than yours, and it's cooler.'

She couldn't argue with that, and she realised she didn't want to, so she nodded, picked up her bag and her keys, set the alarm and followed him out.

She looked awful.

Utterly gutted, and he had no idea what she'd want to do.

Would she keep it? He had no idea, but it was her decision to make, even though it'd kill him to stand back and let it happen. Her right, her choice. Her baby.

He'd brought the car back with him almost the minute he'd got home, and it was hitched up on the kerb outside. He drove them back to his, ushered her in and walked through to the kitchen, crunching over the broken china.

She stopped at the threshold and stared at it. 'What happened?' she asked, her voice shocked, and he gave a short huff of laughter.

If you could remotely call it that.

'I lost it a bit, but I'm OK now.'

'Are you?' she asked, and searched his eyes, her own worried. 'Are you really? Or are you still angry?'

He smiled at her, but it was a sad effort and he could see she wasn't convinced.

'Only with myself,' he said honestly, surprised to realise it was true. 'I just want to talk to you, Georgia, work out where we go from here, how we deal with this. But let's get supper under way because I'm starving. What do you fancy?'

'I don't know. What have you got?'

'All sorts. Why don't you look in the fridge and I'll sweep this up?'

He left her examining the food, cleared up the mess he'd made when he'd hurled the mug across the room, and then stood beside her at the open fridge door.

'Thoughts?'

'Something healthy. The sea bream fillets, maybe, with new potatoes and a salad?'

'Sounds good. Why don't I get you a drink and then I'll start cooking?'

It only took him a few minutes, and while he cooked she sat on the bench under the tree and sipped her sparkling water and breathed in the scent of the nicotiana and night-scented stocks, with the grass cool under her bare feet and her mind in turmoil.

What did he mean by 'deal with this'? It seemed to imply that there were choices, but to her there were no choices, and only one possible option.

Yes, it might not have been planned, and he might not want to have anything at all to do with it, but for her this unexpected pregnancy was nothing short of a miracle.

But it was his baby, too. Would he reject his own child?

No. He'd said he only wanted her not to be pregnant, not that he didn't want a baby. So what did he want, and what did he really feel?

I can't do this again...

Her hands slid down, curling over her baby as if to shield it from harm, and she closed her eyes and told herself to breathe.

He dished up, carried the plates to the door and stopped.

She was sitting on the bench, eyes closed, hands held against her abdomen in a protective gesture that wrenched at his gut, and his heart went out to her.

That was his fault. All of this was his fault, and there was nothing he could do to turn back the clock and take it away.

It was up to him to make it right, in whatever way he could, no matter what the cost to him personally or financially.

He put the plates down on the table and walked over to her. 'Hey. It's ready,' he said gently, and she looked up and smiled.

'Thank you.'

She got to her feet and walked back with him, and they sat and ate in silence, and then finally she pushed back her plate, met his eyes and said, 'What do you want me to do?'

He didn't pretend not to understand.

'It's not my decision,' he said.

'That doesn't stop you having an opinion.'

'My opinion is irrelevant. As long as you're carrying it, this is your baby. Whatever happens, it has to be your decision, and whatever you decide, I'll stand by you.'

Even if it broke his heart.

She stared at him for the longest time. 'Do you

really mean that, or are you just saying it because you feel you should?'

'No, I really mean it.'

'What about your "I can't do this again" comment? What was that about? Because you weren't standing by me then, by any stretch of the imagination.'

He shook his head. 'I was in shock. I didn't mean it, Georgia, and I'm really sorry I said it. I was just pole-axed, but of course I can do it. I'm here for you, whatever you want, I promise.'

'Honestly?'

'Honestly.'

'OK.' She held his eyes. 'I want to keep it,' she said, watching him carefully, and he felt the air go out of him like a punctured balloon.

'Are you sure? You're not just saying that for me?'

She shook her head. 'No. I've wanted a baby for ever, and I never thought it would happen. I'm still not sure I believe it, but I'm more than ready for it. And I can do it. I've got a good support network, so I won't be alone—'

'You won't be alone,' he assured her. 'I'll be there for you, Georgia. Always. And for the baby. We can do this together, somehow.'

Somehow? What did that mean, exactly?

And—together. What did *that* mean? Together as in together, or just shared decision-making? And as for parenting…

She had no idea. 'So how are we going to do this?' she asked, and he shrugged.

'Honestly? I don't know. I suggest we play it by ear, take it a day at a time.'

'OK. That sounds good.'

What does together mean?

'So are we going to tell everyone?' she asked him.

'Everyone?'

'Our colleagues, friends.'

'No. No, not yet. Nobody needs to know.'

'And how does that work? Because it's going to be-come obvious pretty soon and they're all going to want to know whose it is.'

'Do you have to tell them?'

'Dan, they're my *friends*! Be realistic.'

'OK. You need to tell your friends.'

'And how about colleagues? How about Ben Walker? Because he's your clinical lead, and his wife is a friend of mine. And he will ask, I know he will, and I'll ei-ther have to tell him or lie, which I don't want to do.'

He frowned. 'No. I realise that.'

'So—what do I say to people? Do I tell them you're the father, or are we going to pretend we've had noth-ing to do with each other? Because that simply won't work. I'm not that good a liar, and I don't want to have to lie about this.'

He sighed and scrubbed a hand through his hair, and she could understand his dilemma. 'OK, you have to tell Ben, and your friends, but not everyone. At least not yet. Not till your scan.'

'No, I agree. And this—together thing you talked about. What did you mean by that? What kind of to-gether?'

He held her eyes for a long moment, then looked away.

'I don't know. I just know this baby is my responsibility, and so are you now, and I don't shirk my responsibilities.'

'I'm not your responsibility!'

'Yes, you are. Your health and welfare, at least, until the end of your pregnancy and probably longer, so— whatever you want from me, whatever you want for us, I'll consider it. Money, marriage—whatever.'

Marriage? She considered that for a second, but no more, because the last thing she needed after a man who'd left her because she couldn't give him a child was a man who would only be with her *because* she was having a child.

She could understand where he was coming from, but that didn't mean she had to hand over her own responsibility, and she wouldn't. It wasn't necessary.

'I don't want anything from you, Dan, and certainly not marriage,' she said truthfully. 'This is my fault, not yours. I knew the condom had torn, I hadn't had any fertility tests, and common sense would have dictated that I take emergency contraception just to be on the safe side, but I didn't because I genuinely didn't believe I needed to, and that was a mistake. So you're off the hook.'

'I don't want to be off the hook,' he said, to her surprise. 'This is my baby too, and I really want to be involved, from now onwards, for ever.' She felt a wave of relief, and then he added, 'I'd like to supervise your care, too, but obviously I can't.'

She felt her eyes widen, her relief gone.

'No, you can't. It's totally unethical, and for good reasons.'

'I get that, but I would like to be involved where possible, scans and that sort of thing, so I suppose when it comes to that point people will need to know I'm the father.'

He didn't sound thrilled by that. 'Is that a problem for you?' she asked bluntly. 'That people will know you slept with me?'

'No, of course it isn't. In fact it might be good if people already thought we were together by then.'

'What, so it doesn't look as if I'm such a slut?'

He gave a sharp sigh. 'You're not a slut, not by any stretch of the imagination, Georgia, and it takes two, so what does that make me?' He shrugged. 'I'm not ashamed of what we did, and if it makes it easier for you with your friends that we're in a relationship, then tell them that. I'm fine with it.'

'It would be a lie, though,' she said, after a long pause, and then met his eyes. 'Unless we were.'

He looked away, gave another shrug, maybe slightly bewildered as he groped his way through it. Just like her, then. 'We are, in a way. And maybe we should be. It's a long road. Maybe we should travel it together.'

She shook her head. 'No. It's not a good enough reason,' she said, quoting his own words back at him, and something odd happened in his eyes before he looked away.

'No, probably not,' he said, but he sounded almost sorry about that and she wondered what he really did think, what he really did want. Apart from fulfilling his responsibilities, which was something Mark had never understood.

'I don't think we need to lie,' she said eventually. 'Discretion would be good, and I'd be grateful if you didn't talk about us to anyone, and of course I'll share my handheld notes with you, they're about your child, but I don't want you hovering over me like a cross between a helicopter and a guardian angel, watching my every move for the next eight months, because it isn't necessary and it'll do my head in. I'm quite capable of looking after myself and lots of women do this perfectly well on their own.'

He frowned at that, but he nodded, and she realised she'd hit a nerve.

'Oh, Dan, I'm sorry. That was tactless, but I'm fine. I'm fit and well, I know what I'm doing, I know what to look out for, and I know you don't want a relationship really. Nor do I. Certainly not one based on duty and guilt and a misplaced sense of valour.'

'That's not what this is about.'

'Yes, it is. Of course it is. What else could it be about?' She gave a weary shrug. 'Look, I'm sorry, but I'm tired, and I think we've both got enough to think about for now. There's no rush, we don't have to do anything at all for a few more weeks, and if the situation changes, we'll look at it again. But for now let's just do what we said and take it one day at a time, please?'

He nodded slowly, his face more sombre than she'd ever seen it, and then he met her eyes.

'OK. I'll run you home.'

'There's no need.'

'Yes, there is. You're tired, so am I, and I'm not letting you walk home alone, so do me a favour and don't argue about it, please. I haven't got the energy for it.'

She gave a soft laugh. 'Well, since you put it so nicely...'

He rolled his eyes. 'Sorry. I'm just a bit...'

'I know. I am too. Come on, then, drive me home, if you insist.'

* * *

One day at a time.

That was harder than he'd expected because now, after a fortnight of hardly seeing her, he was falling over her all the time. Ever since she'd dropped the bombshell their shifts seemed to coincide again, and he had no idea what to say, how to talk to her in such a public place.

'How are you?' seemed too loaded. How about, 'You OK?' Better, maybe.

And then a few days into their 'one day at a time' regime, they had a day when they were both on duty and it was quiet. Not that anyone dared to say so, but he picked up on it and suggested a coffee, and his phone pinged instantly.

Ugh. No. Maybe fizzy water.

Oh, dear. See you in the Park Café in five?

He got a thumbs-up in reply, and headed for the café. It was the first time he'd seen her that day, and she looked a little pale. She was sitting on their bench—funny, how they'd claimed it—and she smiled ruefully.

'Can you go in for me? I can't face it. The coffee smells horrendous. Oh, and can I have an apple Danish please? I'm starving.'

'Sure.'

He got to the front of the queue, opened his mouth to ask for his usual double espresso, and switched to tea.

'Here you go. Chilled fizzy water, apple Danish and no, I didn't get myself a coffee.'

'You're a star,' she said, taking a huge bite of the pastry and sighing with what sounded like bliss. Or relief.

'So when did this start?' he asked, and she shrugged.

'I'm not sure. I've been getting pickier, but I'm only just over five weeks. It's very early.'

'Probably twins,' he said with a grin, and her eyes widened.

'Don't even joke about it,' she said, and his heart gave a sudden thud. Early nausea could be an indicator of twin pregnancy, which was why he'd said it, but he'd always thought it was a bit of an old wives' tale. Of course it was.

'It's highly unlikely,' he said, trying to convince himself, and took a bite of his chicken wrap. 'So how are you otherwise?'

She shrugged. 'Fine. Sleepy, hungry but I can't stand the sight of food—I don't know. How are you? Have you had any more thoughts?'

'About us?' Us… Even the word seemed odd, never mind the concept. 'I'm not sure I have. You?'

'Not really,' she said. 'I still don't really know what you had in mind.'

That dragged a chuckle out of him. 'That makes two of us. The only thing I had in my mind last week was damage limitation. How could I take care of you, make sure you were OK, make sure the baby was OK. I didn't really get beyond that, and I still haven't.'

She tutted softly. 'You don't need to take care of me, Dan. I can take care of myself.'

He nodded slowly. 'Yes. Yes, I know you can—but even so…'

'Look, as soon as I get to twelve weeks I'll have a scan. We can go from there.'

'You need to see a midwife before then, or your GP.'

She rolled her eyes. 'Dan, I AM a midwife! I don't need to see one. I'm taking folic acid, my diet is healthy—don't look at my Danish like that!—and my blood pressure is fine.'

'What about anaemia? You need an FBC.'

'I'm taking an iron supplement, and I'm eating red meat when I can bring myself to cook it, and dark leafy veg and pulses—really, I'm fine. I know you mean well, but please stop fussing. I told you about that helicopter thing.'

He threw up his hands and smiled. 'Sorry, sorry. It's just the doctor in me coming out.'

'No. It's the man who's been racked with guilt for the past ten years,' she said gently, and he swallowed. 'It's OK, I do understand where you're coming from, Dan, and I'm not going to shut you out, but really, you don't need to worry about the baby. I'm doing that for you.'

He nodded, suddenly swamped with all sorts of emotions, but oddly one of them was joy. And so he smiled, and reached out a hand and took hers, giving it a quick squeeze.

'Thank you. I'm sorry if you feel I'm crowding you, and I'll keep out of your way, but ask, please, if there's anything you need. You know where I am.'

Her eyes suddenly seemed to sparkle in the sunlight, and she blinked and turned away, but not before he saw a tear bead on her lashes.

'Thank you,' she murmured. 'And—you don't have to keep out of my way. Feel free to drop in any time you're passing.'

'I might well do that.'

* * *

He did, just a few hours later, and she was watering
the plants. He only found out because she was en route
from the kitchen sink with the watering can when he
rang the bell.

'What are you doing? That's heavy.'

'It's not that heavy,' she protested, but he tutted and
carried it out and watered the pots for her while she
made them both a drink.

'Here. Peppermint tea.'

He took it without comment, sat down and looked
at her. 'I've been thinking.'

'Oh, dear,' she teased, and his lips twitched.

'Seriously. You talked this morning about eating
if you could bring yourself to cook, so how about if I
cook for you and deliver it? Anything you fancy, but
so you don't have to handle it. Just hold your nose and
eat it.'

She opened her mouth to protest, then shut it, because today she'd been going to cook herself a casserole and she'd ended up with an egg sandwich, and
even that had been a struggle once she'd peeled and
mashed the egg.

'I can't ask you to do that,' she began, but he cut her
off with a raised eyebrow.

'You didn't. I offered. And I'm not helicoptering,
before you say it, I'm just being a friend.'

She swallowed. Why did he have to be so nice? Because it would be all too easy to give in and let him
look after her.

'It's not really practical,' she said. 'You can't be expected to ferry it here every night. And anyway, our
hours are not always compatible.'

'No, they're not,' he agreed. 'So I thought I could do some batch cooking and you could freeze it. Simple stuff. How does that sound?'

Lonely...

She swallowed again, touched by his thoughtfulness. 'That would be really helpful.'

'OK. Give me some ideas of what you think you might like, and leave it with me. Have you already eaten tonight?'

She laughed. 'If you can call it that. I had an egg sandwich and gagged at the smell.'

He sighed and rolled his eyes. 'Write me a list of things you think you could eat, and I'll go shopping now.'

'But it's late.'

'It's fine. Just do it.'

She sent him off a few minutes later with his list, and he hugged her and dropped a gentle kiss on her cheek on the way out.

'Sleep well. I'll see you tomorrow,' he said, and she nodded, locked the door behind him and headed into the kitchen.

She was suddenly starving, so she had a piece of toast because he was right, an egg sandwich really wasn't adequate, and then went to bed, wrapped in a curious warmth.

Maybe being looked after wouldn't be so bad after all.

Her hand slid up to her cheek and rested there, against his kiss, and she drifted off to sleep with a smile on her face.

CHAPTER SIX

HE GOT TO work early the next morning.

He had a tricky case on his theatre list and he wanted time to check on his patient and reassure her, but it wasn't to be. Sally was on the phone as he arrived, and he was about to walk past the desk when she mouthed 'Hang on,' then finished the call.

'Do you need me?' he asked, and she shook her head.

'I don't but someone does,' she told him, and added quietly, 'Patrick's walked out.'

His heart sank. 'Walked out?'

'Yes. Said it was all too much, he was a useless doctor and he'd had enough.'

'Do I need to worry?'

'Maybe. I'm really not sure. I don't think he's suicidal or anything, he mumbled something about breakfast, but he's been on all night and I don't think it was pretty. I don't know, Samira will tell you more, she's still here but she's on her way out so you'll need to catch her quick.'

'OK.'

He found her in the kitchen, and she told him about the delivery Patrick had helped with. 'He dithered a bit, but in the end he got the ventouse on and lifted the baby out at the second attempt and it's fine, it's been checked and it's all good. The mum had a second degree tear, but I was expecting that, and I repaired it because he was blaming himself, but there was nobody else available and he did well. I haven't done my ventouse training yet, and he said he'd only done it once under supervision with you, but it was madness all night, just like the day had been, so there wasn't really a choice, but he was a mess by the end of it.'

'OK. Thanks. I'll ring him.'

Patrick didn't answer, but for some reason, probably because it was saving it all for later, the unit was quiet, so after a quick word to his first pre-op patient Matt headed out to the Park Café. It was Patrick's favourite haunt according to Sally, and he found him there, slumped over a coffee with a croissant shredded into a million bits on the table in front of him.

'Hey,' he said softly, and Patrick raised his head and looked him in the eye for a second before returning his attention to the croissant, pushing the flakes around on the table, arranging them into little rows.

He put his hand over Patrick's to stop him, and he looked up again.

'Talk to me,' he said, and Patrick shrugged.

'There's nothing to say. I can't do it any more, Mr Blake. I'm no good, and I'm never going to be any good.'

'I disagree. You're a good doctor, but you lack confidence and that'll come with experience. We all go through it. I haven't forgotten what it's like to be in your shoes. It can be terrifying, I realise that. Even now there are days when I think I have no idea what the best course of action is, but that's when you fall back on your training, your experience and your intuition. And it won't always work. Sometimes we lose.'

'Yeah, but—babies? I so nearly screwed up last night, and a baby could have died.'

'That's not what I heard. I've spoken to Samira, she said you did well, and the mother and baby are doing fine.'

'But she tore, and the baby's head was really distorted—'

'Stop it. Right there. By the time you were needed, she'd been pushing for two hours, and the baby's head would have moulded to her pelvis.'

'But it was wonky.'

'They often are, especially if they're large, which is why she tore, not because of what you did. And yes, the suction cup will leave a mark, and it might leave a swelling, but you did it, the baby's fine, the mother is fine. Samira stitched her, she's all good, a paediatrician has looked at the baby and is satisfied that it's unharmed—you did a good job, Patrick, and if you hadn't been there, the baby might well have died, so stop beating yourself up over it. Go home, get some rest, and when you come back I want you with me as much as possible. I'll coach you through this rotation. I'm not going to let you give up. OK?'

He swallowed, then nodded. 'OK. But I still don't think I'm cut out for it.'

'Maybe not obstetrics, and maybe not hospital medicine, but if you go into general practice the body of knowledge you've acquired here will be very useful.'

Patrick nodded, and Dan had to hope he believed him, but he was out of time.

'Look, I have to go now, but I'm here for you, OK? You've got my number. Talk to me, Patrick, that's what I'm here for. You're not alone,' he said, and with a pat on his shoulder he left him to it.

The day had been long, complicated and challenging with very few breaks, and by the end of it the only thing that was keeping her going was adrenaline.

She'd spent the last three hours with a woman who'd had to leave her husband with their three other children. She was coping alone and doing really well up to now, but the baby was overdue, it was five years since the last, and she'd had a long second stage. And now, just to add to the list, the baby was wedged in her pelvis, one shoulder jammed over her pubic bone, and when Georgie rang for help Patrick appeared.

Not the midwife she was hoping for, and there were none available because of course everyone had decided to deliver at once and they were all busy, but he looked edgy and unhappy and she'd heard about his meltdown. He was the last person she needed on this because if it didn't work seamlessly the child would be left with damage to the brachial plexus or worse. And time was of the essence.

'Is Jo around?' she asked, and he shook his head.

'She's in Theatre. I think Mr Blake's still here, he was a minute ago. Do you want me to check?'

She felt a rush of relief. 'Absolutely. Tell him it's a shoulder dystocia, and if he's not about, then find someone else. Quick as you can.'

He nodded and ran, leaving her alone with a distressed woman and no way of delivering her without skilled assistance, and she had five minutes to resolve this before it all went pear-shaped.

'OK, Vicky, let's roll you onto all fours and see if that takes the pressure off,' she suggested, and she'd just got her into position and checked the baby's heartbeat when she heard the door open and close and the snap of gloves going on.

Please, please let it be Dan—

'What have you tried?' he said quietly from behind her, and she could have cried with relief.

'Nothing yet, just turned her over. The anterior shoulder's wedged over the pubic bone and my fingers aren't long enough or strong enough to shift it, but the baby's heartbeat is OK at the moment. You've got about a minute before she has another contraction,' she added quietly, and he nodded and laid a gentle hand on the woman's back.

'Hi there, Vicky, I'm Daniel Blake, one of the consultants, and this is Dr Green. He's going to be assisting me.'

He'd brought Patrick with him? Georgie turned, gave him a reassuring smile, and turned back to Vicky.

'OK, Vicky,' Dan said, his voice all confident reassurance. 'Let's see if we can get your baby into a better position. It may not be very comfortable, I'm afraid.'

'I don't care, do whatever it takes to get it out, please,' she sobbed, and he squirted lubricant on his fingers while Georgie rubbed her back to soothe her and to try and ease the strain.

'OK. I'm going to see if I can coax this shoulder round gently, Vicky, so you'll feel a bit of pushing and shoving. Just brace against me, if you can.'

Giving a running commentary, mostly she suspected

for Patrick's benefit, Dan eased his fingers in under the baby's head, frowned, pushed the head back firmly with the other hand and she saw his forearm tense and then the frown went and he eased the pressure off the baby's head just as another contraction started.

'Perfect,' he murmured as the baby's head crowned, and he stepped back with a smile and glanced at Georgie. 'Yours, I think,' he said, and stood back and watched as she took over again and finished the delivery. She almost sagged with relief as the baby was born safe and sound with both arms waving.

'Time of birth: twenty-twenty-six. Shoulder looks good,' he said, and she lay the wailing little boy down and helped Vicky turn over, then laid him on her chest. He was rooting, and with the deft hands of experience Vicky shifted him into position and he started to suckle immediately.

'Goodness, he's a big boy,' she said, and her face was all tears and smiles, the pain forgotten. 'Hello, trouble,' she murmured softly, stroking him with infinite tenderness. 'Your daddy's going to be so proud of you.'

She glanced up at them, tears welling. 'Thank you so much, both of you. I really thought...'

'Shh,' Georgie said, and gave her a little hug. 'You did really well. I expect his daddy will be proud of *you*, never mind your son. You were a star. Well, and Mr Blake. I expect he deserves a little credit for it,' she teased, and he gave a soft chuckle.

'You're too kind. Apgar nine at one minute,' he added, and wrote it in the notes, just as Kat appeared.

'Sorry, Georgie, it's been manic. Anything I can do?'

'Yes, you can relieve Mr Blake and Dr Green.'

Dan chipped in. 'Actually, Kat, you could find another midwife and relieve Georgie, too. She should have finished at seven. And page the paediatrician on call. It was a shoulder dystocia but it's looking good, just needs a check.'

Kat smiled. 'Sure. I'll page Paeds and go and get Samira, she's just finishing up some notes. See you in a minute.'

'You don't need to—'

'Yes, I do, and we're free now and you've done the best bit,' Kat said with a wink.

Vicky reached out and took her hand. 'She's right, Georgie. You look exhausted, love. You go home to bed. I'll be fine with her. As she said, you've done the best bit and you were brilliant. I can't thank you enough.'

'My pleasure, Vicky. It's what I'm here for. I'll come and see you tomorrow before you go home, if I can. And in the meantime, let's take some pictures of you to send to your husband.'

She heard Dan talking quietly to Patrick, and the moment Kat came back they left, probably to debrief.

'Right, where are we up to?' Kat asked, all smiles and business, and Georgie gave a quiet sigh of relief and filled her in on the details.

It was almost nine by the time she'd done the handover and changed, and to her surprise Dan was still there, leaning on the wall in the stairwell with his phone in his hand when she left the ward.

'Don't tell me you waited for me?' she said, feeling a pang of guilt, but he smiled and pressed the lift button.

'No, but I was about to message you, I thought you might want a lift if you hadn't already gone.'

'You've got the car?'

He nodded, and she could have cried with relief. 'I can't believe that. How come?'

'I left early because I had a difficult case first thing and I wanted to make sure I was ready. Plus I knew you were doing a twelve-hour shift that was likely to run over.'

'Oh, Dan, you are such a star. I know I don't live far away, but I am utterly shattered today. I feel as if I could sleep for a week.' She leant against the wall of the lift and met his eyes. 'Thanks again for rescuing me with Vicky.'

'My pleasure. I've been talking through the shoulder dystocia with Patrick, giving him a bit of mentoring and moral support.'

'I heard about his meltdown,' she said, and he rolled his eyes.

'I think everybody has, but I think I've talked him down off the precipice. He'll be OK.'

The lift doors opened and they walked out into the cool of the evening. It was dark, with only the lights of the car park to guide them, and he led her to his car, opened the door for her and she sank into the soft leather seat and sighed with relief.

'Have you got anything to eat at home?' he asked, and she shook her head.

'No, but I don't care. I'm too tired to eat. I'll have a bit of toast.'

'No you won't, you'll have something proper. I did a batch cook last night for you and it's in my fridge. We'll go to mine.'

She couldn't be bothered to argue. She'd eaten nothing but ginger biscuits all day, and she knew if her blood sugar got much lower she'd start to feel sick again, so she gave in without a fight, rested her head back and was almost asleep by the time they pulled up on his drive.

'Cottage pie or chicken and mushroom risotto?' he asked as they went in, and she shrugged, the effort of making a decision almost too much for her.

'Risotto?' she said, not really caring either way because she was starting to feel queasy, and he nodded, wheeled her to the sofa, sat her down and came back six minutes later with a steaming bowl.

'Where's yours?'

'In the microwave. Start without me, I'll be back in a second.'

She tasted it cautiously, then spread it out a bit, picking at the edges until it cooled enough to eat, because it was delicious and she was ready to inhale it.

'Is that OK?' he asked, coming back and sitting down beside her on the sofa.

'Yes, it's lovely, it's just a bit hot.' She turned her head and smiled at him. 'Thank you.'

'What for?'

She shrugged. 'The food, the lift, rescuing Vicky in time. If you'd gone home...'

'You would have found a way.'

She shook her head. 'I don't think so and I nearly had a fit when Patrick walked in because I don't think he would have been deft enough to do it. That kind of controlled force needs to be applied with skill or you can do so much damage, and it would have completely freaked him out. I'd already had a feel and I could barely reach. I couldn't get up over that shoulder far enough to do any good, and I don't think I would have been strong enough anyway.' She summoned the energy to smile. 'It galls me to say it, but I needed your carefully controlled brute force again,' she added, and he chuckled.

'You're welcome—but you could always say skill and experience,' he said ruefully, and she grinned at him.

'That too, then, if you insist,' she said with a little wink.

He gave another chuckle, and then leant over and dropped a kiss on her cheek that made her skin tingle and her heart do something weird.

'That's more like it. Eat up.'

She ate every last scrap, but by the time he'd taken their plates away through to the kitchen and come back with a cup of ginger and lemon tea for her, she was asleep.

He wasn't surprised. She'd dozed off in the car on a five-minute journey, and he had no idea how she'd kept going. She'd looked exhausted when he'd gone into Vicky's room, and that was well over an hour ago.

He sat down beside her and stroked her cheek with his fingers, but she didn't react and he didn't have the heart to wake her. He wasn't even sure he could, but the sofa wasn't long enough for her to stretch out on properly, and the spare bed was covered in clean laundry waiting to be folded or ironed. And anyway, it wasn't made because he didn't even know where the spare bedding was, he hadn't got that far with the unpacking.

That left only one option, and he wasn't sure what she'd think of it.

He ran upstairs, turned back his duvet, went back down and scooped her gently up in his arms and carried her up to bed.

She sighed and rolled over as he laid her down, and he eased off her shoes, covered her with the duvet and left the door open while he went downstairs to tidy up and get some fresh water in case she wanted a drink in the night.

By the time he got back she was snoring softly, and he smiled, undressed down to his shorts and slid in beside her, leaving the door open and the bathroom light on in case she woke, because she'd never been upstairs in his house and he knew she'd be disorientated.

He lay for a while and watched her sleep, watched the slight flutter of her eyelids as she dreamed, and he wondered what she was dreaming about. Nothing scary, he didn't think, because she made a tiny, contented noise and settled again, and he closed his eyes and drifted off to sleep, oddly glad to have her beside him.

Where was she? And what was that weight on her?

She felt a moment of panic, then heard a soft snore and her eyes flew open.

She was in bed—not hers—in a bedroom with a dormer window and a sloping ceiling. Dan's room, in his house, she realised as she surfaced a little more. Why? Why was she here still, and in his bed, of all places?

The last thing she remembered was eating the food he'd given her. She must have fallen asleep, but surely he would have woken her and taken her home?

Unless he'd been too tired himself? She was absolutely certain he didn't have an ulterior motive.

Whatever, he was fast asleep now, and the weight she could feel was his arm draped over her waist, the warmth from his body close behind her.

Very close, and she needed the bathroom, because the baby was pressing on her bladder. How could she get out without disturbing him?

She circled his wrist with her hand and lifted it, then slid out from underneath it and laid it down, and he sighed and stirred slightly.

Nothing more, so she crept out onto the landing and found he'd left the bathroom door open and the light on over the mirror. So she could find it in the dark?

Maybe. She was as quiet as she could be, and while she was in there she took off her bra, sliding the straps out down the sleeves of her T-shirt, and wriggled out of her jeans, but when she crept back to the bedroom he'd moved, sprawling flat on his front all across the bed like a giant starfish. So now what? Did she wake him? Find her shoes, wherever they might be, and creep out and go home?

No. He'd worry then, and anyway his bed was warm and comfy and she was quite happy to get back into it, if she could only find a square inch to lie on.

She tried moving his arm, and he grunted, lifted his head and stared at her for a second, then sat up and scrubbed his hands through his hair.

'You OK?' he asked sleepily, and she nodded.

'I just needed the loo, but you sort of claimed the whole bed while I was gone.'

He laughed softly, lay down again and shifted right

across out of reach. 'Sorry. That's years of having the bed to myself. Is that better?'

'Much.' She lay down again facing him and met his eyes, but it was too dark to read them. She was suddenly acutely aware of him, of the fact that all there was between them was a pair of skimpy knickers and a T-shirt. Unless he had anything on? She hadn't noticed, and she certainly wasn't asking, but his chest was bare and that was bad enough.

'So how come I'm in your bed?' she asked, trying to sound casual.

His smile was a little crooked. 'You fell asleep, and I didn't have the heart to wake you, and I have no idea where the bedding is for the spare room so I did what I could. I hope that's OK?'

She found a tiny smile. 'Of course it's OK. Thank you. I'm sorry I fell asleep like that. I'm tired all the time now.'

'I'm sure you are, and yesterday was a very long day. There's a lot going on in your body. Making babies is challenging.'

'It wasn't that challenging,' she joked without engaging her brain, and then held her breath as he stared at her, their eyes locked, until a slow smile dawned on his mouth. A lazy, sexy, slightly rueful smile that made her heart turn over.

'No, it really wasn't, was it?' he murmured, his voice all smoky chocolate. He rolled to face her and their legs met and settled, and he lifted a hand and cradled her cheek, his thumb grazing softly over her lips and sending her pulse racing and her mind into orbit.

'I thought we weren't going to do this,' he said softly,

his eyes still locked on hers, a question in them that she couldn't answer. Or at least not in any sensible way.

They weren't going to do it. They weren't supposed to be doing it. Doing anything other than being friends, but she wanted to. Was it wise? No. Would they? Maybe...

His thumb stroked her lips again, and she could feel the slight tug on the damp skin as she parted them, feel the hitch in her breath, the beat of her heart against her ribs.

Would they?

This was such a bad idea.

Lying there with her, their legs touching, her lips soft and warm and damp under his thumb, her eyes fixed on his, almost luminous in the half-dark of the bedroom—it was a bad idea. A beautiful, wonderful, really, really bad idea.

He wanted her. So much. If only it weren't so complicated...

He moved his hand away from those tempting lips, stroking the side of her neck in a gentle caress, and he could feel the beat of her pulse under his fingertips.

Was it so complicated? Was it, really? She was having his baby, for heaven's sake. How much more complicated could it get? It couldn't. They were already bound by a relationship deeper than he could ever have imagined.

But it wasn't what they'd agreed, was it? Or was it?

One day at a time, they'd said, and maybe today— or tonight—was the time to make a decision.

Just—what decision?

He wrestled with it for so long that in the end she

made it for him. Her eyes drifted shut, and he let out a soft huff of laughter.

'Come here,' he murmured, and gathered her gently up against his chest, rolling onto his back so she could settle her head on his shoulder.

Their legs tangled, one of hers over his, an arm draped over his chest, palm flat against the skin above his heart. He could feel the soft press of her breasts against his side, the drift of her breath across his skin as she slept, and it felt right.

Torture, but in a good way, because although he still wanted her, now wasn't the time and that was probably a good thing. He'd done enough damage already. The last thing she needed was him upsetting their fragile status quo. It had to last for the next eighteen years or more, and compromising it so soon was never going to be sensible.

He gave a quiet sigh, closed his eyes and drifted off to sleep.

She was woken, as usual, by the pressure on her bladder which was becoming a constant feature of this pregnancy.

She didn't want to move, couldn't bring herself to face the day already, but she had no choice, so she peeled her arm carefully from his chest, pushed herself up and wriggled over the mattress to her side.

A glance at the digital clock on his bedside table told her it was ten to six. She needed to go. She was due back at work at seven, and she wanted to pop in and see Vicky before it all kicked off, so she picked up her clothes and shoes, tiptoed out to the bathroom and dressed while she was in there, then crept downstairs, wincing with every creaky step.

The latch on the front door wasn't deadlocked, to her relief, and it opened smoothly. She clicked it shut behind her, walked briskly home, put some toast in the toaster, showered, dressed and ran back down, grabbing the toast on the way out.

Not the most organised start to her day, but she'd slept well, thanks to Dan. Too well, because she'd thought…

No. It wouldn't have been a good idea.

He was woken by the sound of running water, and by the agonising tingling in his arm of pins and needles. He lay and massaged it until the blood returned, heard the bathroom door open and the creak of the stairs. She must be going down to get something to eat, he thought, but then he heard the sound of the front door closing, and he sat up and realised her clothes were gone, and she'd left.

Wise. He'd woken with a raging erection and an urgent need to bang his head against the wall to knock some sense into it, and if she'd come back to bed…

As it was he was going to be late. By the time he'd had a shower, scarfed down a bowl of breakfast cereal and arrived on the labour ward, it was ten to seven.

Would he end up working with her? And would it be OK?

He had no idea, and he didn't find out for a while, because Patrick collared him for a chat about his night shift, and then he did a quick ward round of his gynae post-ops before going down to the ED to see a pregnant woman who'd been involved in a car accident.

She had a closed fracture of her wrist which needed reducing, but he was worried about the impact of the collision on her uterus and the risk of a placental abruption at thirty-three weeks, so he left instructions that as soon as her fracture was reduced she should be admitted to the antenatal ward for monitoring.

His pager went, and of course the maternity lift was busy, so he ran up the stairs two at a time and arrived at the top as Georgie emerged from the lift.

'Morning,' he said, trying to sound casual, and she smiled at him a little warily.

'Hi.'

'You OK?' he asked, not sure what he was asking exactly but needing the answer.

'Yes, I'm fine.' She looked away, glancing round to check there was nobody there. 'I'm sorry I crept out this morning but you were still asleep.'

'I wasn't, actually. I'd woken by the time you closed the door, but it was just as well because I was nearly late.'

And who knows what might have happened if she'd gone back into the room. Just as well she'd done a runner.

'I've got some news for you,' she went on. 'I've just seen Vicky off with her husband, and they've decided to call the baby Daniel George. How about that?'

He laughed, and felt the tension drain away. 'Oh, that's lovely. I feel properly chuffed by that.'

'Mmm. Good, isn't it? So what's your day got in store?'

He groaned. 'No idea, but we're on take and I've just come back from the ED, so stand by for chaos. It's funny, it's always quiet for Ben.'

'I don't think that's quite true,' she said with a chuckle, but the phone was ringing as they entered the ward and they parted company at the desk, leaving him to deal with another emergency on the way in, a woman with uncontrollable bleeding from fibroids. He took her straight to Theatre for a hysterectomy, and by lunchtime he was in Theatre doing an emergency section on the woman from the ED, but both she and the baby were fine, and his pager was blissfully quiet, so he headed for the Park Café and found Georgie there with another woman.

That was unfortunate. He'd wanted to talk to her, but that wasn't going to happen now. He wondered who the other woman was. He didn't recognise her, but maybe it was just as well that she was there. It might stop him saying anything stupid. He slapped on a smile and went over to them.

A shadow fell over their table, and she looked up and her heart did a little jig.

Stupid. So stupid—

'Dan, hi,' she said, really glad that Laura was there with her because all she could think about was last night. 'Have you met Laura Stryker?'

'No, I haven't. It's good to meet you.'

'And you,' Laura said. 'How's the cottage? Any issues?'

'No, none at all, I love it. Look, I need to grab some lunch. Can I get either of you anything?'

'No, I'm fine, I need to get back to the ED,' Laura said, getting to her feet. 'Good to meet you, Dan.'

'And you. It's good to put a face to the name.'

Laura walked away, and Dan looked down at Georgie, his eyes unreadable with the light behind him.

'So, do you need anything?'

Apart from her head examined? 'I wouldn't mind an apple turnover,' she said, and he nodded and walked off, heading to the café entrance. She stared after him, wondering where they'd go from here.

Back to bed to finish what they'd very nearly started? Or back to square one of being friends and steadfastly ignoring whatever it was that wanted to pull them together?

She had no idea, and she wasn't sure Dan did, either, so when he came back she raised the subject.

'I've been thinking. If I hadn't been pregnant, I wouldn't have been with you last night, would I?'

He met her eyes, then looked away. 'No. Probably not.'

'So, it really isn't a good idea letting it happen again. We so nearly...'

'Yeah. We did.'

'And if I wasn't pregnant, we wouldn't have been in that situation, so why put ourselves in it now? It's so early, Dan. I could lose this baby so easily, lots of people do, and then where would we be? Together, for what? Random sex with someone we work with? That's never a good idea. And I really don't feel ready for anything else, and I'm not sure you are.'

He nodded slowly. 'No. You're right, I'm not sure I'll ever be ready—which doesn't mean I don't like you, because I do, a lot, and if it wasn't for Holly and the baby then maybe I'd feel differently about us, but you're right, it's very early, and if all goes well with the baby we've got plenty of time to think about this. Who knows?'

He glanced back at her, and she smiled at him.

'Yup. I guess we could be in and out of each other's lives for twenty years or more.'

'Or more than that. Graduations, weddings, grand-children.'

'Grandchildren?' She started to laugh, and he gave a rueful grin and shrugged his shoulders.

'Just a natural progression of thoughts. Can I drop round tonight? I've got those meals for you. I put them in the freezer last night, so they're all ready to go.'

'That would be lovely. Thank you—'

'Oh, for goodness' sake!' He pulled his pager out, glared at it and rolled his eyes. 'Sorry, I've got to go. I'm needed on Gynae.'

He looked at his sandwich and slapped his head, and she laughed. 'Go. I'll put it in the fridge for you in the labour ward. Come and get it when you can.'

'You're a star,' he said, and apparently without thinking he bent and dropped a kiss on her mouth and walked away, leaving her lips tingling.

So much for their conversation. All she could see was Dan with grey threaded through his dark hair, bouncing a grandchild on his knee, and she felt a huge knot of emotion swelling in her chest and threatening to choke her.

No. It was way too soon to think about stuff like that. She picked up their food and headed back to work before she totally lost the plot.

CHAPTER SEVEN

HE SHOULDN'T HAVE kissed her.

He hadn't given it a nanosecond's thought, just swooped in and did what came naturally—and that was worrying.

It worried him all the rest of the day, and it was still worrying him when he arrived at Georgie's house a little after seven-thirty with the meals.

He rang the bell, and when she answered the door he held out the carrier bag and she took it and peered inside.

'Gosh, that looks lovely. Thank you so much. Are you coming in?'

He shook his head. 'No, I'll go home and cook for myself now. I'm hungry.'

'Or you could eat with me?' she suggested, and he wasn't sure if she was being polite or really meant it.

'Are you sure?' he asked, and she laughed and walked off into the kitchen. He heard the whirr of the microwave starting up as he stepped into the hall and closed the door, and she turned and smiled at him as he leant against the kitchen doorway and folded his arms.

'I should apologise about last night. I didn't mean to stir things up,' he said, and her smile softened.

'Nothing happened last night,' she reminded him gently. 'You were a perfect gentleman, and you looked after me. That's all, Dan. All it needs to be.'

What about what I want it to be?

Not that that mattered. That was just his body talking, and she obviously didn't want the same thing, if he even knew what that was. He nodded slowly, the fight between his head, his heart and his body too confusing to deal with right now, and their earlier conversation had done nothing to clarify it, at least for his body and possibly his confused and relentlessly optimistic heart. 'OK. I just didn't want you not to feel comfortable with me.'

She laughed at that, but her eyes were gentle and he wanted nothing more than to pull her into his arms and hold her. 'Daniel Blake, you really aren't very observant. I slept like a log. Would I do that if I wasn't comfortable with you?'

He smiled and nodded again. 'OK. I'll give you that. So what are we having?'

'Cottage pie. I thought I'd ring the changes. What do you want with it? Tenderstem broccoli, or some sugar snap peas, or baby carrots, or—ooh, what's this?'

'Ruby chard. You can slice it up and steam it in the microwave for a minute or two like spinach. It's out of the garden.'

'Really? Wow. Let's try that, then,' she said with a smile, and he took it off her, washed it, sliced it and piled it in a lidded dish while she checked the cottage pies.

'Ouch. They're done,' she said, licking the finger she'd stuck in one, and he rolled his eyes and put the chard into the empty microwave.

And then he turned and bumped into her, and their eyes clashed and he stepped away with a hasty apology and a whole host of regrets.

Some for coming in instead of going home again, but mostly for not having followed through last night.

He didn't stay long that evening, and after that they settled into a kind of routine.

He made some more meals for her, simple but tasty things which she would never have been able to cook but managed to eat, like a pea and mushroom risotto, a rich chicken casserole with mushrooms, prunes and apricots for the iron, more of the cottage pies—and he froze them in portions and delivered them on a regular basis, complete with iron-rich fresh vegetables like broccoli, asparagus, peas and spinach, and sometimes more of the ruby chard out of the garden.

He'd certainly done his research, and she was hugely grateful.

They argued about who was paying for the food, and he finally shut up and gave in. Except when they ate together at his, and then he wouldn't hear of it, and he always drove her home afterwards. No more falling asleep on his sofa, and they didn't mention it again.

Sometimes he ate at hers, sometimes she went to his, sometimes she ate alone, and gradually the weeks went by.

And then he started nagging again.

'You need to see a midwife.' 'Have you made an appointment with your GP?' 'When are you going to start accessing antenatal care?'

So she gave up when she hit the ten-week mark in

the middle of October, and went to see Lucy Galla-gher, her GP.

Lucy checked her over, gave her a clean bill of health and then added, 'It's time to book you in for a scan, but you know all that.'

She did, and of course it meant a referral to the hospital.

Her hospital. Her department. Her friends.

So what now?

She left the surgery and walked straight to Dan's house. She knew he'd had the afternoon off, and con-veniently she found him in the front garden digging out weeds round the edge of the drive.

He straightened up, winced and smiled at her.

'Hello, you. How are you doing?'

'OK. You look as if you've done enough for one day.'

His grin was rueful. 'Yes, you're probably right. So what's up?'

'I've just been to my GP.'

He held her eyes for a long moment, then nodded, dusted off his hands, threw the trowel into the weed bucket and led her through the side gate into the gar-den, locking it behind him.

'So is there a problem?' he asked, and she could see the concern in his eyes. She shook her head.

'No—well, not a medical problem, but she's refer-ring me for a scan, so that'll open a whole can of worms any minute now. They're all going to know.'

He nodded slowly. 'OK. Have you eaten?'

She shook her head. 'No. My appointment was at five-thirty.'

'Right. Go and sit down, and I'll stick a couple of meals in the microwave now and we can talk about it.'

Not that there was much to talk about, apart from exactly how much they were going to reveal about their relationship, and who to tell first, because that would be the starting point to kick it all off.

The microwave pinged, and she joined him at the table, picking up her fork and poking her food for a moment. Too hot to eat yet, so she launched in.

'I think I need to talk to Ben before he gets the referral,' she said, and he winced and then nodded.

'Yes, of course you do. Are you going to tell him it's mine?'

She chuckled at that. 'I don't have a choice. He and Daisy are well aware I don't have a social life that involves dating, and they know about Mark, so they'll know this pregnancy is nothing short of a miracle. They will ask whose it is, though, and I will have to tell them.'

'You really think they'll ask?'

'Absolutely, and I can't say it's no one they've met, because although that's true of Daisy, it's certainly not true of Ben, and knowing him he'll work it out in seconds anyway. The fact that my conception date coincides exactly with your arrival is a bit of a giveaway. And then there's the sonographer, and the antenatal clinic reception staff who all know me from the clinics, and all the other midwives—it'll be round the hospital in minutes. And anyway, it'll soon be obvious because my clothes are already tight, but that could be your fault with all the tasty food you keep plying me with.'

'I'll take that as a compliment,' he said, then searched her eyes.

'Do you mind if they know it's me?'

She shrugged. 'No. I thought you might.'

'I don't mind, and it'll cut down all the idle specu-
lation, but I do wonder if we ought to go public about
our relationship before the scan thing comes up. Just
so it's not totally out of the blue.'

She stared at him, surprised by that. 'What relationship? We're friends, that's all. Aren't we?'

His smile was wry, a little strained. 'I don't know.
It's a bit more complicated than that, really, isn't it?'

She sighed and dropped her face in her hands. 'Oh,
they're all going to be talking about us,' she groaned,
and she heard him chuckle.

'You could always go somewhere else.'

Her head snapped up and she stared at him in as-
tonishment. 'Are you serious? I trust these guys! I've
worked here for four years, they know me—why would
I want anyone else looking after me?'

'It wasn't a serious suggestion,' he said soothingly,
and then added with a wry smile, 'although I have to
say if we wanted to keep it quiet the idea has some
merit.'

She sighed again. 'They'll all think we're together,
won't they?'

'We are together.'

'Not like that. Well, only the once.' Although it had
nearly been twice, and it wouldn't have stopped at that.

He hesitated, then said very quietly, 'Maybe we
should be.'

If he'd shouted the words, they wouldn't have had
more impact. She felt her jaw sag, and clamped her
mouth shut.

He was looking at her, his eyes deadly serious, and
she felt her heart lurch and start to race. Surely he
didn't mean that? No, of course not. But—what, then?

'No,' she said slowly. 'We've talked about this and I don't think we should. Not really—not properly.' Because it was only for the baby, and that wasn't a good enough reason, however tempting, and after Mark she was too wary to dare to trust her own judgement.

He shrugged and looked away. 'Just an idea. Don't dismiss it without thinking about it.'

She couldn't think about anything else.

All that night it churned over in her mind, and she woke exhausted, sick and dreading the day. She forced down some toast, promptly lost it and walked to work on legs like rubber.

She needed to find Ben, but it wasn't hard.

He was just leaving the desk when she went in, and he smiled at her, then paused and gave her a thoughtful look. 'Are you OK? You look really pale.'

'I'm fine. Can we talk?'

He searched her eyes, found something there and laid a hand gently on her shoulder. 'Sure. Come with me,' he said, and ushered her into his office. 'So what's up?'

She shook her head, and he steered her to a chair, sat her down and perched on the edge of his desk.

'Georgie, talk to me,' he said gently. 'What's wrong?'

'Nothing's wrong,' she said. 'I just feel a bit rough today.' She made herself meet his eyes, and found nothing but concern. 'I'm pregnant.'

He stared at her for a moment, then gave a low chuckle. 'Well, you dark horse,' he said, and hugged her gently. 'That's amazing. Congratulations. I take it we *are* celebrating?'

She tried to smile, but then her eyes welled and she shrugged. 'I don't know, Ben. I don't honestly know how I feel. Shocked, overjoyed, confused?'

'Not planned, then?'

That startled a laugh out of her. 'How could it possibly be planned? You know perfectly well I've had fertility issues. I didn't imagine for a moment this could happen.'

'Which of course is how it did,' he said slowly, and then added, 'Does Dan know yet?'

She stared at him, not surprised, just... 'How on earth?'

'Are you kidding? I'm no stranger to chemistry, Georgie, and you guys have it in spades. So, does he know, or are we going to have to keep this under wraps?'

'Keep it under wraps?' She laughed out loud. 'Ben, I'm pregnant. With the best will in the world, we can't keep it under wraps—but yes, he knows. He's known for weeks.'

'So how many weeks are you?'

'Ten.'

His eyes widened. 'Ten?'

She sighed and rolled her eyes. 'Yes. Ten. And before you get a calculator out, it was his first day.'

Ben's mouth opened, shut again and he stifled a smile. 'Like I said, chemistry. So have you seen anyone yet?'

'My GP—Lucy Gallagher. She's referring me for a scan, so I'm just telling you before you find out.'

'OK. Well, it's safe with me. Are you going to tell anyone else yet?'

'Jan,' she said, wondering what her boss would make

of it. 'And maybe Liv. I work with her quite often and she doesn't miss a lot.'

He nodded. 'Can I tell Daisy?'

She shook her head. 'No, let me tell her. It's… It's complicated.'

His mouth quirked. 'I can imagine. That's a pretty quick courtship.'

She felt herself colouring and looked away. 'No courtship, Ben. We're not together. Well, not like that. It was a one-off. And he's been amazing, very support-ive, but—well, I'm not looking for a relationship, not after the last time. I don't think I could trust anyone again, and he has issues, too, but he is the baby's father, and he definitely wants to be involved, so we're doing this together and we're friends. That's all.'

'I'm not judging, Georgie. You're entitled to a life, and I'm glad he's being supportive. Does he know you're telling me?'

She nodded. 'Yes, he knows. He's fine with it.' As fine as he was about any of it, and in truth she didn't have a clue how fine he was with it at all.

'Good. So, who do you want to look after you? Be-cause obviously Dan can't, which leaves Nick, Jake and Emily.'

'And you.'

'Are you OK with that?'

She smiled a little sadly. 'Not if you don't think I should be, but I don't think I could be in better hands.'

He gave her a gentle smile. 'Thank you. We'd all look after you, Georgie, but it's up to you who you choose and I won't be offended if you don't want me. You don't have to decide yet, though, there's plenty of

time,' he added, and he shrugged away from the desk
and pulled her to her feet and hugged her properly.

'We're here for you, you know that,' he said
gruffly. 'Me and Daisy. Anything you want or need,
just ask. And I'll do my best to keep it quiet for as
long as we can. And in the meantime, don't shut the
door on Dan. He's a very decent human being, and
you don't know what might happen between you, so
never say never.'

She blinked away sudden tears and hugged him
back.

'Thank you for being so understanding.'

'Don't be daft.' He let her go, gave her a stern look
and told her to go and get something to eat before she
fell over.

He was as good as his word.

He didn't even mention it to Dan, but he didn't need
to because she gave him a heads-up over lunch. Well,
lunch. A handful of ginger biscuits, her default high-
carb stopgap, eaten hastily in the ward kitchen just
before three, so not really lunch, and not much of an
opportunity to talk, but she felt he should know she'd
done it.

She told Liv, who hugged her hard and, like Ben,
offered any help she needed, and she told Jan.

Jan was unshockable, and her main concern was for
the health of Georgie and the baby, so she tore up the
rota and took her off nights, which was kind because
nights on maternity were a special kind of hell, and she
even sent her home on time at the end of her shift, so
she called in on Daisy on the way home and told her
not to yell at Ben because she'd sworn him to secrecy.

Then Dan rang her, and she said goodbye to Daisy and went round to his house and told him everything Ben had said. Well, most of it. Not the bit about not closing the door on him. He didn't need to know Ben was matchmaking, especially when there wasn't a prayer of her letting him into her life in that way just because he felt it was the right thing to do.

And then three days later she got her scan appointment, and it all suddenly felt much more real.

The next week took for ever to pass, but finally it was time, and she met Dan down in the antenatal clinic at five-thirty, right at the end of the clinic.

'Hi, Georgie,' the sonographer said, then looked at Dan, said nothing more but welcomed them both in with a wide and slightly surprised smile.

Georgie didn't really feel like smiling. She was a mass of nerves, still not quite able to believe she could be pregnant. She lay down on the couch with Dan by her side and they watched the screen as Steph ran the transducer over her little bump.

It had been there a week already, popping up out of the constraints of her pelvis. It had been a huge relief because it was no longer squashing her bladder, but she'd been quite surprised that it had happened so soon in a first pregnancy.

The grainy image appeared, changing as Steph moved the head of the scanner over her skin, and then there it was, the image of a baby, the tiny nose clearly visible in its face, the little limbs, all present and correct, the heart beating steadily, a rapid little whoosh that they could hear quite clearly.

She felt Dan squeeze her hand, and she sucked in her breath and pressed her fingers to her mouth.

'I really am pregnant,' she said softly, and Dan laughed.

'Yes, you really are,' he said, his voice slightly choked—and then the sound changed and her breath caught. *Two* foetal heartbeats?

She listened in stunned silence, not quite sure she was hearing what she thought she was hearing, because the sound was becoming drowned out by the roar of her own heart.

'Is that an echo? Or the cord?'

Steph shook her head. 'I don't think so. There's a double whoosh. The cord's more of a thud.'

Her heart hitched, and Steph moved the head again, and she heard Dan suck in his breath as another perfect little baby came into view.

'There are two,' he murmured, and he squeezed her hand.

'Yes, there are. You've got twins in there, Georgie, and I think they're identical,' Steph said with a smile, and then she ran the transducer over the placental area and confirmed it. There was only one placenta, and Georgie's pulse ramped up a notch.

Identical twins were more prone to problems and congenital abnormalities than fraternal twins, but at least they were the same size and both the hearts were beating well, the heartbeats strong and bold, beating in unison, and she felt a sudden rush of love so powerful it took her breath away, and gradually the shock gave way to a flicker of pure, unadulterated joy.

She stared at the screen as Steph went back over the little twins, and she was overwhelmed.

'Twins? Really?' she murmured, and Steph met her eyes and smiled.

'I'll call Mr Walker. He'll want to look at this, he oversees all the twin pregnancies. He's in the clinic now.'

Dan's hand found hers in a firm, steady grip, and she clung to him as Steph made the call. Moments later there was a knock on the door and Ben came in, winked at her and studied the image frozen on the screen, then picked up the transducer.

'Right, let's have a closer look at these little guys,' he said cheerfully, and she lay there and watched as he moved around from side to side, examining every angle until he was satisfied.

'Well, they're definitely monochorionic, there's only one placenta and one chorion, so they're identical for sure.'

'What about the aminion? Are they monoamniotic as well?' Dan asked, and Georgie's pulse hitched up a notch. Not another layer of complication…

'Too early to tell. The amnion's often hard to spot at this stage. How many weeks are you?'

'Eleven plus four.'

'OK. I think we need to scan you again in a week, but it's looking good so far and monochorionic mono-amniotic twins are extremely rare, so it's unlikely.'

He looked at Steph. 'Can you save all these images, please, and we'll compare them next time, and then we might go for a 3D scan and maybe 4D for greater clarity?'

She nodded, and he looked at them both and smiled.

'Any questions?'

Georgie shook her head, still numb with shock, and behind her Dan murmured something that could have been no. He sounded like she felt. Leave it to an obstetrician and a midwife to go for the unusual, she thought.

'OK. I need to get back to my clinic, but if you want to talk about it, my door's always open.'

They walked out of the clinic in a daze. At least he was, and he was pretty sure Georgie was, too, but at least they didn't have to walk home. He'd brought the car because it had been raining that morning, and he was glad he had because his legs were like jelly.

'Yours or mine?' he asked, and she shrugged.

'Yours, I think. I haven't got much food.'

He fired up the car and headed out of the car park, his mind full of the images they'd seen.

Twins? Really?

He turned onto the drive, cut the engine and opened the door, and they walked into the sitting room and sat down as if their strings were cut.

'I can't believe it,' she said, and he squeezed her hand, as much for his own comfort as hers.

'No, nor can I, but it's definitely real. I recorded their heartbeats,' he said, getting out his phone, and he pressed play and they listened.

'What are you thinking?' she said softly, and he looked up at her wary face and tried to smile.

'I think we're having two babies,' he said, and there was a catch in his voice.

She nodded. 'Is that OK?'

He laughed, but it came out more like a sob. 'Yes,

it's OK. It's incredible. It's just a bit much to take in all at once.'

'Will you be able to come to the next scan?'

She was putting on a brave face but she looked a little shocked still, maybe even on the verge of tears, and apart from when she'd told him she was pregnant and he'd behaved like an ass, he'd never seen her like that.

'Of course I'll come. You know that. Come here.'

He reached for her, and she snuggled against him and let him hold her, and his mind went into hyper-drive.

Twins, for heaven's sake! How on earth had that happened? Of all the crazy things.

'Fancy a pasta bake?' he asked, and she nodded.

'Anything. I'm starving.'

'Eating for three?' he said wryly, but she just shook her head slowly, still dazed.

'How?' she asked, following him into the kitchen. 'It's like buses. You wait for ages, then two come at once.'

That made him laugh, and he put the pasta bakes into the microwave and pulled her into his arms.

'They'll be OK,' he said. 'Lots of people have twins.'

'I know, but—really?'

He was totally in agreement with that, and there was no way she'd be able to look after two babies on her own. Twins were hardcore. On top of the demands of two babies on her pregnant body, and the sheer physical effort of carrying them around all that time, there was the probability of a Caesarean section, followed by sleepless nights and the relentless task of caring for two tiny and very demanding little human beings while recovering from major surgery.

It changed everything. And she could argue all she wanted, but he was looking after her, like it or not, because this was his fault, his responsibility.

And he was going to fulfil that responsibility if it was the last thing he did.

'Move in with me,' he murmured, and she lifted her head and stared at him.

'What? Why?'

He shrugged. 'Because I don't want you to be alone? Because I want to be able to look after you without one or other of us running backwards and forwards? This is a whole different ball game, Georgie.'

She looked away.

'So what are you suggesting?' she asked, and he hesitated, because he wasn't sure.

'Honestly? I don't know. I just know that a twin pregnancy isn't a bundle of laughs, and I don't want you getting any more exhausted than you have to.'

'You don't need to look after me. I'm quite capable of looking after myself, and you're doing enough already.'

'At the moment, maybe. But maybe not enough in the long term.'

'Well, can't we deal with that if and when we get there?'

If and when? Or as and when?

'OK,' he agreed, although he didn't really agree. 'But the offer stands.'

She kissed his cheek and moved away. 'Thank you. I'll bear it in mind. Anything I can do?'

'No, you're fine, they're nearly done. Sit and talk to me.'

She did, and then after they'd eaten he cleared the table and loaded the dishwasher.

'Do you want anything else? Yogurt? A hot drink?'

She shook her head. 'No, thanks. That was lovely, but I need to go home now. I'm tired and I ache, and I could do with a bath and an early night.'

He pulled her to her feet and settled his hands on her shoulders.

'It'll be OK, Georgie,' he said, and she stared straight into his eyes.

'Will it?' she asked wryly, and he couldn't answer because there was no way he could tell, and she knew that as well as he did.

'I'll run you home,' he said, and stopped her reply with a finger against her lips. 'That's not negotiable,' he told her, softening it with a smile, and she shrugged and gave in.

The next week was agonising, and she spent much of it doing endless research into twins, mostly about mono-chorionic monoamniotic twins which did nothing to reassure her. But Ben had said it was highly unlikely, and maybe the membrane wasn't visible because it had been too soon.

But by the end of the second scan, there was no doubt about it, and they could see it clearly on the screen.

Her babies were monochorionic, monoamniotic iden-tical twins, growing inside the same amniotic sac, from the same placenta, with nothing to stop them getting en-tangled in each other's umbilical cords with potentially catastrophic results. And that was just the obvious. On top of that were a host of associated conditions caused by the late splitting of the embryo, and the chance of them reaching viability was slim.

And just like that, in the space of a week, her pregnancy had gone from the delightful surprise of a single baby to twins to an ultra-high-risk twin pregnancy with a very uncertain outcome.

She turned her head away, too shocked to talk, too numb to cry, the dreams she'd allowed herself to build in the past few weeks in tatters. It was left to Dan to talk to Ben, to ask Steph for photos, to ask what would happen now.

He gently wiped the gel from her skin, tugged down her scrub top and helped her up, and she stiffened her spine and followed Ben out of the room and into his consulting room, Dan at her side.

Ben was brilliant with them.

Even though they both knew all the risks and technicalities and implications for her pregnancy, he went through them meticulously, one by one, and Dan was grateful for that because his mind was in bits.

He sat by Georgie's side, her hand in his, and every now and again he could feel a shudder run through her. He shifted closer, swapped hands and put an arm around her shoulders, and she leant wordlessly against him while Ben went through it all.

How much of it she heard, he had no idea. He wasn't doing much better himself. He wanted to scream and cry and hurl things, to ask, why him? Why, after already losing one child to an obstetric complication, was he facing the threat of losing not one but two more?

MCMA was a one in ten thousand chance, and the

likelihood of them surviving was slim. How cruel could life get?

'Do you want to do this later?' Ben asked gently, and Dan looked up and met his clinical lead's sympathetic eyes and shrugged.

'I don't know. Georgie?'

'I can't—I'm sorry, Ben. I can't take it in, it's just… Why me?' she asked, her voice so forlorn Dan could have cried for her.

'Hey, come on,' Ben said. 'It's not the end of the world and it could have been a lot worse. We know they aren't conjoined, which they could have been so easily, nor do they have TRAP syndrome—twin reversed arterial perfusion, where only one twin has a heart. We know that because there are definitely two hearts beating happily away.'

'What about TAPS?' she asked, which was just what Dan was thinking.

'Twin anaemia-polycythaemia syndrome means their blood vessels become linked so that one twin becomes anaemic and the other overloaded with red blood cells. It's tricky but not impossible to deal with, but it's also vanishingly rare. TTTS, twin to twin transfusion syndrome, is more likely, but again it can be dealt with. You'd be very unlucky to have either of those, so, yes, it'll be a bit tricky, but once you've reached twenty weeks you're going to have constant monitoring, very frequent scans—you'll be very closely watched throughout this.'

'Have you ever seen this before?' she asked, and he nodded.

'Yes. Yes, I have. Ten years ago we had a patient with it.'

'And?'

He smiled. 'Daisy and I delivered them the night before our wedding, and the girls are at the same school as our children, and they are both absolutely fine. So are Matt and I, and we're MCMA twins, which is pretty much why we both ended up in obstetrics and why he's a twin specialist heading up a referral unit in London. So I have a considerable personal interest in the condition, and a specialist on tap who can't tell me to get lost because I'd never speak to him again. Don't worry, we've got this. We just need to get you through the next twelve weeks, until the babies are viable. If we can do that, then we're well on the way to home and dry.'

CHAPTER EIGHT

HOME AND DRY.

Would her babies *ever* be home? Home with her, back in her little house...

Her too-little house. She'd have to move. She'd need a proper garden, especially if they were boys—if they survived that long.

She could feel the panic rising, the fear she might lose them, the fear of all that could happen to them, the possibility that they would survive against all the odds seeming so remote that she struggled to believe in it.

The doorbell rang, and she stood there, frozen. Who could it be? She didn't care, she didn't want to speak to anyone. She couldn't.

But it rang again, and then she heard knocking, and a voice through the letter box.

'Hello? Georgie? Let me in.'

Daisy. It was Daisy, and she'd never been so glad to see anyone in her life.

She opened the door and Daisy walked in, put her arms round her and hugged her hard.

'Ben told me he'd sent you home, said you might need someone to talk to that wasn't Dan. Are you OK?'

'No. I can't do this,' she mumbled into Daisy's

shoulder, and Daisy tutted and led her into the sitting room, sat her down and made them both a cup of mint tea, then gave her a mock stern look.

'Right. We'll have less of that "I can't do this" non-sense,' she said candidly. 'What happened to our Georgie?'

'I'm just scared for them, Daisy. And it's weeks and weeks until they're even remotely viable. What if something happens? What if the cords get tangled before then? They'll both die and it's just so unfair. And it's not just the cord entanglement. It's all the vascular and cardiac problems—there are so many things that could go wrong that are totally out of my control. They're my *babies*, Daisy, and I can't help them, and I feel so *useless*.'

'You're not useless, and you're not alone. You've got me on tap, you've got Dan, and you've got Ben and Matt. There's no way Ben's going to let anything happen to you if he can possibly avoid it, and his brother's the godfather of twin pregnancy. You couldn't be in safer hands. Now drink your tea. And have you got any biscuits? I'm starving.'

'Only ginger.'

'They'll do. I've had a few million of them over all my pregnancies. It'll bring back fond memories.'

It was a hideous day.

He'd taken an hour out in the morning which had meant leaving his registrar in charge, but he was straight back in with a prolapsed cord needing a crash section, followed by another section with a baby in fetal distress due to a prolonged obstructed labour.

And then to put the cherry on top there was another

placenta previa for his hot button. This time, however, she had notes, a booked elective section for the following day and she was already in under observation when she started contracting, so it was a simple case of taking her straight to Theatre and delivering her baby safe and sound.

Just as well, as his head was all over the place after the bombshell of the scan, and all he wanted to do was get back to Georgie and see if she was all right.

He wasn't sure he was. He'd spent the last week telling her it would be fine, they had to wait, it was too early to see the membrane, but his optimism had just taken a crashing dive and he was struggling. It was too much to take on board in the middle of a working day, too much information to process on a vanishingly rare condition that until last week had been a theoretical thing that he'd learned about in college and never expected to see in practice, and now, after the second scan, he felt out of his depth and overwhelmed by the enormity of it all.

How Georgie was doing was anybody's guess, but one thing he knew. From now on she was staying with him and he was looking after her, because there was no way either she or another baby of his were going to die if he had the slightest chance of saving them.

Always assuming she'd agree to his suggestion, and he was pretty damn sure she wouldn't.

She was about to water the garden when the doorbell rang.

Dan, inevitably. She wasn't sure she wanted to see him. He'd be bound to make a fuss, and she just felt exhausted and emotionally wrung out.

She opened the door, and he was standing there with the car outside. Odd, he almost always walked and it was fine this evening.

'May I come in?'

'If you don't fuss over me.'

He looked at her for a moment, then gave a quiet chuckle. 'How did I know you'd say that?'

He stepped inside, closing the door behind him, and gave her a gentle hug. She could have stayed there indefinitely, propped up by his strong, firm body, wrapped in the warmth of his arms, but he dropped them and let her go. 'Can we talk?'

She felt her shoulders droop. 'Do we have to? I'm so tired, Dan. It's been a hellish day. I just want to go to bed.'

'Ditto. But I have a suggestion. Well, two, really. I don't want you on your own, Georgia, not now we know what's going on, so I'd like you to come back to mine, or if you won't do that, then let me stay here, so I'm here for you.'

Why? What did he know that she didn't? She searched his eyes. 'Why?' she asked, and his eyes changed from concern to anguish.

'Because I need to look after you. I have to. I can't face losing anyone else to an obstetric complication,' he said with brutal honesty.

Oh, Dan. She'd somehow lost sight of the fact that she wasn't the only one struggling. This was the last thing he needed with his history, and for the first time that day she stopped worrying about the babies and switched her attention to him.

'Dan, I'm fine,' she said gently. 'And at the moment, the babies are fine, and even if they weren't, there's nothing you can do about it. Nothing either of us can do about it. We're in the lap of the gods.'

He looked down at her and nodded slowly. 'I know. I still won't rest if I haven't done everything that I *can* do.'

He glanced past her, and saw the watering can in the kitchen sink. 'Like that, for instance. Why are you doing that? Watering the plants with that heavy can? And anyway it's the end of October. Why do they need watering? It rained yesterday.'

'But not enough for the pots. It's not heavy, I only half fill it, and it's only for the evergreen shrubs, the rest are fine. For heaven's sake, Dan, I'm not an invalid! And watering the plants won't hurt the babies.'

He walked past her, topped the can up to the brim, picked it up and carried it out. 'Right, which ones?' he asked, and watered them while she folded her arms and watched, resisting the urge to tap her foot on the floor.

'Dan, I'm OK. I'm feeling a lot better, I've had Daisy here and she's been amazing. She made me lunch, talked sense into me and she's just round the corner if I need anything.'

'She's also got four children and can't drop everything and come, nor can she be here in the night in case you have a problem, nor can she do the little things like make you a cup of tea every time you want one—'

'I can make my own tea! I'm not an invalid!'

'Good. I'm very, very glad to hear it. But you *are* tired, you *are* pregnant with twins, and you're still working. Cut yourself some slack, Georgie, and let me help you, please.'

Light dawned. 'Is that why the car's here? So you

can drive me and all my things back to yours so you can hothouse me until they're born?'

He studied her, and gave a little huff of not quite laughter. 'No. Well, maybe, but I was pretty sure you'd refuse, at least for now.'

'So—why the car? Oh, of course. It's got *your* things in.'

He sighed and looked away. 'I just want to look after you. Indulge me, for God's sake. How hard is it?'

Actually in the end it wasn't hard at all, and it was almost a relief to know she wasn't on her own. Just in case...

But they weren't having a repeat of the situation they'd had before, where she'd ended up in his bed. Far too dangerous. She handed him bedlinen, put a towel in the bathroom for him and went to bed, shutting the door firmly behind herself and leaving him to it.

She heard him pottering around in the kitchen, but it wasn't long before he came upstairs. She heard the flush of the loo, the sound of running water, then a few minutes later the click of his bedroom light switch.

Her retreat would have been more effective, she thought wryly, if she'd remembered to get herself a glass of water first so she didn't have to creep out after he'd gone quiet, but the stairs creaked under her feet, and moments later he came down and joined her in the kitchen.

'Are you OK?'

'Yes, of course I am. I'm just thirsty.'

He grinned ruefully. 'Ditto. I meant to take a glass of water up with me and forgot.' He sighed and leant against the door frame, his eyes trained on her so that she was acutely conscious of the scanty nightdress that ended somewhere well above her knees. It didn't help that it was covered in tiny cats, either. What kind of a look was that? Not that it mattered in the slightest—

'Cute cats,' he murmured, and she turned to look at him. He was wearing a tired old T-shirt with a faded, peeling picture of Superman on the front, for heaven's sake—but with snug jersey shorts that sent her pulse into hyperdrive, and he had a lazy smile on his face that made her heart hitch.

She raised an eyebrow. 'You can talk. Superman, really? How old are you?' she teased, trying to ignore the shorts, and his mouth twitched.

'It was a present from my sister years ago—and anyway, it's comfy.'

'Well, it had to have one redeeming feature,' she said with a stifled smile, and dragged her eyes off him.

She ran the tap till it was cold, handed him a glass of water and headed back upstairs, acutely conscious of him behind her. He'd have a great view straight up her skirt. She tugged the back of her nightie down a bit and kicked herself for not putting on a different one tonight. A long one. Ankle length would be good.

He followed her up without a word, hesitated in his bedroom doorway then set the glass down.

'Wait.'

She sighed and turned back. 'Now what?'

'Don't close your door. Please?'

'What?'

He gave a short, frustrated sigh and scrubbed his hand through his hair, leaving it rumpled and sexier than ever. 'Look—I don't want to invade your space, Georgie, and I know you don't want me here, but I need to know that you're safe. If anything happened to you—'

She wrapped her arms around herself. 'You're making me nervous now. Did Ben tell you something he didn't tell me?'

'No! No, absolutely not. It's just…'

'…what happened…' she finished gently, and he nodded.

'Yes. And I can't just switch that off. It's there all the time, every day at work, every night if I have a case I'm concerned about, because I know what it means when someone dies because you haven't done enough. I've been there, and I don't want to go there again. And if that means I'm doing too much, I'm sorry, but I need to take care of you and keep you and the babies safe, and also give you the reassurance that if something does happen, you're not alone. I couldn't bear you to be alone.'

She felt her eyes fill. 'Oh, Dan. Come here,' she said softly, and pulled him gently into her arms and hugged him.

It was a mistake. Of course it was a mistake, because despite all that had happened, despite the fear and the threat to her pregnancy and his endless hovering, beneath it all was a longing to hold him, to be held by him again.

He rested his head against hers and sighed, and she felt some of the tension go out of him. His warmth seeped into her, calming the fear she was trying so hard not to acknowledge, and gradually she relaxed. But not completely.

She let him go, took a step back and smiled.

'Thank you,' she said softly, and then stepping back,

she pushed the door to, leaving it open a crack, and climbed into bed. The bed where he'd held her in his arms and made love to her. The bed where they'd made their babies.

She wished she could trust him with her heart, and under any other circumstances she might well have done, but she knew he didn't want a relationship any more than she did. He wasn't just doing this because of her, he was doing it because of the babies too, because of his guilt and his fear for their safety.

And in a way she was glad he was here, because underneath her bravado and protests lay a deep well of fear and dread over what the next few weeks and months would bring. That was the reason, and the only reason, she'd let him stay.

It was no kind of a foundation for their relationship, but it was all she could have from him, all he had to offer and all she would accept, and she couldn't let herself forget that.

He stayed for the rest of that week, and by the end of it she was struggling with the forced proximity. She thought he was, too, but probably not for the same reasons. She had a feeling he felt unwelcome, and she felt crowded, hovered over, watched, even when he wasn't. And under it all was the tug of attraction that was driving her crazy.

And his sleep gear didn't help. Why did he have to be so ridiculously well put together? The odd carbuncle or bad breath or a disgusting habit would go a long way towards making it easier.

So she told him it wasn't working for her, and instead of agreeing that it was overkill anyway, he came back with another idea.

'Why don't you come back to mine?' he suggested. 'There's more space there, and I've sorted out the spare room. Or we could alternate? Stay here if we're working late, or at mine if not? And you can spend the days here when you're off duty and I'm on call, so you're nearer the hospital. How about that?'

It seemed a reasonable compromise, and she was surprised to find she actually liked the idea, so they tried it and found it worked. And every day at work he got out his Doppler and they listened to the babies' heartbeats.

So far, so good, and she started to relax. She even allowed herself to feel happy.

And then three weeks after her last scan, when she was nearly sixteen weeks, she had a bleed at work. Nothing much, just a few spots, and not fresh blood, but a bleed for all that, and the bubble of happiness burst and brought her crashing down to earth. She stared at the blood, stark on her pale underwear, and gave up any pretence of courage.

Dan. She had to find Dan, but he'd left the ward, so she sent him a message and phoned Ben, and he sent her straight down for a scan. She messaged Dan again, and he and Ben made it just in time.

She was already lying there, top hitched up, trousers tugged down and her heart in her mouth when they arrived, and Dan stood beside her, her hand clenched in his as Steph scanned her, going carefully over every inch of the placenta, over the babies, the cords...

'Well, that all looks fine,' Ben said with a relieved smile, and they both started breathing again. 'They're both growing well and they're the same size, which is good. I'm happy with that.'

'So what caused it?' she asked.

'I have no idea, but I don't think it's anything to worry about. It's all looking good, but you need to take a couple of days off and rest, just to be on the safe side, and we'll go from there, but I'm pretty sure it's nothing. We just need to keep them in there until they're viable, and longer if possible.'

'So when would you deliver them by choice? Assuming they get to that point?' Dan asked.

'Any time from thirty-two weeks.'

'That's still so early,' she said.

'Not that early, we can deliver them any time from twenty-four weeks onwards if we really can't avoid it, but by thirty-two weeks they'll be safer out than in if we have any worries. If we don't, we might leave them to cook another week or two. But since you have had a bleed, I'm a little concerned about you living alone.'

'She isn't,' Dan said firmly. 'We're together.'

Which made it sound much more than it was, but it seemed to satisfy Ben. 'Good. And in the meantime I want you to have a 4D scan so we have a video of how they move and relate to each other. Some are more active than others. Have you felt them moving yet?'

'I'm not sure,' she said. 'I did wonder yesterday, but I put it down to wind. It's quite early.'

'It's not unheard of, and they're certainly moving well, so it could be. Anyway, at the moment you're OK, they're OK and it's looking good for now, so I'm happy.'

True to his word, Ben had her scanned with monotonous frequency, and he was happy with her progress.

Dan wasn't. Like Georgie, he was living on a permanent knife-edge. The stress in the build-up to each scan
was hell to deal with, and every time it was all right he
relaxed again. Until the next time.

They got to know the babies' faces in the 3D scan,
watched them grow and develop over the next few
weeks, and inevitably with all the scans there was no
hiding the fact that they were girls, and of course that
hit a nerve.

Would knowing they were boys have been any better? He wasn't sure. Either way losing them would
break his heart, and the slow passage of every day was
agonising, but bit by bit they got closer to viability.

Then when she was twenty weeks Ben sent them to
London for a 4D scan with his brother Matt, and they
watched the video of them moving and it suddenly all
seemed so much more real. Matt was more than happy
with the babies, so they went out for dinner afterwards
to celebrate and all the Christmas lights were on, and
it felt oddly romantic, almost like some surreal date.
Only of course it wasn't, and he kept having to remind
himself of that.

They spent Christmas at work, because everyone
else had children, but because there were no scheduled electives the workload was lighter with only
three straightforward deliveries, and everyone loved
a Christmas baby, so it was a good day.

And another day nearer. She was almost twenty-
two weeks, and after twenty-eight it should be safer,
but the suspense was killing him.

At the beginning of January, when she was twenty-
three weeks pregnant, she had a message as she was on

her way to work from Laura Stryker, to say she was in labour and en route to the hospital. She'd seen her the week before at Livvy's, and she'd thought at the time that Laura looked imminent.

Nice to know pregnancy hadn't clouded her judgement, but she just hoped they got their boy, so that Tom wouldn't pass on the Retinitis Pigmentosa gene that was gradually robbing him of his sight. They'd chosen not to find out, but she knew they'd regretted that decision and were desperate to know now.

Georgie met them at the desk and gave Laura a little hug, then changed quickly and went to handover.

'Laura Stryker's just come in,' she told Jan. 'Can I have her, please? And she wants the birthing pool.'

'Of course. No lifting, though, so you be careful and get someone else in to help you if it's tricky to get her out. And use the hoist if she can't help herself. I don't want you doing anything risky.'

She went straight back to them, and found Laura rocking backwards and forwards, one hand on her back, the other clinging to Tom, and Georgie checked the time.

It eased off, and Laura looked up and met her eyes. 'Is the birthing pool free?' she asked, and Georgie nodded.

'Yes. Let's move you in there. It'll take a little while to fill, but there's no hurry and I need to have a look at you and see how you're doing.'

Well, as it turned out. Her contractions were coming every three minutes and she was already seven centimetres, so as soon as the pool was full and Georgie was happy with the temperature, Laura stripped off and climbed in, wearing just a little vest top that she could quickly pull out of the way after the baby was born.

'Oh, that feels so good,' she said with a sigh of relief, and she didn't talk again after that. The odd moan, a bit of shifting around to find a comfortable position, Tom's hands supporting her and rubbing her back firmly during contractions while soft music played in the background.

Georgie checked her again when she came out to use the bathroom an hour later, and her cervix was fully dilated.

'You're doing really well. Want to go back in for the delivery?'

Laura nodded and climbed back into the water, sinking under it with a sigh of relief, then she gave a guttural groan and rolled over, kneeling up with her arms folded on the edge of the pool and pushing, and while Tom murmured gentle words of encouragement, Georgie pressed the button for another midwife and went round to the other side of the pool where she could keep an eye on her progress.

'OK, Laura, the baby's head's crowning, so nice little pants now, no more pushing, just let it happen,' she said, wondering where the other midwife was. Surely they weren't all busy?

They were, and she got Dan instead.

'You again. Having a career change?' she murmured with a smile, and he chuckled quietly and hunkered down beside her.

'Liv's on her way. Anything I can do?'

'Yes, turn the lights down a little more and get a towel ready in case we need to lift them out quickly, but I don't think we will. Here we go… Lovely, Laura, well done, tiny little push—OK, the head's out, so stay well under water and turn over—that's it. Well done.'

She was there beside her now, and as Laura gave one final push Georgie reached down into the water and lifted the baby up and out, so its head was clear of the water as it took its first gasp of air. Tom had pulled her top out of the way, and the baby lay cradled on her chest, blinking up at them in the gentle light.

'Hello, baby,' Laura said softly, but Tom's face was tense.

'What is it?' he asked, his voice tight, and Georgie moved the baby a fraction so she could see, and smiled up at them.

'It's a boy,' she said, her eyes filling with tears, and Tom's face crumpled.

'Oh, thank God,' he said, and he buried his face in Laura's shoulder and wrapped his arms around them both and sobbed with relief.

There was a tap on the door and Liv Jarvis came in. 'Oh, I've missed it!'

Georgie looked up and grinned at her. 'Still plenty to do.'

Dan gave a soft chuckle. 'Over to you,' he murmured to Liv, congratulated the happy family and left them to it.

She was soaked by the time Laura was out of the water and dried, so as soon as the placenta was delivered she left Liv in charge and went to change, a little bubble of happiness inside her for them and their new son.

The babies were busily kicking her in the bladder, so she needed a quick wee and some dry scrubs, and then she'd be back in there to finish off the paperwork and settle Laura into a bed.

Except she didn't make it back, because she realised, now she had time to think about it, that the babies were very active. Worryingly active, and she was only twenty-three weeks. It was still much too soon. Would they make it? She didn't know and she was swamped with fear, but she rang Dan, he rang Ben, and once again they met at the scan room.

'So what's going on?'

'I don't know. A lot of wriggling and tumbling about, and I'm just really worried about the cords. I was doing a delivery, and then I realised how active they were—much more than usual.'

'OK, let's have a look.'

Yet again they watched as Steph scanned her meticulously, checking the placenta for any issues, the cords for entanglement, the babies for any sign they might be distressed, but she found nothing of any major concern.

Ben took them into his office and sat them down.

'Right, I don't think this activity is significant, not this time, and they're quieter now and the cords aren't tangled, so I want you to chart the movements as you've been doing and we'll review it daily and if necessary we can deliver them if the situation changes.'

'It's too early,' she said, her hands instinctively going to her bump. 'They're not really viable, Ben. Not yet. They're so tiny.'

He nodded slowly. 'It's not ideal, I agree, but they're looking well, and they stand a chance now.'

'I want more than a chance!' she said desperately.

'I know. And I realise how tough this is for you both,

but if we can keep you going then every day that passes makes a difference.'

'You're not going to put me on bed rest, are you?' she said, dreading his answer, and he shook his head.

'Not now, and probably not at all if it all proceeds well, but I want you on light duties only now, Georgie. I'll talk to Jan. Clinics only, shorter hours, less running around. If we can keep your workload down to a minimum but keep you here, that's the safest place.'

'Do you really think she should be at work?' Dan chipped in, his voice tight with worry, and she reached out and took his hand, as much for her own reassurance as for his.

'I don't think it'll hurt, but you certainly aren't doing any more deliveries. We can monitor you frequently during the day as you get further on, and once you've got past twenty-eight weeks or so the danger from entanglement doesn't seem to be the issue we once thought it was, so inpatient bed rest and monitoring doesn't seem as necessary as it did and doesn't have a measurable effect on the outcome. So, no, in short, we won't put you on bed rest unless it's absolutely necessary, but you'll be even more intensively monitored from now on. Don't worry, Georgie. We're keeping a very close eye on you and we'll act as soon as we think it's necessary.'

They walked out of Ben's office and Dan glanced at his phone.

'You need to talk to Jan, and I need to see how my registrar's doing and make sure Patrick hasn't lost the plot, and then how about lunch?'

Lunch? She was still in a bit of a daze, but actually...

'Yeah, why not? That's a great idea. It's a lovely sunny day. We can sit in the window of the Park Café and look at the trees. I'll call you.'

She went and found Liv, and she met her eyes and mouthed, 'You OK?' and Georgie nodded.

'Sort of. Had a bit of a hiccup with the babies. They were really active but I've had a scan, it's all OK, Ben's happy, but I'm going for lunch with Dan if you're able to carry on?'

'Yes, I'm fine. They're doing well. Utterly besotted, both of them. That baby's going to be so spoilt.'

'Like you'd never spoil your two,' she said with a smile, and after a quick word with Laura and Tom she left them to it and messaged Dan to tell him she'd see him in the café.

She went down in the lift because she felt suddenly exhausted, and by the time Dan got to the café she could hardly keep her eyes open. He slid into the seat opposite her and took her hand.

'You OK?'

'Tired. So, so tired. I think I'm just emotionally exhausted.'

'Well, not to mention the physical challenge. You need fuel. Stay there, I'll get you something. What do you want?'

'I don't know. Get what looks nice.'

He did. He brought lasagne and a chicken casserole and gave her the choice, and she took the casserole, tasty and filling and full of healthy calories, and almost inhaled it, then sat back with a sheepish smile.

'Gosh, I needed that. Thank you.'

He gave a soft huff of laughter and finished his lasagne, drained his coffee and checked the time.

'Do you need to be somewhere?'

Another laugh. 'Always. It's not critical, I've got ten minutes. Want anything else?'

'An apple turnover for later? I'm so hungry these days.'

'Another one? I need to start feeding you more.'

'No, you don't, I'm going to be carrying enough weight...'

Her face must have changed, because he frowned and reached out a hand and took hers, squeezing it gently.

'You'll be OK,' he said, and she met his eyes and shook her head.

'You can't say that. You know you can't say that. You're a doctor, Dan. Don't promise what you can't deliver. That's the first rule. Don't tell people it'll be OK when you have no control over it. We have no control over this. We just have to wait it out.'

He squeezed her hand again. 'I know. I'm sorry. I just...'

'Want to make it all right?' She squeezed his hand back. 'I know. I understand.' She glanced up at the clock on the wall. 'Shouldn't you be going?'

'What about your cake?'

She shook her head. 'I don't need it. I've got biscuits in the ward kitchen. They'll do. I'll walk back with you. I need to find out what Jan's going to let me do for the rest of the day. If I know her, not a lot.'

They went back in together, and as they parted at the desk he dropped a kiss on her cheek and walked away, and she turned back to see Jan smiling.

'He's a nice man,' she said, and Georgie was on the

point of opening her mouth and changed her mind, nodding instead.

'Yes, he is.' Even though he wasn't hers and never would be. She stifled the pang and smiled at Jan. 'So, what am I doing? Don't tell me, auditing the notes to find some spurious data that nobody really needs?'

Jan raised an eyebrow. 'I have no idea what you mean. The files are there. Go through them and see if you can spot any inconsistencies, anything that we could be doing better, or any patterns emerging that concern you.'

'Really?'

'Really,' Jan said firmly, and left her to it.

CHAPTER NINE

She got home before him—her house, because he was still at work and she'd be closer if the movements got too lively again.

She made herself a drink and propped herself up on the sofa, but it wasn't as comfortable as his and she was fidgety and restless.

Like the babies. Maybe if she went and lay down, it would be better. She climbed the stairs, shocked at how much harder it was now at only twenty-three weeks. She looked as if she were thirty weeks or more, so heaven knows what she'd look like by the time she reached thirty-four.

If she ever did.

She paused and closed her eyes, taking a moment to ground herself, then went on up, turned back the duvet and lay down on her side, her hand resting on her bump, feeling the movement of the babies. The crazy jiggling of earlier had gone, and they were peaceful now, just the odd wriggle or stretch.

'Please be OK, babies,' she murmured. 'I couldn't bear it if you weren't...'

She squeezed her eyes shut, but a great wrenching

sob tore itself out of her chest, and she turned her face into the pillow and sobbed her heart out.

She was crying.

He could hear her the moment he came through the door, and he ran upstairs and found her on her bed, her hand splayed protectively over the babies.

He kicked off his shoes and lay down beside her, his hand finding hers and splaying over it.

'What's up?' he asked softly, and she lifted her head and met his eyes.

'I'm just so scared for them,' she said, her voice clogged with tears, and he eased her into his arms and pressed a kiss to her forehead.

'I know, but Ben's taking really good care of you, and he knows what he's doing.'

'He can't change fate.'

'No, but he can pre-empt it. He's doing a great job, and so are you. You can't do any more than that.'

She let out a shaky sigh and nodded. 'I know. I'm just being silly.'

No sillier than him. He'd struggled all day with this latest reminder of how fragile her pregnancy was, how quickly it could turn to disaster. But she didn't need to know that.

'Let's go back to mine, and I'll cook you a nice meal and we can watch something silly on the TV—a rom-com or something.'

She tilted her head back and looked at him. 'Really? A rom-com? That doesn't sound like you.'

'I like a rom-com. Why not?'

She smiled, in spite of herself, and rolled away from him. 'OK. Let's go,' she said, wriggling her feet back into her shoes and standing up slowly because her blood pressure was low and she got dizzy.

'OK?'

'Yup. Rom-com here we come.'

He sat her down on the sofa while he cooked, and when he called her through there were candles on the table.

'Gosh, that's a bit OTT for a weeknight,' she said with a smile, but he just grinned.

'Getting into the mood for the film,' he said, and brought their plates to the table. A delicious monkfish and roasted tomato penne, with a tiny kick of chilli—Italian food, in keeping with the romance, followed up by a light and delicate lemon dessert served in a dainty cup with an amaretto biscuit on the side.

She all but licked out the cup, then pushed it away. 'That was delicious, Dan. Thank you.'

His smile was gentle. 'You're welcome. Right, let's go and choose a film.'

They curled up on the sofa side by side, but then somehow she ended up lying with her head on his lap, with his arm around her and his hand splayed over her bump. Every now and again the babies would move, and his hand would stroke soothingly over them and they'd go back to sleep.

It wasn't long before she joined them, and she was woken by the click of the TV turning off.

'Time for bed,' he murmured, and she stretched and sighed and shook her head.

'Too comfy.'

'Tough,' he said with a chuckle, and shifted out from under her and pulled her slowly to her feet and into his arms.

It felt so right, so natural, and when they reached the bedroom door she stopped and met his eyes.

'Stay with me,' she said softly, and she saw something flicker in his eyes. 'Not—for that. Just…' She had no idea what he was thinking, but in the end he nodded.

'OK—but in my room. The bed's bigger.'

Why did he agree?

It was every kind of torture, but he wouldn't have changed it for the world. They didn't make love. That wasn't what she needed, and it would have been a bad idea on every level, not least for her pregnancy. But lying with her head on his chest and her leg over his, he could feel the babies move and he knew they were all right.

Not so his arm, but then she rolled away and he winced and rubbed the life back into it, then curled in behind her, his arm draped over her waist and his hand on the babies, and gradually he fell asleep.

They slept together every night from then onwards, and she slept better than she had since the start of her pregnancy.

The weeks passed slowly, and with every check, their babies were that bit nearer to being viable. She wasn't sure how Dan felt about them being girls. Boys might have been better, but maybe the fact that they were girls was just more bittersweet. But he'd never mentioned it, and throughout it all he was wonderful.

Endlessly supportive, kind, funny—if it hadn't been for the fact that he was only doing it because of guilt and to keep his tiny girls safe, she could almost have believed they had a future.

Not that she dared to let herself think about it, because if the babies died, this would all stop. There'd be no need for him to look after her, no need for him to stay with her and hold her while she slept, no need for him to be with her at all, but as it was they were still taking one day at a time and she was doing her best not to be too needy or dependent.

She couldn't let that happen, because letting herself love him would be a recipe for disaster. They weren't together in that way, and never would be, and her pregnancy was still balanced on a knife-edge.

But even so, he was house-hunting.

He'd sold his house in Bristol and was looking for a three or four bedroomed house with a garden. She told him he was jumping the gun, don't tempt fate, pushing their luck, so he didn't go and view any, but he was still searching, and she wasn't sure how he would cope if anything happened to the babies now.

She passed the magic twenty-four-week viability milestone, then the twenty-eight-week one, then thirty—and then it was thirty-two and Ben was talking about delivering her, so she was started on steroids to mature the babies' lungs.

She had a bit of cord entanglement. Not enough to worry about, but enough that she was being monitored even more closely. She had a Doppler scan three times a day, and Dan was doing it morning and evening as well, and she was still doing the movement chart, sitting down for an hour and counting the number of movements in that time.

There were usually in excess of twenty-five, but sometimes more and sometimes hardly anything. They seemed to sleep most often when she was busy, and wake up when her pelvis was no longer rocking them with every stride and sending them off to sleep, so every time she lay down a football match would start.

And then one day towards the end of March, when she was thirty-four weeks and her section was scheduled for the next day, one of them went quiet.

She was at work, sitting at a desk uploading patient notes in the antenatal clinic, and it just felt—wrong.

And it was Dan's clinic.

She tapped on his consulting room door and put her head round, and he beckoned her in, took one look at her face and ended his call.

'What?'

'They've been really active, lots of shoving and pushing, and now the one on the right isn't moving as much. It feels—odd.'

'Right. Scan, now,' he said, and as they walked the few steps to the ultrasound room, he was on the phone to Ben.

Steph was just finishing off, and the moment the couple came out they were in there. Ben arrived as Steph started to scan her, and together they studied the images.

She'd been right to worry. One of them had turned round, the cords were really tangled, and the baby on the right had the cord looped around her neck. It wasn't tight, and the heartbeats were similar, and she was moving a little more again now, but if either of them turned the wrong way she could die. It was seriously bad news, and she knew what Ben would say before he opened his mouth.

'Sorry, Georgie, we can't leave them like this, we'll have to do your section now. When did you last eat?'

'Breakfast,' she said, feeling giddy with fear and anticipation.

'Good, because I don't want to wait, it's too risky, so I need to put you under. I'm really sorry but it's the safest thing to do. If they move again...'

She nodded, and then found herself in a wheelchair being whisked up to Theatre. Her scrubs were peeled off, she was gowned and Peter, the anaesthetist, got the cannula in ready.

Dan was with her, holding her other hand, stroking the hair back off her face, and she could feel the tremors running through him, feel his fear, his dread, the storm of emotion that was going on inside him, but he was there with her, and she loved him for that.

'You'll be OK, Georgie,' he was saying. 'You'll all be OK. I'm here for you.'

They were the last words she heard as she slipped into unconsciousness.

'Are you coming in?' Ben asked through the doorway, but Dan's heart was pounding, adrenaline coursing through his body, and he thought he was going to throw up.

He shook his head. 'I'm sorry, I can't. I can't do this again. I can't lose anyone else. Just—don't let them die, Ben. For God's sake, don't let them die.'

Ben's eyes held a thousand questions, but he didn't have the words to explain and Ben didn't have time to listen. He took a step back, then another, and turned on his heel and strode out of Theatre, out past the lifts, down the stairs and out into the park, sucking in lungs-ful of air.

Please don't let them die. Don't let them die. Don't let them die...

He sank down under a tree and leant against it, star-ing blindly out across the park. He felt sick. He should be up there with Georgie, not down here wallowing in self-indulgence. He was such a coward. He should have been with her.

He buried his face in his hands, and then he felt a touch on his shoulder and looked up.

Patrick, hunkering down beside him, concern in his eyes.

'Are you OK, Mr Blake?'

He just laughed at that, but the laugh caught in his chest and came out as a sob. 'Georgie's in Theatre,' he said.

'I heard. So why aren't you there? She needs you.'

He shook his head. 'I can't. I can't do it again. I've been here before, and I can't—I just—'

'Yes, you can. Come on, Dan. Get up. I'll come with you. You're not alone, I'm here. Come on.'

He sucked in a huge breath, let it out again slowly and got to his feet, then made his way back inside, Patrick beside him all the way. Patrick, the junior doc-tor who'd nearly driven him insane, and who now had come of age and found his strength.

There were seats outside the theatres, the seats where he'd left Rob on his first day, waiting to find out if Susie and the baby would survive.

Like the seats where he'd sat waiting for a cry from his baby, the cry that had never come.

'Sit down, Dan,' Patrick said gently, and he sat beside him, a hand on his shoulder, and they waited. Then Patrick's pager went off and he had to leave, and Dan felt lost without him there.

He didn't know how long he'd sat there staring at the door before it opened and a nurse came out. Ten minutes? An hour?

'Mr Blake? Your babies are with the NICU team, they're working on them but they're doing well, and Mr Walker's just closing. He said to tell you they're all OK.'

He closed his eyes, squeezing back the tears, but they fell anyway, tears of joy, disbelief, regret that he hadn't been there, guilt because his other baby had never had this chance. He had no idea how long he sat there as emotion ripped its way through him, wave after wave of pent-up feelings finally finding their release, until in the end he felt an arm around his shoulders, a solid shoulder to cry on.

Ben, who'd been there for them from start to finish, who'd saved his babies and his beloved Georgia, was there with him, saying nothing but offering his silent support.

He pulled away from him, hauled in a breath and scrubbed his hands over his face, and Ben handed him a tissue.

'Sorry. It's—it's been a hell of a pregnancy,' he said, and then he saw a glitter in Ben's own eyes as he smiled.

'I know. Congratulations. I'm so glad it's turned out so well for you both,' he said, his voice a little unsteady, and Dan laughed and hugged him hard.

'Thank you. Thank you so much. You have no idea what it means to me.'

'My pleasure. She's in Recovery now, and the babies are about to go up to NICU soon. Let me take you through so you can see them before they go.'

'Georgie? Georgia, I'm here.'

She opened her eyes and looked up at him, and his face swam into focus. His eyes were red-rimmed, his lashes clumped with tears, but he was smiling with every part of his face, and she was so happy to see him.

'Ben said they're alive,' she said with a little sob of joy. 'They're both alive.'

'I know. I've just seen them. They're beautiful, Georgie. So beautiful.' There were tears coursing down his cheeks, and his eyes were full of emotion as he put his arms around her and hugged her gently, her head cradled against his shoulder.

She could hardly believe they'd got so far. Their babies had made it against all the odds, and now it was down to the NICU staff to keep them safe.

Not quite out of the woods, but almost.

'Go and be with them,' she said to him tearfully. 'Tell them I'll come and see them as soon as I can. Tell them I love them.'

He nodded and got to his feet, then bent and kissed her.

'I love you, Georgia,' he said gruffly, and then he thanked Ben again and left, and Ben looked at her and winked.

'You OK?'

'I think so,' she said. 'Thank you so much.'

His eyes creased in a smile as broad as Dan's.

'It's my absolute pleasure. I couldn't be happier for you.'

But she hardly heard his words, because echoing in her head were Dan's last words before he'd gone.

'I love you...'

He hadn't meant to say that.

It had just come out, and it shocked him. Was it true? Did he love her? Actually, really *love* her? Like that?

Maybe. Possibly. He was certainly immensely proud of her, of the courageous way she'd coped with a complicated pregnancy that had had them both balanced on a knife-edge for weeks. And there was no doubt that he was attracted to her; even during the ordeal of this terrifying pregnancy she'd been beautiful to him, and he'd wanted her so much it had trashed his peace of mind and messed with his sleep. Until he'd had her in bed with him every night, and then it just felt right.

But—love?

He didn't think it was reciprocated.

She pushed him away at every turn, she'd accepted his help grudgingly because she was so fiercely independent, and she'd only done that out of common sense and pity for him because of his past.

No. That was unfair, and she was better than that. It was empathy, and her understanding of where he was coming from had made it easier, but she still hadn't cut him any slack if he helicoptered, as she put it. And being with her wasn't an easy ride. She was as sassy as hell, highly opinionated, knew her own mind and he didn't often win an argument. Although even that had been better recently, and she'd leant on him more and more as the weeks had crept by, but she was still fiercely independent.

So how could he love her, this contrary, awkward,

prickly, defensive woman who'd fought her corner and
stood up for herself against all odds?

How he could *not*? After all, she'd given him something he'd thought he'd never have. A family.

He watched through the glass as the NICU team
worked on their babies. Wires, tubes, the endless beep-
ing of machines were all around them. How would they
cope with that?

And they were so tiny. So, so tiny. Well, not really.
They were both just under two kilos, slightly over four
pounds, and he'd delivered so many babies of that sort
of weight who'd sailed through it, but these were *his*,
his and Georgia's, and the sight of them, so small and
so vulnerable, brought back all the painful memories
that he'd tried so hard to subdue.

Memories of a baby who hadn't made it, who'd
weighed the same, who he'd held in his arms and loved
with all his heart. He couldn't do that again. Please, let
him not have to do that again.

Please let them live. Please let them be all right…

Someone was walking towards him, opening the door,
smiling as she beckoned him in. 'Hi, Dan, I'm Sarah and
I'm one of the team looking after your babies. Do you
want to come in? They're all settled now.'

He nodded, and she checked his wristband, gave
him a gown and a mask and led him over to the cot.

It wasn't the first time he'd been in there. He and
Georgie had been given a guided tour a few weeks ago
as it had been anticipated that the babies might need
to be in here, but also he'd come up here to see Susie's
baby on his first day, right after he'd left Georgie in
her bed on the night their twins had been conceived.

He would never have imagined on that night that

he'd end up being the father of a baby in here, never mind two, but there they were, alive and apparently doing well.

They were in a twin cot, lying side by side with their scrawny little arms touching, just as they had been all their lives to now. So close they were almost one. It brought a lump to his throat. And he had to swallow hard before he could speak.

'I'm so glad they can touch each other. They're so used to it. They've never been apart. I can't believe they're actually here, that they've made it this far.'

'No. They're pretty special babies.'

'Yes, they are.' He swallowed the lump again and pulled himself together. 'So which is which?' he said, staring down at two identical little faces, or what he could see of them with the tubes taped to their cheeks.

'The one on the left is twin number one, the one that had the cord around her neck, and the one on the right is twin two. Have they got names?'

He shook his head. 'No. We haven't talked about it yet.'

Hadn't dared, for fear of tempting fate, just like he hadn't bought a house yet, and they had no cots, no baby car seats, no buggy—nothing. Not even a packet of nappies, because she wouldn't hear of it until she knew they were OK. And as for names…

'We ought to do that,' he murmured, staring down at them in awe, watching their little chests rising and falling steadily.

'You might find it helps. Bonding with a baby you can't hold or touch is very difficult, but giving them names somehow makes them seem more real, so people say.'

He nodded. His baby had never had a name, or not one he'd ever known, and that still broke his heart, but in his head she was Emily, because she'd just looked like an Emily.

'I'll talk to Georgia. She's probably got some ideas.'

They talked a bit longer, about the care they'd need, how long they'd be in there, how they were being fed, and then Sarah gave him a chair and left him there, and he sat beside them, staring through the clear walls of the cot, watching them breathe. That in itself was a miracle. He pulled out his phone and took a little video of them for Georgie, and as he was about to stop twin two stretched and yawned, and he didn't know whether to laugh or cry. He ended up with a bit of both, then after a while Sarah came back.

'Georgie's back on the ward and she's asking for you,' she said, and he nodded and got to his feet.

'You will let us know if anything changes?'

'Of course we'll let you know, and you can come back and see them any time you want to. We'll bring Georgie in here to see them later, once she's settled in her room. She's just down the corridor on the left.'

He took one last look at them and headed out to find her.

'Hi, you.'

She smiled at him. 'Hi.'

He came over to her and took her hand. 'How are you doing?'

She wasn't sure. She was still trying to work out if he'd actually meant what he'd said. 'I'm fine, but never mind me, how are the babies?'

'They're amazing. I took this for you.' His smile was

a little crooked, and he perched on the edge of the chair by her bed and pulled out his phone and showed her a little video clip of them, and her eyes filled with tears.

'Oh! Oh, that's really sweet! I can't believe that little yawn. Which one is she?'

'The second. Twin two. They need names, Georgia. They should have names.'

There was something in his voice, and she looked up at him and caught a hint of sadness in his eyes. He'd never mentioned his baby by name. Maybe she'd never had one?

'Yes. Yes, they should,' she said gently, and then, 'Have you got any ideas?'

He looked a bit surprised at that. 'I thought you would.'

She shrugged. 'A few. I didn't really want to let myself think about it. Not until they were safely here.'

'No. I didn't either.' He settled back in the chair. 'So let's hear your thoughts, then.'

'I don't know. Should they start with the same letter? Should they be completely different?'

He chuckled softly. 'I don't think there are rules.'

'They need to go with Blake.'

'Or with Seton.'

'Seton-Blake?' she offered, and he smiled.

'That's quite a mouthful,' he said, and pulled out his phone. 'I think we might need help. Shall we start with the As?'

They worked through the list, and she was on the point of giving up when they reached the Es.

'Emily's nice,' she said, and his face froze.

'Not Emily,' he said.

He didn't say why, but he didn't need to. It was

enough that he didn't want it, so she let it go. 'OK. Elizabeth? Eva?'

'They'd work together.'

'Put them on the shortlist, then,' she said, and they moved on, reaching the Is without any further consensus.

'India's interesting.'

'With what?'

He shrugged. 'Isla? Iona? Isabel?'

She shook her head. 'One of my friends has an Isabel and the others are all place names.'

He put his phone down and looked at her. 'D'you know what? I like Elizabeth and Eva. Beth and Evie. They all work with Seton-Blake.'

She smiled, liking the sound of them—and the sound of Seton-Blake. 'Yes, they do. Happy with that?'

'I think so, if you are. They're your babies.'

'No. They're *our* babies,' she said firmly, then added, 'I wonder when they'll let me see them?'

'Soon, I think. They're going to wheel you in there on the bed for a little while.'

She felt a shiver of excitement. 'I want to see them now.'

'Shall I go and ask?'

'Could you?'

It wasn't long enough, but then it never would be, she realised, because if she looked at them for ever she'd still struggle to believe that they were hers.

They were so beautiful, so tiny and perfect and vulnerable, and yet they were apparently doing well. She could hardly bear to leave them, but Ben was on his way up to see her and they needed to be fed. Just a tiny bit, a few mils every hour, but they at least had names now.

Beth was the first one to be born, the one who'd had the cord around her neck, and Evie was the second, the one who'd obligingly yawned for their video, and when Georgie spoke their names they'd both turned their heads towards the sound.

'They recognise your voice,' Dan said, and she felt the comforting warmth of his hand as he squeezed her shoulder.

She nodded. 'They've heard enough of it for today. We need to leave them in peace,' she said, and as her bed was wheeled back out to her room she was swallowing back tears. She should be holding them, feeding them, being a mother instead of a post-op patient forced to take a back seat to the NICU team.

'Hey,' he said softly, taking her hand as the nurses left them. 'They're doing well. You'll soon be able to hold them.'

'I should be expressing my colostrum for them,' she said, wondering if they'd ever be able to breastfeed or if their reflexes would be dented by the ease of tube and then bottle feeding. Breastfeeding was hard work for prem babies, and lots of them failed to establish it.

Please let them make it.

She shut her eyes, but the tears slid down her cheeks anyway, and she felt Dan's arms around her, hugging her gently.

'Don't cry,' he murmured. 'They'll be all right.'

'You don't know that. Nobody knows that.'

'Hey, come on, chin up, they've got this far and they're doing well. Mop yourself up. Ben's here.'

She felt the soft touch of a tissue on her cheeks, and

opened her eyes to find Ben standing at the foot of the bed watching them.

'How are you doing?' he asked, all matter-of-fact despite the warmth in his eyes, and she was glad he was there, glad he'd been there for all of them.

'I'm fine. Thank you so much for everything you've done for us.'

'Don't be daft, it's my job and I wasn't going to let you down, I'd never hear the end of it,' he said, brushing it aside. 'Let's have a look at your incision. I have to say I'm pretty proud of it.'

'Modest with it, aren't you?' she teased, and he grinned.

'No point in denying my genius,' he said, but behind the cocky grin was a kindness fathoms deep, and she knew how much of himself he'd invested in her care.

He was a good friend, and she was hugely grateful for all he'd done for them. Only apparently she wasn't allowed to tell him that, so she lay there and smiled as he checked her over, nodded in satisfaction at her wound under its dressing and covered her up.

'How's the pain level?'

She shrugged. 'It's quite sore now.'

'OK, first things first. We'll get you some pain relief, then get you out into a chair and see how you feel, and then you maybe need to think about feeding those babies, but the midwives will deal with all of that, and I'll come and see you again later.'

It was the third day before she could hold the babies in her arms, and it seemed like a year, but when the time came it was the most wonderful thing that she'd ever known.

They'd been able to lose the feeding tubes on the second day, and without the tape on their faces she started to be able to tell the difference between them. Beth was quieter, more watchful than Evie, and Evie was a bit more active, but they were breathing normally for themselves without supplementary oxygen.

And they were both hungry. They'd lost weight, which was normal, but there was little enough of them so of course she worried. She was expressing her milk for them, but there wasn't much at first, and they were being topped up with donated breast milk, for which she was hugely grateful.

She was grateful for Dan, too.

He was back at work, but popping up all the time to check on her and his tiny daughters, saving his paternity leave for when she left hospital. He spent as much time as he could with them, but he didn't tell her again that he loved her.

He probably hadn't meant it, or at least in the way she'd rather hoped he had. Foolish, really. She knew he was only here for the little ones, she'd been reminding herself of that for months, and it was stupid to let herself believe otherwise.

Then her milk really came in, on the day that Beth had a minor setback and had to have a feeding tube again, and she hit the four-day blues with a vengeance.

Dan found her curled up on her bed, sobbing silently, and he sat down beside her and stroked a tendril of hair off her face and kissed her.

'Hey, you. Bad day?' he murmured, and she nodded.

'Beth's got a feeding tube again,' she said.

'I know, but she's doing OK. It's just a little setback, nothing major.' He hoped...

'I know. I'm just being stupid,' she said, and he smiled and hugged her gently.

'No, you're not, it's your hormones.'

She gave him a look through tear-clumped lashes. 'You do know if you say that to me under any other circumstances you're dead meat?' she said, and he chuckled.

'Fair enough, but for now at least it is true. You know what's going on. Why don't you mop yourself up and we'll go and see the girls together?'

She nodded, sniffed and scrubbed at her cheeks, and he handed her a tissue and helped her off the bed. She winced, and he frowned.

'Do you need more pain relief?'

'No, I'm fine, I just want to be able to go home with my babies.'

'I know. It won't be long. They're doing really well. Let's go and give them a cuddle.'

He put his arm round her and gave her a gentle hug, and then walked slowly with her through to NICU. She was leaning on him, but then she was leaning on him for so much these days that it was becoming a habit.

A habit she probably needed to wean herself off, because it wasn't for ever—was it?

But in her head was a persistent echo of his voice, saying, 'I love you.'

If only she dared to believe it.

CHAPTER TEN

TWO DAYS LATER Ben let her go home, and Dan stayed with her. Her mother had been for a flying visit to meet the babies, but she was unable to take time off from running her guest house at the start of the Easter holidays, and her father lived in New Zealand with his second wife and in any case didn't know one end of a baby from the other, so there was nobody who could be at home with her apart from Dan, and she didn't know what she would have done without him.

They were based at her house so they were closer to the hospital in case there was a problem with either of the babies, and he looked after everything. The food, the shopping—he even watered the plants which were starting to grow again.

He was back in her spare room, though, not in her bed as he had been for weeks now. He said it was because of her incision, but she thought it was probably because the babies were safe now and so his vigil wasn't necessary any more, but she missed his presence and her bed felt lonely and empty without him.

He was still at work because they wanted to preserve as much of his paternity leave as they could, and every morning he took her to the hospital and brought her home at the end of the day.

The babies had been moved out of NICU into the neonatal ward, and she spent most of her time either with them or attached to the breast pump, and someone—Livvy or Daisy, usually—would take her home in the middle of the day so she could rest for a while, then take her back, and gradually both she and they grew stronger.

They were gaining weight fast now, making huge progress, and by the time they would have been thirty-six weeks she was able to breastfeed them both when she was there. And on the eighteenth day after they were born, she was allowed to take them home.

His home.

Needless to say she'd protested, but his arguments were reasonable. His bedroom was bigger, which would allow more room for the cot, and as the weather was warmer she'd be able to sit out in the garden with them in the shade of the trees.

But it was Laura, living just around the corner with her little baby James, that clinched it for her. They'd be able to spend time together once Dan was back at work, and Livvy with her baby Esme was also within easy walking distance. She'd have Daisy, too, not far away, and she'd never been so grateful for the close community that had been forged in the hospital.

And anyway, it was only until she was properly back on her feet and the babies were in a sensible routine.

So she agreed, and the night before they were discharged he took her there so she could make sure she was happy that it was ready for them, and when she walked into his bedroom her eyes filled with tears.

He'd somehow, with very little spare time, built the

hastily ordered cot and made it up with a freshly washed new sheet, and hung a lovely little mobile, a gift from Ben and Daisy, from the ceiling. There was a chest of drawers with a changing table on it, a comfy chair with low arms for breastfeeding, and in the drawers were all the tiny little clothes they'd need for the first few weeks, and his bed was made up all ready with fresh linen.

'I thought you and the babies would be better in here,' he said. 'But I won't be far away, just next door.'

'Next door?' she said, and she felt a wash of guilt that she'd turned him out of his room, the room they'd shared. But maybe that was how he wanted it.

'Happy with it?' he asked, and she nodded, even though she would have been happier with him in there with her, but that was being unrealistic, she realised. Time to get real.

'Very. It looks perfect. Thank you.'

'Don't thank me, they're my children too.'

They were, but it still seemed unfair.

'It feels so wrong to turn you out.'

'It's fine. We've agreed—and anyway, I haven't slept in here for ages, I've been at yours since they were born, and I can sleep anywhere. And besides, I've moved all my stuff.'

'If you're sure…'

'I'm sure,' he said firmly. 'Come on, let's take you home so you can pack your things ready for the morning and get an early night.'

She packed her clothes ready for the morning, which didn't take long as there wasn't much that fitted her now, then perched on a seat in her little garden while he made supper, wondering when she'd be here again.

CAROLINE ANDERSON   189

The plants were starting to emerge from their winter
rest, the leaves opening, small shoots pushing up out
of the compost, and there'd be nobody there to water
them. How would they survive?

'It's ready. Want to eat out here?' he asked, standing in the doorway, but it was getting chilly and she
shook her head.

'No, it's too cold now. I'll come in.'

She gave it one last look and stepped inside, and he
frowned and tipped her head up with a gentle finger
under her chin. 'What's up?'

'My plants. They're all going to die, aren't they?'

'No,' he said, and then surprised her yet again. 'I've
got a plan for them. I thought we could move them to
mine and group them around the edge of the patio.
I can look after them that way, and you'll be able to
enjoy them.'

She gave a ragged little sigh. 'I don't know what
I'd do without you,' she said, choked, and he gave her
a crooked smile.

'I hate to state the obvious, but without me you
wouldn't be in this situation.'

She wouldn't—and without him, she wouldn't have
her beautiful little girls, either. She smiled and kissed
his cheek. 'No, I wouldn't, would I? Shall we eat?'

'Is this everything?'

She nodded and followed him downstairs, taking
one last lingering look at her bedroom before she left
it. Had she just spent her last night here? She had no
idea. She couldn't really afford anything bigger on her
own, and Dan really wasn't part of that equation. Well,

at least, she didn't think he was, although he'd talked a lot about houses. If only she could read his mind...

She closed the door, went downstairs and by the time she reached the bottom he'd stashed her bags in the boot of the car and he was waiting for her.

'All set?'

'What about the fridge?' she asked, but he'd already thought of that, as he'd thought of everything else. It was open, emptied, washed and left ajar to keep it aired, and everywhere was immaculate. Goodness knows what time he'd got up, or when he'd come to bed.

She had one last look at her sitting room, then closed the door on that, too.

It seemed oddly symbolic. Would she ever live here again? She wasn't sure, and even if she did, it wouldn't be the same. Nothing would ever be the same again.

She set the alarm, stepped outside and closed the door on her old life for ever.

They were escorted out of the hospital by a fleet of well-wishers, with Dan carrying Evie and Ben carrying Beth, strapped into their little car seats side by side, and as they drove away from the security of the hospital she felt a shiver of apprehension.

How would they cope? One would be hard enough, but two tiny babies who needed feeding every two hours—she was going to be on her knees. How would *she* cope? Because Dan couldn't breastfeed them, with the best will in the world.

He glanced across at her. 'Hey, stop worrying, it'll be fine.'

'Fine?' she said, and gave a hollow little laugh. 'It'll be hard, Dan, is what it'll be. And relentless.'

'Yes, it will, but it'll get easier.'

'Will it? I don't know. I think we'll just get used to it.'

If it doesn't break us first...

She closed her eyes and rested her head back, and after a few minutes she felt the car stop and he cut the engine.

'Hey, sleepyhead.'

She opened her eyes. 'I wasn't asleep, just...'

'Gathering yourself,' he said, and she realised he was doing that, too. Gathering himself for what was to come.

Please let it be all right.

He wouldn't let her lift a finger.

Probably just as well, because by the time she'd fed them, which was the first and most important thing, she was so tired she could barely manage to drag herself upstairs to change their nappies and settle them in the cot.

'Why don't you get ready for bed?' Dan said softly. 'I'll give you a few minutes to get settled. Do you want a drink?'

'Oh, yes. Tea would be lovely, please,' she said, and he nodded and ran lightly downstairs, leaving her to undress.

He'd unpacked her clothes and put them away for her, and to her surprise they were all in a logical place. It shouldn't have surprised her, really, he was a very logical and methodical person, and he always paid attention to detail.

It was one of his best and yet most irritating features, she thought with a smile. She pulled out a clean sleep bra and her cat nightie, mostly because it was short so it would be easy to pull up to feed them, but also because it was the most comfortable.

When he came upstairs she was sitting on the edge of the bed looking at the babies, and he put the tea down and came and sat beside her and put his arm around her shoulders.

'You OK?' he asked softly, and she nodded.

'I can't believe we're here with them. I never thought we'd get to this point, not like this.'

'No, nor did I.'

His voice was sad, and she turned her head and looked at him, searching his eyes. 'I'm so sorry about your baby, Dan,' she said quietly. 'I didn't really understand until I had ours just what it would mean to lose them. No wonder your heart's broken.'

There was a flicker of his lips, not really a smile, and it didn't reach his eyes before he turned back to them. 'She looked so like they did when they were born. It was almost as if I'd been given her back.' He met her eyes again. 'I had a bit of a meltdown while you were in Theatre.'

'I know. Ben told me you'd said you couldn't do it again, couldn't lose anyone else, so I told him what had happened to you. I hope you don't mind?'

He shook his head. 'No, of course I don't mind. I'm glad you did, but I'm sorry I wasn't there for you. I felt really guilty about it, but I couldn't stay, I was in bits, and afterwards I hated myself for abandoning you like that, for abandoning them, but I couldn't watch—'

'Hey, Dan, it's OK. It's OK. It must have been incredibly hard for you, the whole pregnancy.'

'It was, but looking at them now it was worth every single second of it. They're so precious.'

'They are.'

He took a deep breath, let it out slowly and smiled at her. 'I have an idea. You and the babies need to sleep, and we can't leave them alone, so I can lie in here with them and you can sleep in the other room until they need feeding again, if you like.'

'Or you could stay here with me,' she said softly, and for a moment neither of them moved a muscle.

'I'm not sure that's a good idea,' he said eventually, and she plastered on a smile and tried not to feel rejected. Of course he didn't want her. That wasn't what this was about.

'No. Probably not. There's no point in us both being exhausted.'

He frowned at her. 'I wasn't thinking of me, I was thinking of you.'

'Then stay,' she said. 'You can pick them up and give them to me when they need feeding, and you can change their nappies. You'll enjoy that—and you need the practice,' she added, just to lighten what seemed suddenly a very intimate moment.

Again he hesitated, then he gave a wry little smile and nodded. 'OK. Why don't you go first in the bathroom and I'll sort myself out and come and join you?'

They sat up in bed drinking their tea, and then he put his arm around her and gave her a hug.

'I'm so proud of you. That pregnancy must have been hell for you, but I never once heard you grumble or complain.'

'Oh, I did.'

'No. Not really. You just gritted your teeth and got on with it. I'm in awe.'

She tilted her head and looked up into his eyes, and he leant over slightly and kissed her. It was a chaste kiss, but filled with tenderness, and it gave her courage.

'There's something I want to ask you,' she said quietly.

'Well, two things, really, but the second one might not be relevant.'

'Why don't you start with the first, then?'

'I'm not sure I want to. I'm not sure I'm brave enough, because if the answer's no, it'll spoil everything, and I know it's not really what you want anyway.'

'Spit it out, Georgia. The suspense is killing me.'

But he was smiling, and she didn't want that to end, so she took a mental photo of it before she ruined it all.

'I might start with the second one. I was thinking, we've been living together for months now, sort of, and—well, now we've got the babies, it might be really rather nice if we kept that going.'

'I thought we were.'

'But—only for now.'

'It doesn't have to be. I didn't think you'd want more,' he said, and she searched his eyes.

'So what do you want?'

He smiled again. 'I want to know what the first question was.'

'Oh.' She looked away, her heart picking up, and took a deep breath. 'When I was in Recovery, you said you loved me. Did you mean it?'

'Yes. Yes, I did. Did you want me to?'

She nodded, feeling a warmth spreading inside her.

'Yes, I did, because I love you, too. I didn't want to, because I thought you didn't want a relationship.'

'No. I didn't want to be in a position again where I could be so vulnerable to hurt, to loss, but that was rather taken out of our hands. And the more I've got to know you, the more I've grown to love you, even though you pushed me away as hard as you could.'

'Only to protect us both.'

He laughed softly. 'Yeah. We should have thought of that earlier, but I can't tell you how glad I am that we didn't.' His smile faded, and he became all serious. 'You asked me what I wanted, and I think you've just given me the answer, so I have a question for you now. Will you marry me, Georgia Seton?'

'Ma—?' She sucked in a breath. 'Oh, Dan. Really? Do you mean that? It's not just because of the babies? Because the last thing I want is someone pretending that they love me—'

'I'm not pretending, Georgia. I wouldn't pretend about something as important as that. I want to marry you, to live with you, and bring up our babies here, in this house, together.'

She felt her eyes widen. 'Here? But—I thought you were going to buy somewhere?'

'I am.' He looked a bit guilty. 'I didn't discuss it with you first because I wasn't sure what you'd say and you didn't want to talk about it, but I've spoken to Tom, and he might be willing to sell it to us. It'll need extending of course, in time, but if that was done sympathetically we could have a lovely house with plenty of room for—'

'Yes.'

He stopped talking and looked hard at her, and then he started to smile. 'Yes, it'll need extending?'

She started to laugh. 'No, you idiot, although it will. I mean yes, I'll marry you. I'll marry you,' she said again, the laughter gone, replaced by total and utter conviction. 'I love you, Daniel Blake, more than I could ever have imagined, and I'd be honoured to be your wife.'

He swallowed hard, drew her gently back into his arms and kissed her. She could feel all the pent-up love and tenderness that he poured into it, and when he lifted his head his eyes were brim-full of emotion, with a touch of humour.

'I can't believe you said yes without arguing. You've just made me the happiest man alive, Georgia Seton-Blake.'

She looked into his eyes. 'You can't call me that yet,' she said, and he smiled that lazy, sexy smile that made her heart turn over.

'Just practising...'

* * * * *

THE PERFECT MOTHER FOR HIS SON

EMILY FORBES

MILLS & BOON

To my Book Club Girls,

After eighteen years it's time to thank you
for many hours sharing wine, laughter, some tears
and dozens (possibly hundreds) of books!

To those of you still standing since day one—Kate,
Tamara and Vicki and Wendy—this book is for you.

With love,

Emily

CHAPTER ONE

'DR PATEL, WE have an incoming ambulance. Unconscious sixteen-year-old diabetic patient. Can you take that?'

Ajay put his phone into a drawer of the nurses' station and slid it closed. He didn't like to keep his phone on him at work, it could be too much of a distraction, but he liked to keep it near in case of an emergency. Leaving it at the nurses' desk meant they could check the caller ID and notify him if it was important. Although there could only ever be one call that wouldn't go unanswered and that would be related to his son.

He'd actually been about to call home to check on Niki, but that would have to wait now. His son had seemed a little out of sorts that morning, and even though he knew that Mrs Singh, his housekeeper and part-time nanny, would have let him know if there was a problem, he was still concerned.

Ever-present worry ate at the back of his mind. He knew he was overprotective; he knew he was always prepared for bad news. From what he'd seen doctors who were parents behaved in one of two ways—either checking on every little cold and scrape or ignoring any illness or injury unless the kid was critically ill.

Niki had been a premmie baby; his arrival into the world had been traumatic for everyone and he still had additional needs. As sole parent to a child with a disability Ajay knew he had a heightened sense of responsibility, and he suspected his concerns wouldn't be disappearing any time soon.

Niki's needs were the reason he'd applied for the position in the emergency department at Bondi General Hospital. They lived in Bondi, but Ajay had been making the long commute across the harbour to North Sydney Hospital, and the time spent travelling had eaten into his time with Niki and sapped his energy. It had become a burden, and he'd needed to make a change.

He'd figured he had two options: move house or change jobs. He hadn't wanted to uproot Niki from the only home he'd known and the house that Ajay loved. He had enough to deal with already. He hadn't needed the additional stress of moving house. He was still the new kid on the block at Bondi General, but he hoped the move would solve a lot of problems once he settled in.

He heard the approaching sirens and headed for the ambulance bay. The heat and humidity still surprised him as he stepped out of the hospital. Summer in Bondi was often hot and sticky, and humidity had never bothered him—he'd grown up in the tropics and was accustomed to it—but the contrast between the air-conditioned comfort of the hospital and the muggy Sydney weather was always stark, and he could feel perspiration begin to gather at the base of his spine.

But then the ambulance swung into the driveway and there was no time to think about the weather or to worry about Niki. He had a job to do.

He reached for the back door of the vehicle and pulled it open. A young female paramedic climbed out. He recognised her; he'd been at Bondi General for three weeks now, and faces were becoming familiar, although names were not always so easily recalled.

His eyes flicked to the name badge sewn onto her shirt. Mei. 'Hi, Mei, what have we got?' he asked as Mei pressed the button to release the stretcher.

'Unconscious sixteen-year-old girl, Type One diabetic. Hypoglycaemic episode. We picked her up near Campbell Parade.'

Ajay knew Campbell Parade. As a local, he was familiar with the road that ran parallel to the famous beach. It was only a ten-minute drive from the hospital—less in an ambulance with flashing lights and sirens.

He stepped to the head of the stretcher. 'What are her vitals?' he asked.

'Blood glucose three point three mmol per litre, heart rate one-forty. We've given her one milligram of Glucagon and we're running ten percent glucose through the IV.'

The paramedics had managed the patient well, and there wasn't a lot more Ajay could do except monitor her and hope she regained consciousness.

'Do you know her name?'

'Breanna,' Mei replied as the second ambulance officer appeared from the driver's side and another young girl approached from the left. The girl had obviously been crying, but otherwise seemed fine. Ajay assumed she was a friend, no one had mentioned a second patient.

'Is she going to be okay?' the girl asked.

'And you are…?'

'Isobel.'

'You were with Breanna?'

The girl nodded.

'Tell me what happened.'

'I'm not really sure. She said she didn't feel well and then she collapsed.'

'Has she been drinking?'

The girl nodded and replied, 'Vodka.'

Ajay wasn't surprised. While Bondi Beach was a dry zone, the area around Campbell Parade, which bordered the beach, was well known for its party atmosphere. Alcohol and diabetes were not a good combination for Breanna, but Ajay would save his lecture for later—right now he needed more details.

'Vodka and what?'

'Lemonade.'

'Diet lemonade?'

Isobel shook her head. 'No—why?'

The sugar in the mixer made the risky situation worse, but he ignored her question for the moment as he focused on treating his patient.

'Has she eaten anything?' he asked as he and Mei started pushing the stretcher into the hospital. 'You knew she was diabetic?' he added, when Isobel shook her head a second time.

'Of course.'

'Has this happened before?'

Another shake of the head.

'Did you try to get her to have something sugary? A soft drink? Jelly beans?'

'No. She didn't have her emergency kit with her and

it happened so quickly. One minute she was fine—the next she was on the ground.'

Ajay suspected Isobel's recollection was a little hazy, but it was all he had. 'Did she hit her head?'

'I don't think so.'

'Has she taken anything else? Anything illegal? Smoked anything? Tablets?'

It was the summer holidays, two days after Christmas, and people were in full party mode. Not that it really made any difference. Ajay had worked in hospital emergency departments for long enough to know that kids partied at any time of the year, but he swore it was getting worse.

Was he getting old? No, he knew drugs were more commonplace, cheaper than alcohol and had fewer calories. Young girls in particular had taken up popping pills in numbers he hadn't seen before, and he needed to know exactly what he was dealing with.

Isobel was wringing her hands and having difficulty maintaining eye contact. He wondered what else she wasn't telling him.

'I'm not judging,' he said. 'Just trying to make sure I have all the facts so I can treat her properly.'

'We didn't take any drugs. Is she going to be okay?' Isobel repeated.

Ajay had no idea, but the odds were in her favour. 'I hope so. Has anyone called her parents?'

'You're not going to call them?' Isobel was agitated now.

'Breanna is only sixteen. We'll have to notify them.'

'We'll get in so much trouble.'

Ajay thought that was highly likely, but also irrelevant. 'You'll need to wait here while we assess her,' he said when Isobel continued to follow them as they pushed the stretcher towards the treatment area. 'You'll need to give us some details about Breanna—do you think you can do that?'

He nodded at Julie, the triage nurse, and she guided Isobel to the waiting area. There was nothing else he needed from her at this stage.

Ajay knew that giving Isobel a task to keep her occupied was going to be the best thing for everyone. It would make her feel useful and stop her getting in the way.

'On three.'

Breanna was transferred from the stretcher onto a barouche and Ajay forgot about anything else for the moment. All he was focussed on was treating his patient. He positioned an oxygen mask over her face as one of the nurses connected her to the monitors. He ordered routine blood tests and a blood alcohol test and instructed the nurse to continue with the intravenous ten percent glucose.

He would wait, hoping Breanna would regain consciousness before he called her parents. He knew Julie wouldn't have called them yet—she'd be waiting for more information about Breanna's condition and more than likely waiting for him to make the call as the treating doctor. It went with the job.

Julie stepped into the treatment bay. She had a piece of paper in her hand. 'Breanna's parents' names and number,' she said as she tucked it into the top pocket of his scrubs. 'They're in Western Australia for a birthday party. The girls were staying by themselves for a few days. You can call them, but there's no way they can make it back tonight.'

He nodded in acknowledgement, realising that it was late and Breanna's parents were two and a half thousand miles away, on the opposite side of the country. 'Well, we're not releasing her,' he said. She was only sixteen and he wouldn't release her into someone else's care. 'She'll have to be admitted to the paediatric ward. I'll call her parents if you can organise a bed for her?'

He went to find Isobel, wanting more details before he spoke to Breanna's parents. Had she had a hypoglycaemic episode related to alcohol before? If so, would the parents know? What questions would they ask? He wanted to be able to allay any concerns if possible.

'Has this happened before?' he asked Isobel.

'Are we in trouble?' she asked, evading his question.

'With me? Your parents? Breanna's parents? Or the police?'

'The police!'

'The paramedics said they picked Breanna up on Campbell Parade, near the beach,' he continued. 'You're both under eighteen. Were you drinking in public?'

'No! We had a few drinks at home before we went out.'

Ajay suspected it was more than a few, but that was irrelevant now, and at least if they couldn't be charged with underage drinking in public that was one less thing to worry about.

Julie was waiting for him as he ended his phone call with Breanna's distraught parents. He had tried to allay their fears but, as a parent, he knew all too well that they would be frightened, and being four thousand kilometres away would only add to their fear and feelings of helplessness.

'I've got a team coming from Paediatrics to take her up to the ward,' Julie told him. 'Speaking of which…'

Julie was looking over her shoulder, but Ajay had already sensed that someone was standing behind him.

He turned around and forgot to breathe. Forgot what he was doing.

Standing before him was a petite blonde vision. Five or six inches shorter than him, she was wearing light blue scrubs that matched her eyes. Her pale hair looked like spun gold and was held back from her face by a headband decorated with artificial flowers. Her lips were pink and her skin luminous. She was stunning, and not at all who he'd been expecting.

'Hello, Daisy. Hello, Bill,' Julie said.

Until Julie had spoken again Ajay hadn't noticed the orderly standing beside the woman. An oversight—but in his mind a completely understandable one. No one would be looking at anyone else.

'Our patient is in here,' she said, gesturing towards the treatment bay. 'Dr Patel can fill you in.'

He wasn't sure that he could remember anything about the patient. It wasn't like him to lose his train of thought—he prided himself on his focus, on his ability to compartmentalise—but his mind was blank. He needed a moment to gather his thoughts.

'I'm sorry, have we met?' he said as he stalled for time. There was something familiar about her. A sense of déjà vu. 'I haven't been at Bondi General for long,' he said with a smile, hoping he didn't sound rude, 'and I'm still sorting out who I should and shouldn't re-member.' He didn't think he would have forgotten her.

She shook her head. 'No, we haven't met. I'm a

nurse on the paediatric ward. I'm Daisy Carlson,' she said as she stepped into the treatment cubicle.

Carlson? He frowned. That surname was familiar even if Daisy wasn't.

'You will have worked with my sister Lily. She's doctor in A&E,' she added.

Was that it? She looked familiar because he knew her sister?

There was definitely a similarity—they were both blonde and pretty—but he didn't think that explained the sense of connection he felt, although he was at a loss to put his finger on exactly what had triggered that feeling.

'Of course. Daisy, you said?' He smiled as he spoke.

She nodded, and he was aware that she was watching him intently. He wondered if she was as intrigued by him as he was by her. The idea was flattering.

'This is our patient?' she asked.

She glanced at the patient, but returned her attention to Ajay as she finished speaking. He got the sense that her attention was less about her being intrigued by him and more that she was sizing him up. That was less flattering, and he wondered if she doubted his skills. He was new, but he knew what he was doing. What was she waiting to hear?

He nodded. 'Breanna. Type One diabetic, brought in unconscious, hypoglycaemic, blood alcohol level of zero point zero nine. She'd recovered consciousness, she's stable and sleeping, but she's only sixteen and I'm not discharging her without an adult.'

'Where are her parents?'

'Interstate for the weekend. They're in Margaret River in Western Australia. I've spoken to them, but they've got a three-hour drive back to Perth, meaning they'll miss the midnight flight. The earliest flight they can get is at six in the morning.'

Daisy nodded. 'Okay.'

Daisy was surprised that she was able to string any words together. She hoped her sentences were co-herent, but she was finding it difficult to concentrate while Dr Patel was watching her. His smile had burned through her, making her dizzy. She'd almost found herself reaching out, looking for something solid and stable to right her axis and support her.

She tried to concentrate on what he was saying, but to do that she had to focus her attention on his lips—and that didn't help her cause at all. His lips were full and she found herself waiting, hoping, they'd break into another smile.

She lifted her gaze to his eyes instead. His eyes were amazing. Dark and intense, they looked like pools of molten chocolate, liquid and sensuous. She was a sucker for eyes. And lips. She knew it was because she focused on those areas. She could read people's lips, but she'd also learnt to read their expressions, and much of that came from their eyes. The windows to the soul. Eyes could tell her how someone was feeling—which was helpful when she couldn't hear their tone.

She picked up the patient's notes as Bill attached a bed-mover and prepared to steer Breanna out of A&E. She flicked through the pages, scanning the blood test results, the list of medications, even as she knew she wasn't absorbing any of the information.

She held on to the side of the bed as Bill moved it along the corridor. He didn't need her help—the bed-mover was doing the work—but Daisy needed the support. Her knees were shaky and her heart was racing. She was a bundle of nerves. But it had nothing to do with the patient and everything to do with the new doctor in Emergency.

She could feel his eyes on her, following her progress towards the lift, but she resisted the urge to turn around.

She leaned against the wall of the lift as it took them up to the paediatric ward and took slow, deep breaths as she tried to calm her heart rate.

CHAPTER TWO

Ajay was at work early. He'd raced through his regular early-morning swim and foregone his second cup of coffee to give himself time to check on Breanna before officially starting his shift.

Breanna's parents were expected to arrive this morning and he wanted to be up to date. Even though she had been transferred out of his care to one of the paediatricians, he was the initial treating doctor and he wanted to meet with her parents.

He checked in with Kerry, the paediatric nurse unit manager, who advised him that Breanna's parents had landed at the airport and were coming directly to the hospital. He had time to catch up with her.

Breanna's bed was in a side room. She was a lot older than most of the patients on the paediatric ward and had been given her own space. Through the window in the door Ajay could see that Daisy was in with her. Daisy's back was to the door, but he knew it was her.

Her blonde hair was plaited in an extended braid that started near her crown and finished below her shoulders. She'd tucked several yellow daisies into the plait. Her arms were elevated as she adjusted the drip, and his eyes were drawn to her slim forearms and delicate wrists. She was petite.

'Good morning,' he said to her as he stepped into the room and closed the door behind him. 'I wasn't expecting to see you again today.'

He spoke quietly, not wanting to disturb their patient who was sleeping. He hadn't been expecting to see Daisy, but he had been hopeful, and seeing her there made him smile. It had been a long time since he'd been happy to see anyone other than Niki.

Happiness, anticipation and excitement had all been missing from his life in recent times, and he'd forgotten what it felt like to look forward to seeing someone.

He waited for Daisy to acknowledge his greeting. To respond. But she ignored him.

Had he spoken too quietly? He stepped further into the room and tried again. 'Hello. How is our patient?'

There was still no response.

Ajay frowned. This was all rather odd.

He walked around to the opposite side of the bed, into Daisy's line of vision. Her head swivelled in his direction and her hand flew to her chest as she jumped.

'Oh, you startled me.'

'You didn't hear me come in?' he asked.

'No.'

She was watching him closely. In the same intense way that she'd watched him last night. As if he captured her attention. Her focus flattered him. She shook her head and the morning sun coming through the window caught her, illuminating her golden hair and making her glow. He was dazzled and dazed—so much so that he almost missed her next sentence.

'I'm deaf.'

Ajay frowned. He seemed to do that a lot around Daisy. 'Did you say you're deaf?'

She nodded.

He hesitated. Opened his mouth and then closed it again. He wanted to say her speech was perfect, but he knew that was just stating the obvious. He wanted to ask how she spoke so clearly, but didn't want to offend her. He waited, hoping something would come to him that didn't make him sound insensitive or ignorant.

'I wasn't born deaf,' she said, by way of an explanation, obviously anticipating his questions, and obviously used to people's curiosity. 'I went deaf when I was a child. I can speak but I can't hear.'

He found himself looking for hearing aids in her ears but finding nothing. Nor could he see any sign of a cochlear implant. Her hair was tied up—he'd be able to see that.

'I lip-read and sign,' she continued.

Now he felt foolish. *That* was why she watched him so closely when he spoke. He didn't enthral or fascinate her. She was watching his lips, reading his words. He felt like an idiot.

He was used to being with hearing-impaired people. It was an everyday occurrence for him. But he wasn't used to having nothing to say for himself. For the first time he realised how the fear of saying the wrong thing could make him mute.

He let his hands do the talking. *I didn't know.*

'How could you?' Daisy responded to his signing without pause, but he could see by the expression on her face the moment it dawned on her what he'd done. That he'd signed.

She raised her eyebrows, posing a silent question.

My son is deaf, he signed in reply.

She smiled, and he swore his heart skipped a beat.

This was crazy. He was standing in a hospital room, having a silent conversation with a virtual stranger, and his palms were clammy and his insides were churning. He felt like a schoolboy. A tongue-tied schoolboy.

'Really?' she said.

He nodded and found his voice, knowing that he would not be able to keep up an adult conversation using sign language. 'But,' he admitted, 'my sign language is limited. My son is not quite two. I haven't had to learn very much yet.'

He wondered how she managed. It was strange to find himself curious about another person. He'd been existing in a bubble for the past two years, focused solely on work and his son, and to find himself interested in something else was almost refreshing.

'You've come to check on Breanna?' she asked, bringing the conversation back to their patient and deflecting the focus from herself.

He wondered if that had been deliberate, but he followed her lead. 'Yes. I thought I'd get a quick update before her parents arrive. How is she doing?'

'She's doing well, she's stable, and she remembers going out last night. Her vital signs are all normal and her last two blood glucose levels were both above four mmol per litre.'

Kerry stuck her head into the room as Breanna stirred and opened her eyes. 'Breanna's parents are here.'

There was no time for discussion as the door opened wider and Breanna's mother, a short woman with a worried frown, hurried in, followed by her husband.

They both went straight to their daughter's side, not stopping for introductions, and Ajay thought they probably hadn't even registered that he and Daisy were in the room.

Daisy had stepped away from the bed, giving them space, and he noticed she had moved towards Breanna's head, to stand beside the monitor. He knew it was so she could see everyone's faces and read the conversation.

'Breanna! My darling, what happened? Are you okay?' Her mother wrapped her in a tight hug as Breanna burst into tears.

The woman lifted her head and looked at Ajay, obviously expecting an answer from him since her daughter wasn't able to speak.

'I'm Dr Patel,' Ajay said. He made sure that he turned slightly towards Daisy, so she would be able to see his lips and follow the conversation. It was important to him that she felt included. She was the one taking care of Breanna. 'We spoke on the phone last night. Breanna is fine. She was very lucky.'

He had already told them their daughter was fine, but he knew they needed to hear it again. It was very likely that they had retained nothing from the previous conversation, and they needed to see Breanna for themselves before believing that she was okay.

'I still don't understand how this happened?'

'The usual way,' Ajay answered drily. 'Too much alcohol.'

'You're only sixteen!' Breanna's mother protested as she turned back to her daughter. 'How did you get the alcohol?'

Breanna's sobbing increased in volume, but if she

thought that was going to get her out of answering her parents' questions she was mistaken.

'Bree?' her father queried.

Breanna's sobs subsided. 'We have fake IDs.'

'Not any more, you don't.'

'I'm sorry. I didn't mean to do it.' Breanna's lip wobbled again. 'I didn't think I'd had very much to drink.'

'You shouldn't have had *anything* to drink.'

Ajay spoke up. 'Your father is right, Breanna. Alcohol and diabetes are not a great combination. I'm sure your specialist has told you that too?'

Ajay was certain that her specialist, or Breanna's GP, or both, would have explained the dangers to her. Even though she was only sixteen it wasn't unusual for teenagers to drink alcohol, and the risks needed to be outlined.

Breanna nodded. 'She did, but I didn't really understand.'

'You said she had a hypoglycaemic episode?' the father queried. 'Wouldn't the sugar in the alcohol elevate her blood sugar?'

Ajay was standing next to Daisy, on the opposite side of the bed from Breanna's parents. He had deliberately kept a bit of distance between himself and Daisy—partly to make sure that he could turn towards her slightly and allow her to read his lips, and partly because he knew that if he stood to close to her, close enough to smell her perfume, he might become distracted.

He moved towards her now, just slightly, trying to make sure she focused on him, making sure she watched him speak. His hand brushed her forearm. Her skin was cool and soft, but he felt a very slight spark arc between them, as if together they generated heat. Daisy jumped and he knew she felt it too.

He focused on his answer as he tried to ignore the fizz of energy that continued to burn between them.

'That's true for small amounts,' he said. 'The sugar content can initially raise blood glucose levels, but this will be followed by a fall once the effect of the alcohol on the liver has kicked in. And with excessive amounts, the liver becomes overloaded.'

He had been going to say *large amounts* of alcohol but had changed his mind. He wanted to frighten Breanna—she needed to understand the dangerous consequences of her actions. He thought the ramifications of her decision would stay with her for some time, but it was hard to know with teenagers. She had made a full recovery—there would be no lasting side effects, no permanent damage—and who knew if she'd got a big enough scare to make her more cautious next time? He needed her to understand the risk.

'The liver will *always* process alcohol first. It wants to remove it from your blood instead of regulating your blood sugar by releasing stored glucose, which can lead to a hypo. That's why it's critical not to drink alcohol on an empty stomach when your blood glucose levels are already low. The risk of a hypo occurring is possible both during the time you are drinking and for many hours after. Alcohol can also make it harder to recognise the symptoms of a hypo. A hypo can look and feel a lot like being drunk. Alcohol can make you feel dizzy, sleepy, and disoriented—the same symptoms as hypoglycaemia. Isobel said you complained of feeling unwell and she put that down to the alcohol. She didn't think you were having a hypo.'

'Where *is* Isobel?' Breanna's mother asked.

Ajay could tell by their tone that Breanna's parents were upset, and he could feel Daisy's tension mounting. Her spine straightened as she stiffened beside him, and he got the distinct impression she was about to go into battle. Ajay was sure that the parents were relieved, and worried more than angry, but he also knew that Daisy wouldn't be able to hear the concern in their voices. She would be able to follow the words but not the tone.

He looked at her, waiting for her to glance his way so he could allay her fears. She turned to face him and he mouthed the words silently, just for her benefit. *It's okay. They're worried, that's all.*

He hoped he could calm her down. Everyone was already on edge, with heightened stress levels, and no one needed the tension ramped up further with an argument. But Daisy chose to ignore him.

'Isobel has just left,' she said. 'She was here first thing this morning. She's been worried about Breanna. She was concerned that she should have done something earlier but, as Dr Patel said, the symptoms of a hypoglycaemic episode and excessive alcohol consumption can look very similar. If it wasn't for Isobel having the presence of mind to call for assistance Breanna's situation would be very different.'

Part of him was surprised that he could read her so well and recognise that she was going to voice her opinion, and part of him was impressed that she was so forthright and passionate. While a small part of him was concerned, because she wasn't helping Breanna's cause, he didn't want to overrule her. In actual fact he agreed with her, and her opinion wasn't putting Breanna's health at risk, so there was no need to shoot her down. He wouldn't hesitate to intervene if he thought patient care was being compromised, but that wasn't the case here.

'Breanna made a bad choice,' Daisy continued. 'Both girls did. But they're teenagers, and Isobel did the right thing. She got Breanna the help she needed.'

Breanna spoke up and all eyes, Daisy's included, turned to her as she said, 'It wasn't Isobel's fault. She didn't make me drink.'

'Isobel came to the hospital with Breanna,' Ajay explained. 'She called 000 and got her the help she needed.'

'She called the police?'

Ajay shook his head. 'Isobel called an ambulance. The police aren't involved.'

'Aren't there charges for underage drinking?'

'There can be,' he replied. 'But the girls were drinking at a private house before they went out. They weren't drinking in public, and from what I understand there were no adults present at the house. If there had been they would be liable for prosecution, but it was just a group of teenagers. Isn't that right, Breanna?'

She nodded.

'Isobel did the right thing,' Ajay stressed. He didn't want Isobel to take any blame. She had done her best to care for her friend. 'I've seen before where kids panic in these situations and leave their friends. If Isobel had done that we might not be here in this room, talking to Breanna. While the girls were doing the wrong thing by drinking alcohol, Isobel did the right thing when it counted. She called an ambulance, she stayed with Breanna, she came to the hospital with her and made sure we knew Breanna is a diabetic.'

Breanna's mother picked up her daughter's hand and looked at her wrist. 'Where's your bracelet?' she asked.

'I wasn't wearing it.'

'Breanna!'

'You know I hate wearing it.'

'But one day it might save your life,' her father said. 'You do understand that, don't you? Think about what might have happened if Isobel hadn't been with you. That bracelet might have been the only way for the paramedics to know what was happening.'

'May I make a suggestion?' Daisy asked. 'I know this isn't everyone's preference, but a medical tattoo is a good option for teenagers with life-threatening allergies or medical conditions.'

'A medical tattoo?'

'Yes.' Daisy nodded and stretched out her right arm. She turned it so her palm faced the ceiling and the underside of her wrist was exposed. 'It's just a small tattoo and it goes just here.' She tapped her wrist. 'Right where the bracelet would be.'

'I don't know about a tattoo,' Breanna's mother said.

'You can get temporary tattoos,' Daisy added. 'That could be a compromise. It might be worth a discussion in a few days' time?'

'And what about now? When can we take Breanna home?'

'In a few moments,' Ajay told them. 'I just need to make sure she has a follow-up appointment with her specialist.'

'Her specialist? But you said she's fine.'

'And she is. But her specialist needs to know what has happened. I will send an update, but her condition needs to be managed—and that includes managing alcohol consumption.'

'She's sixteen!' Breanna's father said.

And at the same time Breanna insisted, 'I'm never drinking again.'

Ajay smiled. 'I hear you both, and I know that right now, Breanna, that's how you feel and what you think. But again, like the tattoo, working out how to deal with alcohol is a conversation that's worth having. An insulin pump can be a good option in general for teenagers. Has that been discussed before?' The family nodded and Ajay continued. 'You have a lot to think about, but none of it needs a decision this minute. We'll give you some time together. I'll email Breanna's doctor and Daisy will organise her discharge. She'll let you know when you can go home.'

Daisy followed Ajay out of the room. He touched her arm as they walked down the corridor and felt another spark. It was a disconcerting sensation. Not unpleasant— far from unpleasant—but definitely unexpected.

He couldn't keep letting it catch him unawares. He'd have to remember to be ready, he thought.

'Are you okay?' he asked her.

Daisy stopped walking and turned to look at Ajay. 'Why do you ask?' she said.

'You seemed a little uptight in there.'

Daisy was about to pretend that everything was fine, but Ajay's big brown eyes were full of concern, and she got the sense that he was asking because he did want to know.

She knew he'd made sure she felt included in the discussion with Breanna and her parents and she appreciated his efforts. Throughout the exchange he had positioned himself where she could see him, enabling her to read his lips. She'd thought initially he hadn't done it deliberately, but then she'd wondered if he had. He'd turned to her when he spoke, making sure she could see him, and he'd touched her arm to get her attention.

She imagined she could still feel the warmth of his fingers on her skin, a buzz from where his fingers had made contact with her, and she didn't want to lie to him.

'I was,' she replied. 'I thought her parents were about to read her the Riot Act, and I didn't think it was the right time for that. And I certainly didn't want them criticising Isobel. Their daughter owes her life to Isobel and they didn't even ask if Isobel was okay! They owe Isobel their gratitude, and I felt it was important to point that out.'

Ajay was smiling.

'What?' Daisy asked.

'I think they got your message.'

'Good,' Daisy said, adamant that she'd done the right thing. 'And, just so you know, if you disagree with me you can say so. It won't be the first time I've been told off for speaking my mind.'

'I'm not going to tell you off. I happen to agree with you. But if your comments ever affected patient care I wouldn't hesitate to step in. I was just concerned you weren't reading the room right. Breanna's parents were concerned about her. They'd flown across the country, not really knowing what was happening for those several hours they were in the air. Fear and then relief can make parents a little crazy.'

'I get it. Breanna was lucky—and she *is* lucky her

parents care about her.' She wished she could say the same for all the parents she came across in the hospital, but unfortunately that was not the case. 'But I'll warn you now: it probably won't be the last time I express my views, even if I know I really shouldn't. If something upsets me I'll let people know. It's a trait that has got me into trouble with the nurse unit manager before.'

'What sort of things upset you?' he asked.

'Injustice. Kids who've sustained injuries from abuse—physical and emotional. Kids who get sick because they haven't been vaccinated. Kids need a voice, and sometimes I find myself giving them one. I might not be able to hear, but there's nothing wrong with my voice. Working in paediatrics, I'm never quite sure which way things are going to go. Not all parents are good ones. Plenty of kids end up here *because* of their parents.'

She paused for breath and waited for the comment she was sure would be forthcoming. She had expected him to have an opinion about her strong point of view—most people did—but he was silent, seeming to accept that she was entitled to an opinion.

She appreciated that. Most people didn't seem to expect her to *have* an opinion, as if her deafness made her mute and compliant, and when she made her opinions known they then seemed to assume she must be wrong. She'd learned over the years that due to the combination of her looks and her deafness people assumed she must be stupid. But that was their issue, not hers.

Was it possible that Ajay was different?

She watched his eyes, looking for a clue as to what he was thinking. Lacking the ability to pick up emotions from someone's tone of voice, she had become an expert at reading people's emotions from their body language and expression—in particular, from their eyes. Some emotions were easier to read than others. Anger manifested as tension in the shoulders, as a stiffness in posture and often a tightness in the jaw. Nervousness could be seen in the eyes and a restless spirit. Happiness and sorrow were straightforward, while someone who was confident had a relaxed demeanour.

Empathy was harder to determine. It wasn't really in a smile, or in a tilt of the head. It went deeper than that. It came from the heart, from the soul, and she'd learnt to look for that in people's eyes. She needed to see in through those windows.

She saw empathy in Ajay.

He had a good heart. She sensed that.

He touched her arm, drawing her attention as her mind wandered. Her skin tingled and a delicious sense of warmth spread through her.

He nodded. Just once. 'Good on you,' he said. 'Sometimes kids need someone to advocate for them. If I write the email to Breanna's specialist are you able to start the discharge notes?'

'Of course.'

'Thank you.'

He smiled at her and her knees wobbled. Daisy could feel herself blushing, and breathed a sigh of relief when Ajay headed for the lift to take him back to the emergency department. She stayed in the corridor, giving herself a moment to gather her scrambled thoughts before heading to the nurses' station to organise Breanna's discharge.

But her mind kept wandering.

Her nerves were going crazy, but she needed to gather her thoughts and her senses. She had to put a lid on this attraction she felt towards him. He was off-limits. He had a child, and most likely a wife.

He wasn't wearing a wedding ring, but that wasn't unusual amongst the hospital staff. A lot of the medical staff didn't wear jewellery on their wrists and hands as infection control meant they were forever washing or sanitising, and rings in particular got in the way.

But he'd talked about his son and he seemed like the type of man who would be happily married. He was kind, considerate and gorgeous. He would have been snapped up quickly, and Daisy couldn't imagine anyone wanting to let him go.

CHAPTER THREE

DAISY FINALLY ORGANISED Breanna's discharge, and after checking her other patients headed to the cafeteria for her morning tea break. She exited the stairwell and saw a familiar figure walking towards her. Blonde-haired, blue-eyed, oval-shaped face, tall and slim. Her features were almost identical to Daisy's, with the exception of her height. At five foot ten inches tall, Lily was almost half a foot taller than Daisy.

She was Daisy's eldest sister—a doctor currently doing her residency in A&E. Despite their height difference there was no mistaking them for anything other than sisters. They were physically comparable, and their personalities were also similar—although in Daisy's mind Lily was far more confident.

Daisy wasn't shy and retiring, but she was quieter than her siblings. Her deafness has played a part in that, but neither Daisy nor Lily were as loud or as outgoing as their other siblings, middle sister Poppy and their brother Jet, second oldest. But despite that, when the Carlson siblings were together, all blonde, tanned and attractive, there was no doubting they were related.

There was a very close bond between the four of them—to the extent that they were on rotation moving in and out of Lily's house on Moore Street, over-looking Bondi Beach. Currently it was Daisy and Jet's turn to live there. Although, to be exact, the house belonged to Lily and her husband Otto—but Otto was studying in London, and had been for the past two years. In the meantime the Carlson siblings had been making the most of the convenient and comfortable accommodation.

Poppy had lived there briefly, when she'd first transferred to Bondi Ambulance Station from Brisbane, but she had recently moved out with her fiancé, Ryder, and Jet had taken her place. It was a busy house, but Daisy loved it. She loved having her siblings close.

She was seven years younger than Lily, six years younger than Jet, and five years younger than Poppy, and by the time Daisy had been thirteen all her siblings had left home, leaving her alone in Byron Bay. She had hated being left behind. She had hated being alone.

She'd already lost so much before they'd left her. At the age of eight she'd stood in a cemetery and said goodbye to her identical twin, and she'd never recovered from that. Losing Willow had been traumatic, and Daisy still felt as if a piece of her was missing. She often wondered if her life would have been different—if *she* would have turned out differently—if she had been able to grow up beside her twin. Instead she'd grown up with a sense of loss, which had been compounded years later by a sense of resentment and abandonment.

She knew her siblings would hate to know she'd felt abandoned by them, but losing her twin sister and then losing her older siblings one after the other had been almost more than she could bear. She never wanted to feel that way again. Now she always made sure that if anyone was leaving it would be her. She made a point of keeping her distance in relationships, of not getting too close, not getting too involved. She was always ready to leave at the drop of a hat, to be the first to bail.

But when it came to her siblings she was relishing having her family together again after ten years, and she intended to keep the status quo.

Daisy loved all her siblings, but Lily was the one Daisy had always wanted to be when she grew up. She smiled at her sister as Lily met her outside the cafeteria door.

'Talk about perfect timing,' Lily said as she linked her arm through Daisy's and continued into the cafeteria.

'How was your morning?' Daisy asked.

'Just the usual,' Lily replied, her head carefully turned towards her sister. 'The ED is always madness at this time of year. The crazy combination of holidays, sun, surf, parties and backpackers—too many people having too much fun.' She slid her tray along the bench and picked up a plate containing a slice of banana bread as Daisy added carrot cake to the tray. 'I'll get this and two coffees—can you grab a table?'

Daisy chose a table against the back wall of the cafeteria. It wasn't busy, but she preferred to be away from the servery, away from the hustle and bustle. Her mind wandered as she waited for Lily to pay for their purchases. She blinked and gave a small shake of her head when Lily placed the tray on the table and waved a hand in front of her face.

'You look like you're a million miles away,' she said. 'What's on your mind?'

Daisy wondered what her sister would say if she replied with, *The inexplicable reaction I'm having to a married man.*

She toyed with the idea of telling her, before deciding it would be prudent to keep her thoughts to herself. There was absolutely no point in admitting she was attracted to a married man—a husband and father. He was completely off-limits, so discussing her feelings was irrelevant.

But that didn't mean she couldn't talk about him at all. She couldn't resist. She was desperate to know more about him.

'I looked after a patient who was admitted by Dr Patel. He works with you in the ED,' she said, before switching to sign language to continue the conversation. She didn't want to be overheard, and being able to converse in silence with her siblings was one benefit of her disability. *He's new, I think, but he knows you.*

He is new, Lily said, signing in return. *He started about three weeks ago. He seems good. Everyone likes him.*

Daisy was pleased Lily had responded using Auslan. Apart from the fact that it allowed her to keep the conversation confidential, Daisy also found reading sign language easier then reading lips. If the person she was conversing with was proficient at signing she found that it often took her less effort to interpret their words.

Even Kerry likes him, Daisy signed with a smile.

She'd had a few run-ins with the nurse unit manager, and she knew she wasn't alone, but Dr Patel didn't look to be in danger of getting on Kerry's notorious bad side.

He was fantastic with the patient and her parents. Lots of the doctors—present company excepted, I'm

sure, she signed, *seem in a hurry to get out of the room
as quickly as possible. They come in, say what they
want to say, don't encourage questions and go, leaving the family with more questions than they had before. But Dr Patel listened.*

Daisy had been impressed with his bedside manner,
but it was the way he'd made *her* feel that had put the
sparkle into her day. He'd made sure she knew what
was going on, which she appreciated. He'd recognised
that it was hard for her to follow conversations that
were not one on one.

Did you know he has a son who is deaf? she signed.

*No. I know he's a single dad, but I didn't realise his
son was deaf.*

Single? Daisy touched the tips of her index fingers
together, asking the question before she'd thought about
it.

He was single? As in not married? The memory of
his smile sprang to mind, bringing with it the memory of how it had made her feel, the warmth that had
spread through her.

Is he divorced? she continued.

I don't know, Lily replied. *I haven't asked.*

Daisy knew her sister wouldn't ask probing questions about her colleagues' personal lives because it
might invite reciprocal questions—and, while Lily was
married, her husband had been living in London for
the past two years, and Lily avoided talking about him
at all costs. Lily and Otto had left for London together,
but Lily had returned home alone after a few months.
Lily didn't like to talk about what had gone wrong,
about the heartache of her failed pregnancy, and there

was no way she would want her personal life being discussed on the hospital grapevine.

Not that Ajay's marital status mattered. It was irrelevant. Daisy had no interest in dating someone with a child. She was happy working in paediatrics, and she loved caring for kids, but she was more than happy to say goodbye at the end of a shift.

Why are you so interested?

Lily waited for an answer that Daisy wasn't ready to give. But Lily didn't need it confirmed.

You like him!

Don't be ridiculous, she denied. *I've spoken to him for ten minutes, in a patient's room. I barely know him. I just thought he had a good bedside manner. And I thought he was married.*

But now you know he's not.

I'm not interested in dating someone who has a child. I'm twenty-three. I don't want or need that responsibility, she signed, knowing she wasn't being completely honest.

She had no intention of adding that kind of complication to her life at any point but, knowing how Lily felt about motherhood, she kept that to herself. Daisy did want to find love, and she wanted to find someone to replace the hole in her heart that losing Willow had left, but she believed that one person could fill that hole. There was no need to bring children into the mix.

She didn't want to risk letting a child down the way her parents had let *her* down. She had suffered two traumatic events in her childhood, losing her sister and her hearing, and she blamed her parents for both of those. The idea that she might let children of her own down in a similar way terrified her. She did not want to be judged and found wanting. She wasn't convinced that nurture would rule over nature; she wasn't convinced that she could do a better job than her own parents.

Of course she saw examples of good parenting when she was caring for her patients at work, but she also saw the bad, and having experienced the bad herself it made her extremely wary. And nervous. The best and safest option, in her mind, was to avoid having children altogether, and that was what she intended to do. She didn't want to raise a child, and negotiating raising a child of divorced parents was a minefield, in her opinion—one she had no intention of navigating either.

So you want footloose and fancy-free? What else is currently on your list? Lily asked.

'He has to be kind and non-discriminatory,' said Daisy, switching to speech. She wanted someone who was accepting not only of her disability but the disabilities of others too. She wanted someone who accepted the differences in people. 'He can't assume I'm stupid because I'm deaf.'

'I think sometimes people—men *and* women— think you're not smart because you're so pretty. I don't know why people can't accept that you can be both.'

'It's more than that,' Daisy argued.

She knew that Lily and Poppy had both come up against that assumption, based on their looks, but she knew that her deafness added an extra layer of ignorance to people's attitudes. It was something that she found endlessly frustrating.

Many times in the years since she'd lost her hearing she'd had people assume she was stupid. Or rude. Usually once she'd explained her hearing impairment people understood that she wasn't being rude, but it didn't stop some of them from still thinking she was stupid. She had yet to figure out why someone would think that just because she couldn't hear. It was one reason she had tried cochlear implants, when she'd been told that hearing aids wouldn't correct her issues. But that hadn't been as successful as she'd have liked.

'He needs to listen to me,' she continued.

She often felt that men were not interested in what she had to say. They just wanted someone decorative by their side.

She thought of Ajay. How he'd listened to her. How he'd made sure to include her. How he had, unknowingly, ticked a lot of her boxes. But there was one that he couldn't tick.

'He has to be family-oriented,' she said.

That was non-negotiable for her. Someone who didn't value family was always going to create friction for her. She needed him to understand and accept how important her siblings were to her.

'He should be able to make me laugh. He should have a job he enjoys and that he takes pride in doing well.'

'Does he need to be rich?' Lily asked.

'No.' Daisy and her siblings had not grown up with money. It wasn't a dealbreaker.

'What about good-looking?'

She nodded. She didn't have a clearly defined image of what 'good-looking' meant, but she wanted someone who made her catch her breath. Someone with kind eyes and a kissable mouth. Someone who made her feel excited and jittery when he entered the room.

Someone who made her feel that *she* was the only one in the room.

'And he needs to make me feel special,' she added.

She wanted to be important to someone. She wanted to be their priority. She needed to know that she wasn't going to be abandoned. She wanted to know she was loved. She wanted to know she wouldn't be alone.

She'd been alone since she was thirteen. She and her siblings had been raised on a commune by parents who hadn't ever seemed to want the responsibility of a family, preferring to leave child-raising to anyone else, and the minute her siblings had been old enough to leave they had done so.

She hadn't blamed her siblings. She hadn't been their responsibility, and she'd known they had all wanted to get as far away from Byron Bay and their childhoods as possible. She'd felt the same way. But she still resented her parents for their lack of interest in their offspring. That was a different sense of abandonment altogether, and she had vowed never to give anyone else a chance to walk away from her.

She knew that had led her to create unreasonable expectations for potential partners, so the minute they stumbled she cut them off, leaving them before they could leave her.

'That's some list! Is anything negotiable?' Lily wanted to know.

In her opinion her list was completely valid and acceptable, but perhaps she could be flexible about a couple of things. 'Maybe they don't need to make me laugh every day,' she said. 'If they give me a chance to show them I'm not stupid maybe I'll give them two chances.'

'Perhaps you'll meet someone on New Year's Eve. What are your plans?'

'Poppy has got me a ticket for that party at The Pavilion. I thought she got one for you, too?'

Lily nodded. 'She did, but I don't think I'll go. I might just go to dinner with Jet and Mei at Mei's parents' restaurant. You can have my ticket—use it to invite someone else.'

Daisy waited, wondering if Lily was going to be more specific about who she could offer the ticket to. 'I don't think so,' she said, when Lily stayed silent. 'I'm not sure if I'll go either. I'm working a late, so by the time I get there I will have missed the best part of the night, and you know I find it hard to follow conversations in a crowd.'

'You'll be there in time for midnight, though. Isn't that what it's all about? Maybe you'll kiss a frog and find your prince without having to worry about conversation.'

'Maybe.'

She wondered whether Ajay had plans for New Year's Eve. Did he have a girlfriend? A partner? Who would he be kissing at midnight?

That shouldn't be of any concern to her. She wasn't denying she was attracted to him, but men with children were not on her list, so she'd just have to ignore the attraction. Ignore him.

They worked in different departments. That shouldn't be difficult.

'Ajay, is your patient stable?'

Ajay was inserting a cannula into his patient's hand

in preparation for a saline drip. He turned at the sound of Julie's voice. 'What is it?' he asked.

'We've got three ambulances incoming.'

'Three?'

Julie nodded. 'Surf rescue. Five patients.'

'How far away are they?'

Ajay was treating a woman who was in the early stages of her first pregnancy and had been vomiting ferociously, to the point where she'd become dehydrated, but once the drip was running he could leave her under supervision of the nurse.

'Two minutes,' Julie replied.

'I'll be there.'

The ED was already busy, and Ajay tried not to look at the full waiting room as he headed for the ambulance bay. Julie would have prioritised the patients, and if she needed him to meet the ambulances that was what he would do.

Julie was waiting, standing beside Dr Lily Carlson, and immediately his thoughts went to her sister. To Daisy. He'd been thinking about her a bit, wondering if she would be a good sounding board for an issue that was plaguing him about Niki. He felt her opinion would be helpful. Not only because of her hearing impairment, but because he knew she would give him an honest opinion. She certainly hadn't hesitated to share her thoughts with Breanna's parents. He didn't like to admit it, but at times being a single parent and having no one to bounce ideas off, especially when it same to Niki's disability, was difficult, and there were times when he doubted whether he was doing the right thing.

He'd discussed Niki's potential surgery with his sister and his parents, but they had conflicting views which hadn't helped. His parents were both doctors and they supported the procedure, having the view that if something could be fixed with medicine or science then surely you'd choose that path. Asha, on the other hand, thought that if something wasn't broken it didn't need to be fixed.

And that was what Ajay was struggling with. He didn't think Niki was broken, but would he benefit from being able to hear? Would cochlear implants be helpful for Niki? He didn't know the answer to that but maybe Daisy would. She had a foot in both camps. Would she mind if he asked her opinion? he wondered as he stopped beside Julie and dragged his focus back to the task at hand.

'What are we expecting?' he asked, as he prepared for what was to come.

'The patients are all part of a Chinese school group. Two adults, three students. They were caught in a rip, I believe. One resuscitation. The rest less serious,' Julie said as two ambulances pulled into the waiting bay.

Ajay opened the rear door of the first ambulance and Mei Chen climbed out.

'I've got two teenagers, both with lacerations. One with a dislocated shoulder, the other with a fractured ankle,' she told him.

'From being caught in a rip?' Ajay frowned. Those injuries weren't consistent with being swept out to sea.

Mei shook her head. 'They were on the rocks at South Bondi—do you know the spot?' Ajay nodded and she continued. 'They misjudged the sea and three of them got swept off the rocks by a wave. They were caught in Backpackers' Rip. These two managed to stay on the rocks but sustained serious injuries.'

'And the others?' Ajay looked around for the three other patients. He could count two more—an adult and the third student.

Mei nodded in their direction. 'Water inhalation and a concussion,' she said.

'And the fifth?' he asked as he started to push the stretcher into the hospital. 'I thought there were five patients. Where's the third ambulance?'

'Still coming. They've got the resus.'

'Do any of them speak English?' Ajay asked.

'No.'

Ajay turned to Julie. 'Is there anyone who speaks Cantonese in the hospital at the moment?'

Julie shook her head.

Ajay bit back his frustration. He knew the hospital could call interpreters when needed but, given the number of international patients that were treated at Bondi General every day, he really thought there should be some interpreters on permanent staff. He realised it would be hard to choose which languages were needed, but Cantonese, German and Spanish would be a good start.

'I can hang around to translate for a bit while you wait for an interpreter,' Mei offered. 'But if we get another call I'll have to go.'

'Thank you. I'd appreciate that.' He glanced over his shoulder into the ED waiting room as they moved the patients inside. 'We're going to need more staff. Can we call for extra hands?' he asked Julie.

Julie nodded and headed for the desk. 'On it.'

'Can you call me when the third ambulance arrives?' he added before turning his attention to the patients they did have.

There was a lot to organise, but he liked to be busy. He liked being at work. He had to focus and there was no time to dwell on things. At work he knew what he was doing, he felt in control, whereas at home he often felt out of his depth, trying to raise a child on his own.

Mrs Singh helped with Niki, of course, but it wasn't the same as having a wife, and it definitely wasn't the same for Niki as having a mother. But there was nothing Ajay could do about that. He still blamed himself for not saving Priya, even though he knew it hadn't been his fault. It hadn't been his job. But still, he *was* a doctor...

He would do his best to save any patients who presented to him in Emergency. He had vowed to do his job to the best of his ability, so no other family would experience what he'd gone through, and no other family would have to suffer like he and Niki had suffered.

He ordered chest X-rays for the adult with suspected water inhalation, needing to see if there was sea water in his lungs. The concussed student needed observation. The kid with the fractured ankle he handed to Lily, and he took the dislocated shoulder.

His patient lay on the stretcher, still clutching the 'green whistle' the paramedics had provided him with, sucking on it frequently and inhaling the pain relief that it dispensed.

He called for Mei's help to explain what was going to happen. He needed to check his patient for signs of fractured bones before relocating the arm in its socket. He ran his fingers over the bony surfaces, feeling for crepitus, watching and listening for pain responses, knowing the pain relief in the whistle might be masking some. He ordered midazolam in preparation for the relocation, and just as he was debating whether or not to order X-rays Julie advised him that the third ambulance was pulling in.

Relocating the shoulder would have to wait, he thought, as he returned to the ambulance bay.

The ED would normally be the last place she would choose to work, Daisy thought as she entered the department for the second time in three days. It was noisy and chaotic, and fast-paced and stressful, and even without her hearing impairment she knew she would find it difficult. Add that in and the stress escalated.

She knew it was not the area for her—you couldn't afford to make mistakes in here, and she was certain her deafness would mean she'd miss a vital piece of information at a critical time. Yet, when the call had come through for extra hands she hadn't hesitated to volunteer to help.

She had just finished her shift on the paediatric ward, and she didn't have anything she needed to do or anywhere she needed to be, but she knew there was one reason and one reason only, why she had offered her services. And that reason had chocolate-brown eyes and a killer smile.

Despite telling herself that she should, and could, ignore him, she had immediately volunteered to assist, unable to resist seeing him again. But that didn't constitute a problem, did it? No harm could come from seeing him at work.

She searched the space, looking for a tall man with dark hair and a perfect mouth. There was constant movement. Four people crowded around one bed, three were at another, and other staff hurried around the department, carrying things, moving things, pushing things, ducking and weaving around each other, hands and feet and lips all in constant motion.

She wasn't sure how they managed to avoid colliding with each other or tripping over, but for the most part they seemed to work as a well-oiled machine. Each had their own roles.

She watched the flow of people for a moment and imagined the noise. She knew her deafness would prevent her from ever working in the ED, but she wouldn't choose it even if she could hear. She liked calm. And even without the noise there was no way this could be described as a calm environment.

She knew a lot of people would think the paediatric ward was chaotic too, and it could be at times, but it was a different type of chaos. Controlled chaos. There were plenty of moments when it was quiet. Peaceful, even. Times when she was one on one with her tiny charges. When she could sit and cuddle a toddler.

The staff on the paediatric ward tried to foster a sense of calm—sick kids didn't need excitement. They didn't need emotional or physical stimulation. In contrast, the ED was a hive of physical stimulation.

All these thoughts whirled through her mind as she took four steps into the ED, looking for Ajay.

She could see Lily and she could see Mei, her brother's fiancée, but she couldn't see Ajay. She knew she couldn't just stand there waiting for him. She'd offered to help, and she needed to find someone who could tell her what to do. But everyone she could see was busy. She couldn't see anyone to interrupt, so she headed towards the triage desk.

The external doors slid open as she crossed the

department, and she saw Poppy pushing yet another stretcher through the doors. The ED was already over-flowing, Daisy wasn't sure where this patient was going to go—but that wasn't her issue, and she forgot about it almost immediately when she saw Ajay walk-ing beside Poppy.

She read his lips as she watched him direct the traf-fic. 'Bring her through here,' he said, as he gestured towards a treatment bay in the corner of the ED.

She ducked out of the way as one of the orderlies pushed a patient in a wheelchair past her. She stood by the triage desk and kept one eye on Ajay and an-other peeled for someone who might be able to give her a job to do.

He was in his element. Measured and calm in the eye of the storm. She had a moment to watch him be-fore the triage nurse noticed her, and Daisy had to turn her attention to her instead.

'Hello, Daisy. Have you come to lend a hand?'

She nodded. 'Where do you need me?'

Julie pointed at a young Chinese boy who was lying on a bed three bays along. 'Can you run a set of obs on him? He's got a suspected concussion, but we haven't had time to get to him yet. His name is Chi.'

Daisy nodded, and was heading his way when chaos erupted around her. People came running from all di-rections. She'd thought the ED was busy before, burst-ing with patients and staff, but now it seemed as if the numbers had doubled. She saw Lily racing across the department. She'd left her patient and was heading in Ajay's direction. She grabbed a crash cart on the way, and Daisy figured out what was happening. Ajay's pa-tient was in cardiac arrest.

Daisy reached her patient. There was nothing she could do to help Ajay and Lily—her deafness made emergency situations impossible—so she focused on the job she'd been given.

She drew the curtains around Chi's bed. There was still frantic activity in the ED, and she could just imagine the noise. Neither she nor Chi needed to see what was unfolding in the treatment bay across the room.

'Do you speak English?' she asked him.

The young boy shook his head. Daisy was relieved—it meant she wouldn't have to have a conversation. She could concentrate on taking his obs, recording them. She could do that.

She checked his vital signs. His oxygen levels were low, so she slipped an oxygen mask over his nose and mouth and turned up the flow. She put an oximeter on his finger and wrapped the blood pressure cuff around his arm.

Julie had said he had a suspected concussion, but Daisy wasn't sure how she'd be able to check for that. His pupils looked to be an equal size, but it was hard to tell as his eyes were so dark, and the language barrier meant she couldn't ask the usual simple concussion questions: *How many fingers am I holding up? What day is it?*

She recorded his obs on the chart that had been left on his bed, but she wasn't quite sure what else she could do. He had a bandage wrapped around his head, and abrasions on his hands and legs. He was wearing shorts and a sun shirt, which might have protected his body a little, but she figured she'd clean up the abrasions to make sure he didn't get an infection.

She peeked out of the curtain to check what was

happening, and was relieved to see that order seemed to have been restored to the department. The paramedics had disappeared, Mei and Poppy included, and Lily and Ajay were working on Ajay's patient, but without the urgency of before. Daisy hoped that meant she'd been successfully resuscitated.

She drew back the curtain fully, leaving it open now that the drama had subsided, and got started on cleaning Chi's cuts and scrapes.

She attended to his legs first, before moving her attention to a long graze that ran up the inside of his left forearm. He winced in pain as she lifted his arm away from his body to assess the damage.

'Sorry,' she said automatically as she relaxed her hold. She hadn't meant to hurt him.

She moved his arm again, trying to be gentle, but even so she was aware of his resistance. She looked at him, trying to figure out how to explain that she wasn't trying to hurt him but that she needed to move his arm, when she saw the colour drain from his face. Sweat coated his upper lip and his skin had turned grey.

Her eyes flicked to the monitor. His heart rate had escalated and he was obviously in pain—and then Daisy got really worried as, despite the oxygen mask, his oxygen levels plummeted.

She looked back at Chi. He was pointing at his chest. They didn't need to communicate verbally. She knew he was suffering chest pain.

She pulled a pair of scissors from her pocket and cut away his shirt. A sixth sense told her it wasn't his heart, and she needed to take a look. She peeled his shirt back to reveal his ribcage and saw the problem.

A section of his chest wall was not expanding as he breathed.

She looked for Ajay. This was not something she could handle.

'Dr Patel!'

CHAPTER FOUR

'DR PATEL!'

Ajay was talking to Lily, no longer working frantically on his patient, so Daisy assumed his patient had stabilised. But she didn't have time to worry about that anyway. She was desperate. She needed help urgently—she was way out of her depth.

Ajay took one look at Daisy's face and hurried over to her side. 'What's wrong?' he asked.

'It looks like a flail chest. He presented with concussion and abrasions, but I think he might have multiple rib fractures.'

Ajay pulled his stethoscope from around his neck and pressed it against Chi's chest. Daisy stepped out of the way as Ajay assessed her patient. He listened to his breathing, checked the monitor, watched the uneven rise and fall of his chest.

'Julie!' he called. 'This patient needs a chest X-ray.'

Daisy sank into a chair as Ajay issued instructions and Chi was wheeled out of the ED. Adrenalin rushed through her body and her legs were shaky. She looked up when she felt a hand on her shoulder. Lily was standing in front of her.

You okay? she signed.

Daisy nodded. 'I think so, but it was a little more dramatic than I bargained for.'

Ajay was standing in the empty spot where Chi's bed had been. He was looking around the ED. 'Is that it?' he asked.

Lily nodded. The ED had emptied while Ajay had worked on Chi. 'The cardiac arrest has gone to the coronary care unit,' she said. 'The water inhalation patient is still in Radiology and the fractured ankle is in Theatre. The dislocated shoulder has been discharged with a sling and painkillers and is waiting to be collected. We've just got a few in the waiting area to deal with.'

'Anything urgent?' Ajay asked.

Lily shook her head. 'I've checked. I don't think so.'

'Good. Why don't you take your break while I wait for Chi's results? Go and get a coffee with Daisy. She looks like she could use one.'

'I can wait for Chi. You started before me,' Lily replied. 'You go and I'll call you if things change.'

'Okay.'

Ajay didn't argue, and Daisy wondered if Lily was sending them off together on purpose.

'I'll buy you a coffee,' he said as he headed for the door with Daisy beside him. 'Thank you for your help and well spotted on the collapsed lung.'

Daisy smiled. 'It was pretty obvious something was wrong, but I'm not built for emergencies.'

'You handled yourself well.'

'Thank you,' she said, hoping she wasn't blushing under his praise. 'But I'll be happy to go back to the kids' ward. Organised chaos is more my scene. I imagine you're used to it, so you wouldn't notice, but there's a lot of fast conversation—between the staff, the patients, the paramedics, the patients' families. There's a lot going on and I'd be worried that I'd miss something important.'

Ajay was silent for a moment, considering her words. 'I hadn't thought about that.'

'There's a lot of information to gather. Pieces to put together. Decisions to make. I know not all of your information is gathered verbally, there's obviously the physical exam as well, but there's no ignoring the fact that you really need all your senses. I'm more than happy to go back to Paediatrics and leave the emergency stuff to the rest of my family.'

'The rest?'

'Lily, Jet and Poppy. My siblings. Poppy is a paramedic. I assume you've met her since you started? She brought the cardiac arrest patient in today.' Ajay nodded and Daisy continued. 'And Jet is a lifeguard.'

'There's a few of you... You're all in Bondi?'

'We are. We've been spread around the country and the world for the past few years—it's only been a few months since everyone has been together here. It's great to have everyone in the same place again,' she said as they reached the cafeteria.

'What would you like?' Ajay asked as they stood in line.

Daisy ordered a green tea. Ajay waited for his long black coffee, but then looked irritated when he got to the cashier. He was patting the pockets of his scrubs.

'What's the matter?' Daisy asked.

'I forgot to grab my phone from the triage desk. Do you think they'll take an IOU?'

Daisy pulled her phone from her pocket. 'I can get this.' She always carried her phone with her. She kept it on vibrate but she needed the talk-to-text message function in case someone needed to contact her. Pagers had been replaced by mobile phones and the hospital intercom, but she couldn't hear the intercom.

She held her phone over the machine to pay as Ajay first protested and then thanked her. 'Thank you. I'll get it next time. Where would you like to sit?'

Unusually for late in the day the cafeteria was busy, and there were only a few spare tables. Daisy preferred the cafeteria when it was less crowded, and she'd hoped it would be quiet—she needed a chance to recover from the ED.

'Follow me,' she said.

'Where are we going?'

'To check out the surf.'

'I can't leave the hospital,' Ajay replied. 'My shift isn't over. And I don't have my phone if someone needs me.'

'We're not leaving the hospital. But I need some fresh air.' She unlocked her phone and searched for the extension for the ED. She handed her phone to Ajay. 'Tell the ED to call me if they need you. I'll get a message through talk-to-text.'

She waited at the fire escape until Ajay had made the call and returned her phone. She swiped her security card and headed up the stairs. They emerged on the flat roof of the hospital. Air-conditioning units and solar panels took up the majority of the space, but one corner had been co-opted as a dining space, with a collection of plastic chairs and a table partially sheltered from the elements by a small pergola. A few fake plants tried to brighten up the space. It wasn't exactly picturesque, but the view of the Pacific Ocean made up for what the space lacked in ambience.

Daisy led the way to the chairs, pleased to find they had the rooftop to themselves. It was after five, so everyone was either working or had gone home, but there were still a few hours of daylight left at this time on a summer's day. A light breeze blew across the roof, carrying the scent of the sea. Clouds drifted overhead and, looking over the railing at the edge of the roof, they could see the waves rolling into Bondi.

'I had no idea this was here,' Ajay said.

'It's not part of the induction tour.' Daisy smiled. 'It's not often we get time to sit out here, but it can be a good spot to catch your breath and recharge.'

'And check out the surf?'

Daisy nodded. 'I prefer to come up here if I have time. I don't like the cafeteria when it's busy.'

'Why not?'

She could see he was confused. He would know a noisy environment wouldn't bother her. 'The more people there are, the more conversations I have to have,' she explained. 'A lot of people use their time in the cafeteria to socialise, catch up on gossip, that sort of thing.'

'You prefer to be left alone?'

No.' Daisy shook her head. 'But it's difficult for me to follow conversations in a group. Lip-reading is hard when there are lots of different people talking, jumping in, cutting each other off. A large group makes things complicated, and it's exhausting for me. When I need a break from the ward, sometimes the cafeteria is not the best place for me to recharge.' She fell silent as she sipped her tea.

'Ah, I get that,' he said, just before he tipped his head back and closed his eyes—perhaps to give her the respite she'd said she needed.

Daisy took the opportunity to study him. He could use a shave, she thought. He had the shadow of a beard. It wasn't thick—maybe a few days old—but she found it easier to lip-read if a man was cleanshaven. Lily would say he could use a haircut too, but Daisy liked his hair. It was shiny, dark and thick, with an unruly curl. It made him seem approachable and relaxed, which were probably good traits to have when you worked in an emergency room. Certainly Breanna and her parents had responded to him.

He opened his eyes and Daisy knew she was blushing, very aware that he'd caught her watching him.

'Do you mind if I ask you a question?' he said.

'Of course not,' Daisy replied.

'I need your advice.'

'*My* advice?' What could he possibly need *her* advice on?

He nodded.

'What about?'

'Niki.'

Daisy frowned. She didn't recall any patient named Niki. Was that one of the Chinese students? Was he getting the patients confused? Her patient had been Chi. 'Who's Niki?' she asked.

'My son.'

'Your son?'

Ajay nodded. 'I told you he was deaf?' he said.

She hadn't forgotten that. In fact, it had made her feel even more of a connection to Ajay—it had made her feel as though he might understand her more than most people.

'I had a call from his ENT specialist today,' he continued when she nodded. 'Niki is on the list to have cochlear implants fitted, and there's a spot in January available to him.'

Daisy waited, unsure what response was required... uncertain what advice Ajay was seeking.

'No comment?' he queried.

'I didn't realise you'd asked me a question.'

'I don't suppose I did, but most people have an opinion when I mention Niki getting the implants.'

'Which is?'

'One of two standard responses. They either say, "That's great", or, "He's young to be having major surgery. Aren't you worried?"'

'*Are* you worried?'

'I am,' he admitted. 'Not about the surgery itself— it's not that major —but I am wondering if I'm doing the right thing, and that's what I wanted to speak to you about. I'd like your opinion.'

'About...?'

'About Niki's options. He's profoundly deaf—he has bilateral deafness—and while he's a candidate for cochlear implants, I'm not sure if it's right for him.'

'You're a doctor. Niki is your son. Surely you've considered the options and formed an opinion?'

'From a medical point of view, of course I have, but that doesn't tell me if it's the right option. Everyone I talk to seems to have an opinion, but I haven't spoken to anyone who has a hearing impairment. I'd like to know what you think.'

'You want my opinion on cochlear implants?'

'Only if you have one. I guess what I really want to know is should I be doing anything and everything I can to fix Niki's hearing? As a doctor I want to fix people, heal people. But Niki isn't broken. He's just deaf. Some people I've spoken to insist that I must put Niki through the surgery. Others say I should wait and let Niki make the decision when he's older. Some say it's important to get it done before the age of five, and others have said I shouldn't do it at all—that he doesn't need to hear. So you can see my dilemma. The more people I ask, the more varied opinions I get given.'

'Maybe you should stop asking,' she said, half serious.

'Maybe I should,' he replied with a smile, and Daisy felt her heart jump again in an immediate response to his grin. 'How about if I make you the last person?' he added.

Every moment she spent with Ajay increased her opinion of him. His concern for his son was so obvious and heart-warming. He was clearly anxious, wanting to know he was doing his best by him, *for* him, and Daisy wished she'd had someone like Ajay in her corner when she was a child.

When she'd lost her hearing at the age of eight she hadn't known that it could have been avoided. That her parents' views on vaccination had cost her her hearing and her sister her life. When she'd learned later that both those losses had been potentially preventable it had caused her more heartache, and she'd never forgiven her parents for what she saw as their negligence.

She wished they'd done better by her and by Willow. She wished they'd cared for their children like Ajay clearly cared for Niki. She wished she'd felt loved.

She wanted to help Ajay, but she didn't know Niki and she didn't feel she could comment on anything specific. What she did have to say might not be what he wanted to hear, but she supposed that was up to him to decide.

'You might not like what I have to say either,' she told him.

'No. But it will take me one step closer to making a decision.'

'Oh, no,' she said as she held up her hands. 'I'm not sure I want the responsibility for your decision resting on my shoulders.'

'I thought getting him the implants would be the right thing to do,' Ajay explained. 'That it would make it easier for him to communicate. But then I met you and you communicate so well. You don't seem to miss hearing. I just wanted your opinion as someone who sees it from the other side. From Niki's side.'

'How old is Niki?'

'He turns two in a few weeks.'

'And he was born deaf?'

Ajay nodded.

'I'm not sure I'm the best person to ask. I think my experience and Niki's are probably quite different. I wasn't born deaf, as you know. I lost my hearing at the age of eight as the result of a viral infection.' She'd lost a lot more than her hearing, but now was not the time to bring that up. This conversation was not about her. 'So Niki and I are different. I lost my hearing after I learned to talk.'

'But you lost hearing in both ears?'

Daisy nodded. 'I was told that was quite unusual. But,' she said with a sight shrug, 'that's what happened.'

'And you haven't ever used aids?'

'I can't use hearing aids as they only amplify sound, and you need some hearing for them to work. I did have a cochlear implant when I was thirteen, but I didn't like it.'

'Why not?'

'Have you listened to any examples of what hearing through implants sounds like?' She knew there were videos that tried to explain the sound. 'You know it's not like hearing normally? The sound is far from perfect. It's quite distorted.'

Ajay nodded. 'It's like listening to a radio with bad static.'

'Underwater,' she added.

'But I assumed that would be better than nothing?' He looked really concerned now.

'I think in the past ten years the technology has probably improved—I hope it has—but I struggled with the implants. I found I had to concentrate really hard. And I had just started high school, which was hard enough without expending all that energy on listening. I preferred to shut the world out at times.'

'Why?'

'Because I was different.'

Daisy had been teased and isolated by her peers because of her difference. Her deafness had been one thing, but that difference had been magnified by the fact that she lived on a commune, which had not been seen as an acceptable lifestyle choice even in the bohemian region of Byron Bay. Navigating her teenage years without Willow by her side had been immensely difficult. Teenage girls could be awfully cruel, and only by avoiding them had she avoided misery.

But that was a lot more information than she wanted to unpack today, so she settled for a simpler explanation. 'I preferred to ignore the fact that others saw me as different. If I couldn't hear what they were saying I didn't have to let it affect me.'

She'd been able to lip-read in class. There'd been no need for her to be able to hear. Her siblings had all moved off the commune by then, so even at home there had been no one she needed or wanted to be able to talk to, and her parents certainly hadn't seemed perturbed by her silence. Lily had been the one who had organised the implants for Daisy. She doubted her parents would ever have suggested them.

'It wasn't the right solution for me—mentally or physically. The external parts can't get wet, so every time I went for a surf or a shower or a swim I had to remove them. I found I was always taking them off. And then I just left them off more and more often, until I stopped wearing them altogether.'

Growing up, Daisy had been constantly in the water. Surfing had been her escape and she had been in the ocean every chance she could get. That alone had made the implants impractical, and meant she had them out more than in.

'So you're not a fan?'

'I can only tell you about my experience. But I do think it's important to be able to communicate. I can sign and lip-read, and that is my preference, but that's not to say implants aren't the right thing for Niki. They might give him the best chance of learning to communicate. I'm not really helping, am I?'

Ajay smiled again, and Daisy's stomach did a languid flip. 'No, you are. It's good just to have this conversation. I appreciate it.'

'You will have been told that Niki can expect the best results if the implants are fitted before the age of two?'

Ajay nodded. 'The specialist has said if not now then at the latest before the age of five.'

'It's a big decision, isn't it?' Daisy said. 'To put your child through surgery. I imagine if it was critical the decision would be a bit more black and white, but at the end of the day only you can decide. What does Niki's mother think?'

A shadow passed over Ajay's face. It wasn't sadness she saw. It was something more complicated. Regret? Guilt?

'Niki's mother died. The decision is all mine.'

'I'm sorry. I didn't realise.'

Daisy hadn't imagined *that* scenario when she and Lily had been gossiping about Ajay and, despite knowing she wasn't to blame, she felt as if she'd overstepped a boundary.

But Ajay was gracious. 'It's something we're learning to live with, but it is hard at times. I didn't realise how many decisions I'd have to make on my own, and some decisions would definitely be better made with two heads.'

'You didn't have any conversation at all with her about Niki's hearing?'

'No. She died before we knew Niki was deaf,' he said.

Daisy felt as if she'd opened her mouth and exchanged one foot for the other. She wondered how recently his wife had died, but she wasn't about to ask.

She thought it was perhaps wiser not to bring up the topic of Ajay's wife again until he did.

But Ajay unwittingly answered her question anyway. 'He was diagnosed with profound hearing loss when he was eleven months old.'

Niki was almost two, so by Daisy's calculations, his wife had died at least a year ago. But she knew from experience that it didn't mean Ajay would be healing. He might *never* heal, and she figured he would always have scars.

'You hadn't suspected he was deaf?' she asked.

Ajay shook his head. 'No. His early development seemed normal, and I was dealing with a lot of other things when he was a newborn, so his hearing problems went under the radar. In hindsight I realise there were probably indicators, but I spent so much time with him one on one that I didn't ever need to catch his attention. He responded to me in what I thought were appropriate ways, but what he was responding to was visual stimulation rather than auditory. He was a quiet baby, but I just thought he was content and I was happy with that. He did vocalise, and he wasn't old enough for me to be thinking about delayed speech development.'

'How did you figure it out?'

'We were at a birthday party—the child of a friend— and a balloon popped. It gave everyone a fright, adults included, and several of the children started crying. I just happened to be watching Niki at the time, and I remember I was startled by the bang but Niki didn't react at all. I thought that was odd. And then, when he saw the other children crying, so suddenly and en masse, I could tell he had no idea why. He looked quite puzzled. It was clear that he was aware of the other children—their movements, their expressions—but he had no reaction to the noise of the balloon bursting. He was watching them all quite intently. I called his name and he didn't turn. I did wonder if he was being distracted by the other children—he was used to it being just the two of us—but in my gut I knew it was more than that.'

'What did you do then?'

'The birthday child was the son of a colleague—so, of course, when you're in a room full of medical professionals there's always an opinion to be given. I asked the question, and once we started looking for signs of hearing loss it was pretty obvious. He's had all the tests and scans now, and I've been given the options, so I just have to figure out what to do to help him.'

'Well, whatever you decide, promise me for Niki's sake that you will continue to learn sign language. Both of you. He might want that option when he's older,' Daisy said. 'He might want a chance to be a part of both communities. The hearing and the deaf. I do think it's important to be able to communicate, but that doesn't just mean verbally. I'm lucky. My siblings can all sign and I can lip-read and speak, I just can't hear. But I know there are a lot of deaf people who rely on Auslan and prefer to sign. It might also be good for you to have a network of people in the deaf community to help you navigate this. You say you haven't spoken to anyone other than me whose had this experience?'

Ajay shook his head. 'Okay, that sounds like sensible advice. I'll remember that. Thank you,' he said as he stood up from the chair. 'You've given me a lot to think about, and I appreciate your opinion, but I'd better get back to work. And don't forget I owe you a coffee.'

As she watched him go she hoped she'd been able to help him, but he had left her with more questions than answers. What had happened to his wife? Had it been an accident? An illness? How traumatic had it been? One thing was certain—it couldn't have been easy and it was obviously still difficult.

Losing someone you loved was devastating. How was he coping? How was Niki coping? Who did he have to support him? Could she provide some of that support?

She certainly had experience with both loss and hearing impairment, so she was well positioned to be a friendly and sympathetic ear—figuratively if not literally. She could offer friendship. There was no danger in becoming his friend...

Ajay's thoughts were scrambled, and had been since yesterday, when he'd sat with Daisy on the hospital rooftop.

He'd gone for his semi-regular early-morning swim in the tidal pool at Bondi, hoping to settle his mind, but that hadn't helped. He usually found the routine of lap swimming calming, but today he hadn't been able to get into the zone. His thoughts had continued to tumble around in his head and he'd eventually given up on the laps, rinsed off the salt water and was now heading home to shower and have breakfast with Niki.

As he walked along the beach his thoughts continued to swirl. He had the day off and he had a long list of things that needed to get done—among them calling Niki's specialist and booking his surgery. But that wasn't what was occupying his thoughts.

It was Daisy. One hundred percent Daisy.

His head was full of thoughts of her…of her golden beauty and calming nature. She had been the perfect balm for his muddled mind. She had been the voice of reason and just what he'd needed. Her insight had been invaluable.

Swimming laps normally gave him time to work through his problems and find solutions—it had worked on many occasions over the past twenty-three months, since Niki's birth—but talking to Daisy had helped to clarify his thoughts in a more concise way and he was indebted to her. She had helped him to clear his head, freeing up space that was now, ironically, occupied with thoughts of her.

She was easy to talk to…to confide in. Was it because she was such an attentive audience? Was that her nature or a product of her hearing impairment? He had no idea, but he knew he enjoyed her company and looked forward to seeing her again.

He hadn't looked forward to other people's company in a long time. He had deliberately shut himself off, distanced himself from others and buried his emotions. It had been a defensive strategy—he had a lot going on and work was always hectic—but losing his wife and raising his son had added another layer of complexity. In order to cope he couldn't afford to be introspective; he needed to look outwards, not inwards.

He'd blocked out most of his feelings in the past two years, using the excuse that he was busy at work, busy with Niki, too busy to focus on himself. But that wasn't completely true. He hadn't wanted to focus on his emotions, hadn't wanted to acknowledge his feelings. Not because he was devastated, and confused, but because he felt guilty.

He'd had a few conversations with his sister Asha about how he was managing, and each time she had asked if he would consider seeing a counsellor and each time he'd refused. He didn't need someone else to give him strategies. He didn't want to be judged. How could he explain that although losing his wife unexpectedly had been a huge shock, that he was grieving, and that he was devastated that his son wouldn't know his own mother, his overriding emotion was guilt?

Guilt that he was alive and would get to see their son grow up and Priya wouldn't.

Guilt that she'd died giving birth to their son and he hadn't been able to save her.

Guilt that Niki was never going to know his mother.

Ajay knew Priya's death hadn't been his fault, but that didn't stop the guilt. It didn't stop him from feeling as if he had a penance to serve.

He couldn't change the outcome and no amount of counselling could change it either. But he could try to make things better for Niki. He couldn't bring his mother back, but perhaps he could fix his hearing.

He couldn't heal him, but he could help him. That was what Daisy was telling him.

Would Priya have agreed?

He knew she would have wanted to do anything in her power to help Niki, to give him the best chance of fulfilling his potential.

She had been so excited about her pregnancy—as had he. They'd known they were having a boy, and Priya had spent hours preparing for his arrival. Like everything she did, her preparation had been meticulous, culminating in an idyllic nursery filled with bright colours to stimulate his mind, books, toys and a wardrobe full of clothes.

Ajay was glad Priya had been able to do that at least. He was pleased he would be able to tell Niki that his mother had been so excited about him, had loved him, had had hopes and plans and dreams for him. He knew Priya would have done anything and everything to help Niki achieve his dreams. Ajay would do that too. He would do it for Niki and for Priya.

He might not have been able to save her, but he could care for Niki.

Ajay and Priya had shared similar views, dreams and goals. It was why he had been attracted to her initially. They had met through a friend of his mother's. Ajay's mother had introduced him to plenty of prospective brides, but Priya had been the one to capture his attention. The marriage hadn't been arranged in the traditional sense, it had been their decision, but their meeting had certainly been arranged, and together they had soon been making plans for the future.

Plans that Priya would never get to fulfil. Leaving Ajay to do the best he could. Alone.

And he'd thought he was managing. Coping, at least. Work was good and Niki was happy. But Niki still couldn't hear, and Ajay was still adjusting to the idea of being a single dad. He'd thought he was okay with being alone, but talking to Daisy, hearing her thoughts, had emphasised to him how very alone he was.

In his day-to-day world he had no one to talk to about Niki, no one to bounce ideas off, no one to share the decision-making. His parents lived in Fiji, his sister in LA—they were not part of Ajay and Niki's daily life.

He hadn't realised how tough being a single parent was going to be. And Niki's health issues complicated things further.

Priya would have been able to share the worry. But Priya wasn't here.

And until he'd met Daisy he hadn't thought about what came next.

He wasn't looking to date. He had enough to focus on, enough on his plate, and there were plenty of women who would be willing accomplices if he needed comfort. But meeting Daisy had made him reconsider his choices. Made him realise that he was missing *company*, and that was different from needing comfort. He had enjoyed talking to Daisy. It had been easy, natural, and it had reminded him of what was missing in his life.

He loved Niki, and being a dad gave him immense pleasure, but at the end of the day it had been nice to have someone to share an adult conversation with. He'd missed that more than he realised.

He was halfway along the beach now, and the morning sun was warm, but it didn't have the bite that was forecast for later in the day. The beach was quiet—it was only a little after seven o'clock—but the water was busy. The waves were good—not big, but what looked like neat, consistent sets. Ajay had grown up in the water, but he was a swimmer and a scuba diver, not a board rider.

He stopped for a moment to watch the surfers. A young dark-haired girl—small, no more than six or seven, he guessed, jumped off her board and stood in the shallows. She was looking out to sea and Ajay wondered who she was with. She was too young to be at the beach alone. He drew level with her and followed the direction of her gaze.

Two surfers were sharing a wave as it curled towards the shore. One of them was female, wearing a long-sleeve top and bathers. Blonde hair fell over her shoulders. Bare legs. Good legs. Tanned, lean, strong.

His gut tightened in an unexpected visceral response. Desire coiled in his belly and the turbulent thoughts in his head were replaced with recognition.

It was Daisy.

She didn't notice him. Her gaze was fixed on the little girl.

'One more wave,' he heard the child say, as Daisy nodded and they turned and headed back out to sea.

He watched them paddle out from the beach and wondered who the girl was. Not Daisy's daughter, surely? She looked far too young to have a daughter of six or seven. But he realised he had no idea how old Daisy actually was. He knew almost nothing about her. He knew she had three siblings, and that she was a nurse, but for all he knew she could be married, have a partner, have a child... He'd asked for her advice regarding Niki, but he hadn't asked a single question about her. He'd learned nothing more about her yesterday than he'd known before.

He felt awful. He'd been so self-absorbed. He wanted to know more about her, and he vowed to remedy that at the earliest opportunity.

His eyes still rested on Daisy. Her hair was bright, shiny and golden in the morning sun as she lay on her board. Her hands dug into the water as she pulled herself through the waves. Her head was turned towards the little girl and he could see her talking as she paddled, could see the curve of a cheekbone, the curve of her lips...the curve of her bottom. She was all curves, and Ajay could feel his heart thudding in his chest as his temperature rose.

He watched her until she was far from shore and her features blurred. He knew he should keep moving, he had a busy day planned with Niki, but he couldn't make himself walk away. It was just one more wave.

He watched as they caught the wave and then came out of the water. Daisy was carrying the boards as the little girl skipped beside her.

He walked towards them, planning to offer to help while trying to appear as though he hadn't been standing watching but had just happened to be walking past coincidentally. 'Good morning, Daisy.'

'Dr Patel—hello.'

'Please, call me Ajay,' he said.

Hearing her refer to him so formally made him feel a thousand years old and he was relieved when she nodded in agreement.

'You're out and about early.'

'It's the best time of the day.' She smiled. 'I couldn't resist a surf.'

He looked down at the little girl at Daisy's side, curious to know who she was. She had jet-black hair and dark eyes, and he couldn't see any resemblance to Daisy. 'And you are one of the youngest surfers I've ever seen,' he said, waiting expectantly to be introduced.

'This is my niece, An Na. An Na, this is Dr Patel. He works at the hospital with me.'

Ajay was relieved. If An Na was Daisy's niece then perhaps Daisy was single. He couldn't deny that he liked that idea, but he tried to convince himself that it was just because that would mean he could talk to her without worrying that he'd upset someone or make her uncomfortable.

He enjoyed talking to Daisy and wanted to be able to do that again. Not because she was a good listener— which was ironic—but because she seemed to understand him. He could sense a connection—that somehow she got what he meant without him having to be completely forthcoming or explicit.

'Can I carry a board for you?' he asked.

'Thank you.' She handed him her board. 'Have you been for a swim?'

He nodded. 'At Icebergs.'

'I want to see the icebergs,' An Na chimed in, looking up at Daisy as she spoke.

Daisy laughed. 'There's no icebergs. He's talking about the pool down by the surf club.'

'Why did he say icebergs, then?'

Daisy pointed towards the southern end of the beach, where the tidal swimming pool jutted out into the sea below the four-storey white clubhouse that housed the Australian surf lifesaving headquarters and the Bondi Icebergs' winter swimming club.

'It's the name of a club for people who like to swim in winter, because the water can be as cold as ice.'

Seemingly satisfied with that answer, An Na said, 'I'm going to see if Daddy is in the tower,' and ran ahead.

'Are you an Icebergs member?' Daisy asked.

'No. I don't swim competitively, and I can't commit to the regular sessions needed to keep up a membership.'

He knew members of the club had to compete against other swimming clubs throughout the winter, on at least three out of every four Sundays, in order to maintain their membership.

'But you swim often?'

He was aware of her checking out his physique, and he couldn't deny he was flattered by her attention. He knew he was in good shape physically, and he hoped she liked what she saw.

'As often as I can.'

'You don't like swimming in the sea?'

She smiled as she spoke, and he knew he was testing her.

'Technically, Icebergs is the sea,' he argued. The pool was a tidal pool, filled with salt water, so he thought he had a valid case.

'You know what I mean,' Daisy said in disagreement.

'It's much safer in the pool.'

'Are you worried about rips or sharks?' she asked.

'I'm more worried about getting hit on the head by an errant surfboard.'

Daisy laughed.

'Where's your car parked?' he asked as they approached the base of the lifeguard tower.

'You can leave the board here, thanks,' Daisy said, pointing underneath the tower to a storage area. Ajay could see surfboards stacked against the wall, mingling with other assorted pieces of equipment—trailers with jet skis, all-terrain vehicles, and the iconic blue boards used by the lifeguards for surf rescues.

'I didn't realise this was a public storage area,' Ajay said as he propped the board up in the space Daisy indicated.

'It isn't,' Daisy replied. 'My brother Jet is a lifeguard here. One of the perks of his job is keeping his daughter's surfboard here, and I figured if I'm taking her surfing he can keep mine here too.'

'An Na is your brother's daughter?'

'Yes. And you know Mei, don't you? One of the Bondi paramedics? She's my brother's fiancée—An Na is their daughter.'

It was all starting to come together now, he thought, as Daisy grabbed a towel that was hanging near the surfboards and headed for the stairs that led up to the promenade. The same stairs that An Na had raced up on her way to the lifeguard tower.

Ajay followed Daisy up the steps, trying to watch where he put his feet rather than watching Daisy's rather shapely bottom that bobbed in front of him.

She stopped at the outdoor shower near the tower and threw her towel over the railing. 'You're not working today?' she asked as she turned on the taps.

He was clearly showing no sign of being in a hurry. He shook his head. 'I have today off. I'm taking Niki on a play date.'

'A play date?'

'Yes.'

Daisy closed her eyes as she stood under the shower spray. She tipped her head back as she rinsed her hair and Ajay had to remind himself to stop talking as Daisy could no longer read his lips.

Niki didn't go to childcare any more because of the communication difficulties. While that hadn't been an issue when he was a baby, Ajay had concerns now that Niki wouldn't be able to make himself understood which may impact on his care. He knew it was important for Niki to socialise with other children, and he did try to arrange outings for him. Today they were catching up with a colleague from Ajay's last hospital. Someone who had supported him when he'd lost Priya and had made an effort to keep in touch. Ajay had never got involved with a local parents' group—he'd had neither the time nor the inclination—and he appreciated this effort of his colleague to support both him and Niki.

Ajay watched the water running down Daisy's face, following the curve of her cheeks and lips. The morning light caught the droplets, making Daisy shimmer and sparkle. He knew he really should turn his back—the whole scene was affecting him in unexpected ways—but he couldn't make himself look away.

Daisy lifted the bottom of her rash vest and pulled it up over her head, removing it in one swift movement. Her hands swept across her stomach and up over her breasts as she removed her top, and Ajay's eyes followed her hands. He only just managed to avert his gaze before she opened her eyes.

She turned around to rinse her shirt, giving Ajay a few well timed moments to compose himself. He knew he was in trouble now. He already enjoyed her company—she was easy to talk to and her face was angelic—but he hadn't realised she was also hiding a spectacular figure underneath her hospital scrubs. Now she was standing before him in her aqua bikini, tanned and toned, and he couldn't recall ever seeing a woman with such perfect proportions.

Daisy turned off the taps and reached for her towel. She dried her face before squeezing the water from her hair. She wrapped the towel over her breasts, shielding her body and allowing Ajay to breathe again.

'I'd better go and fetch An Na,' she said as she spun back to face him. 'Enjoy your day.'

'Are you working?' he asked, eager to keep the conversation going…eager to keep her there for a little longer.

'No. I have the day off too.'

'Do you have plans?'

Daisy shook her head, and Ajay felt the words burst from his mouth before he had time to think.

'Would you like to have dinner with me tonight?'

'Dinner?'

'In lieu of the coffee I owe you.'

'I'm happy with a coffee.'

'I'd like to take you to dinner if you've got time. A coffee doesn't seem reward enough to thank you for listening to me yesterday, and it would give me a chance to prove to you that I am not one of those parents who has nothing else to talk about other than their kids. You'd be doing me a favour,' he added, in an effort to persuade her, when she still looked hesitant. 'I'd get a chance to eat something other than pasta or crumbed chicken for a change. Will you keep me company?'

He waited, inexplicably nervous. He hadn't dated since meeting Priya, and even then he hadn't had to find the courage to ask her out. Their meeting had been arranged, even if their marriage hadn't. Even though he hadn't mentioned the word 'date', he hoped Daisy would accept. He didn't think he could handle the rejection.

After what felt like a lifetime, Daisy finally replied. 'Thank you. I'd like that.'

Now he had to think of somewhere to go. He hadn't been anywhere that didn't cater to children for two years, and found himself at a loss. 'Do you have any preference?'

'Do you know Lao Lao's Kitchen in Bondi Junction?'

'No.' He shook his head. 'But I'm sure I can find it.'

'It's Mei's parents' restaurant. If you like Asian food, I can recommend it. And they have options other than noodles and fried chicken.' She smiled.

The old advice on what not to eat on a first date sprang to his mind—noodles with chopsticks was one thing, because it was inevitably messy and hard to eat gracefully, but he was happy with the choice. After all, it wasn't a date.

He was about to offer to pick her up when she took the matter out of his hands.

'Shall I meet you there?' she asked, before he could speak. 'Is seven-thirty okay?'

He hesitated, his inherent manners making him feel he should offer to fetch her—but would that make it seem like a date? This wasn't a date.

'That sounds good,' he replied, knowing that it didn't matter how they got there, and it didn't matter what he called it, he was just looking forward to a spending some time with Daisy and having a meal that wasn't consumed at half past five with Niki or by himself at close to midnight, which seemed to be the case more often than not lately.

CHAPTER FIVE

DAISY GREETED MEI'S father when she arrived at the restaurant. Chen looked after front of house while Mei's mother Li ran the kitchen.

He kissed her on both cheeks and said, 'Your date is already here.'

Daisy thought about correcting him. It wasn't a date—if it had been she would have turned it down—but as she looked past Chen's shoulder she saw Ajay standing up from a table and forgot what she'd been about to say.

It was the first time she'd seen him dressed in casual clothes. She'd thought he'd looked good on the beach today. He was lean and muscular, and he had a swimmer's physique, but she'd been very conscious of making sure she'd kept her eyes on his face. He'd been bare-chested, and his long, lean limbs and smooth olive skin had been hard to miss, but seeing him now, standing in the restaurant, dressed in a slim-fit white shirt that highlighted his broad shoulders and narrow waist and contrasted perfectly with his dark hair and tanned skin, took her breath away.

How was it possible to look good in a pair of swimming shorts, barely dressed, and then look even better with clothes on?

She let Chen lead her across the room, although she suspected her feet would have taken her straight to Ajay without any thought on her part. Her brain had completely disengaged, and she felt an irresistible force propelling her forwards.

He has a child...this isn't a date, she reminded herself, as Ajay smiled and pulled out her chair for her.

But, despite not wanting to call it a date, she felt the fluttery feeling in her stomach, the dryness of her throat and the racing of her heart, which were sure signs that, no matter what she might think, it certainly *felt* like a date.

She needed to find a neutral, safe topic of conversation—something to give her heart rate time to settle down. Something to keep her mind off how good he looked sitting opposite her at the table. Something to make her think she hadn't been super-foolish in ignoring her pledge to avoid him and instead accepted his invitation to dinner without hesitation.

'How did the play date go?' she asked, after they'd ordered drinks and Chen had offered to bring them some starters.

Ajay groaned. 'It was a disaster. I transferred to Bondi General because it would give me more time with Niki, but after half an hour I thought I would rather be at work. I know that makes me sound like a bad father, but disastrous is the only way to describe it.'

'What happened?'

'Niki was completely out of sorts. He's usually quite a happy little boy, but today he was clingy and obstreperous, and I ended up cutting the play date short.'

'Is he not well?' Daisy had heard plenty of stories from her patients' parents, and knew how often a change in behaviour pre-empted an illness, but Ajay was shaking his head.

'I don't think so. I put it down to being overtired, and he did have a long sleep once we got home, so hopefully he's back to his normal self tomorrow.'

'When you'll be back at work?'

'Yes.'

'Have you had a busy time over Christmas?' she asked, wondering if there was a reason Niki might be overtired.

'Not really...nothing out of the ordinary. We didn't really celebrate Christmas this year, as my family is all overseas.'

'You don't have any family here? What about on your wife's side?'

'I have no one here. My wife's family are all in India.'

She couldn't imagine being so far away from her siblings. She'd hated it as a teenager, when her siblings had all left home, but there had always been at least one of them in the country. And although she hadn't seen them often, knowing that one of them was only a few hours' drive away at any given time had been reassuring.

'That must be difficult.'

'I'm used to it. My parents sent me here to boarding school when I was thirteen, so it's been a long time since I've had family around. I don't suppose you can imagine what that's like? You can't turn around in Bondi without bumping into one of *your* family.'

'That's true,' she said, although she could imagine what it was like to be alone more easily than he suspected.

'You don't find it annoying?' he asked.

'Not at all.'

'Not even a little?' he teased.

Daisy laughed and shook her head. 'No. I love it. In fact, Lily, Jet and I are sharing a house too.'

'You really all get along that well?'

'For the most part, yes. By the time I was thirteen the others had all left home, and for the next five years I was on my own, so I enjoy having us all back together in the same place.'

'Where did everyone go?'

'We grew up in Byron Bay, and then for a long time we were spread up and down the east coast of Australia. Lily and I both came to Sydney to study, but Lily came here when I was eleven, and I followed seven years later. All three of them spent some time overseas too. Jet has been in Sydney for a while, but Poppy moved here from Brisbane just a few months ago.'

'And you're the youngest?'

'By five years.' She hadn't always been the youngest but that wasn't something she was prepared to talk about tonight.

'And your parents?'

'They're still in Byron.'

'What do they do? Are they medical, like you and your sisters?'

'No. Mum works in retail and Dad was a professional surfer. He runs a surf school—or he did,' she said, realising she didn't actually know if he was back at work after a recent medical emergency. 'He had surgery recently for a ruptured brain aneurysm.'

'That sounds serious. How's he doing?'

'Okay, I think.'

'You *think*? You haven't spoken to him? Seen him?'

'We went to Byron and saw him before his surgery, but the op was done in Brisbane.'

'Is he still there?'

'No, he's back in Byron Bay, but only just.'

'Byron is only a day's drive away,' Ajay said, and she could hear the confusion in his voice.

She knew she could get to Byron in a little over ten hours in the car, or on a short flight, but neither Daisy nor her siblings had a close bond with their parents and not even her dad's health scare had altered that. Daisy in particular had a lot of unresolved issues with them, and she didn't think that was likely to change.

'I'm not close to my parents.'

Her comment was met with only one raised eyebrow, and she knew that he wasn't going to probe, but also that he would listen if she expanded.

Was she willing to discuss her family?

'We didn't have the most conventional upbringing,' she said, deciding her childhood should be no secret, and realising part of her was curious to gauge his reaction.

'No?'

She shook her head. 'We were raised on a commune. It was certainly not the normal family dynamic. We were raised collectively by the adults, but sometimes it felt like no one was raising us. I spent more time with my siblings than my parents—they certainly didn't take responsibility for us. My father had rebelled against his conservative parents, and my mother ran away from home at the age of eighteen. I don't know if they even wanted to *be* parents. I disagree with the way they raised us, with some of the things they believe in, and I feel they let me down. I wish I didn't feel that way but…' she shrugged '…that's how things stand. I certainly don't feel that we were ever important. It was always very obvious that their relationship was more important than any relationship they had with us, and we've never even met our grandparents. Fraught familial relationships seem to run through the generations with us. But I'm lucky to have my siblings. *They're* my family. They're all I need.'

Ajay had a slightly incredulous expression on his handsome face.

'I assume from your expression that your family is more traditional,' she said, as Chen brought more food to the table. 'Tell me about them. Where did you grow up?'

For a moment she thought Ajay was about to ask her more questions, but thankfully he took her cue to change the direction of the conversation and obliged her with an answer. 'In Fiji. My parents are still there—they're both doctors—and my sister lives in LA.'

'If you have no family here, who helps you with Niki? Who's watching him tonight?'

'I have a live-in housekeeper and nanny—Mrs Singh. She looks after the house and also Niki. She's a widow, and I guess she's kind of a surrogate grandmother for Niki. He adores her. It's been a good solution for us.'

'So you have Mrs Singh instead of childcare? Or do you use both?'

Ajay shook his head. 'I cancelled his enrolment when I became aware of the communication barrier. I don't want Niki at risk because he can't make himself understood or can't hear others. You were right when you said it was important for him to be able to communicate. It had already affected my choices for him, and you made me think about what that would mean for him going forward, and how it could potentially affect the choices he might want to make for himself.'

'You've made a decision about his surgery?'

'Yes. I spoke to his ENT surgeon and booked him in. I hope I've done the right thing.'

'You're doing something, and with the best intentions. That's what counts. He's lucky to have you.'

But was he going to be enough? Ajay wondered. Niki had no one in Australia other than Ajay. No mother, no grandparents, no cousins, no siblings. Ajay hadn't thought about it in that context until listening to Daisy. She didn't know her grandparents, and had a complicated relationship with her parents, but at least she had her siblings. Who would Niki have?

In every recent conversation he'd had with his mother and sister they'd asked him about his social life, about whether he was ready to meet anyone new. So far he'd resisted, but were his mother and sister right? Did he need to think about what his future looked like for Niki's sake as well as his own?

And what would his family think of Daisy?

He knew the answer to that. Daisy was not what his mother would have in mind. His mother would deny it, but her list of suitable wives for Ajay would be unlikely to include a blonde-haired, blue-eyed, Caucasian Australian girl.

But that didn't stop his mind from wandering as their conversation naturally progressed to a discussion about the hospital and their colleagues, and it was only when Chen gently interrupted to ask if he could get them anything else that he realised the restaurant was empty. He was reluctant for the evening to end, but he needed to get home to relieve Mrs Singh.

'No, thank you,' he said, before settling the bill and walking Daisy to her car. 'I enjoyed dinner. Thank you for keeping me company.'

He would like to invite her out again, but he needed to consider what that would mean. Did he have time to date? Did he *want* to?

Maybe he should take a moment to think things through logically. He didn't want to make a hasty decision without consideration of what it would mean for Niki as much as for himself.

He decided he would take his cue from Daisy. He'd see how she said goodnight.

When she thanked him for dinner and got into her car without a kiss on the cheek, without any suggestion that they meet up again, he had to take that as a sign not to rush things.

It was probably sensible, he thought as he drove himself home, but that didn't mean it wasn't disappointing.

Ajay stretched his back and rolled his shoulders, easing the knots that had developed during the course of his marathon shift.

It was almost guaranteed that a New Year's Eve shift would be hectic, and tonight's had been no exception.

Extra staff had been rostered on to cope with the anticipated chaos that usually accompanied New Year's Eve on Bondi Beach. The beach was fenced off for a ticketed event, and while alcohol was banned on the beach there was plenty of alcohol in the pubs and bars in the surrounding streets—and, judging from the events of this evening, plenty of illegal drug use as well.

Even with the additional doctors on the roster Ajay should have clocked off hours ago, but a regular schedule as an A&E doctor was one thing he'd learnt not to rely on. While he'd had better shifts, with fewer weekends, since moving to Bondi General, there was never any guarantee of getting out of the hospital on time.

And tonight he'd been caught in a true emergency.

Tonight's shift had been both hectic and tragic.

A group of teenage boys had been involved in a serious car accident and four of them had been brought into Emergency, three in a critical condition. Two had been stabilised, but the third hadn't survived. As a doctor, Ajay knew he had done his best. But as a parent Ajay was devastated, and it had dampened his enthusiasm for celebrating what was left of New Year's Eve.

Not that he'd felt that excited about it at any stage.

He had made plans to meet friends for dinner, but it was now after eleven, meaning he would have missed dinner altogether. There was probably no point heading to the restaurant now. He knew he was looking for reasons to avoid the party—that was partly why he'd offered to assist in Theatre, knowing it would delay his departure, but he hadn't expected it to end the way it had.

If he could go back he might reverse his decision, but hindsight was a wonderful thing. If he could go back there were a lot of things he would do differently.

Starting with saving Priya.

He wanted to go home and see his son, sleeping safely and soundly in his bed. That would make him feel better. He was feeling old. The things he'd seen, professionally and personally, had left him exhausted. He was tired, but knew he wouldn't sleep.

He'd go home, try to sneak into his own house so that Mrs Singh didn't catch him, and toast the new year with a beer on his balcony. Alone. Sad. Pathetic.

But being alone was something he'd done many times on many nights in the past two years. And he knew if he went home without a good reason Mrs Singh would tell him off.

He changed out of his scrubs as he wondered what his options were. The more he thought about it, the less he wanted to join his friends after their dinner. It would be just another occasion when he would be late and single, joining in with friends who were all married. He should celebrate the end of another year, or at least drink a toast to the New Year, but he didn't feel like braving the crowded bars or joining in with revellers who had started celebrating hours before him.

He wondered if Daisy had made it to her party. If she was enjoying it. It had sounded like one for the young and the single—and he only met one of those criteria.

He'd like to see her, but he felt far too old and jaded and he didn't think it would be a wise decision. Besides, although she'd told him about the party, she hadn't invited him to join her. She hadn't said if she was going with anyone. He didn't want to make a fool of himself. He was attracted to her, he wasn't going to deny it, but he had no idea how she felt.

He sighed and headed for the exit—and found himself walking out of the hospital at the same time as Daisy.

His spirits lifted instantly.

'Hello. You've had a long night.' He knew she'd been working a late shift—she'd mentioned it at dinner the night before.

'So have you,' she replied. 'But I expected to work late. I don't suppose you did.'

'No.' He shook his head and ran his fingers through his hair, realising for about the fourth time in recent weeks that he needed to make an appointment for a haircut, and probably find time to shave as well.

'Rough night?' she asked.

'A little,' he said. 'We lost a patient—a teenage car accident victim.'

He was exhausted, and knew he must look it too. In contrast, she looked as fresh as a daisy. She'd been well-named, and the thought made him smile.

'What are you smiling at?' she asked.

He could tell she thought it was an odd time to be smiling, but just seeing her had improved his mood and made him feel that there were still some things in the world that were beautiful and good and right.

'Just thinking how well your name suits you,' he said, taking care to make sure he faced her, so she could read his lips. 'Are you going to your party?'

She was still wearing scrubs. Her name badge had a sticker with a daisy on it and tonight pink daisy earrings hung from her lobes.

'I'm supposed to be. What about you? Are you still meeting your friends?

'I'm pretty sure I've missed dinner by now.'

'I'm sure they'll still be up. It's not midnight yet.'

'The truth is I'm happy to have a reason to pull out of the commitment.'

'Why?'

'Everyone there will be part of a couple,' he said with a slight shrug. 'It's awkward now that I'm single.'

'So what will you do?'

'Go home.'

'Would you like to come with me to The Pavilion? Lily had a spare ticket, but she gave it away—we could see if you can get in at the door?'

He was tempted, but if he was honest he didn't really feel like partying. A drink with Daisy had some appeal, but not going to a big event where he would probably lose sight of her in the first minute.

'Thanks, but I'm not really in the right frame of mind for that after tonight's events.'

'Would you like to come and have a drink at my house instead?' she asked, as if she could read his mind. 'Lily and my brother and Mei are there. You can have company without having to make too much effort.'

'I don't want you to miss your party,' he said. He would love to accept her offer, but he didn't want her to feel obligated to entertain him.

'I'm not much of a party person,' she admitted. 'Poppy bought me a ticket, but I'm happy to have an excuse to go home. It's not really my thing. I don't like big crowds. By now everyone will be dancing, and I can feel the music, but I can't hear it. I don't really feel like joining in at this late stage, and then at midnight I'll be expected to kiss a random stranger.'

'A random stranger?'

'Well, probably not completely random.' She smiled. 'Bondi is a small community—everyone knows everyone. But I don't have a date, so it's a little bit unknown.'

Now all he could think about was someone kissing Daisy. Someone who wasn't him.

'I'm going to call a taxi and then let Poppy know I'm going home,' she said as she pulled her phone from her pocket.

'Let me drive you. You won't get a taxi tonight,' he said, even though he knew that was probably not quite accurate. Before midnight she had a slight chance. But he had his car at the hospital, and nothing else he wanted to do, nowhere else he wanted to be…no one else he wanted to see.

She looked up at him. 'If you give me a lift you have to promise to come in for just one drink. At least then we can say we did *something* to celebrate the New Year.'

Ajay followed Daisy's directions and pulled into Moore Street, stopping in front of a tall, narrow house near the top of the hill. It hadn't taken much persuading to get him to agree to go in and have a drink with her.

Daisy opened the door and he followed her inside. A long passage ran along the left-hand side of the house, which appeared to be just one room wide. There was a room to his right, then a staircase, and next a lounge. A Christmas tree still stood in the corner of the living room. It was covered in blue and silver decorations, and he noted that the blue was the colour of Daisy's eyes.

The lounge opened into a kitchen that spanned the width of the house. Lily was in the kitchen, but there was no sign of Daisy's brother or of Mei. He saw a fleeting look of surprise on Lily's face as he entered the kitchen behind Daisy, but it didn't last long and she quickly covered it with a welcoming smile.

'This is a nice surprise,' she said, somehow managing to sound pleased while at the same time making it clear that she expected some kind of explanation.

'I invited Ajay in for a drink,' Daisy explained. 'He worked late and missed his dinner party.'

'I thought you were going to the party at The Pavilion?' Lily said as she glanced past Daisy's shoulder to look again at Ajay, as if trying to work out what he was doing in her kitchen.

'I changed my mind. I didn't feel like joining in when it was almost midnight and everyone else would have been there for hours. I thought we could come here and see the New Year in with you and Jet and Mei,' she said, and she looked around, as if expecting the others to pop out from the kitchen cupboards.

'Jet and Mei have gone to bed.'

'Already?'

Lily nodded. 'They're both working tomorrow—early shifts. Jet starts at five.'

'That's an early start to the year,' Ajay said.

'It's usually six o'clock, but on New Year's Day it's earlier. Mei starts at seven, and I'm watching An Na. so I was just about to go to bed too.'

'Would you mind keeping Ajay company while I get changed?' Daisy asked. 'I'll only be a minute,' she added, before disappearing without waiting for an answer.

Ajay turned to Lily. 'You don't mind Daisy inviting me here?' he asked, still trying to decipher Lily's reaction.

Lily smiled. 'No. I just wasn't expecting her to bring anyone home.'

'I can't imagine many people say no to an invitation from Daisy.'

'That's true. People are drawn to her. They always have been. We think she sprinkles them with fairy dust.'

Lily was smiling. He thought she was joking, but he wasn't a hundred percent sure, and he couldn't pretend he didn't know what Lily was talking about. He certainly felt as if Daisy had cast a spell of some sort on him.

'But I can't remember the last time she invited someone home,' Lily added.

He was flattered to think that Daisy had extended him an invitation, but he tried to remain humble. 'I think she felt sorry for me.'

Lily just smiled again, and he realised he still had no idea what she was thinking.

'What would you like to drink? Mei and I opened a bottle of champagne, if you'd like a glass. Or there's beer or wine?'

'I should say champagne, given that it's New Year's Eve,' he replied, 'but I'd really prefer a beer.'

'Beer it is, then.' She opened the fridge, and a cupboard, and handed him a bottle of beer and a glass. 'Why don't you take that out onto the deck?' She pointed towards the doors at the end of the kitchen, 'I'll just make up a quick platter—I'm sure you're both starving.'

He *was* hungry—he'd missed dinner—but he didn't want Lily to wait on him. 'I don't expect you to do that.'

'It's no trouble. We all had a platter earlier; I always buy too much, so I can assemble one quickly enough.'

She began pulling things out of the fridge, making

it clear that she was going to put one together whether he agreed or not. She poured a glass of champagne and handed that to him as well.

'Take this for Daisy. I'm sure she won't be long,' she said, and she dismissed him to the deck.

He was too tired to argue any further, so he did as directed and took the drinks outside.

Fairy lights wound around the railing and festoon lights hung above the deck. Unlit candles, grouped in jars, were clustered in the centre of the table. The night was warm, but a faint breeze carried the sound of music from the concert on Bondi Beach, which stretched out below the house. The lights of the buildings along Campbell Parade and through the surrounding streets glittered under the moonlight. It was a romantic scene.

Lily brought out the platter, an assortment of cheese, grapes, olives, crackers, dips and pâté. 'There you go,' she said as she placed it on the table.

'Aren't you joining us?' Ajay asked as Lily turned to leave. He was trying to be polite—it was her house, after all—but he hoped she would say no.

'No, I'm about to go to bed,' she replied as Daisy stepped out onto the deck. 'An Na will be up at the crack of dawn, and I promised to take her surfing if the conditions are good.'

'You're a surfer too?'

'We all are,' she said, before she turned to Daisy. She hugged her and said, 'Happy New Year,' followed by something he couldn't hear.

Daisy shook her head in reply, leaving Ajay curious as to what had been said.

'Happy New Year, Ajay,' Lily said to him.

'You too,' he replied as Lily left the deck, leaving him alone with Daisy.

She had changed into a pale blue camisole top that highlighted her tan and brought out the colour of her eyes. Her feet were bare and her slender legs extended from a pair of short white shorts. He tried not to stare, and was relieved when she spoke, as it brought his attention back to her face.

'Do you mind if I light the candles? I need more light so I can lip-read,' Daisy asked, and Ajay was reminded that only he could hear the music that drifted through the night.

'Of course. Let me,' he offered, and he passed her the glass of champagne and held out his hand for the box of matches.

She placed the box into his palm and her fingers brushed his skin. He had an overwhelming urge to wrap his fingers around hers, to hold her to him and not let go. But, in an instant her soft, warm hand was gone, replaced by the hard matchbox.

He opened the box and struck a match, lighting the candle wicks one by one until they flickered and glowed in their jars. He sat opposite Daisy, so she could see his face clearly, and picked up his glass.

'Here's to a new year and new friends,' he said, as he raised his glass in a toast.

Daisy smiled and repeated, 'To new friends.' She waited while he drank and then asked, 'How are you feeling now about your shift?'

'I'm trying not to think about it. I've had personal losses but, as a parent, I can't imagine anything worse than getting that phone call. I'm glad I wasn't the one who had to make it. At least I know we did everything we could. That boy made a poor decision and it cost him his life. His family and friends will have to live with that, and I'm not sure how they'll do that—especially the boy who was driving the car.' He sipped his beer.

'I'm glad you didn't have to make that phone call too,' Daisy said. 'I've seen too often how the doctors in Paediatrics struggle in those instances. It's an awful part of the job.'

Ajay hadn't considered that it would be a scenario Daisy was all too familiar with. 'How do you handle it?' he asked.

'By trying to make it as calm as possible. I imagine it's a different experience in the paediatric department, but it's still horrible, and I want to help make it less traumatic. Fortunately, we have more good days than bad.'

'You're happy working with kids?'

'I love it.'

Her face lit up, and Ajay vowed to keep her talking about something that made her glow.

'Kids are uncomplicated, really, and I much prefer caring for them than for adults. They aren't fazed by my disability. Some adults seem to think that my hearing impairment makes me incompetent. The kids are far more accepting. I think that sometimes, if they aren't well, they actually like the fact that there's something wrong with me too.'

'There doesn't seem to be too much wrong with you.'

'You don't know me very well yet,' she said.

'Agreed. But I'm just telling you what I see. And you should accept a compliment when you get one.

Make that your New Year's resolution—to graciously accept a compliment.'

'I'll try.'

'Try now,' he said. 'The colour of your top looks lovely on you—it brings out the blue of your eyes. You should wear it often.'

Daisy looked back at him silently.

'That's your cue to graciously accept my compliment,' he told her.

Daisy smiled as she thanked him, and he thought he detected a faint blush on her cheeks in the light of the candles.

'So, what is your resolution going to be?' she asked as she lifted her champagne glass.

Ajay shook his head. 'I try not to make them. Things don't ever seem to go according to plan.'

'That doesn't seem fair. If I have to make one, you should too.'

'I could start with something simple, like cutting back on my coffee intake.'

'That doesn't sound nearly ambitious enough,' she said, and smiled.

'Well, I'm not about to start training for a marathon, so what would you suggest? Do you have something in mind for yourself?'

'Other than learning how to accept a compliment?' She sipped her champagne before continuing. 'I have, but it's a hard one because it's not completely up to me.'

'What is it?'

'I want to find my happily-ever-after.'

'You think that exists?' he asked.

'Don't you?'

He could see the horror on her face when she re-alised what she'd said.

'Sorry—that was thoughtless. Of course you don't believe in happily-ever-after. Not any more.'

But Daisy had misinterpreted his question. Priya's death hadn't been what he was referring too. He and Priya certainly hadn't ended up with their happily-ever-after, but there had been no guarantee that they would have managed it anyway. He might have had his chance at love, and he might think that he didn't deserve an-other shot, but he didn't want to talk about Priya. Or himself. He wanted to know more about Daisy. That was the goal he had set himself. That could be his resolution.

'I'm not saying I don't think you'll find it,' he said. 'Tell me what you're looking for. Is it the fairy tale? A husband? A family?'

She shook her head. 'No. There's a space right here,' she said, and she placed her hand over her heart. 'A space for one person that I need to fill. I'm not looking for a family, I'm not necessarily looking for a husband, I'm just looking for my person.'

Ajay wanted to ask her what her person would be like. What if her person already had a family? What would she do then? But before he could delve deeper, he heard the crowd of revellers on the beach begin the countdown to midnight.

'Ten... Nine... Eight...'

He turned his head towards the sound and then back to Daisy. 'It's almost midnight,' he told her. 'I can hear the countdown from the beach.'

Daisy stood up and held out her hand. He took it,

and a heady mix of completeness and excitement came over him. It felt as if he was coming home.

He followed her to the corner of the deck, where she leant against the railing and let go of his hand as the first firework burst in the sky over the ocean. She was standing right beside him, but the minute her hand pulled out of his he felt as though she was miles away.

Her face was tilted towards the heavens as she watched the fireworks explode in a colourful fiery display against the night sky. But Ajay ignored the fireworks, choosing instead to watch Daisy. The colours played across her face and reflected in her eyes. Red and gold, white and green... She looked as if she'd been painted by van Gogh. As if she belonged with all the artistic masterpieces.

She turned to face him as the final explosion burnt out and faded, its sparks falling towards the sea. Her hip brushed his as she turned to him, bringing her closer to his side, and Ajay's skin tingled as she rested her hand on his forearm. She was watching him closely, and he had no idea if it was because she was waiting for him to speak or because she was as caught up in the moment as he was.

He was enthralled and entranced. Her face was tilted towards his, and now it was his reflection he could see in her blue eyes. His face had taken the place of the fireworks. Daisy looked calm and peaceful. He felt the complete opposite. He was excited and nervous, a maelstrom of emotion.

Looking into her eyes, he had no idea if she felt the same crazy emotions. He couldn't tell if she felt the irresistible pull of attraction as strongly as he did and he was scared to ask, worried that the answer wouldn't be the one he wanted to hear.

His reaction to her scared him. His feelings for her shocked and surprised him. They'd been sudden and intense from the first moment he'd laid eyes on her. And standing beside her now, under the midnight sky, he felt like a firework, full of energy and ready to explode.

He'd never had a response like this to a woman before. His introduction to Priya had been orchestrated and he'd had expectations—a sense of what she was like—before he'd met her. But Daisy had burst into his world when he'd least expected her, and he was having trouble thinking about anything else.

He wanted to pull her into his arms and hold her close. Instinctively he knew she would feel right in his embrace. The weight of her head resting on his shoulder, the smell of her hair, the curve of her cheek against his chest, the warmth of her hand in his and the curve of her hip against his side would all feel perfect.

His body had been waiting for her. He knew how she would feel pressed against him. Again, he had a sense of coming home. Daisy had cast a spell and he could feel himself falling under it.

After losing Priya he hadn't contemplated finding a partner again. Instead, he'd made a conscious decision to focus on his son and on his work. His relationships in the past year had been brief—physically but not emotionally satisfying. He hadn't been in a place where he'd had the emotional energy to invest in a relationship, but being here with Daisy made him want to change his mind. She made him think about future possibilities. She made him remember how it felt to experience the first heady rush of desire.

'Happy New Year.'

Her voice was a whisper, but to Ajay's mind it carried with it myriad promises. Perhaps it was the idea of a new year. Perhaps it was the stars above, the fireworks, the magic of a new beginning. But he had to know how she felt. He had to know how she tasted.

Deciding on actions, not words, prepared to be rebuffed but hoping otherwise, he bent his head, waiting to see what she did. Would she step back? Would she put up a hand to stop him? Or would she close the gap between them, as small as it was already?

She lifted her chin a fraction higher, coming to meet him. Her eyes were wide, her pupils large. Her lips were soft, pink and parted.

Was he going to be crossing a line? He hoped not.

Her name spilled from his mouth as a soft breath before he brushed his lips over hers. He heard her sigh and watched as her eyelids fluttered and closed.

She tasted like champagne. Exciting, but familiar, making his blood effervesce. She tasted like happiness.

Perhaps he did deserve some after all.

CHAPTER SIX

DAISY HAD SPENT the first day of the New Year lying in the garden, reading, working on her tan and trying not to think about last night.

About 'The Kiss'.

About the way Ajay's eyes had darkened as he'd lowered his head and the sense of delightful anticipation she'd felt, knowing he was about to kiss her. The excitement. The warmth of his lips on hers. The touch of his thumb on her cheek. The firmness of his fingers in her hair. The taste of his mouth. The feel of his body against hers.

She had wrapped her arms over his shoulders, holding him to her, holding herself up as her bones had melted under the heat of his touch.

She'd closed her eyes as he'd kissed her, leaving her blind and deaf, but her other senses had been working overtime. Touch, taste and smell had been enough. She knew she would have been overwhelmed if all her senses had been functioning. The way he tasted, the way he felt, was now imprinted on her memory.

There had been no awkwardness, no bumping of noses, no sense that it was their first kiss. It had felt as if she already knew him. As if they had shared a thousand kisses before. A thousand lifetimes. She'd fitted into his arms as if she'd always been there and she'd never wanted to leave.

The kiss had been amazing, but that didn't mean it hadn't been a mistake. Daisy knew she'd got caught up in the moment. She didn't deny that she'd wanted to kiss him, but she knew it couldn't happen again.

She needed to fix things.

She needed to steer clear of him.

She didn't want a relationship—especially not with a man who had a child. That was a complication she didn't need or want.

Ajay had said he'd text her today and she'd deliberately turned her phone off. She wished, as she so often did, that Willow was there beside her. She and Willow would have dissected every second of 'The Kiss' and worked out a plan, but now it was all up to her. She had to work out how she was going to play this.

The kiss had been a mistake.

She was just going to have to ignore the fact that it hadn't felt like one.

She showered and got ready for work before switching her phone back on, only to see she had no messages. She remonstrated with herself when she felt disappointed. Wasn't this what she wanted? No complications?

Perhaps in the clear light of the morning Ajay was also having second thoughts. Maybe he had got caught up in the moment too. Perhaps the occasion, the warm summer evening, the stars and the fireworks overhead had seduced them both into doing something they hadn't planned.

If that was the case, she hoped there would be no awkwardness. She hoped 'The Kiss' hadn't ruined any chance of a friendship. She might not want a relationship with him, but he was a nice guy, and another friend was always welcome.

Daisy stepped on to the paediatric ward and forced herself to focus on patient hand-over, blocking out all thoughts of last night and any and all possible ramifications from her mind. She watched Kerry carefully, to make sure she didn't miss any important information about the small charges she was going to be responsible for this shift.

'Daisy, we've got a toddler, twenty-three months old, admitted this morning with a severe reaction to a funnel-web spider bite.'

The funnel-web spider, found in New South Wales, was one of Australia's deadliest spiders, and while there hadn't been a fatality in several years all Sydney-siders still had a healthy respect for, if not a fear of, these large, aggressive spiders. Daisy knew that children fared worse than adults when bitten—the spiders' fangs were large, and could inflict a large amount of venom quickly, meaning children were more at risk because they were smaller and the venom was therefore more lethal. But it was reassuring that this child had been admitted to hospital. That he was a survivor and not a victim.

'He's had three vials of antivenene and is stable, but we're keeping him overnight for observation.'

That was good news, Daisy thought.

And then Kerry continued, 'You know Dr Patel from A&E?'

Daisy nodded and hoped she wasn't blushing as she wondered why Kerry was bringing Ajay into the conversation. Had someone said something? Had someone seen them leaving the hospital together last night? It was quite possible. Anyone could have seen them— Daisy hadn't been paying attention to who else had been around as they'd left.

'The patient with the spider bite injury is Niki Patel—Dr Patel's son.'

Daisy's blood froze in her veins. Niki was the patient! Ajay must be terrified.

Her heart ached for him, and she wanted to go directly to Niki's room, but she forced herself to check her other patients first, knowing that would leave her time to spend with Ajay, time to check up on him as well as on his son.

When she got to Niki's room she saw Ajay sitting in a chair beside Niki's cot. He looked exhausted.

'Ajay!'

He stood up as she entered the room. She went straight to him and wrapped her arms around him. It was a reflex gesture. He looked as if he could use a hug, and she instantly forgot her decision that they could only be friends. Forgot that they needed to have a serious discussion about 'The Kiss' and the fact that it couldn't happen again.

He was warm and solid. She fitted neatly against his chest, her head tucked into the curve of his shoulder. He held her to him for a half a minute, until she came to her senses and realised where they were. Realised what she was doing.

She released him and stepped back. She tilted her head up to see his face. 'Sorry,' she said, 'that wasn't very professional.'

'It's okay. I needed that.' He smiled, but the smile only just reached his eyes. There were lines at the side of his mouth that she hadn't noticed before—she would swear they hadn't been there yesterday—and his face was drawn.

She looked more closely. Looked not just at his face but at the whole of him. His hair was messier than normal, and he looked as if he'd dressed in a hurry. In fact, he was dressed in the same clothes he'd had on last night when they'd left the hospital.

When he'd driven her home.

When he'd kissed her.

She took another step back as she felt her cheeks redden. 'Have you been here all day?'

He nodded and ran a hand through his hair, messing it up even further.

Maybe that explained why he hadn't messaged her, she thought. 'Sit down,' she said. 'Let me check Niki and then you can tell me what happened.'

'Niki was playing on the floor. He was putting blocks in and out of a toy truck and I heard him scream. He's normally pretty quiet, so that was a shock. He was holding his finger and I could see the puncture wound. The spider was in the truck. I'd never seen a funnel-web in the house before.' Ajay was shaking his head, as if he still couldn't believe what had happened. 'I bandaged his hand, but he was still crying, and within minutes he was sweating and then he vomited. I put him in the car and brought him to the hospital. He had a seizure on the way here.'

'You must have been beside yourself.'

Ajay nodded.

'You drove him here yourself? You didn't call an ambulance?'

'I should have, but I wanted to get him here as fast as I could. We're only a few minutes away, and I knew the roads would be quiet early on New Year's Day. I didn't want to wait for the paramedics. I called the hospital on the way—they knew we were coming. They had the antivenene ready. Thank God I knew what type of spider it was.'

'It must have been a horrific experience. For both of you,' Daisy said as she checked Niki's vital signs.

An IV ran into his little arm, replacing the fluids he would have lost through vomiting, rehydrating him. Niki was lying on his back in the cot, wearing a nappy but nothing else. Daisy looked for traces of Ajay in him. His dark lashes curled against his cheek as he slept and his thick dark hair was damp and curled sightly, like Ajay's. She wondered if he had the same deep chocolate eyes as his father.

'Has he had any more seizures?' Daisy asked as she looked back at Ajay.

Ajay shook his head. 'No. Fortunately he seems to have come through well. But because he's so young he's staying overnight, just to be on the safe side.'

Ajay's skin, normally a healthy bronzed colour, was decidedly pale. 'Have you eaten?' she asked.

'No. I haven't left his side.'

'You could have texted me,' she said.

'I'm sorry. I know I said I would. But Niki had to be my priority.'

'No,' she said, with a shake of her head. She wasn't

talking about the message he'd promised to send her—the one she'd avoided by turning her phone off—she was talking about offering support. 'I meant you could have messaged me and I could have come in earlier,' she explained. 'Given you a break or some company.'

'I didn't think of it.'

Of course not. Why would he? There would have been plenty of other things on his mind. Plenty of other things to worry about, to occupy his thoughts. She would have been far down his list.

'Why don't you go and grab something to eat while I stay with Niki?' Daisy offered.

Ajay knew she must see the look of hesitation on his face. 'I don't know...' he said.

'Ajay, you need to eat, and it won't do you any harm to get some fresh air for a few minutes. Niki is stable and I will stay here with him. Text me your number and I promise I'll message you if anything changes.'

'Are you sure?'

'Positive. He'll be fine.'

'I left his toy koala at home. I know he'll want it when he wakes up. Do you think it's okay to leave?'

He was normally so decisive, but seeing his son suffer, and the worry and concern he'd had for Niki's wellbeing, made it impossible for him to think clearly. His thoughts were scrambled and he was looking to Daisy for guidance.

She was nodding. 'I promise I will message you. I'll even get the hospital to call you, if necessary. You're not far away, are you?'

'No. A few minutes.'

'Go. I'll take care of him.' She smiled. 'I do this for a living, you know.'

He let Daisy convince him. 'I won't be long,' he said.

He really did want to fetch Niki's stuffed toy—he knew how attached Niki was to it.

He appreciated Daisy's level-headedness. It felt good to have someone to talk to—someone to bounce ideas off. He knew that Niki was his responsibility, his concern, that the buck stopped with him, but having someone to whom he could verbalise his decision-making process helped to crystallise his thoughts and calm his nerves.

Niki had slept well—better than Ajay had thought. He'd been given a hospital bed beside Niki's cot, and he was looking forward to getting home and having a long, hot shower. But seeing Daisy arrive for her early shift brightened his mood.

'Good morning. Why am I not surprised to find you here?' she asked as she handed him a brown paper bag and a takeaway coffee cup.

'What's all this?' he asked.

'Breakfast. I know the hospital will feed you, but I figured there's always room for a blueberry muffin and a decent coffee.'

'Thank you.'

'My pleasure. And it will keep you busy while I check Niki,' she said as she turned her attention to his son.

'Good morning, little man. Are you feeling better today?'

Ajay saw Niki smile in response to Daisy's smile.

He knew Niki couldn't hear her but, like everyone else, he couldn't resist her smile.

Daisy kept up a steady stream of conversation as she changed Niki's nappy. She made sure to look at Niki the whole time, involving him in what she was doing, giving him the chance to follow the movement of her lips, to see the words forming even if he couldn't hear them.

Ajay realised then that a lot of people didn't talk to Niki, not bothering to make the effort because he couldn't hear. Daisy was different. She was a natural with children and he watched Niki respond to her easy manner and engaging smile.

'I can see why you enjoy paediatrics,' he told her. 'You're a natural with kids.'

'I love working with them,' she replied, 'but I'm not sure I could handle them twenty-four-seven. Nursing them and raising them are two very different things.'

'Why do you say that?'

'Nursing is the easy bit. I'm trained for that. And at the end of the day I get to go home. I'm not responsible for these little people until they reach adulthood.'

'No one is trained for parenthood. You learn as you go.'

'I'm sure that is partly true, but I also think you learn from others around you. From how you've been raised. From what you've experienced. I'm happy to look after them at work, but I couldn't imagine being wholly and solely responsible. I'd be afraid of disappointing them.'

Ajay thought that was an odd response. 'Why would you think that?'

'I didn't have great role models.'

'Yet you seemed to have turned out pretty well,' he said with a smile as he tried to lift her sprits. He could see she had become a little downcast.

'I told you I had an unusual childhood,' she said. 'Of course at the time I didn't realise that—not until I was a teenager, really—but a few things happened that *really* affected me…things my parents could have controlled.'

Ajay was worried now. He remembered the comment she'd made when they had treated Breanna. She'd said, *'Not all parents are good ones.'* His blood went cold as he wondered what she'd been referring too.

'What things?' he asked.

'Losing my hearing, for one.'

Ajay frowned. He wasn't sure he was following her train of thought. 'Losing your hearing?'

'When I was eight years old I contracted mumps— that's how I lost my hearing. It's unusual, apparently, to lose the hearing in both ears but…' she shrugged '…it does happen. It wasn't until I was older that I learned we kids could have been immunised. My parents could have—*should* have protected us against the virus, but they didn't believe in vaccinations. My father was the son of a doctor—he should have known better. But my parents' beliefs cost me my hearing and cost my sister her life.'

'Hang on…your sister?' He was really confused now.

She nodded. 'My identical twin. Willow. We were inseparable. My parents' beliefs robbed me of the most precious thing in my life and I can't forgive them for that. I lost my hearing, but Willow lost her life.'

'Daisy! I am so sorry.'

Tears welled in Daisy's eyes and Ajay's heart ached for her. Without thinking he took a step towards her and wrapped his arms around her, held her as the tears flowed. He felt her relax against him, but he didn't let her go. He rubbed his hand on her back, making small circles, calming her like he did Niki. But he was very aware that she felt nothing like Niki in his embrace.

'I still miss her. Every day,' she said. 'She was my person.'

Eventually her tears subsided and her breathing returned to normal. He let her go just enough to let her see his face, see his lips. 'Your person?'

Daisy had mentioned her 'person' before, but he hadn't realise she'd already had one in her life.

She nodded. 'She was special to me and I was special to her. We'd been together every minute since we were born. And then one day, she wasn't there. One day it was just me. And nothing was ever the same. I wasn't special to anyone any more. I'd lost my person. I was eight years old and I'd lost my person. Willow and I even had our own language, as lots of twins do, but I stopped talking after she died. Everyone assumed it was my way of dealing with the grief and that I would talk again when I was ready. They were right. But what no one realised until later was that the virus that had taken Willow had also taken my hearing. Losing Willow was my first experience of loss. She was gone, and a few years after that the rest of my siblings left Byron Bay, one by one, until by the age of thirteen I was really alone. But if my parents had vaccinated us in all likelihood I would still have had Willow. I've never forgiven my parents for that. I can't. They let Willow down. They let me down. I've never recovered from losing Willow and I don't want to go through anything like that again,' she said.

She grabbed some tissues from beside Niki's bed and wiped her face. She took a deep breath and gave him a half-smile.

'I'm sorry, I have no idea why I downloaded all that on to you.'

'Don't be sorry. I'm glad you trusted me with your story,' he said honestly. And he was—it had given him an insight into her and he felt he knew her better now.

He could only imagine how she must have felt— losing someone who had been a part of her since before they were born. Losing Priya had been devastating, but they hadn't been two halves of a whole. He had existed separately from her. Their identities had not been irrevocably entwined. Daisy, on the other hand, would have had much of her identity wrapped up in being an identical twin. Her loss must have been unimaginable.

The only thing Ajay could relate it to was losing Niki, and he couldn't imagine his life without his son. He'd been absolutely terrified when Niki had been bitten by the spider. All he'd been able to think about was that he couldn't lose Niki as well as Priya.

But his mission now was to try to make Daisy feel better.

He gathered up the pile of mail that he'd brought with him when he'd fetched Niki's toy koala and a few overnight supplies. A pale green envelope caught his eye, and he realised he might have just the thing to take Daisy's mind off her confessions.

He reached out and touched her arm, drawing her attention back to him. 'Before we go, there's something

I want to ask you. I want to invite you to this,' he said as he handed her the envelope.

'What is it?' she asked as she pulled out a piece of printed cardboard.

'An invitation to a fundraising ball.'

'It says it's this weekend.'

He nodded. 'I've organised a table of ten. I'm going with colleagues from my old job at North Sydney Hospital, but they all have partners so I had one spare ticket. Would you like to come with me?'

'As your date?'

She sounded uncertain.

'Yes. I thought after New Year's Eve…'

He trailed off when Daisy shook her head and his heart plummeted. He'd been on a few dates in the past two years, but they had been arranged purely to satisfy physical urges. Daisy was triggering a very different reaction—an emotional one as well as physical—and at no other time had he been so eager for his offer to be accepted.

The kiss they'd shared had got him through the dark hours of last night, as he'd sat beside his son's bed. Once he'd known Niki was going to be okay he'd been able to think about other things, and his mind had kept returning to Daisy and the kiss. The buzz he'd got had been enough to convince him that he needed to make room in his life for the possibility of a relationship. All his focus recently had been on Niki and work, but he needed to make time for himself too. Niki was going to be okay. Now Ajay had to take care of himself.

He enjoyed Daisy's company—which was not something that could be said for his few other dates in the past year. He knew he hadn't been in the right emotional state previously, and hadn't wanted to make an emotional connection with those women, but he realised he'd be happy to spend time with Daisy platonically if that was all she wanted. Although after that kiss he wasn't denying that he'd be happy if it developed into something more...something intimate.

'I wanted to talk to you about New Year's Eve...' she said as he held his breath. 'I shouldn't have kissed you.'

'I kissed you.'

'And I kissed you back,' she said. 'But I'm sorry if I gave you the wrong idea. I'm not looking for a relationship.'

'I thought you were looking for your person?'

'My *person*—singular. I don't date men who have children.'

That was twice now that she'd verbalised a lack of interest in children, in having a family of her own. Was she giving him a warning? Was a platonic relationship the best he could hope for?

He decided that at this point in time he would be happy with that. 'What if we don't call it a date?' he suggested. 'We don't need to be specific, and I don't need to take a partner, but it seems a shame for the ticket to go to waste.'

'Isn't there anyone else you could offer it to?'

'Probably,' he admitted. 'But I'd like you to come. I promise not to kiss you again,' he added, hoping to reassure her even as he desperately hoped she would welcome another kiss. 'It's a fundraiser for the Deaf Society. I organised the table to support Niki. If you don't want to come for my sake, will you come for his?'

'You're not playing fair.'

'Maybe not. But I think you'd enjoy yourself. You've got my number. Think about it and let me know.'

He didn't want to pressure her, but he really wanted her to say yes.

CHAPTER SEVEN

AJAY PICKED UP his phone when it rang. He looked at
the photo that appeared on the screen and smiled as he
answered the call and heard his sister's voice.

'Hey, big brother.'

'Hello, Asha,' he greeted her. 'How are you?'

'Good. I want to know how *you* are. I just spoke to
Mum and she told me Niki's surgery is scheduled for
Monday. I didn't realise it was so soon. I thought Mum
and Dad were going over for the surgery, but Mum said
that isn't happening. Are you okay with that?'

'It's fine,' Ajay told her. 'The surgery was brought
forward, and Mum and Dad didn't have time to arrange
a locum for the clinic. The surgery isn't major. Mum
will try to come a few weeks later, to be here when the
processor gets turned on.'

'A few weeks? He won't hear straight away?'

'No. It's a two-step process,' he explained, not for
the first time.

'Tell me again how it works?'

Asha lived in Los Angeles. She was a script writer,
married to a movie director. He knew understanding
medical procedures was not something she had to trou-

ble herself with unless it was something that occurred on screen.

'The first step is putting the implants in,' he told her. 'That's done under anaesthetic. The surgeon will make a small incision behind each of Niki's ears and place the implants under the skin. Then he'll drill a couple of tiny holes to allow him to insert an electrode into the inner ear.'

'Ouch. That sounds painful.'

'Apparently it's not too bad,' Ajay said. 'The wound will be closed with stitches, his head will be wrapped to prevent infection, and that's the first part done. It's not major surgery. It only takes a couple of hours and he'll be out on the same day.'

'But he won't be able to hear?'

'Not at that stage. They'll test the implants during the initial surgery, to make sure they're working, but they get paired with a sound processor and activated once the wound has healed. So that's usually a few weeks later.'

'And that will be around the same time as his birthday?'

'Yes.' Ajay was pleased with the timing of the surgery. It would serve as a distraction on the day of Niki's birthday.

He had conflicted feelings about the day. He'd become a father and a widower on that same day. It was still a difficult concept to get his head around—although he hoped, with time, that his guilt would ease and he'd be able to separate his feelings and celebrate the day properly. For Niki's sake.

'I'll let you know how he goes with the surgery on

Monday,' he said to his sister, 'but right now I've got to run.'

'Where are you off to?'

'A fundraising ball at the Opera House.'

'That sounds fancy. Who are you going with?'

'People from work.'

'Work? I thought you promised to make more of an effort this year. To try to be a little more fun.'

'It's only January—give me time.'

He thought about telling Asha about Daisy, before deciding to keep his own counsel. He knew Asha would approve, but he kept silent for two reasons. Firstly, he didn't know what was happening between them yet, and it was far too early to be putting his feelings into words, and secondly, he knew Asha would be straight on the phone to their mother, and he did not need her getting any ideas. It wasn't as if he was going to marry Daisy—he had no plans to get married again—but he knew he had no way of explaining that to his mother.

He said goodbye to his sister, picked up his dinner jacket and went to collect Daisy.

Ajay stepped out of the limousine and straightened his bow tie, even though he knew it was already perfectly straight, and tugged at his shirt-cuffs. He couldn't remember the last time he'd been this nervous.

He rang Daisy's doorbell and waited for her to answer. His nervousness doubled when she opened the door.

She looked incredible. She wore a pale blue dress the colour of her eyes—the colour he'd told her she should wear often—and he wondered if she'd chosen it because of his compliment. The bodice of the dress was covered with hundreds of tiny sequins that sparkled in the light, and it had a full skirt that floated around her legs as she moved. She had small silver daisy earrings in her ears, but otherwise wore no jewellery. She didn't need any other adornment.

She turned to pick up a small silver purse from the hall table and Ajay caught his breath, glad for the first time that Daisy couldn't hear him. While the front of her dress was fairly demure, the back was something else altogether. It plunged to her waist, revealing the length of her spine and highlighting her amazing shoulder blades, toned from surfing, and the small of her back.

He'd never realised that a woman's back could be so sexy. He clenched his fists by his sides, stopping himself from reaching out to rest his hand on her skin, stopping himself from tracing the curve of her spine with his fingers.

Her hair had been pulled back in a loose knot at the base of her neck and a few loose tendrils curled softly around her face. She looked stunning, and he really wished he hadn't promised not to kiss her. There was nothing he felt more like doing at that moment, but he restrained himself, offering a compliment instead.

'You look beautiful.' He signed the words as he spoke them.

'Thank you. I didn't know you knew how to sign that,' she said as he took her hand to help her down the two small steps from the front door to the path and the street.

His driver was standing by the car, the door open, and Ajay helped her into the waiting limousine, letting the driver close Daisy's door as he went to the opposite side.

'I've been practising,' he said as he clicked his seat belt into place. 'I thought that would be a good phrase to learn, and I hoped I'd be able to get away with a compliment even on a non-date.'

Daisy smiled. 'You're having Auslan lessons?'

'I thought it was important, given what you told me about your experience with the implants and your hearing journey. If Niki decides he doesn't like the implants then I want to make sure we still have a way to communicate.'

'So Niki will learn Auslan too?'

'Yes. But tonight we are not talking about Niki or his surgery or work. I want tonight to be about having a good time,' he said as he poured her a glass of champagne and handed it to her.

He was looking forward to the evening, even if Daisy had insisted that it wasn't a date. It had been a long time since he'd looked forward to anything. When he'd organised the table for the fundraiser he'd done so out of a sense of obligation, but now he couldn't think of anything else he'd rather be doing than attending the event with this gorgeous woman by his side.

The limousine joined the queue of chauffeur-driven cars delivering guests to the Opera House. The building's sails were golden in the early-evening light, the sun setting in the west reflecting off the thousands and thousands of small tiles that covered the sails. Lights glowed from within the iconic building, in readiness for the night's event.

Their driver opened the door and Ajay stepped out. He turned and offered Daisy his hand. She slid her own

hand into his and let him help her out of the vehicle.
Flashlights popped as photographers snapped pictures
of the guests. Ajay could see plenty of celebrities—
actors from the stage and screen, sports stars, business tycoons and politicians rubbed shoulders, and the
paparazzi jostled for the best position to capture their
images.

Daisy blinked and hesitated beside him. 'I feel like
Cinderella arriving at the ball,' she said.

He gave her a moment to look around and take it
all in. Close to seven hundred people were expected
at the event, and he knew the numbers could be overwhelming.

Then he tucked her hand into the crook of his elbow
and said, 'Ready?'

She nodded and smiled up at him, and let him lead
her to the steps. A red carpet tumbled down the centre
of the stairs and they joined the procession of guests
making their way up to the Opera House.

Daisy paused when they reached the top to look up
at the sails that seemed to unfurl above their heads. She
reached out and ran one hand over the small diamond-
shaped mosaic tiles that covered the sails.

Ajay had noticed on several occasions how tactile
Daisy was. She was constantly touching things. He
imagined she used her other senses to compensate for
her loss of hearing. She touched him often, usually on
the arm—probably a habit she'd adopted to make sure
people looked at her when they spoke to her.

'I didn't realise the sails were tiled.'

'No?'

She shook her head. 'I've never been to anything

at the Opera House before. I've never even set foot inside it.'

That surprised him. 'Really? Why not?'

'It seemed like a touristy thing to do. And opera and plays are not really my scene. Following someone signing during a live performance is difficult. It's often only possible to watch the stage or the interpreter—not both. So one way or the other I miss what's happening.'

Her comment reminded him again of what life without hearing must be like. There were so many things he hadn't considered when he'd thought about the impact of a hearing impairment on someone's day-to-day life, and he was pleased he'd decided to book Niki's cochlear implant procedure. Hopefully that would make a difference to him. But for now he was going to focus on Daisy.

He loved the Opera House; he thought the building was magnificent and the architecture fascinated him. He'd assumed every Sydneysider would have visited it at some point, even just to walk around it, but he was pleased to know that he was the one who would share this experience with her.

'I look forward to hearing what you think, then,' he said as they stepped inside and made their way to the event space.

Daisy paused, as if soaking in her surroundings as she took in the view of the harbour and the famous bridge through the large windows. Ajay collected two glasses of champagne from a passing waiter and they watched green and yellow ferries and sailboats of all sizes criss-crossing the water before making their way into the function room.

He introduced Daisy to the other guests at their

table—colleagues and friends from his previous job, the people he should have spent New Year's Eve with— and asked one of them to take a photograph so he could prove to his sister that he had actually gone out.

The evening ran like clockwork. Meals were served, auctions were run and speeches given. Everyone on their table appeared to be enjoying themselves, but even though he knew them well, he couldn't help wishing that he and Daisy were in a quiet restaurant at a table for two.

He'd noticed the eyes of every man in the room turn to her when she'd entered, looking at her in admiration, and a fair number of the women's eyes had too—although they might have been a little envious. Ajay couldn't blame them, but he wanted to keep her to himself. Daisy was stunning. She glowed, effervescent, ethereal, as if sprinkled with the fairy dust that Lily had spoken about, and the more time he spent with her the more he believed it.

The formalities were over now. The speeches were finished and the silent auction had ended. Ajay had made the winning bid on a night's accommodation at Taronga Park Zoo, in one of their new habitat rooms overlooking the koala enclosure. He'd bid way over the reserve price, but he knew it would be worth it. Niki would love it.

He returned to the table after paying for the auction item and felt his heart skip a beat when he saw Daisy sitting there, knowing she was there with *him*. But as he got nearer he saw that her brow was a little furrowed, her expression tired.

'Are you okay?' he asked.

'My brain needs a rest,' she said. 'I might just go for a walk. It's tiring, trying to follow all the conversations.'

He felt terrible. He hadn't thought about how hard it would be for her, sitting at a table with nine other people and trying to keep up with multiple conversations that she couldn't hear. The fact that he recalled she'd previously pointed out the issue to him, on the hospital rooftop, and still he'd forgotten made him feel even worse.

He vowed to do better when it came to understanding her difficulties. He needed to do better for Daisy and, in the future, for Niki too.

The band had been playing quietly during dinner, unobtrusive background music, but now they began another set with a quicker, more upbeat tempo.

'Would you like to dance?' he offered, thinking she might enjoy that more than a walk.

'I don't dance. I can't dance,' she replied. 'I can't hear the music.'

'You don't need to hear it. You can follow me.'

'You can dance?'

'I think so.' He grinned, trying to relax her with humour. 'I had a boys' boarding school education, remember? Along with cricket, rugby and French lessons, they thought teaching us how to dance would be a useful skill to have.'

'And is it?'

'I'll let you know in a minute,' he said, and he held out his hand to her, inviting her to accept his offer.

Daisy stood and put her hand in his. His fingers closed around hers and the warmth of his hand flowed up her arm and spread through her like wildfire. Despite the heat, little goosebumps rose on her skin, and the contrast of hot and cold perfectly captured the turmoil inside her—the juxtaposition between right and wrong, between her head and her heart.

She was conflicted in so many ways, but this was the reason she'd said yes to his invitation tonight. Because of the way he made her feel. The way the touch of his hand, his smile, his kiss, lit a fire inside her. She wanted that feeling, and so she had made a choice and accepted his invitation.

She knew she could always justify something if she wanted it enough, and she wanted to spend time with Ajay. It didn't have to be anything more than an enjoyable evening. She didn't need to worry about the future—she could enjoy the way he made her feel and then move on.

She was looking for her person—the one who would fill the hole left by Willow—but she didn't have to find him right now. It didn't have to be Ajay. She was only twenty-three. She had time. And therefore there was no reason why she shouldn't enjoy his company. They could spend some time together. She didn't have to marry him. She didn't have to take on a child.

The whole night had had a dreamlike quality about it. She was out of her league amongst these rich and influential Sydneysiders who could afford to drop thousands of dollars on hosted dinner parties, chartered yachts and flights over Antarctica. She completely understood how Cinderella had felt, and she'd been worried she'd be spotted as an imposter and have to flee on the stroke of midnight.

But now Ajay had taken her hand and she forgot about not belonging, not fitting in. She forgot about all the other guests, their money and their fancy lives. Ajay's touch centred her, focused her, and took her mind off everything else as he led her to the dance floor. There was no room in her head for anything else other than the way her hand felt wrapped up in his. The way her fingers slid between his and her body swayed instinctively towards him.

His hold was light, gentle and reassuring. She felt safe. But that still didn't mean she felt as though she could dance.

He sensed her hesitation and put the fingers of his free hand under her chin. He tipped her face up to look at him and said, 'Trust me. I've got you.'

He pulled her closer. His hand was in the small of her back, holding her close. It was warm on her bare skin and she could feel every millimetre of his fingers pressed against her. Her heels made her several inches taller, and her head tucked beneath his collarbone. She fitted there perfectly.

There were other couples on the dance floor, and their lips moved in silent conversation as they danced to music she couldn't hear. She let her other senses guide her instead. She breathed in, inhaling the scent of his freshly laundered shirt and his aftershave, which was a heady blend of sandalwood and bergamot.

The dress she'd borrowed from Mei's sister-in-law, Su-Lin, floated around her. Daisy had never worn anything as beautiful. The bodice was heavy—the front was encrusted with hundreds of shimmering sequins—but the back dipped low, exposing the skin on her spine, which tingled under the touch of Ajay's slim fingers. The skirt of the dress was gossamer-light…like wisps of cloud brushing across her skin.

She couldn't hear the music or the other guests. All her information was visual, olfactory and tactile. She closed her eyes, but then she was overwhelmed. She felt as if she was floating, but the heat of Ajay's hand and the lightness of his touch left her powerless, defenceless, and she wasn't sure if she liked it.

She opened her eyes and stumbled, treading indelicately on his toes. She looked up at him. His eyes were dark, but she felt their immediate and now familiar connection.

'Don't think,' he said. 'Lean into me...feel the music through me. One, two, three... One, two, three...'

She rested her head on his chest and felt his heart beating against her cheek. *One, two, three... One, two, three...*

She closed her eyes again and concentrated on the beat of his heart and the rise and fall of his chest. She matched her rhythm to his and wondered if this was what it would feel like to make love to him.

Would they match?

Would they find their rhythm?

After her initial stumble she relaxed, and eventually she felt as if she belonged in his arms. They danced together for the rest of the night, but Daisy felt she could have danced until sunrise.

But the night had to end, and now Ajay had taken her home and was walking her to her door.

She was aware of him as the sleeve of his shirt brushed her arm as they walked up the steps. She turned to face him. She was standing close enough that she could feel the heat of his body rising off him.

She looked up at him. 'Thank you for inviting me to the ball. I had a fabulous night.'

She didn't want the night to end. She was a conflicting mess of emotions. They'd agreed to a platonic evening, but her feelings on the dance floor had been anything but. Would she be making a mistake to take things a step further? Could they have a fling, knowing that they had no future?

Perhaps if they agreed on some boundaries, some rules, they could. Perhaps it wasn't impossible. Not if they both agreed. She could give herself a time limit. A few weeks. Long enough to scratch the itch but not long enough to fall in love.

She took a chance and asked, 'Would you like to come in?'

He ran a hand through his curls as he briefly closed his eyes. When he opened them they were dark, and his expression was tortured as he replied, 'Believe me, I'd love to, but I can't. Mrs Singh is going to visit her sister tomorrow, so I'll be up early with Niki. And, more importantly, I made a promise to you, and I don't know if I can keep it if I come in.'

She wasn't sure she *wanted* him to keep his promise any more. She was sorely tempted to tell him to forget about it. To kiss her again. But before she could say anything his fingers were under her chin and his touch left her speechless.

'Thank you for keeping me company,' he said as he tilted her chin up.

Daisy held her breath, wondering if he was going to break his promise after all, but his lips just brushed her cheek in a light, feather touch, before he smiled and walked away, leaving her tormented and unfulfilled.

But she knew she only had herself to blame.

She went to bed alone, wishing she'd been brave

enough to hold on to him, to pull him back to her and kiss him goodnight.

She felt like Cinderella—the night had been like a dream, but at the end of the day she was home alone, without her prince...

'How was the ball?' Poppy asked when Daisy arrived for dinner.

Amazing,' she replied, unable to keep the smile off her face.

'You look like you enjoyed yourself. Have you got any photos?'

She showed Poppy the photo of her with Ajay. The one he had sent to his sister.

'You look gorgeous,' Poppy said as Jet and Ryder waked through the door, 'and Ajay looks pretty fine too. You make a good looking couple.'

Daisy thought they looked good together too. Ajay's dark hair and eyes were a striking contrast to her fairness. They were standing close together, looking at the camera, not touching, but Daisy knew that a few hours later they had been much, much closer. She had been in his arms, held against his chest as they'd danced, and the memory made her blush.

She took her phone back from Poppy and looked around the room, eager to find another topic of conversation before her tell-tale blush invited questions. 'Isn't Lily coming?' she asked. She'd thought all four siblings were having dinner together, but the table was only set for four.

'No,' Poppy replied. 'I need to ask your opinion on something and I don't want Lily to know.'

'What is it?' Jet asked.

Daisy clasped her hands together beneath her chin and brought her fingers to her mouth. She could only imagine one secret Poppy would want to keep from Lily. One secret that could shatter Lily's fragile heart.

'Are you pregnant?'

'What? No!' Poppy exclaimed.

But Daisy was pleased to notice that neither Poppy nor Ryder looked horrified at the idea. Perhaps another niece or nephew would be on the way before long. She hoped so. Daisy loved being an aunt to An Na, but she regretted that she'd missed An Na's baby years and was eager to welcome more nieces and nephews into her life—babies and children she could love without having to raise them, could love without worrying she would fail them.

'I want to invite Otto to our wedding, and I need to know if you think that is a good or a bad idea.'

'Oh.' Daisy hadn't expected that, but she could understand why Poppy might want her and Jet's input. It could be a tricky situation. Given that, by the time of the wedding in March, it would be almost two years since Lily had returned from the UK, it would be almost two years since Lily had seen her husband, and none of them really knew what the situation was.

Lily didn't talk about him—or only very rarely. They weren't divorced but they were definitely separated, living on opposite sides of the globe. The pandemic had added an extra layer of complexity to their relationship, but even without that it was difficult to know where things stood.

'He's still family after all,' Poppy added. 'And maybe this could be the catalyst that gets them back together.

It would give Otto a reason to come home. It certainly doesn't look as if Lily is going to ask him to.'

'Do you think she wants to?' Jet asked.

Poppy nodded. 'I think so, but I think she's afraid of what will happen if he says no. Despite everything, I don't think she's ready to let go of the relationship. Of him. I think she's still hoping for a miracle, but she's scared of reaching out to him. Scared of being rejected.'

'Well, neither of them has mentioned divorce, which is a positive sign,' Jet said.

'Lily hasn't. How do you know what Otto is thinking?' Daisy asked, wondering how Jet could make that statement.

'I've spoken to him.'

'What? When?' Daisy and Poppy both spoke up.

'We speak every couple of months. He calls to check in.'

'Why haven't you told us this before?'

Jet shrugged. 'There are lots of things I don't tell you. It didn't seem important. It's good to know that he still cares, but he doesn't want Lily to know he's checking up on her.'

'I'd forgotten how good you are at keeping counsel,' Daisy said.

'I hadn't,' said Poppy. 'I haven't forgotten that you didn't tell me Ryder was in Sydney.'

Jet laughed. 'You might also remember that, for one, I never knew about your history with my best friend, so you're just as good at keeping secrets as I am—probably better—and, two, you had a boyfriend at the time. So, again, it didn't seem important to tell you that Ryder was here.'

'I haven't forgotten but I have forgiven you,' Poppy

said to Jet, before she leant across to kiss Ryder. 'It's turned out perfectly—which is why I want to help Lily and Otto find their way back together, if that's what they want.'

'Otto hasn't found anyone else?' Daisy asked, crossing her fingers under the table, hoping to hear Jet say no.

'No. I don't think he wants to,' Jet replied.

Daisy let out a sigh of relief. She knew Lily hadn't looked once at anyone else, let alone twice, since coming back from London.

'Is Otto Lily's person?' Ryder asked, making his first contribution to the conversation.

'Definitely,' Poppy said.

'How do you know?' Daisy asked, looking around the table at Jet, Poppy and Ryder, all of whom had found their true love. 'How did you all know you'd found your person? Was it love at first sight?'

'Probably not that instantaneous,' Jet admitted. 'I travelled the world thinking I would find what Mei and I had had many more times, not realising what we'd had was rare. At first it's just a sense that there's something special about this person. A sense of knowing them even if they're a stranger. A sense of them knowing *you*. You don't recognise it as love. I didn't, at least. Not until later. I am content when I am with her— complete. And I know things will be okay while we're together. She makes the world better, brighter, bigger.'

Daisy didn't realise she was nodding until she became aware of Poppy watching her closely. 'Is that how you feel about Ajay?' she asked. 'Are things serious between the two of you?'

'No. We had a good time last night, but he won't be the one.'

'How do you know?' Jet asked.

'How did *you* know that Mei was the one?' Daisy countered.

Jet and Poppy had both ended up with their first loves. Did Mei and Ryder tick all their boxes, or were some things more important than others? Ajay didn't tick all *her* boxes, but she couldn't pretend she'd ever felt like this before. When he'd held her in his arms she'd felt as if she was where she belonged, but that thought terrified her. She'd spent too many years convincing herself that she couldn't…*shouldn't* be a mother, and therefore she knew she couldn't have a future with Ajay.

She just hoped that there was more than one person in the world for everybody.

'Experience,' Jet replied. 'Experience taught me that it was special—that *she* was special. When I was twenty if thought there would be a thousand girls who would make me feel the way Mei did. But I was wrong. There were plenty whose company I enjoyed, but none who made me feel that I'd come home. I never felt that connection with anyone else. Mei and An Na are everything to me. They hold my soul, my happiness and my life in their hands.'

'Do you think it's like that for everyone? If you hadn't found Mei, do you think you would have fallen in love with anyone else? Is there only one person for each of us?'

'I don't think so…but there is the best one.'

'Would you like me to add Ajay to the guest list,

Daisy? He's more than welcome at our wedding,' Poppy said.

'No,' Daisy replied with a shake of her head. 'Not yet.' She knew that would be taking a step she wasn't ready for. 'And we still haven't answered the question of what to do about Otto. He will have finished his fellowship. He could come home… And maybe he does need a reason.'

Poppy nodded. 'I think we should invite him,' she said. 'I think he and Lily need some gentle persuasion. Jet, do you think he will come?'

'I think there's a good chance. He would have come home before now, but Covid made things difficult. Now that he's finished studying and is fully vaccinated it should be easier.'

'Excellent!' Poppy clapped her hands with excitement. 'Decision made,' she said.

Daisy drifted off into a daydream of Lily and Otto back together, living happily ever after, and of her with Ajay, dancing at Poppy and Ryder's wedding…

CHAPTER EIGHT

AJAY WAS GRIPPING the railing in front of him so hard his knuckles had turned white. Daisy could understand that watching his son undergo surgery must be difficult, but Niki's scheduled operation—stage one of the cochlear implants—was relatively minor, and no serious complications were anticipated.

He had asked her to keep him company while Niki was in Theatre, and she hadn't hesitated to offer her support, but she certainly hadn't expected him to be wound so tightly. He was far more tense than Daisy would have expected, and she was at a loss as to why that should be the case.

They were standing above the operating theatre, looking down on the scene through the windows of the viewing area. Niki was covered in sterile sheets, and all that was visible of him was the side of his head and one ear, covered in orange antiseptic paint.

She wondered why Ajay had insisted on watching the surgery if he was going to find it so stressful. Perhaps she should suggest that they go and get some fresh air.

'Ajay, shall we go for a walk? You might feel better if you take a break.'

The surgery was going to last two hours, and Ajay had already been standing, watching intently for almost an hour.

'No. I can't leave him.'

'What's bothering you?' she asked. 'I imagine watching your child go through surgery isn't easy, but the operation itself is fairly routine, and you and I both know that Trent is an excellent surgeon.'

'I can't leave him,' he repeated. 'If something happens to him I'll blame myself.'

'Nothing's going to happen.'

'You can't guarantee that. And I've made the wrong decision before.'

'When?' Daisy frowned.

'The day I lost Priya. I can't go through another day like that,' he said as he shook his head.

'Like what?'

He ran his fingers through his hair—something Daisy had noticed he always did when he was thinking deeply.

'I still don't know how to describe that day. It was the best and worst day of my life. It sounds impossible, but it's true. I lost Priya on the day Niki was born.'

Ajay hadn't talked much about his wife, and he'd never mentioned how she'd died. Had Priya died in an accident? In childbirth? From a medical episode?

'Ajay, that must have been horrific,' Daisy said. 'Was it to do with her pregnancy or something else?'

'Her pregnancy was perfect. And Niki was perfect too. Priya was healthy and strong all through her pregnancy and she delivered Niki a little prematurely but safely. She was holding him, and then all of a sudden she went pale and her blood pressure dropped abruptly.

Some of what happened next is a blur, but other parts are still so vivid. A nurse snatched Niki from Priya—I remember that. I was standing there, frozen, trying to make sense of what I was seeing, and the midwife grabbed Niki—ripped him out of Priya's arms before we knew what was going on And then there was blood. So much blood... I was pushed out of the way. Then I was holding Niki. I don't even remember the midwife handing him to me. The bed rails were pulled up and then Priya was being wheeled out of the room, whisked off to Theatre. I'll never forget the look on her face. She looked terrified. She told me to take care of Niki. Told me she loved us. I could see in her eyes that she was scared. I think she knew she wasn't going to make it. I don't remember answering. I think I nodded. I didn't even have time to kiss her. I should have gone with her. I shouldn't have let her go alone. I couldn't fathom that she wouldn't come back.'

Daisy understood now why Ajay was refusing to leave Niki.

'Her uterus had ruptured during the delivery. It's extremely rare, and even at the time I didn't consider the possibility that that was what was happening. Afterwards no one could explain *why* it had happened, and that just made it more difficult to accept. I'm grateful that Niki survived—there's usually a risk to the baby in these cases—but there's no way I'm going to leave him alone on that operating table. I promised Priya I would take care of him.'

Daisy put her hand on his arm, trying to reassure him through touch. 'It's okay, Ajay. I get it. And I'll wait with you until you can see him in Recovery.'

Ajay and Niki's tale was a tragic one. Daisy had her

own history of tragedy, but to have Niki's birth tied to his mother's death must be an incredibly hard thing for Ajay to live with.

'At least I can tell Niki that his mother's last words to him were "I love you". We didn't know at the time that Niki wouldn't have been able to hear her. We didn't know that he'd never hear his mother's voice.'

Daisy heart ached for Ajay and for Niki. Ajay had clearly loved Priya, and she could understand now why he was so terrified—why he was so fearful that something would go wrong. She understood all too well that just because something was out of your control it didn't stop the fear or the guilt when things went wrong.

She squeezed his arm gently, offering comfort in the only way she could. 'This will be all over soon, and Niki will be home with you before you know it.'

'Which brings me to another problem,' he replied. 'What to do with Niki at home.'

'What do you mean? You'll need to keep him quiet for a few days, keep his bandages dry, and he might need some pain relief. But he won't need any special care.'

'I know all that, but Mrs Singh needs time off. Remember when she went to visit her sister?'

Daisy nodded. 'The day after the ball.'

'Her sister is undergoing heart surgery—nothing major, but she needs someone to stay with her for a while post-op, and Mrs Singh is it. Which means I'll have to organise leave from the hospital—which might be tricky, seeing as I've only been there less than three months.'

'I can help you,' Daisy offered. 'I have some rostered days off coming up.'

'Thank you, but I'm sure there must be something you'd rather do if you have time off.'

'Not really. I don't have any plans.'

'Are you sure? I know you enjoy paediatrics, but I didn't think you were keen on looking after children outside of the hospital.'

'I don't mind temporary responsibility,' she said. 'I do it often enough with An Na. There's not too much I can mess up in that regard.'

'It's not that I don't appreciate your offer, but I don't want you to use your days off.'

'I'm happy to help. And you have to agree it makes sense. Niki already knows me, and I understand his disability. I can manage his post-op wound care and I can teach him some more sign language. It's only for a few days and I can work around your schedule. I'll be able to look after Niki when you're at work.'

Her role would be like that of an au pair or a nanny. Not a mother. And she couldn't deny the idea of spending extra time with Ajay wasn't without appeal.

'If you're sure, that would be amazing.'

'I'm sure,' she reiterated.

Ajay was looking forward to getting home. It was his first day back at work since Niki's surgery, and Daisy's first day of minding Niki. She had visited each day following Niki's surgery, and the two of them had already established a good relationship. He knew Niki was perfectly happy to be at home with her. She had an affinity with children, and even though they couldn't hear each other it was obvious that Niki had taken to her.

He, on the other hand, had taken a little longer to adjust to Daisy's presence in his house. Other than his sister, his mother and Mrs Singh, no other woman had been in the house since Priya's death, and it had been a little unsettling at first to see Daisy there.

He'd returned from the shops one day and she had been sitting on the couch with Niki on her lap while she read to him, showing him the pictures in a lift-the-flap book. Seeing his son curled up in Daisy's embrace had tugged at his heart strings. It hadn't been unpleasant, but it had made him a little regretful. Niki had never had the chance to sit with his mother like that, or to have his mother read to him, hug him or kiss him, and it reinforced to Ajay what was missing in Niki's life.

Not that Ajay was looking to replace Priya. He wasn't thinking about remarrying. After losing Priya he wasn't willing to risk going through anything like that again, but he'd be lying if he said he wasn't looking forward to having some adult company.

Daisy's company.

He loved his son more than anything in the world, but he was looking forward to seeing Daisy and to spending time with her without interruption.

He had hoped to be home hours ago, and having his shift go well over time on Daisy's first day alone with Niki wasn't ideal. He had messaged her to let her know he'd been delayed, and he was hoping she had waited up for him.

He knew that was one reason he'd accepted her offer of help. He was keen to have her under the same roof. Keen to see if they could take their relationship past the platonic stage. His few dates in the past two years had satisfied his sexual needs without forming any personal connection. It was different with Daisy, and he was starting to think that perhaps she could put

some enjoyment back into his life—both in and out
of the bedroom.

The stair lights leading from the garage to the first-
floor living area were on, but the lounge room was in
darkness. Had Daisy already gone to bed?

He sighed, disappointed, and went to check on Niki
before reheating something for dinner.

Niki's door was open and light spilled into the passage. The light was much brighter than his usual night
light.

Ajay stepped into the room and found Daisy, tucked
into the occasional chair in the corner of Niki's room,
reading. Why was she in there? His immediate thought
was that Niki must be unwell. But why hadn't she messaged him?

She looked up, obviously having detected his movement from the corner of her eye.

'What's wrong? Is something the matter with Niki?'
he asked.

She shook her head and stood up, marking the page
in the book. He bent to kiss Niki's forehead, and followed her out to the kitchen.

'So, Niki is fine? No dramas?' he double-checked
as Daisy opened the fridge.

'No dramas. We had a good day—a great day,' she
said with a smile.

He saw she had left a plate of food for him in the
fridge. She pulled it out, uncovered it and popped it
into the microwave to reheat. He took a bottle of wine
from the kitchen bench. He offered her a glass, but
she declined in favour of herbal tea. He poured himself some wine and they moved around the kitchen

in synchronicity, as if it was something they'd done a thousand times before.

'Why were you reading in his room?' he asked when she'd handed him his plate and carried her cup of tea to the couch.

'I went to bed and then I realised I wouldn't hear Niki if he needed me.'

'He has a baby monitor.'

'That's fine during the day, because it lights up when it makes a sound so that draws my attention, but if my eyes are closed…'

He got it then. He was an idiot. 'Daisy, I am so sorry. I didn't even think.'

'It's okay. I don't expect you to think of everything. It's not an issue for you. But I was worried that I wouldn't know if Niki needed me, and also, if there was any other emergency, I might not know about that either until it was too late.'

'What sort of emergency?'

'If the smoke alarm went off, for instance, I wouldn't hear that.'

'You'd wake with the smell of smoke.'

'Possibly. But by then it's often too late. People die in house fires all the time. I have a responsibility to Niki to keep him safe.'

'No.' He shook his head. 'It's *my* responsibility to make sure both of you are safe.'

'It's not your fault. And I didn't want to go to bed. I should have thought of it before. It didn't really matter—it just meant I stayed up.'

He felt terrible that she'd felt unsafe in his house, and wondered what she normally did. 'What do you do at home? Surely it's the same situation when you're by yourself?'

She shook her head. 'I have a bed shaker alarm.'

'A what?'

'It's a monitor that's connected to the smoke alarm. It has a pad that goes under the mattress, and if the smoke alarm goes off it triggers the monitor. That sets off a strobe light and also the pad. That vibrates and shakes the mattress. That wakes me up,' she explained.

That sounded like a simple yet perfect solution. 'I'll go and fetch it for you tomorrow,' he offered.

'I can get it.'

'I know. But I want you to feel safe. You're taking care of Niki, let me take care of you.'

She was touched that he'd offered but she could manage. 'Thanks, but you're going to work. Niki and I are meeting Mei and An Na for a milkshake tomorrow. I'll get it while we're out,' she replied, breaking into a yawn as she finished speaking.

She'd been too nervous to go to bed. She'd been terrified that something might happen to Niki on her watch, and she knew she wouldn't sleep anyway—wouldn't be able to sleep—while she was alone in the house. Niki was her responsibility tonight, just as Willow had been her parents' responsibility. But, unlike her parents, Daisy was going to make sure nothing went wrong.

So she'd stayed up because she knew she wouldn't sleep, but also because she'd wanted to see Ajay. It was silly—she was sure he hadn't expected her to—but she was glad she had.

'Time for bed,' he said now, as he stood to clear the dishes.

She was tired, but reluctant to get up, and nervous about going back to bed. Which was unwarranted. Ajay was home now—she knew she'd be safe.

'Would you like me to stay with you?' he asked, sensing her hesitation. 'Would you feel safe then?'

'You'll come to bed with me?' she asked. If that was what he was offering, then *yes* and *yes*.

'If you're nervous about going to sleep we can always stay awake for a little longer.'

She looked up at him to see him smiling. She almost lost herself in the dark depths of his chocolate-brown eyes. But what was he suggesting? What was she seconds away from consenting to? It would be as simple as nodding…as natural as moving an infinitesimal degree closer to the warmth of his body.

He held out his hand.

'What are we doing?' she asked.

'Whatever you want,' he replied. 'I want to take you to bed. I want to spend the night with you in my arms. But the choice is yours.'

She knew she could accept his offer. She wanted to spend the night with him and she wasn't going to pretend otherwise. She could share a night with him. It didn't have to be anything more than that. It didn't have to *mean* anything more than that.

She took a deep breath and reached for his hand.

There were always ways to justify a choice.

His fingers closed around hers and then there was no hesitation, no room for questions or doubts. He pulled her to her feet and into his arms and she knew this was where she needed to be, where she was meant to be.

A tremor ran the length of her as his thumb traced her mouth. His fingers rested on the curve of her cheek and she tipped her head backwards as his fingers brushed lightly against the side of her face. Her heart skipped a beat as he bent his head and kissed her. His lips were warm and soft, but commanding. She responded instantly, parting her lips, opening her mouth and her heart to him.

Her eyelids closed and she drifted off into a moment of pure bliss, unable to think of anything beyond the fact that he was making her melt and her limbs now felt like liquid.

She swayed against him and he lifted her into his arms as though she were weightless. He held her firmly against his chest as she nestled her head into his shoulder. She breathed deeply, lost in a sense of awareness and anticipation as his scent surrounded her, cushioning her. She could almost picture the waves of desire that surrounded them, wrapping her in a kaleidoscope of virtual colour.

He carried her along the hall and she felt him nudge his bedroom door open with his foot. She knew he was carrying her to bed, and his step was steady and, oh, so certain. She felt safe. Beautiful. Desirable.

He lowered her to his bed and she opened her eyes, blinking as he switched on the bedside lamp and bathed them both in dim light. He eased himself above her, supported by his arms, and she reached up and ran her hand over his biceps, marvelling at how his muscles rippled as he supported his weight.

She could see the rise and fall of his chest. Her breath was coming fast, as was his. It was warm on her face.

And his gaze was hot and intense and dark as it moved over her.

The waiting was agony, but it was also exquisite.

A delicious sense of anticipation was doing battle with her competing need to pull him down to her and demand him *now*.

'Ajay...'

She whispered his name and her stomach flipped as she recognised the look of desire in his eyes.

He lowered his body until it covered the length of her. She wanted to feel his weight on her, needed to wring every last sensation and know that this was real and happening to *her*.

She felt his lips on her neck, but she needed them on her mouth. She took his face in her hands, placing one hand on each side of his gorgeous face, and kissed him firmly, urging him on, letting him know she was willingly giving herself to him, giving him permission to take her and make her his...

Daisy couldn't remember being this happy in a long time. Even knowing that Mrs Singh was returning in a few days, meaning Daisy would no longer need to stay at Ajay's, couldn't dampen her spirits.

The initial few days had stretched into two weeks, when Mrs Singh's sister had had some post-op complications, but Daisy hadn't minded. She and Ajay had tag-teamed their shifts in order to make it work. When she'd finished her rostered days off she had swapped some of her day shifts with other nurses. She'd enjoyed every minute of looking after Niki, and revelled in every minute she'd spent in Ajay's bed.

Today, the January sun had been shining on them

since they'd left Bondi, enhancing Daisy's mood even further. She smiled as she looked out of the window. Sunlight on the harbour made the water sparkle like silver as they drove across the Harbour Bridge, and it followed them still as they headed for Taronga Zoo on Sydney's north shore.

Ajay rested his hand on her thigh, drawing her attention to him, as the movement had been designed to. She felt the warmth of his palm through the thin cotton of her summer dress and welcomed the accompanying rush of heat that spread up her leg and into her belly. Even through a layer of clothing his touch never failed to excite her.

She turned her head to face him and read his lips as he said, 'You look happy.'

'I am,' she said, as her smile widened. She was about to create another memory with Ajay and Niki, and even though Ajay had bid on this adventure at the silent auction with Niki in mind, Daisy was just as excited about the excursion. 'Did I tell you I haven't visited the zoo since moving to Sydney?'

The zoo had been in line with the Opera House in her mind—somewhere tourists visited—but she was seeing things in a different light through Ajay's eyes. She was seizing any opportunity that involved going somewhere or doing something with him, agreeing to anything that allowed her to spend time with him.

Over the past fortnight she had gradually let her defences down with Ajay and Niki. She hadn't intended to, and she knew it wasn't real life. She was just like a nanny. She didn't have any real responsibility with Niki. She wasn't at risk of mucking things up.

She had been looking for one person to fill the hole

Willow had left in her heart, and had convinced herself that one person was all she needed. But what if she had room for two? Could she do it?

Niki was a delight, and things had gone surprisingly smoothly, but it had only been two weeks and she still wasn't convinced that raising a child was something she had capacity for. But the idea wasn't scaring her as much as it used to and she knew she would miss Ajay and Niki when she moved back to Lily's and no longer saw them every day. It wasn't going to be easy to say goodbye, so she'd vowed to make the most of the time she did have left. Who knew? Perhaps, together, they could find a way forward.

Daisy opened the rear passenger door once Ajay had parked the car. Niki had fallen asleep in his car seat and was stirring sightly now that the vibration of the engine had ceased. She still took care to wake him gently, not wanting to startle him. She unclipped his harness as he opened his eyes. He smiled at her in recognition and Daisy's heart swelled with love. He was such a sweet little boy, inherently good-tempered, and he'd quickly wormed his way into her soul.

Do you want to see the koalas? she signed.

She had taught him the Auslan signs for all the Australian animals when they had been looking through his picture books, getting ready for their overnight visit. He knew kangaroo, wombat, emu—and, of course, his favourite: koala.

Niki smiled and put his arms out, asking to be lifted from his car seat. Daisy picked him up and cuddled him and he wrapped his arms around her neck. She loved the weight of him, his smell, his eagerness to be cuddled. She loved everything about this little boy.

Ajay was unloading Niki's stroller from the boot of his car, along with their overnight bags.

'I'll carry Niki, if you like,' Daisy said, reluctant to put him down, not knowing how many more opportunities she would have to hold him.

He clung to her like a koala joey while Ajay locked the car and piled the bags into the stroller.

'Welcome to Taronga Zoo.' Their guide greeted them at the gate and explained the schedule for their visit as she accompanied them to their room. 'I'll let you settle into your room and then, if you'd like to meet me in the hotel lounge, I'll take you on your tour of the Sanctuary.'

Before she left she went to the curtains and drew them back with a flourish to let the light in. Niki ran to the window as Daisy gasped in delight. Their room had a view across the harbour—Daisy could see the bridge in the distance—but it was what was directly outside the window that had caught their attention. The room looked out over the koala enclosure, and in the tree right in front of them was a koala with a joey.

'This is amazing,' Daisy said, turning to find Ajay grinning delightedly behind her.

Niki was engrossed with the koalas, and it took a fair bit of persuading before they could entice him to leave the room so they could make their way to the Australian animal sanctuary for their tour.

Ajay had organised for an Auslan interpreter to accompany them for Daisy's benefit, enabling her to follow along with the information about the animals, but she was just as happy watching Niki's reaction as they wandered through the enclosure and came face to face with dozens of adorable animals.

They were introduced to Robbie and Wednesday the echidnas, as well as wallabies, pademelons and the koalas. The guide gave Niki a handful of pellets to feed the wallabies, but the obvious highlight for him was feeding eucalyptus leaves to a koala and being allowed to stroke its soft fur.

Niki had held Daisy's hand and dragged her all around the enclosure, delighting in the animals just as Daisy had delighted in seeing his reaction. For a brief moment she'd allowed herself to imagine what it would be like to spend every weekend like this, in the company of Ajay and Niki. As a family.

But she knew it was just a fantasy. She wasn't cut out for a normal family life. She wasn't prepared for the ongoing responsibility.

So she held Niki's hand, and at times Ajay's, and as the afternoon drew to a close, and they'd returned to the hotel for dinner, she knew she'd made some memories. She stored them away to sustain her in the days to come. In the days when she'd find herself alone again.

Niki had finished his meal and was searching his paper placemat intently, trying to find all the animals that were hidden in the illustration of the Australian bush, when the restaurant lights dimmed and the staff brought out a cake with sparklers fizzing on top. They carried the cake over to Niki as they sang 'Happy Birthday'. His eyes were wide as he watched the procession, and even though he couldn't hear the singing he was smiling happily, and when the song finished and he saw everyone clap their hands he joined in vigorously.

The waiter placed the cake on the table in front

of Niki. It had been made in the shape of a koala's head, round with two semi-circular ears. It had been frosted with pale chocolate butter icing, sprinkled with cocoa-dusted coconut to look like fur, and had a large, oval-shaped chocolate biscuit for a nose, with chocolate button eyes and long liquorice lashes.

It was an elaborate cake and Niki was fascinated.

But Daisy was confused. 'It's not his birthday today, is it?' she asked.

Ajay shook his head. 'No. But I can't bring myself to celebrate on the day. I'll have to as he gets older, and understands which day it is, but I want him to have some birthday memories, and I thought that today was as good a day as any. I find it hard to celebrate his birthday, knowing it's the day Priya died.'

'You must have loved her very much,' Daisy said, thinking that Ajay's tale was tragic, but also heartbreakingly romantic.

Priya had been kind, intelligent and beautiful. She had been a good wife and would have been a wonderful mother. He had loved her—of course he had—but he was finding it harder and harder to remember exactly how she had made him feel. How he had felt about her. When he was with Daisy all he could think about was how Daisy made him feel, and his past was receding little by little each day.

'How did you meet her?' Daisy asked. If she'd noticed that he hadn't responded to her previous comment she didn't mention it.

'Through my parents. My mother, actually. And her network. She arranged it.'

'An arranged marriage! People actually do that?'

'It's far more common than you would think. Indian mothers are very partial to the idea. And some people think it's convenient.'

'Convenient!' Daisy was aghast. 'It's not like ducking out to buy a loaf of bread from the service station or ordering a pair of shoes online. Marriage shouldn't be about *convenience*.'

Ajay laughed. 'Relax. I didn't say *I* was looking for convenience. And my marriage wasn't arranged... only facilitated.'

'What does *that* mean?'

Ajay shrugged. 'My mother decided it was time I got married, and it suited me to be introduced to women who were looking to settle down.'

'Couldn't you find your own person?'

'I hadn't met anyone who I could see a future with.'

'But you had dated, yes? Hadn't you ever been in love?'

'Of course I'd dated,' he said, wondering if he should be offended. 'I had girlfriends through med school, but nothing serious. I was focused on my studies. I didn't put a lot of energy into dating. And I didn't marry the first girl I met through my mother. I did have a say in the matter. I wasn't expecting love at first sight, but I was looking for someone I could see a future with. Priya was the one.'

But Ajay didn't want to talk about Priya. He didn't want to think about her either. He only had room in his head for Daisy.

The pull of attraction he felt for Daisy, that immediate reaction he'd had to her—he'd never felt that with Priya. Theirs had been more of a slow burn. Shared ideals, common interests and mutual respect had led to love. With Daisy, he knew he wouldn't have cared even if they'd had nothing in common. There was no way he would have been able to ignore the feelings she stirred in him.

Were those feelings something else he was going to suffer guilt over?

No, he told himself. He was entitled to have feelings for someone else. His only concern was that Daisy had made it clear she wasn't looking for a man like him. A man with a child. She had no interest in an instant family. No interest in a family at all.

He felt a definite physical and emotional connection, but he wasn't about to label his feelings or express them to her. He didn't want to open himself up, to expose himself to rejection or loss. He knew it was going to be hard to let her go, but he would have no choice. He and Daisy didn't have a future.

But they did have a present. So he'd keep his feelings to himself.

He didn't want to talk. He just wanted to take Daisy to bed.

CHAPTER NINE

DAISY SAT BESIDE Ajay in the darkened movie theatre, their hands clasped together and resting in his lap. Daisy had been worried that moving out of Ajay's house and back to Lily's would mean she spent less time with him but, although she wasn't seeing Niki as often, she and Ajay were still spending time together.

They had agreed not to publicise their developing relationship at work—neither of them wanted to be the subject of hospital gossip—but she had no idea where their relationship would ultimately go.

She'd grown fond of Niki, and they'd developed a strong connection, but she still wasn't convinced that she could manage the responsibilities tied to raising a child. She also had no idea what Ajay thought. What did *his* future look like in his mind?

Daisy might have allowed herself to believe that Ajay could be her person, but she'd made it explicitly clear that she wasn't looking for an instant family. Therefore, there was only one way this could go.

She knew she couldn't afford to get any closer to Niki and Ajay. She knew she needed to start to put some distance between them. But she couldn't bring herself to do that yet. She enjoyed his company far too much. So she told herself that a few more days, a few more weeks, wouldn't hurt anybody.

For their date night, Daisy had chosen a movie that was showing as part of the French Film Festival. She needed to watch films with subtitles, and foreign films were guaranteed to have them, so naturally they had become her preference.

She leant against his shoulder as the opening credits ended and the lights dimmed completely, but within a few minutes Ajay became restless.

He released her hand and she saw the screen of his mobile phone light up as he pulled it from his pocket. He'd had several text messages from Mrs Singh during the course of the evening—Niki had been running a slight temperature and Daisy had initially thought Ajay might cancel their date—but it was the final night of the festival, and he'd seemed happy enough to let Mrs Singh give Niki paracetamol and monitor him while they went out.

But this time it wasn't a text message, Daisy realised as she saw Ajay stand and swipe his screen to answer the call as he strode up the aisle without a backward glance.

Her heart skipped a beat. What was so important that he was answering the call? Was it Niki?

She stood and hurried after him, following him out of the theatre. She found him standing on the footpath, facing her, and she read his lips as she approached.

I'm on my way.

He shoved his phone into his pocket and said to her, 'I need to go. Niki's temperature is thirty-nine point four degrees, and he's not responding to paracetamol.'

'I'll come with you.'

'No. You should stay and watch the movie.'

Why on earth would she want to do that? she wondered.

'I can manage,' Ajay continued. 'He's my responsibility.'

That stopped Daisy in her tracks. He was dismissing her. She wasn't required.

It shouldn't hurt—she had made it very clear that she didn't want the responsibility—so how could she blame him for not sharing it with her? She knew she couldn't. But that didn't stop the sharp pain of rejection that cut through her. To find herself so easily and quickly relegated to the sidelines was a blow she hadn't expected.

'Can you get a taxi home?' Ajay asked without apology. 'I don't have time to drop you off.'

Daisy nodded, dumbfounded. What else could she do? What else could she say?

Nothing. There was nothing she could say, and in the blink of an eye Ajay was gone. Leaving her standing on the footpath in front of the cinema, feeling like she'd been discarded. Feeling unwanted, unneeded and unimportant.

She closed her eyes, blinking back the tears, as an image of his face appeared on the back of her eyelids, his words repeating to her.

'He's my responsibility.'

Reminding her that she hadn't wanted any responsibility.

'He's my responsibility.'

Telling her she wasn't required.

'He's my responsibility.'

Making it clear he was choosing Niki over her.

Not for one moment would she expect him to put her before his son, but to know he didn't need her, didn't want her to be part of this, hurt her deeply.

Knowing he could so quickly and completely shut her out was soul-destroying. She'd pretended that she didn't want to become part of his life, that he wasn't the man for her, but as he'd walked away and left her standing there, alone, she'd realised that wasn't true.

He was her person. But, just as she'd feared, he was abandoning her.

He could have chosen for her to go with him. He could have chosen her as well. Instead he had walked away, leaving her standing there alone, abandoned.

The pain of her past rushed in and collided with the pain of her present, crushing her, destroying her.

Ajay sat beside Niki, sponging his little body, cooling him down. His skin was covered in tiny red pustules, but at least he was sleeping comfortably for the moment. He felt warm to the touch, but not dangerously so, and his temperature, while still elevated, wasn't alarming any more.

Lesley, the nurse, had just read Niki's oxygen levels, blood pressure and temperature, prior to finishing her shift. She had checked his drip and his notes, to see when he was due for more paracetamol, and had now left the room, leaving Ajay alone with his son.

He wondered who would be assigned to take care of Niki for the next shift. He'd asked Kerry not to put Niki on Daisy's roster. He didn't want to get Daisy into trouble, but he didn't want to see her at the moment. He didn't want to be reminded of the fact that he had been out with Daisy when he should have been at home with Niki. He didn't need any more guilt added to the weight already on his shoulders.

But he hadn't considered that she would come and see him anyway. He could only blame that oversight on the fact that he was sleep-deprived, scared, and not thinking clearly.

Daisy would know Niki had been admitted and of *course* she'd check on him, he realised when he heard her voice.

'Ajay! Niki's got chicken pox?'

She was wearing the dangly pink daisy earrings, and she looked bright and sounded cheery, but the usual shine in her eyes was missing. The shine that he realised now was what he looked for to make him smile. He knew he didn't deserve to have her make him smile. Not after the way he'd treated her last night.

She wasn't smiling either, and he waited for her to berate him. He felt terrible that he hadn't made sure she got home safely last night, but he'd been so concerned about Niki. He waited for her to scold him, knowing he deserved it, knowing it would add to his guilty conscience. But she said nothing.

He knew he should apologise for his behaviour, but the words stuck in his throat. His apology would be insincere. He felt bad, but he knew he would behave in exactly the same way if the situation were repeated. Niki had to come first.

'Kerry said he's been vaccinated?'

Ajay heard the query in Daisy's voice. He knew how she felt about the importance of vaccinations, and at least he could set her mind at ease on this topic. 'Yes, of course. I know there have been a few cases of chicken pox recently, and I know vaccinations are not one hundred per cent effective, but I didn't expect him to catch it or for it to have such serious complications. Niki is all I have left in the world. I don't know what I'd do if I lost him. I knew he wasn't well… I shouldn't have left him with Mrs Singh. He's my responsibility.'

He wasn't blaming Daisy. It had been his decision not to postpone dinner and the movie. He'd known the film festival was finishing and he hadn't wanted to disappoint her, but the fact that he'd prioritised seeing a movie with Daisy before his own son's welfare sat heavily on his conscience.

Daisy didn't stay long. She had her own patients to attend to, and he wasn't about to encourage her to stay by his side. She soon left Ajay sitting by Niki's cot, nursing his guilt.

He wished he could have turned to her for comfort, but he couldn't look at her without being reminded of his choices and the fact that he'd let both Niki and Priya down. He'd broken his promise to Priya to look after Niki. He'd abandoned his responsibility when Niki was unwell in favour of dinner and a movie.

It wasn't good enough.

He wasn't good enough.

He vowed he'd make it up to Niki. He should have never had left his son. He should have listened to his instincts. But he'd let his heart rule his head and Niki had suffered as a result.

Niki had suffered enough already, and Ajay wouldn't make that mistake again. His behaviour was inexcusable. Unforgivable. Niki had to come first. Niki had to be his priority.

Ajay would have to make some changes.

* * *

Daisy looked around the cafeteria for an empty chair as she stood in line, waiting to order something for her afternoon tea. Ajay was sitting by himself at a table in the far corner of the room and there was one vacant chair pushed in beside him.

Niki had been discharged from hospital four days ago, but Daisy hadn't seen or spoken to Ajay since. He hadn't replied to her text messages and she was beginning to think he was avoiding her. She hoped it was just her paranoia taking hold, her expectation that she would be rejected making her feel that Ajay was shutting her out, but she needed to know.

She had no idea what was going on, what had changed, but he'd barely said two words to her since he'd left her at the movies, she could hardly count their brief conversation in the paediatric ward, and although the cafeteria was not the ideal place for his conversation, what choice did she have?

The cafeteria was busy, but for once Daisy didn't mind. The noise might make it difficult for Ajay to hear her, but it would also make it difficult for anyone else to eavesdrop, and she could manage a one-on-one conversation surrounded by noise. She only had to read one set of lips.

She took her tea over to his table. 'Do you mind if I join you?'

She sat down before he had a chance to answer. He had a half-finished slice of cake and a mug of coffee in front of him and she knew he wouldn't get up and leave—his inherent good manners would ensure he stayed at the table at least until he'd finished, because doing anything else would appear rude. She could trust his manners not to let her down.

'You haven't replied to my messages,' she said, getting straight to the crux of the matter.

There was no point making polite conversation about work or the weather. She didn't have time to waste. There was no guarantee he wouldn't finish his cake in one bite and hightail it out of there, back to the emergency department.

'I've been really busy,' he said, with no trace of an apology in his expression.

'It doesn't take a minute to answer a text. I wanted to find out how Niki is.'

'He's recovering well.'

'And the implants? Are they working?'

She knew Niki had been booked in for an appointment to have his cochlear implants switched on two days ago, and she wanted to know how he was going with those too.

Ajay nodded. 'He will start regular speech therapy next week and he's hearing sounds—I'm not sure how well yet, but he is responding. He seems quite interested in the noises around him.'

'That's a good sign. It will take a while for his brain to make sense of what he's hearing, but it's perfect timing in terms of developing speech.'

'I'm hoping so.'

'I've bought a couple of books for him.' She had spent ages in the local bookstore, choosing books that made sounds. Books with farm animals and jungle animals, trucks and tractors. Books that made noises when buttons were pushed. She'd thought they would be perfect stimulus for Niki. 'When can I pop over and give them to him?'

'Why don't you bring them to work? I can take them home to Niki for you.'

'I would like to see him.'

'There's a lot going on for Niki at the moment. I don't want him to get overwhelmed.'

Daisy couldn't see how a brief visit from her, someone Niki knew well, could be overwhelming, but she bit her tongue. Niki wasn't her child. She didn't get a say in his life. But surely Ajay could see how ridiculous his reasons sounded.

'Have I done something to upset you?' she asked, not able to bite her tongue on every topic. 'Why are you shutting me out?

'I need to concentrate on Niki. He needs me at the moment,' he said, only answering part of her question.

'That makes no sense. I'm not trying to take you away from Niki. There's no reason why I shouldn't see him.' She would never expect to come between Niki and Ajay. 'Why don't you just tell me the truth? What is bothering you?'

'Daisy, I don't have time for this.'

'"This"?'

'This discussion, this relationship—any of this. My son needs me. He is my priority. I should have been clear about that from the beginning.'

Daisy's heart missed a beat. And another. She felt her blood freeze in her veins as her heart turned heavy. It felt like stone in her chest and his words cut her painfully and deeply.

But why was she surprised? she wondered. She should have expected this. She'd always known he would leave her. Everyone did. Willow, Lily, Jet, Poppy. One by one, they had all left.

She forced herself to stand. Her knees were wobbly, her legs weak, and she wasn't sure they would take her weight, but she had to get out of there. She was either going to cry or vomit, and she wasn't about to do either in public. She wasn't going to let him humiliate her. She wasn't going to suffer the indignity of being rejected in full view of the hospital.

She picked up her empty dishes and headed for the exit, wishing she had been wiser. Wishing she had left first.

Daisy was gone.

He'd pushed her away and she'd left without a backward glance.

He hadn't been completely honest. He did have time for a relationship—there was no denying that. In his mind they were *in* a relationship.

But Daisy couldn't be his priority and he should never have put her before Niki.

He had lost Priya and he could so easily have lost Niki. He never would have been able to forgive himself for that. He had made a promise to Priya to look after their son, and instead of being home with him when he was sick he'd been out with Daisy.

His feelings for Daisy had shocked him. They'd been sudden and intense. It had been like being hit by lightning from the first moment he'd laid eyes on her.

But the way he felt about her had brought more guilt—just as he'd feared. His feelings for her were so much stronger than his feelings for Priya had ever been, so much more intense—which just made him feel that he'd let Priya down in more ways than one.

But Daisy wasn't to blame. *He* was.

Would he never be free from guilt?

He hoped she'd be back, but he didn't have time to worry about that now. He needed to focus on what he had in his life—his son. Niki needed him. Niki had to be his priority.

He might have let Priya down, but he could redeem himself now. He would take better care of Niki.

'You're not going out with Ajay tonight?' Lily asked, when she came home to find Daisy sprawled on the couch.

'No. Not tonight. Not any night.'

'Oh, Dase…what happened?'

'He told me he wasn't looking for a relationship.'

'I thought you were *in* a relationship.'

'I thought so too. But then Niki got sick and everything changed.'

'What changed?'

'I don't know. He told me Niki had to be his priority. That he'd made a promise to Priya.'

'Priya?'

'His wife. Niki's mother,' Daisy explained.

'What did he promise her?'

'He promised that he'd take care of Niki.'

Lily frowned. 'Did he think you were stopping him from doing that?'

'I don't know. I don't think so. But…'

'But what?'

'Remember how I always said I didn't want to date a man who had children?'

'Yes, but you obviously made an exception for him. Why would that be an issue?'

'Because I told him I didn't *want* children. Why would he choose me when I'd made that clear?

'You don't want children?'

'I thought I didn't. Given our childhood, I thought there was a good chance I'd be a terrible mother, that I'd mess it all up, but after spending time with Niki I started to think maybe I could do it.'

Niki had got into her heart and she thought that maybe, with Ajay's help, she could do it. But Ajay obviously thought differently. He didn't need her help. He didn't *want* her help. Ajay didn't need her and neither did Niki.

'Have you told him this?' asked Lily.

'How can I? He hasn't been replying to my messages.' She had sent Ajay a couple more messages, but her phone had remained stubbornly silent for the past five days.

'You could go and see him.'

Daisy shook her head as tears welled in her eyes. 'There's no point. He's made his choice. I should have listened to my head in the first place. I should never have got involved with him.'

Lily sat beside Daisy on the couch and wrapped her arms around her, offering a comforting hug. 'I know how it feels to have your heart broken, but is he worth fighting for? Do you think you should give up so easily?'

'He let me walk away. He hasn't come after me. If he loved me he wouldn't have let me go.'

It was inevitable, she figured, as she always did. Everyone left her eventually.

Daisy wanted to be special to someone. Ever since she'd lost Willow she'd been looking for her person, and she'd started to hope that she'd found her person in Ajay. She hadn't expected him to prioritise her over Niki, but she had foolishly started to dream of a future.

Now her heart was broken, and she wasn't sure how she was going to survive, knowing he didn't feel the same way. She'd been foolish to think she could find love. She'd been foolish to ignore the voice in her head that had warned her she would find herself alone—warned her that no one would think she was special.

She had lost Ajay and Niki.

She had no one.

Daisy pushed open the restaurant door, half hoping her date wouldn't show up.

Poppy had organised a date for her with Marcus, a paramedic from her station, telling her that it would get her mind off Ajay. Daisy didn't see why she needed to be going on a date, why she couldn't just stay home and nurse her broken heart, but Poppy had insisted, in her usual straightforward manner, that if Daisy wanted to find 'The One' she had to go looking.

Daisy would have cancelled it herself, except that after a week spent moping on the couch she'd run out of excuses, and she knew Poppy would keep nagging her until she gave in. But she had no idea how Poppy expected her to find 'The One' when her judgement was so terrible.

'Hello, Daisy,' Chen greeted her cheerfully as she stepped into the restaurant. 'You look hungry.'

Chen's observation almost made her smile. She

knew it was his way of saying she'd lost weight. Heartache had that effect on her.

She'd chosen Lao Lao's Kitchen for dinner because
it was familiar, and she felt safe there, and she knew
Chen would look out for her. If Marcus didn't turn up
she could always get a takeaway and go home.

That idea was suddenly very appealing, but it was
too late, she realised, as Chen said, 'Your date is here,'
and pointed to a table halfway along the side wall.

Marcus stood up when she reached the table, scor-
ing a point for good manners, and pulled out a chair
for her, settling her into a seat that faced the front of
the restaurant.

He had a pleasant face, an easy smile and he was
nice enough, Daisy decided over dinner. But the date
felt like hard work. She had to concentrate to lip-read.
She wanted it to feel effortless. Like it did when she
talked to Ajay.

She never had to try hard with him. For some reason when she was with Ajay it never even felt like lip-
reading. It was almost as if she could sense what she
was going to say...as if she felt his words rather than
read them. Almost as if she could hear him.

She tried not to compare Marcus's each and every
mannerism, figure of speech and expression to Ajay,
but it was difficult. Everything about Ajay was firmly
imprinted in her mind.

It had been a mistake to come to Lao Lao's Kitchen.
All she could think about was the last time she'd been
there and Ajay had been sitting opposite her. If she
closed her eyes she could recall the way he'd listened
so intently to everything she'd said. How he'd watched
her with his dark chocolate eyes. How he'd made her

feel comfortable. Comfortable enough to share some of her past with him.

And all for what? For nothing.

She felt like a fool.

She would focus on Marcus, she decided. She'd make an effort. It wasn't his fault that Ajay had stolen her heart.

She forced herself to pay attention to Marcus and tried not to think about Ajay.

But that didn't last long.

The front door of the restaurant opened and her heart skipped a beat as Ajay walked in. Her breath caught in her throat as she took stock of the familiar set of his shoulders, the tilt of his head, the curl of his hair.

What was he doing there?

She didn't want him to see her. She couldn't explain why, but she felt exposed. Perhaps he wouldn't notice her.

But the moment she thought that was the same moment he looked in her direction.

Their eyes locked.

She saw him look from her to Marcus and back again.

She breathed out and relaxed as Chen handed Ajay a bag of takeaway, assuming he would take his dinner and leave, but instead he began to cross the room.

He was heading her way.

What was he doing?

CHAPTER TEN

'HELLO, DAISY.'

After ignoring her for over a week, why was he choosing this moment to speak to her? she wondered as Ajay stopped beside her table. He looked expectantly from her to Marcus, and back to her, and Daisy knew she had no choice but to introduce the two men.

'Hello, Ajay. Marcus, this is Ajay—you might have met him before? He's one of the doctors at the hospital. Ajay, Marcus is a paramedic—he works with Poppy.'

'Am I interrupting?' Ajay's eyes were dark, his expression unreadable.

Daisy was normally good at judging people's emotions by studying their faces, but she couldn't tell if Ajay was angry or upset. Curious or confused.

'Yes,' she responded.

But if she was hoping he would go and leave them in peace she was mistaken. Ajay continued to stand beside their table. He was frowning.

'Daisy, what's going on?' he asked.

'Marcus, will you excuse me for a minute?' She stood up, not waiting for Marcus's permission.

She didn't feel she owed Ajay an explanation, but she sensed he had some questions. The restaurant was small and intimate, and she got the feeling this conversation would be better off in a less public space.

They were barely outside, the door hardly closed behind them, before Ajay said, 'Are you on a date with him? What the hell is going on?'

'Poppy set it up.'

Daisy wasn't sure why she was dragging Poppy's name into it. Did she want to shift responsibility? Poppy might have been the instigator of the situation, but Daisy had agreed.

'Why would she do that?' he asked. 'I thought we were dating?'

'And I thought you didn't have time for a relationship. Isn't that what you told me?'

'Niki needs me,' he said, for what felt like the hundredth time.

'I'm not disagreeing with you on that, but he'll need you for the next twenty years. Does that mean you're going to put your life on hold? Did the promise you made to Priya include giving up your life to care for Niki?'

'No,' he admitted, 'and that's not what I'm doing. But Niki is a child. My child. And he needs me.'

'I wasn't trying to compete with Niki. I didn't expect to be your priority. But I am looking for someone who values me. Who thinks I'm special. Who thinks I'm worth something. I told you I wanted to find my person. I'm not going to find him sitting at home.'

'I don't understand why you're out looking. I'm not giving up everything to look after Niki. All I meant was that my priority for now had to be Niki.'

'But that's not what you said. I didn't need to be the most important person in your life, I'd have been happy to be second to Niki, but I'm not even next on your list. Next is your guilt, and then the promise you made to Priya. You made it clear you don't have time for me and I want to matter.'

'You matter to me.'

'But not enough.' She felt like screaming. Or crying. Or both. But she knew that wouldn't help. 'I don't blame you. We want different things. We've known that from the beginning, and if we can't give each other what we want we're always going to end up here.'

'Here? Where's "here"?'

She waved a hand around non-specifically. 'Dating other people.'

'I don't want to date other people.'

'Maybe not. But I don't think you want to date me either. It doesn't matter if you need to prioritise Niki "for now" or "for ever". What matters is that you're not looking for a partner. You're content to be alone.'

'I'm not alone.'

'No,' she agreed, 'you have Niki. But you won't have him for ever. There has to be room in your life for more than just raising your son. What will you do when Niki is grown and leaves home one day?'

'I'll have my work.'

'Trust me, that's not enough. Work is no substitute for love. And the love of a child or a sibling isn't the same as the love of a partner. One day that child will leave you and you'll be alone. I lost Willow, but even I know that eventually she and I would have led separate lives. I'm not trying to replace her, but there is space in my heart, in my life, for someone else. I was prepared to drop my defences for you. I was scared, but I thought it was worth a chance. I thought you were worth it.' *But he didn't want her.* 'But you've made it clear that you don't want a new partner…and you don't want me,' she said as she spun around and turned away from him.

'Daisy, wait!' He reached for her arm, holding her lightly, not enough to hurt her, but enough to stop her from leaving.

She turned back to him.

'Wait,' he repeated, now that she could see him.

'No,' she said as she pulled her arm from his grasp. 'It's okay. This is on me. I should have listened from the start. I thought I could do this. I thought I could explore our connection without becoming involved. But it turns out that's not the case. You told me you didn't need anyone. I should have known that meant you didn't need me.'

She left him standing on the footpath, watching her walk away. Again. Knowing that it wasn't what he wanted.

He had to work out how to fix this—how to convince her to give him another chance. But now was not the right time, he realised, as the door to the restaurant slammed shut behind her.

He felt physically ill. How had he got this so wrong? How had he screwed this up? This wasn't on her. This was on *him*. He hadn't made things clear. He needed to focus on Niki, but that didn't mean he didn't want Daisy to be a part of his life.

His heart still ached for Niki, his motherless son, and he was still angry that Priya hadn't got to live her life, that she hadn't got to know her son, but it was losing Daisy that was hurting him now.

He knew that by distancing himself from Daisy he

had been trying to extinguish his guilt. But it hadn't worked. His feelings for Daisy were so much stronger than his feelings for Priya had ever been—which, again, just made him feel that he'd let Priya down in more ways than one. That he hadn't loved her as she'd deserved to be loved. That he hadn't loved her the way he loved Daisy.

His heart skipped a beat and his legs felt weak as his feelings swamped him.

He loved Daisy.

That beautiful, kind, generous woman had captured his heart.

And she was walking away.

He watched her through the restaurant window and saw her return to her seat at the table. To sit opposite a man who wasn't him.

He was an idiot.

He'd been afraid of opening up to her. Afraid of being rejected. Afraid of letting Niki down. Afraid of breaking his promise to Priya. Afraid of so many things.

So he'd pushed her away and she'd given up on him.

He'd abandoned her.

He'd done the one thing he knew she lived in fear of.

This was on him.

Would he be able to get her back?

Would she want to come back?

His thoughts collided against each other in his head. Daisy didn't want a family. She might not love him. Was he going to be a lonely man? What would his life look like without her?

He couldn't imagine.

He didn't want to know.

He had to fix this.

* * *

Ajay was slumped in a chair at the triage desk when Lily arrived in the ED.

'You look like you've had a rough night,' she said as she took in his rather dishevelled appearance. 'Is Niki okay?'

He'd barely slept last night, but it hadn't been his son keeping him awake. He'd tossed and turned thinking about Daisy.

'Niki is fine,' he replied as he ran his fingers through his hair. He knew he looked a mess. Like a man in pain.

Lily was watching him closely. She reminded him of Daisy and his heartache intensified. He hadn't thought it was possible to feel any worse.

'Are you okay?' she asked.

'Not really.'

He wondered if he could confide in Lily. He had no doubt she would take Daisy's side, if push came to shove, but she was one of the people who knew Daisy best. She might be able to give him a clue as to how he could fix this. As to whether she thought he had a chance of fixing this.

He needed a sounding board. For the past few weeks Daisy had been the person he'd turned to, and he realised now how quickly he'd come to rely on her and her honest and straightforward opinions. Lily was still watching him, waiting. He took his opportunity.

'It's your sister,' he said. 'Did you know she went on a date last night?'

Lily nodded.

'Why would she do that?'

'You told her you didn't have time for her.'

'At the moment,' he clarified. 'Not for ever.'

'That's not how she interpreted it.'

He knew that. 'What do I do? How do I fix this?'

'That depends on what you want.'

'I want Daisy.'

'Are you serious about her?'

He nodded. He'd been shocked by the intensity of his feelings but there was no denying them. Not any more.

'Does she know that?'

'No.'

'Well, if I were you, I'd start there. Talk to her.'

'But what if she doesn't want to hear what I have to say?'

'There's only one way to find out. Would you rather stay quiet and never know the answer? Daisy needs to know you love her and won't leave her. That's it. If you think you can do that, the rest is up to her.'

'You're forgetting about my son. I'm a package deal. What if that's too much?'

'If you think you can promise her the security she needs, if you're her person, you might have a chance of changing her mind about everything else.'

He knew Daisy wanted to be loved, that she wanted security. And after seeing her with Niki he also knew she could definitely raise a child. All he had to do now was convince her that she would be the perfect mother for his son.

Daisy was home alone when the doorbell rang, triggering an alert on her phone. She was feeling lonely and neglected, and was tempted to ignore the door, but when the alert flashed a second time she dragged herself off the couch.

She swung open the door and was greeted by a bunch of pink and white daisies so enormous that she couldn't see the face of the person who was holding them.

But she recognised his hands.

'Ajay? What are you doing here?'

The daisies were lowered and Ajay's gorgeous face appeared. 'I came to apologise,' he said, offering her the flowers.

'For what?' she asked, automatically reaching for the bouquet and taking it from him.

'For being an idiot. For being afraid. For hurting you. The list is fairly long.'

He had a haunted expression in his dark brown eyes and Daisy knew she couldn't send him away. 'You'd better come in.'

She needed to see what he had to say. She *wanted* to see, even though the thought of any potential conversation terrified her.

Ajay followed her to the kitchen and waited while she searched for a vase large enough to hold the flowers. She was avoiding eye contact, delaying the conversation, while she fought to get her heart rate and her nerves under control. She gripped the vase tightly as she held it under the tap, attempting to disguise the tremble in her fingers as she tried to read between the lines. As she tried to figure out if Ajay dropping in was going to be a good thing or if it was just going to bring her more heartache.

She unwrapped the daisies and arranged them in the vase, shaking them out a little to separate them before placing them on the kitchen island, gathering her thoughts before meeting Ajay's eyes.

She led him out onto the deck. It was a glorious day. If he was about to break her heart all over again perhaps the sunshine would soften the blow.

She sat, took a deep breath, and mentally prepared herself for his words. 'Okay, I'm ready.'

Ajay sat beside her and reached for her hand. She didn't resist. He held it in both of his and she looked at their hands, joined together, and knew she was where she wanted to be. What she didn't know was how long it could last.

'I'm sorry for telling you I didn't want a relationship,' Ajay said when she'd lifted her eyes to his face. 'I am sorry for pushing you away. I was afraid of my feelings for you. I was afraid that I wasn't being the father Niki needed because I was so enamoured with you. I pushed you away because I was afraid of letting Niki down, but instead I let *you* down. I came to ask you to give me another chance.'

Daisy wanted to say yes. She wished she could. But she still had so many questions. 'I don't know if I can. As long as we want different things, I don't see that's there's much point. You'll just break my heart again.'

'And what if we want the *same* things?'

'But we don't.' She shook her head. 'I'm not your person. I thought your person was Niki, but now I think your person was Priya.'

'What do you mean?'

'I have spent years imagining what it would be like to fall in love. Years imagining how it would feel to find that person I could spend the rest of my life with.

To find that person who would complete me. I want to be loved. I want to love like my siblings love their partners. I've seen what it looks like and I want that. I want to be someone's first choice. I want to be special. The relationship you have with a partner is different from the one you have with a child. You don't have to choose me or Niki. You could choose both. But you've chosen Priya. You've chosen her memory. I want to be loved like you love Priya.'

'Like I love Priya?'

'Yes. You pushed me way because of a promise you made to her. Because you believed you'd let Niki down by spending time with me. Because you believed you'd let *Priya* down. You can't even celebrate Niki's birthday because that's the day you lost your wife. I want to be loved that much. I want *you* to love *me* that much.'

'Daisy—'

She held up a hand. 'You have to let me finish. Unless you let Priya go, just a little, you'll never have room for me in your heart. I want to find love,' she continued. 'If you're not serious about me, I need to know. If you don't think you can love me, I want to know now.'

'I didn't love Priya the way you think I did. I wish I had. But she didn't make me catch my breath. She didn't make me nervous. She didn't make me forget what I was thinking. She didn't surprise me. I didn't fall in love with her the same way I've fallen in love with you.'

'What?'

She wasn't sure if her eyes had been playing a trick on her. She held her breath as she waited for him to repeat his words.

Ajay pointed at himself, then crossed his arms over his chest, making the shape of an X, with his fingers extended from his palms, before pointing at Daisy. *I love you*, he signed.

Her heart skipped a beat. There was no misinterpreting his signs. 'You love me?'

Ajay nodded. 'I love you,' he repeated. 'You were completely unexpected. The moment I saw you I felt as if the ground beneath my feet had shifted and my whole world had changed. Time stopped and all I could see, all I could think about, was you. I was unsettled, and it was only as I got to know you, bit by bit, that my world was put back together. But when it had finished reassembling it didn't look the same any more. It had changed—you'd changed it. Suddenly I wasn't just looking at a life of going to work and trying to raise Niki as best I could as a single parent. Suddenly I had something to look forward to for myself. Some hope that there would be more for me—a future. I still wasn't sure what that would look like, but in my head, and in my heart, I knew that you were part of it. And then Niki got sick… You're right. I pushed you away because I felt guilty that I had put you before Niki. I pushed you away and made a conscious decision to put Niki first, to take care of him like I'd promised Priya, and I know you feel like I abandoned you. As if I chose Niki over you. That wasn't my intention. I never intended it to be you or him. Not ever. It hurt me when Priya died. My heart ached for Niki, and I was angry that my idea of a future had been taken away from me. But what I thought she and I could have together was nothing like what I know you and I can have. My feelings for you have completely taken me over.

'You are my person,' he said. 'I love you. I will always love you and I want to spend the rest of my life with you. You are already a part of my heart and you always will be. There is room in my heart for you and for Niki. But I need to know if I can be a part of your life. Your future. I need to know how you feel about me. And Niki. We're a package deal, and I know that's not something you wanted, but I'm hoping I can change your mind. I wasn't looking for love, but now that I've found it—found you—I don't want to let you go. I'm convinced we can build something together. The three of us. But you've told me that's not what you want. Now I'm here, hoping I can convince you to change your mind. Begging you to give me a chance. Me and Niki.'

'I don't know if I can do it…' Daisy was on the verge of tears. This was what her heart wanted, but her head still had doubts.

'Do what?'

'Be a good mother.'

'I've seen you with your patients. I've seen you with An Na. I've seen you with Niki. You are patient and kind and loving. All Niki needs is time and love. I believe you can give him that. Together we can give him that, and I believe that you will reap the rewards too. Niki loves you already.'

Daisy closed her eyes briefly and pictured Niki's little face. Recalled how it felt to hold him in her arms as he cuddled into her. She loved the weight of him, his smell, his eagerness to be cuddled. She loved everything about that little boy. When she held him she could even imagine having a child of her own.

She opened her eyes as tears gathered. 'Do you really think I can do it? Do you trust me to help you raise Niki?'

'I have complete faith in you. I *know* you can do it, and I know you will do it better than you can imagine. Do you think you could love us? Love me?'

Bolstered by Ajay's confidence in her, Daisy nodded and smiled. 'You have changed my life. I was looking for one person to complete me but I've found two. I love you both.'

'Daisy, I love you with every part of me. You have captured my heart, my mind, my body. You are my future,' Ajay said as he moved from the couch to kneel in front of her. 'I know we haven't known each other for long but I want you to believe me when I say I will always be here for you. I want to be by your side from now until for ever. I've known since the day we met that I wanted to end up here. You are the one for me. Would you do me the honour of becoming my wife? Will you build a life with me? A family? Will you marry me?'

The tears spilled over now as Daisy thought about how Ajay made her feel. From the first time he'd smiled at her, turning her dizzy, to how she felt now, when she was in his arms. When she was with him she was happy, whole, complete. This was what she'd been looking for. This was *who* she'd been looking for.

He'd come back for her and she knew she had to take her chance. He believed in her, and she had to give herself to him if she wanted to find her happily-ever-after.

She'd survived losing Willow and she'd vowed to live for both of them. Ajay loved her. He was offering her everything she wanted. And more. He was offering her himself and a family of her own.

'Ajay, you are my person—the one I'm supposed to spend the rest of my life with. I love you. I love Niki. I promise to give myself to you for the rest of my life. I *will* marry you,' she said as she pulled him up into her arms and kissed him.

Once. Twice. For ever.

* * * * *

COMING SOON!

We really hope you enjoyed reading this book.
If you're looking for more romance, be sure to
head to the shops when new books are
available on

Thursday 17th February

To see which titles are coming soon, please visit

millsandboon.co.uk/nextmonth

MILLS & BOON

Coming next month

THE VET'S UNEXPECTED FAMILY
Alison Roberts

Finn's smile faded. He was standing very close to Hazel and she was still smiling at him. Without thinking he reached up and touched her cheek with the back of his forefinger.

'It's a good thing that Michael is long gone,' he said. 'The guy was a complete jerk.'

There was something in Hazel's gaze that he'd never seen before despite it looking like something that could have been there forever. Something… lost? It made him want to take her into his arms and hug her. Instead, he just held her gaze.

'Don't let anyone think you're not beautiful just the way you are,' he added softly. 'Because it's not true.'

It felt like time had stopped. Or maybe Hazel had just frozen, shocked by what he was saying. She didn't believe him, did she? But what else could he say that might convince her?

Maybe he didn't need to say anything. The idea of showing her was a lightbulb moment, like tempting her to stay here by offering a place for Ben to recuperate. Only this flash of inspiration wasn't purely intellectual. It was more of a physical thing.

Because… because Hazel really was beautiful and… and he really did want to kiss her.

Just gently. Good grief, he wasn't trying to seduce her or anything. He just wanted her to know that he meant what he'd said. And that she deserved something a hell of lot better than someone who didn't think she was perfect just the way she was.

And… maybe it was his imagination but it looked as though Hazel wanted him to kiss her. She certainly wasn't ducking for cover as his mouth drifted slowly closer to her own. And then his lips brushed hers and it was Finn who felt like he needed to duck for cover because there was a strange sensation that came with that barely-there kiss. A tingle that felt like static electricity or something. A strangeness that was disturbing, anyway.

So Finn backed away fast. He put on his most charming smile, as if that kiss was nothing out of the ordinary for two friends and turned away to pick up the tray on the table.

'Call me,' he said. 'If you need any help in the night. With Beanie or Ben.'

Continue reading
THE VET'S UNEXPECTED FAMILY
Alison Roberts

Available next month
www.millsandboon.co.uk

MILLS & BOON

THE HEART OF ROMANCE

A ROMANCE FOR EVERY READER

MODERN

Prepare to be swept off your feet by sophisticated, sexy and seductive heroes, in some of the world's most glamourous and romantic locations, where power and passion collide.

HISTORICAL

Escape with historical heroes from time gone by. Whether your passion is for wicked Regency Rakes, muscled Vikings or rugged Highlanders, await the romance of the past.

MEDICAL

Set your pulse racing with dedicated, delectable doctors in the high-pressure world of medicine, where emotions run high and passion, comfort a love are the best medicine.

True Love

Celebrate true love with tender stories of heartfelt romance, from the rush of falling in love to the joy a new baby can bring, and a focus on the emotional heart of a relationship.

Desire

Indulge in secrets and scandal, intense drama and plenty of sizzling hot action with powerful and passionate heroes who have it all: wealth, status good looks…everything but the right woman.

HEROES

Experience all the excitement of a gripping thriller, with an intense romance at its heart. Resourceful, true-to-life women and strong, fearless m face danger and desire - a killer combination!

To see which titles are coming soon, please visit

millsandboon.co.uk/nextmonth

t might just be true love...